CATACOMBS

Barry

Hope you enjoy this book.

Remember, within the boundaries, there's probability. However, it takes more than "chance" to cross the bonds.

Larry Slossa

Apr 2010

CATACOMBS

A MYSTERY

LARRY MASSA

AUTHOR *of the* BEST-SELLING BOOK *ARMAGEDDON NOW*

WINEPRESS WP PUBLISHING

WinePress Publishing (PO Box 428, Enumclaw, WA 98022) functions only as book publisher. As such, the ultimate design, content, editorial accuracy, and views expressed or implied in this work are those of the author.

Unless otherwise noted, all Scriptures are taken from the *Holy Bible, New International Version*®, NIV®.Copyright © 1973, 1978, 1984 by the International Bible Society. Used by permission of Zondervan. All rights reserved.

ISBN 13: 978-1-57921-926-0
ISBN 10: 1-57921-926-8
Library of Congress Catalog Card Number: 2007934239

Printed in South Korea.

ACKNOWLEDGMENTS

I owe a tremendous debt of gratitude to my editor, Rosey Dow. She channeled my creativity and coached me in ways to add life to the book. Her innate talents and gifts for conciseness and clarity made her an invaluable ally. She is a word artist and an absolute pleasure to work with.

I want to thank the WinePress sales team for their efforts in promoting the book and to the art department for making an eye-catching cover.

AUTHOR'S NOTE
THE BIBLE CODE

It is a fact that in the mid-1980s, Israeli scientists discovered encoded information about the past and future within the first five books of the original Hebrew Bible. These scientists, Doron Witztum, Eliyahu Rips, and Yoav Rosenberg, wrote a paper with the intent to study the phenomenon systematically and to disclose their methods so scientists around the world could use them.

They submitted their article "Equidistant Letter Sequences in the Book of Genesis" to the prestigious journal *Statistical Science*. Of course, the journal was skeptical and ordered an unprecedented three separate, independent reviews of the work. The outcome of each review confirmed the Israelis' conclusions. In fact, the odds of finding the encoded information in Genesis simply by random chance were calculated to be 1 in 10 million.

Even Harold Gans, a senior cryptologic mathematician in the United States National Security Agency conducted an independent study and verified the Israeli's conclusions. *Statistical Science* ultimately printed the article in 1994 (Vol. 9, No. 3, pp. 429–438).

PROLOGUE

Jerusalem, 743 B.C.

Ahaz's sandals made scuffing noises as they slid across the cold stone floor of the cavernous palace throne room. The palace was hallmarked by great cedar pillars supporting the walls and cedar beams supporting the ceiling, both covered with cedar paneling and decorated with a hundred golden shields.

Streams of bright morning sun flowed through three tiers of windows, each tier consisting of three rows of fourteen. The massive gilded throne mirrored light onto the golden shields, which ricocheted to other shields in a slow-moving light show.

King Solomon had built the elaborate palace before the twelve tribes of Israel split into Judah (a southern kingdom of two tribes) and Israel (a northern kingdom of ten tribes). The kings of Judah had ruled from this very palace in Jerusalem for over two hundred years. It was currently the center of King Ahaz's dominion.

Ahaz had a thick salt-and-pepper colored beard shrouding the lower half of his face, but it did not hide the tortured expression on his leathery features. His shoulders slumped as he stood near the throne. *If Israel finds an ally, how can our two tribes defeat those ten? The city is protected, but we could hold out for only so long. Maybe I should seek help . . . The Egyptians might . . . for enough gold.*

Onam, a gangling man with a bald, bare head sneaked into the chamber. He held a large scroll. The fine weaves of his outer garment looked out of place over his coarse tunic that earmarked him as a servant.

He came before Ahaz and froze, except for his trembling jaw. "K . . . K . . . King Ahaz, it's nearly time to start the day's business. Do . . . do you want me to preview the cases you will be hearing today?"

Ahaz did not disguise his anger as his head jerked around. "Haven't you heard the rumors about Israel invading us? If they do, we cannot prevail alone." He glanced at the scroll hanging from Onam's hand. "I know today's agenda fully, but put everything off."

The servant swallowed hard as his body quivered. With obvious effort, he forced himself to meet the king's glare. "My King, I . . . I am aware, but . . ."

Ahaz stomped his foot, his voice a bullhorn. "But nothing! I said no routine business today."

The servant dropped the scroll as he bolted from the throne room, barely avoiding a collision with a large, bearded man. He was dressed in a short tunic covered with a leather breastplate and an outer coat pulled back like a cape.

The bearded man pointed his spear toward the ceiling, gave Onam a bemused glance, and marched in. As governor of Judah, Shaphan had the immediate task of reconnaissance of all elements who might threaten the kingdom. He was tall, well built, and carried himself with confidence.

Ahaz stared into the man's dark orbs, an ominous feeling crushing him. "Shaphan . . . have you been able to obtain any information about our enemies?"

The governor held the king's gaze and set the butt of the spear near his foot. "My king, our spies have reported that Israel has allied herself with Syria."

Ahaz cringed, his hands betraying a faint tremble. He had dreaded what he was sure would be Shaphan's assessment of the situation. A Syrian-Israeli alliance would result in the loss of his kingdom and likely his life. Hearing the news caused the alliance to become more real than he had ever allowed himself to feel it before.

Frowning, Shaphan continued, "They intend to destroy us by splitting Judah in two and each getting half. They also intend to replace you with a son of Tabeel."

Ahaz reeled, his voice a hiss. "Surely, this cannot be true. Can your spies be mistaken?"

Shaphan shifted his weight and breathed a haunting sigh. "No, they are my most trusted agents. And worse . . . the news is spreading in the streets. Our citizens are beginning to panic."

Ahaz staggered the short distance to the throne and slumped against its back.

Again, Onam appeared at the door, shuddered, and cleared his throat. "King Ahaz."

Ahaz swung his lion-like head to glare at the attendant. "What!"

"Sir, you have a visitor. He says he urgently needs to talk to you about Syria and Israel."

"Who is it?"

"Shear-jashub, son of Isaiah."

Noticing Isaiah's son standing a distance beyond the door, Ahaz moved to a more stately position. Isaiah was the most well-known and renowned prophet in both Judah and Israel. He clearly spoke the word of God. His prophecies always were accurate, although not always pleasant. "Send him in."

Fear squeezed the king's throat as he watched the young man's advance to the throne. Shear-jashub wore a short, white, tightly woven robe. A finely braided rope drew the robe snug and showed his thick quads rippling with each step. "What news do you have?"

Shear-jashub genuflected, his expression stoic. "My king, good health to you. I have no news, but my father does. He wants to talk to you"—he glanced at Shaphan—"in private."

"He does?" The request piqued Ahaz's interest and hope chinked at his depression. "Where in private?"

"He wants you to meet him at the end of the aqueduct for the Upper Pool on the highway to Fuller's field about the ninth hour today."

The small seed of optimism started to flower in Ahaz's mind, for he knew God spoke through Isaiah. "I will be there. My attendants will accompany me but will remain far from the upper pool."

▸ ▸ ▸

Although the aqueduct for the Upper Pool had been constructed one hundred years earlier, the chiseled stone flow channel had worn very little by the continually running water. The channel was supported by cut stones and stacked to form arches where the ground level was not high enough to support it in a continual descent.

Ahaz stumbled as he followed the dirt path weaving in and out of the stone supports. The soft gurgle of water flowing into the Upper Pool floated through the air, providing a calming, almost musical score for the meeting. Ahaz wore no crown and continually combed back his long hair with his stiff fingers as he trudged along the path.

Isaiah sat with Shear-jashub on a rotting log and scanned the path for Ahaz. He caught sight of the king passing through the last arch and stood, the sweet smell of rotting wood still in his nose.

The two men heard only the soft sound of trickling water, occasionally pierced by the caw of a crow announcing its territory as the king lumbered toward them.

Isaiah's long white beard and white hair danced in the balmy breeze, which did little to soothe his foreboding. He scrutinized the approaching king and winced at Ahaz's cowering body language. Isaiah had a long and close relationship with God and had passed to the Jews many of His prophecies, but he was very impatient with people who did not believe God's words. As he evaluated Ahaz's manner, internal doubts probed his being.

Ahaz faltered as he gawked at the two standing men. "What did you want to talk to me about?"

Isaiah's weathered appearance held the formal expression fitting for conversation with a king, his voice pleasant. "Long life to you, King Ahaz. I have a message from the Lord."

Ahaz grimaced and he swallowed hard. "What is it?"

Isaiah sensed the internal pressure he always felt when he had a message to deliver. It began to ease as he took a deep breath. "The Lord says to not be afraid of these two smoking stubs . . . Rezin, King of Syria and Pekah, the usurper of the throne of Israel. Though they devise a plan to combine forces and split the land into two parts, the Lord says it will not happen."

Ahaz avoided Isaiah's look and remained silent.

Knowing the intent of the Lord's message was to remove Ahaz's fear of the alliance, Isaiah was surprised at his unchanged expression, but continued, "In fact, the Lord says in sixty-five years, Israel will become so shattered a people, they will no longer remain a nation."

Ahaz nearly collapsed onto the fallen tree trunk with a fearful countenance. He held his head in his hands with his elbows propped on his knees. "What if that doesn't happen? I need a way to defeat them, not out-wait them."

Isaiah sneered and stepped uncomfortably close to the king. He had heard this type of blatant disbelief before but coming from the king of Judah, it cut him deeper than usual. Anger bubbled just below the surface as he said, "Ahaz, ask for a sign from the Lord your God . . . one that will convince you the Lord has really spoken to me and that He will keep His word."

Ahaz continued staring at the ground in front of him. He placed his hand on his brow as though trying to hide his look of despair. "No . . . I will not ask for a sign . . . neither will I tempt the Lord."

The wind felt sweltering as Isaiah's pulse pounded. He took a menacing step toward Ahaz.

Shear-jashub moved between the two.

Isaiah stopped. He shook his head in disbelief as he rose to an imposing stance. "Hear then, you leader of the house of David. It is a small thing for you to try the patience of men, but will you also try the patience of the Lord?" Isaiah's jaw clenched as he took a single step to leave but wheeled back and leveled his finger at Ahaz, his voice filled with disgust. "The Lord Himself shall give you a sign . . . Behold, the young woman who is unmarried and a virgin shall conceive and bear a son, and shall call His name Immanuel . . ."

CHAPTER ONE

Jerusalem, approximately 770 years later:

Malchus scrunched his forty-year-old body through the narrow opening next to the inside of Jerusalem's city wall and felt the chilly air wash over him. A dank smell permeated his nostrils. Although his torch burned brightly, darkness swallowed the set of stairs immediately in front of him. An invisible creek babbled over random rocks as it coursed under the city, providing a familiar, almost comforting sound.

Malchus' dark brown hair and beard were well trimmed, a requirement for serving royalty. He was a large man. His muscles rippled in the flickering light, but fatigue from a full day's chores closed in upon him. He had spent much of the last ten nights searching the catacombs. Although a lead servant, his daily activities prevented him from fully recuperating during the day. He leaned against the clammy rock entrance and sucked in the damp air. *Maybe tonight will be the night.*

He shook his head, held the torch high, and tramped down the steps. Reaching the corridor, he headed off, ignoring the tombs on the right and the left. Soon he would be back to the area housing the oldest ones. After several minutes, he turned into a side corridor and then another and another.

As he traveled, his thoughts went back to the late afternoon when Bukki, the lead servant for his master's father-in-law had sent a new clue on a standard small scroll. Malchus had deliberately turned the scroll to its seal. It was authentic—the letter *A* embedded in the wax— just as all the others. He had carefully placed his index finger under one edge of the papyrus and inched it through the wax, breaking the seal and allowing the scroll to pop open. He had read the two letters: *P* and *R*.

He continued weaving through the catacombs until he reached a part he had not yet searched. He stopped and fished a hand-drawn map from a pouch tied to his belt. *Let's see . . . where have I not been? Yes . . . this is the way.*

He shoved the map back into the pouch and patrolled the new corridor. He scrutinized each tomb's stone covering, his brain fixed on the letters *P* and *R*.

Suddenly, he froze. His peripheral vision had caught something farther down the corridor. His muscles went rigid as he strained to hear. His ears captured the soft shuffling of sandals on the dirt-covered stone floor, then voices.

Malchus panicked. He flew back through the corridors he had earlier traversed. His master had selected darkness as the time for Malchus to make his search, knowing no one ventured here at night, except to occasionally entomb a body. But his master always involved Malchus in those burials.

Malchus stopped at the bottom of the stairs leading back to the alley by the city wall. His breathing was labored from more than running. His fear of being caught in the catacombs gave way to the realization someone else could be searching as well. The revelation paralyzed him. He had to be the one to find Melchizedek's Tomb—his entire future depended on it.

CHAPTER TWO

Joseph Justus inched his way up the gangplank, jostled by crewmembers carrying supplies and other passengers carrying their luggage. Being much taller, he could easily see where he was going, though he squinted from the low morning sun beaming directly at him.

Justus travelled much of the latter part of his thirty-two years and was quite seasoned, but he still became excited by the boarding process. It always marked the beginning of a new adventure. He had arrived at the dock as the sun peeked over the treetops, his spirit soaring, though this mission was sure to be difficult.

He grinned as he weaved his way onto the main weather deck, easily hefting his massive trunk over the luggage and around the people on deck. It was a beautiful late-autumn day. He loved this time of year. Rather than immediately going below to the cabins, he strolled to the pier side of the ship, lowered his trunk to the deck and leaned on the exquisitely carved railing. The Alexandrian ship had the Twin Brothers, Castor and Pollux, as its figurehead.

Since it was already past the Feast of Trumpets, these ships would soon be wintering at various ports in Crete like the one here at Phoenice, an ideal location. Fortunately, none of them were wintering yet. Unfortunately, this voyage would be packed to capacity because everyone was trying to get as close to their destination as possible before the winter storms made travel almost impossible.

Justus gazed down the gangplank filled with the haphazard movements of crewmembers and passengers and tried to ignore the pounding and screeching of their loading cargo. Not only did his height cause him to stand out in this crowd, but being clean-shaven and having short hair made him even more conspicuous. He watched the boarding passengers, trying to guess where they were from and what their standing in society might be.

Wearing an orange robe, a black man with three large gold rings about his neck and two smaller ones hanging from one ear pushed past Justus. As he did, Justus glimpsed large gems attached to rings on three fingers of each hand, and concluded he was a wealthy Ethiopian, likely close to Queen Candace.

A pasty, white-faced man with a head full of dark brown curly locks, a beard trimmed in a sharp angle from each ear, and a finely woven outer coat followed the Ethiopian. Justus detected bits of a red and yellow undergarment and deduced him to be of a royal family from the recently Roman-conquered country of Spain.

The more varied the passengers, the more exhilarated he felt until he focused on two chained men. Both were skin and bones and wore ragged, dirty tunics. Each wore anklets connected by a single chain, their hands tied together in front of their bodies. And even though they were planted on the dock behind many of the boarding passengers, Justus assessed they were both Jews. *Aha! We have royalty mixed with prisoners . . . and the two Roman centurions following them are sure to be my roommates, one of the many penalties of being the son of a Roman proconsul.*

The last of the passengers was climbing the gangway when Justus sighted a wagon wildly careening down the street toward the pier. The driver reigned in two black stallions—their heads reared back, their hooves grazing the edge of the pier.

Passengers and crew paused to gape at the commotion. A moment later, three women climbed down from the wagon.

A gnarled crewmember near Justus said, "Crazy women. What do they think they are trying to prove?" Leaning into his load, he continued across the deck to the storage hold.

Justin grinned and stretched up on his toes to follow the women's progress. All three appeared to be about his age. This voyage may be even more interesting than he'd imagined.

Two of the women moved to the gangplank but remained on the dock, waiting for the third to register. One kept looking at the water between the ship's hull and the pier, which caused Justus to question whether she was afraid of it. The other looked at ease. Justus could tell from the style of their clothes they were from Greece. He would enjoy meeting either one of them, until the third turned from registering with the captain.

Her gait was fluid, and she held her body upright with a hint of arrogance. Her robe was fine linen and pulled back revealing a short dress, intricately bordered with miniature pomegranates. Her well-proportioned body was accentuated by the cut of the dress, and her deep tan emphasized by her garment's alabaster color.

The other two women started up the gangway as the third arrived. Justus tried to resolve the contradiction between last woman's royal mannerisms and dark tan, but he couldn't figure it out. He ended up simply gawking at the trio.

In seconds, they reached the deck. The front two brushed by Justus, making no eye contact.

The tanned woman, however, stopped directly in front of him looking galled, her short black hair wafting back from the breeze coming off the harbor, and her voice bold. "You have a question?"

The woman's surprising candor rattled Justus. He raised his right hand slightly toward her. "Ah . . . well . . . yes. What's your name?"

The woman hesitated as if evaluating his request, but raised her chin and displayed a challenging expression. "Michal." She used the Jewish soft pronunciation of *ch* as in the name *Michelle*, rather than the harsh Greek *ch* as in *church*. "And yours?"

Justus snapped to attention and replied, "Justus."

Michal's eyebrows raised and the corner of her mouth turned up slightly. "Spoken like a true Roman." She turned and followed her friends below.

Justus was frozen. All he could do was swallow his machismo and stare at her captivating back until she disappeared through the hatch.

CHAPTER THREE

High up in the Jerusalem Temple, the room was the size of a thirty-person synagogue with three windows looking over the city wall. The Mount of Olives lay in plain view. Four long, flat boards were propped up on benches to stand unusually high. Three were covered with opened scrolls. The fourth held a stack of thinly sawn acacia boards, reed pens, and dye ink. The only other furniture was a bench and a cot.

The single door creaked open, and Asher shuffled in. His snowy hair and beard contrasted with his purple robe. Deep lines in his face testified not only to his age, but to the victories and defeats of a long life.

He had worked in this room for the ten days between the Feast of Trumpets and Yom Kippur, but it still felt foreign to him. When he had become a sage forty years ago, his priestly duties in the Temple were suspended, so he rarely visited here, which added to the unfamiliarity of the place.

Perez, a shriveled, middle-aged man with a gaunt profile, filed in behind him. He wore the clothes of a servant but carried himself with confidence from years of working in the presence of royalty. He held a flask of wine and a cup, and looked troubled. "Master Asher, do you need help carrying your supper plate?"

Asher softly snorted. "No, thank you. A loaf of bread and a little boiled lamb isn't hard to handle, even at my age." He plopped down at the stand holding the wooden sheets and pushed them away with a scraping sound to make room for his plate.

Perez placed the wine and cup near the plate and pivoted to go. He hesitated, his head down and his voice soft. "Master Asher, is there anything else I can get you this evening?"

"Yes, Perez. I need a sharp knife."

Perez did a double take. "Sir?"

Asher felt a tinge of impatience with Perez's question. "I will be cutting the acacia wood into strips this evening."

Perez looked mystified. His voice reverted to the tone of a servant. "As you wish, Master. I will get one and return soon."

Perez glided out the door, closing it behind him.

The familiar click of the lock rang in Asher's ear. Pouring himself a cup of wine from the flask, he pushed aside his flowing white beard to sip it. After breaking the bread into four pieces, his quivering legs ultimately allowed him to stand. He selected one piece, lifted the cup, and made his way to the middle window. He spilled only a little wine.

Working the bread through his beard, he bit into it and absent-mindedly gazed over the Garden of Gethsemane as he chewed. The sweet aroma of freshly stomped grapes floated through the window, but their fragrance did not catch his attention.

I should not be doing this, he thought. *My purpose is to find deeper meanings from the Torah.* Asher was to receive the Way of Truth, the essence of this world, things that astonish and frighten. All knowledge and history were in the Torah. All people were in the Torah. In his spirit, he knew he was close to finding the end of Roman rule—the coming of the Messiah. But now, he must stop. Now, he was forced to be a treasure hunter . . . a treasure hunter.

Asher trudged back toward the stand that was holding the rest of his supper. As he passed between two others, he paused to lovingly stroke a scroll with two fingers. Shaking his head, he continued to the one with the bench and slumped onto it.

A quiet knock on the door was followed by a whisper. "Master Asher?"

"Come in."

Perez unlocked the door and plodded in, carrying a small knife. His air was quizzical. "Will this do, Master?"

Asher examined the knife and glanced at Perez. "Yes, it should work nicely."

Perez bowed his head, stepped toward the door, and murmured, "Master, will you need anything else?"

"No, I'll be fine. Soon, Perez, it will be over."

"I'm sure, sir," he softly replied as he exited through the door and locked it.

The setting sun was darkening the room and caused Asher to squint at the knife. *Presently, I will be lighting the lamps, but this night I will be cutting wood, not searching. The scribes should be here tomorrow, and I must be ready.*

He strained to rise and returned to the stand where he had paused earlier. Selecting a scroll, he worked his way back to the one where the thin boards lay. He grasped a single panel, laid it flat and held the scroll against it, slightly below its edge.

Very carefully, he measured the width of 1 letter and marked the board with the knife. Then he measured the distance of 2 letters and marked it with the knife. He continued increasing the width of his marks until he had measured the expanse of 10 letters. He repeated the notching process on the opposite edge of the same slat.

Asher returned the scroll to its original site, but his step became stronger as he headed back, the notched board in his shaking hand. His lips turned up into a half smile as he selected an unmarked board and laid it on top of the marked one, forming a straight edge between the notches on each side. He dragged the blade through the branded wood with a soft splitting sound. He proceeded by moving the straight edge to the 2-letter marks and cut a new strip 2 letters wide.

This would make searching go much faster. With enough strips cut tonight, perhaps he'd find the answer quickly after the scribes' visit tomorrow. Asher regained new energy and determination as he continued cutting the boards into wider and wider widths. While he worked, his thoughts shifted to the bolted door and he felt tears gather. This idea must work, for there was little time left. The Feast of the Booths started in four days and after that, he'd only have until Hanukkah.

CHAPTER FOUR

Justus felt stuffed as he climbed onto the weather deck. The supper the first night of every voyage was the best, for the pheasant was freshly prepared, the cucumbers, melons and leeks were all fresh, and the bread recently baked. Few ships carried live animals for all sailing days, so salted meat, aging vegetables, and moldy bread tended to be the fare for most of the journey.

He circled the weather deck several times, hoping to alleviate the discomfort in his overfull stomach, sidestepping the crew as they checked the main sail and riggings. After completing his circuit, he felt better. Although the wind was light, waves slapped the hull as the bow cut through the sea, lending a hypnotic effect to the evening.

He leaned against the ship's railing and watched a centurion marching towards him. The soldier was classic Roman—clean-shaven, rippling muscles and a square chin with blue pupils that could pierce one almost as effectively as his sword. He was in full uniform—leather breastplate, helmet, sword, and shield. His knobby-bottomed Roman sandals clattered on the deck with every step.

Justus grinned. "Claudius, that was surprisingly good food."

"Yes, it was a very good supper, Honorable Justus. I predict the closer we get to Tyre, the worse the food will be."

Justus chuckled. "I'm sure you are right."

"Sir, I must relieve Cornelius from watching the prisoners. He will be in our cabin this night." Although both centurions had been assigned as Justus' roommates, one was always guarding the two prisoners.

As Justus watched the centurion leave the weather deck, he thought, *He has taken his training seriously.*

Justus' father had required him to train frequently with the soldiers under his command, the reason for the young man's muscular body and agile movements. Although not officially a Roman soldier, Justus had learned most of the techniques of hand-to-hand combat from war-weathered veterans. He was proficient with a spear and crossbow, but he had become an expert with a double-edged short sword. His father often said if he could only pick one person for close quarters combat, he would select Justus.

Justus' solitude was interrupted by Michal and her two companions' arrival on deck. His thoughts instantly changed direction.

Michal ignored him. She led the way to the rail near the navigation area and exclaimed, "Look! It is turning orange."

The sun continued its slow plunge into the ocean, turning from orange to deep red amid the *Ooo's* and *Ahh's* of the three women. When the last sliver disappeared from the horizon, the trio exchanged small talk about the setting.

As they gabbed, Michal casually moved toward Justus until the girls ended up next to the railing where he was leaning. "Good evening, Justus," she said.

Justus observed her studied, casual air and anticipation rose in him. "Good evening, Michal," he murmured.

She twisted slightly and held her palm up. "My attendants, Helen and Thorakis."

Justus nodded. "Ladies, my pleasure."

Helen was dressed much as Michal—short, finely woven white dress, knee-touching robe and mid-shin laced sandals. Thorakis was boyish in appearance. Her dark brown hair was short cropped, and her purple robe was belted tightly around her. Justus noted her tendency to lag behind the other two.

Michal looked pleased and dismissed the other women. "You may return to the cabin now."

"As you wish, my lady." The two scurried to the staircase and descended out of sight.

Michal reversed directions and viewed the sea, her short hair gently rustling across her ears in the faint breeze. The arrival of evening had diminished the wind, and the sea had become very calm. She wrapped her robe tighter against the evening chill, rested against the railing and gave Justus a fleeting look. "What a beautiful sunset."

A surprising feeling of timidity came over him. "Yes, it was. Also, a perfect evening for it."

Michal looked nonchalant and waited several moments before speaking. "I thought you Romans liked surnames."

"Most of us do."

"Well . . . what's yours?"

"Justus."

Michal gave him a mischievous look. "Justus Justus?"

"There's a long story about that."

Michal mused for a moment and looked delighted. "Does the long story include why you have a Roman name but look like a Jew?"

Justus looked down. His cheeks felt hot. When he first arrived in Rome, people had often said that he looked Jewish, but those comments had ceased years ago. He glanced at Michal. "As a matter of fact, it does."

"Well, by all means, tell me."

She had a knack for catching him off guard. He gave a nervous cough and took a deep breath. "My father was a Roman centurion stationed in a small town in Galilee called Nazareth. His name is Marcus Justus. He was very kind to people there. Once he even used some of his own money to build them a synagogue. A man named Joseph lived on the outskirts of Nazareth. He had one daughter, Leah."

"And, of course, they were Jewish?"

"Yes. Joseph's wife died during Leah's birth, so the man raised Leah by himself. My father frequently talked with Leah, and they fell in love. He married her and not too long after, I was born. She named me after her father, Joseph."

"A Roman marrying a Jew . . . A popular idea, I'd guess."

Justus squinted. "It is taboo."

"I know," she said as she shrugged. "Please continue."

Justus gave her a short questioning glance. Placing his hand on the carved railing, he felt light moisture from dew forming as the balustrade cooled. He absently moved his hand across the surface, causing the wetness to pool on his fingers. "Joseph nearly disowned her. Most of the Jews at Nazareth would have nothing to do with us."

Michal's expression softened. "Bet that was hard."

"Very. I think the only reason the town tolerated the union was because Father was so kind to them."

Michal perked up. "So, you were named Joseph."

"Yes. My parents called me Barsabbas when we were around my grandfather to keep us straight."

Michal gazed intently at Justus. "But . . . where does 'Justus Justus' come from?"

"The Jews in Nazareth called me by my surname, 'Justus'. Even after my father was promoted to tribune, and we moved to Rome, the name stuck."

Michal smiled softly. "An interesting story, Justus Justus . . ."

"No . . . simply Justus."

"OK, Justus."

Frozen, Justus gazed at her and felt a mysterious force.

Michal finally broke the trance. "Does your journey stop at Tyre, or are you going back to Nazareth?"

"I'm going to Jerusalem."

Michal canted her head. Her expression brightened and the corners of her mouth faintly pulled up, yet her voice remained unchanged. "Why to Jerusalem?"

Her question brought him back to reality. He swallowed hard, and his eyebrows furled. "To save a friend."

A bewildered expression came over her. "Save him from what?"

"From himself."

CHAPTER FIVE

As she tumbled about in the bouncing wagon, Miriam's thoughts raced through a kaleidoscope of fear. Would she be raped, killed, or maybe sold into slavery? Why would anyone do this to her? If her husband were still alive, he would have protected her.

Miriam's head pounded into the side of the wagon. Her hands were tied behind her and allowed no protection. The desire to scream had long since been quelled by a tightly fitting gag. Her blindfold blocked all light, but she was sure she wouldn't be able to see anything anyway as she felt the rubbing of rough wool material covering her.

The wagon groaned as it came to a standstill. She felt the wool material scrape across her skin as someone pulled it off and growled, "Stand up."

Panic welling up in her, Miriam obeyed. It had been nearly two weeks since a thug had dug through a wall of her home while she slept. She had awakened with a knife at her throat. She had a petite body and seldom did any strenuous labor in her thirty-five years, so within minutes, she was overpowered, rendered helpless, gagged, blindfolded, and bound. She had been carted off to a daily series of different rooms, stables, and barns. She had eaten little and slept even less. The constant fear of death was starting to affect her. She couldn't take this punishment much longer.

The man cut the ropes wrapped around her ankles and helped her to stand. He grabbed her bound hands and guided her to the back of the wagon. As he clutched her arm, his voice was harsh. "Jump."

Overcome more by fear of the man than concern she couldn't see a landing spot, Miriam leaped and hit the ground hard, but the man's grip kept her upright. She had no time to adjust her feet, for he immediately pulled her up a steep incline.

The warmth she felt from the sun on her arms abruptly evaporated. She stumbled as he pulled her several more steps, then stopped her.

His gruff voice echoed. "Stay here."

Miriam again obeyed, shivering in the cool air. Her robe had remained in the house during the abduction, and the only garment she wore was a now-filthy tunic. She swayed, the blindfold hindering her balance, when suddenly he ripped it from her head. The darkness of the enclosure allowed her sight to adjust quickly. She peered at her captor. Only his eyes were uncovered by the dirty white scarf that hung down from his turban and pulled across his face.

She panned the enclosure. It was a cave with openings in the walls that were covered by stones: a catacomb. A chill shot through her. *I'm among the dead.* Would he kill her and bury her in one of these tombs?

Why does he want me dead? I have done nothing to anyone.

Miriam's captor hooked her bound hands and spun her in front of a large oblong stone. Why was it propped open by a small log when all the rest were closed?

"Crawl into the tomb."

Miriam hesitated, unable to make the connection between the command and the small opening before her.

In one motion, the man sliced through the ropes on her hands and pushed her roughly onto the cave floor, he bellowed, "I said, get into the tomb!"

Miriam rolled onto her hands and knees and snaked through the small opening. She had barely made it inside before the man knocked the log away, allowing the stone to crash onto the cave floor. It blocked all but a small part of the tomb's opening.

Still lying on the floor, she struggled to make her near-useless hands remove the gag. Eventually, she succeeded not only in freeing her mouth, but her long, light brown hair puffed away from her head. She moved to the small opening and glared at the man whose body blocked much of the soft light from the catacomb's entrance. "Why have you done this to me? Why do you want me to die in this tomb?"

"Shut up or you will die in this place." He loosened a pouch tied to his waist and pushed it through the opening. "Here, this is food and water. You'll get more tomorrow. Scream all you want, but I assure you, only the dead will hear."

Miriam remained riveted to the empty opening as she tuned in to her captor's departing steps. After several minutes of total silence, she pivoted. The tomb was softly lit by four small cracks in one wall. It took only seconds to establish the six-foot-square tomb was empty except for a narrow ledge just wide enough to lay a body. She shivered as she noted no body was on the ledge.

She could almost hear her heart beat blood through her wrists where her flesh was still indented by the ropes. Claustrophobia skirted her intellect. She felt the prickly feeling in her hands from returning circulation as she limped to the source of light—the cracks. She peered through the largest one and saw the sides of a mountain and in the distance some others, but nothing familiar. And, there was no evidence of people. She worked her fingers into the crack, but the stone was unyielding.

Wobbling, she returned to the stone covering the tomb door and pushed with what little strength remained in her. It wouldn't move.

The events of the last two weeks avalanched into her psyche. She lurched to the narrow shelf and slumped onto it. Her chest convulsed as sobs worked their way up her body to her throat. She burst out crying aloud and tears flooded her face. For several minutes, despair blocked out all her other senses.

Finally, exhaustion took over and quieted the outpouring of despair. She stretched out onto the ledge. As she laid a hot cheek on the smooth, cool surface, a shiver coursed through her body.

Her face held a vacant stare, her head unmoving on the stone. Her red, swollen eyes caught the forming of a single drop of water on the tomb's ceiling. She fixated on it, as the drop slowly grew larger and larger. Finally, gravity took over and it plummeted to the tomb floor. Miriam's body lurched reflexively as the tomb's silence was broken by the single drop's impact. Stillness blanketed her again, as she drifted off. *They would not have done this to me if they knew who my father . . .*

CHAPTER SIX

The walls of the small galley area were lined with shelves about stomach high on an average-size man. A railing was positioned a foot above them, so that diners could hold their standing position while they ate if the seas were rough. Most were crowded with passengers assigned to this particular mealtime.

Justus and Claudius stood in a corner slightly separated from the others. The room echoed with the chatter of passengers getting to know each other or talking with companions. The mixed aroma of fish and bread permeated the air.

Michal stepped through the narrow door and inhaled deeply. She checked the room for an empty spot, saw Justus, and strolled to him. "May I join you?"

Justus moved his hand toward the open area on the shelf next to him. "By all means. Claudius, this is Michal."

Claudius gave a polite nod. "My lady. I'm sorry, but I must take lunch to the prisoners and my fellow centurion. Forgive me."

Still fixing his attention on Michal, Justus said, "We understand, Claudius."

Claudius squeezed past two of the ship's crew who had noted Michal's entrance and approached her, each with a serving bowl.

Unlike ships that transported less wealthy clientele and served meals on bronze plates or in clay bowls, one server slipped a silver plate in front of Michal.

Michal gave the waiter a sheepish look. "Please . . . could I have another?"

Justus watched as the server placed a second plate in front of Michal, but remained silent.

The first waiter held out a bowl filled with salted fish.

Michal ignored Justus and placed a generous portion on one plate, less on the second. She repeated the strategy from the second bowl filled with boiled eggs and bread.

Justus stared at the two plates as his thoughts turned playful. "Do you always skip meals one day, and then eat twice as much the next?"

Michal slanted a scowl at him. "You know exactly what I was doing yesterday. Helen told me you asked where I and Thorakis were."

"Is she better?"

Her soft smile reappeared, and she gave a wave of dismissal. "Yes, she is fine. The sea has calmed a bit, so she was finally able to fall asleep. She was still sleeping when I left the cabin a few moments ago. I'm glad I don't get seasick . . ." She picked up a small piece of bread and threw it on Justus' plate, and faked a sneer. "The other plate is not mine. It's for Thorakis and Helen."

Justus grinned. He finished eating what little food remained on his plate, including the tossed bread piece.

Michal took a bite and looked at Justus, waiting for him to speak.

He wiped his mouth and cleared his throat, with a look of curiosity. "Night before last, you found out all about me . . ."

"Not all."

"Well, not all . . . but, a lot. Now it's your turn to tell me about yourself. Helen said yesterday you had come to Crete from Athens. So, you are Greek?"

Michal pitched her head and feigned displeasure. "I'm sure you already knew I was from Greece. We Grecians dress and act much differently than you Romans."

"Guilty as charged. What I don't understand is why your attendants have Greek names, but yours is Jewish. How is that?"

Michal blushed but did not break eye contact. "Like you, I am half Jew."

"I suspected as much. Care to share?"

She gave him an awkward laugh. "Are you sure you want to hear this long story?"

"It's only fair. I told you about me. Besides . . . I do have the time."

"OK." Michal pushed her half-empty plate away, leaned on her left elbow, and inhaled deeply. "My ancestors moved to Greece while our people were slaves in Babylon. All of the family moved back to Judea except my grandfather. His only child was my mother. My father was a Greek nobleman. My mother says I closely resemble him."

"So, he must have been beautiful."

His comment stopped her for a second. Finally, she smiled and went on, "I look Greek, but I am half Jew. You look Jewish, but are half Roman. Funny, isn't it?"

Justus beamed as he processed her story. "Then you're a Hellenist?"

Michal sobered. "Yes, very liberal."

Justus realized he was close to crossing a line he didn't want to cross, so he quickly changed the subject. "Why are you going to Tyre?"

"Not Tyre . . . Jerusalem."

Justus stood straighter and smiled. "You are? Why?"

Michal's manner became haughty, but her facial features laughed at him as she lifted the plate of untouched food. "Well, certainly not to save anyone." She paused to change her tone. "I'm going to visit my cousin. I haven't seen her for a long while, so I decided to visit her. I'm looking forward to catching up on everything since we last were together."

He grinned. He had become dazzled by her charm and strained to hold his emotions in check. "What's your cousin's name?" he asked.

"Miriam."

CHAPTER SEVEN

Several hundred miles southeast of the Alexandrian ship, James plodded across the courtyard from his workshop and stopped at the door of his room. He brushed wood chips from his clothes and ran his fingers through his medium length beard to assure no wood flakes were embedded there. It had been a hectic day, and he was glad the setting of the sun drew it to a close. Dusk marked the beginning of each Jewish day, so James usually began his day with supper. This was to be no exception.

A large water barrel sat close to the door, so he drew a bowl of water from the barrel and ceremonially washed his hands and arms to the elbow as required of Jews. His forearms and biceps bulged from years of daily carpenter work.

He paid no attention to the chitchat from his brother's wives as they prepared the evening meal in the courtyard. Still, even though he was thirty-two and unmarried, their familiar banter caused him to feel at home as he picked up the lighted lamp next to the water barrel and went in.

His small room adjoined those of his brothers and mother. An advantage of being a carpenter was to have more furniture than most people did. He had built for his room a stool and two benches. A small bed frame was erected from the floor and filled one corner. Crossing the room to a strategically placed shelf, he set down the lamp and sighed in satisfaction. He'd finished the bench and winnowing fork, even though for a while he doubted he'd have them done before the Festival of Booths. Old man Stephen would have them on time.

James removed his outer coat and ambled back to the door. His reach for the door handle was futile, however, as it disappeared and was replaced by Joses. He was James' youngest brother and, although married, he had not outgrown a youth's impatience. His body language showed agitation.

James shook off his surprising appearance. "My brother . . . Welcome. How is work on the farmer's barn coming?"

"Guess who is back in town."

James' shoulders slumped forward. "So, that's why you came."

Joses bustled to a nearby bench but remained standing. He was shorter than James and seven years younger. His meaty forearms and calloused hands confirmed he, too, was a carpenter. His beard and hair were trimmed to prevent interference with his work. His austere expression left little doubt he did not like the news. "James, what are we going to do? The authorities are getting more upset with him every time he teaches. The crowds keep getting bigger. He is going to get himself arrested or worse."

James suddenly wished for days past. After their father Joseph died, Jesus was heir-apparent to the family carpentry business, but a few years back he'd basically turned the reins over to James and began roaming from region to region, teaching people about what he called the Kingdom of God. The family had never been very popular in Nazareth, but this new proclivity had worsened their relationship with many of the townspeople to the point that it was hurting their business.

James felt his throat tighten. "There's nothing we can do to divert him. You were at that one house last fall. Remember, we tried to get him out of there, but he wouldn't talk to us . . . and Mother was even with us."

Suddenly, a handsome, well-built man with wavy dark hair and the family trademark—a meticulously trimmed beard and moustache—stepped in. "Peace to you, my brothers," he said, his voice lively.

James stood a little straighter. His thoughts churned, but he managed a pleasant smile. "And to you, Jesus. Where have you been recently?" Even though the town's gossip about Jesus ran rampant, his presence quieted James. Seeing him again generated a surprising feeling of peace.

"Capernaum." Jesus drifted to the center of the room near his brothers. His countenance was pleasant as he lightly touched Joses' shoulder. "Do not be so concerned. Everything is all right."

Joses' jaw clenched. "Tell that to everyone who thinks you've lost your mind."

Jesus shook his head slightly, but remained silent.

Joses appeared filled with anger, as he spat, "Are you going to the Feast of the Booths?"

Jesus answered with a calm exterior. "No. I am not."

"Why not? Why stay in Galilee? Go into Judea. This is no place for you here. If you must continue to act this way, show yourself openly. Make yourself known to the world." Joses spun and wearily collapsed onto a bench.

Jesus stood his ground during the onslaught of words and leaned closer to Joses, his voice strained. "My opportunity has not yet come. It is not the right time for me."

"So, you say."

"Any time is suitable to you," Jesus said. "Your opportunity is always there." He stepped to the door, but rather than exit, rotated, his voice sounding like a teacher. "The world can not be expected to hate you, but it does hate me, for I denounce it for its wicked ways. I reveal its doings are evil . . . My brothers, go to the feast yourselves."

➤ ➤ ➤

Kore smoothed his long, flowing robe. He used both hands to adjust the finely woven rope holding on his long head scarf, then combed his white speckled beard with his fingers as he entered the Temple enclosure. His palms were sweating, and his stomach churned. The Feast of the Booths started tomorrow, and Caiaphas had sent for him. Caiaphas was a treacherous man, and although half Kore's age, the most powerful Jew in Judea, the high priest. The procurator and King Herod had more authority, but they both tended to do what a high priest desired.

Although Kore was average in appearance, build, and intellect, he had worked diligently in the Jerusalem synagogue for twenty years and had become known as a Pharisee of distinction. He had wormed his way into many social gatherings of the ruling priests and gained their acceptance to the point he was sure he would be selected for the Sadducee-dominated ruling body of the Jews: the Sanhedrin.

As he neared the chamber of Caiaphas, Kore came upon two guards framing the door. Both had bodies hardened with rigorous physical training and wore the Temple uniform with leather breastplate and leather helmet. One held a spear and wore white garments. The other had a long, straight, single-edged sword strapped to his waist and wore black.

Kore addressed the guard in black with a respectful tone. "Jehu, I'm surprised Caiaphas wants the captain of the Temple guards to attend this meeting."

Jehu had an obstinate set to his jaw. "I think you will soon find out why." He gestured to the guard in white. "In case you don't remember, this is Attai."

Attai made no acknowledgment, but held his steely gaze on Kore.

More than Kore's palms began sweating now. He nodded to Attai but did not greet him. His throat felt parched.

Jehu opened the door. "Caiaphas awaits you."

Caiaphas regally posed his thirty-one year old, average-sized frame as the three men entered the meeting room. Intricate black embroidery on his fine white robe showed his lofty position. He wore a headdress and a wide scarf around his neck, both beautifully woven and solid black, his personal style. He was young and had allowed his black beard and moustache to grow long and untrimmed. He eyed Kore unexpressively and gave a curt nod. However, his voice was cordial. "Good evening, Kore. Please, sit down."

Kore sat on a bench near a man who was already seated.

"I'm sure you know Sethur, the scribe."

"Yes, for years."

Jehu and Attai remained standing behind Caiaphas.

Caiaphas staged himself in front and assumed a posture of authority. "As I have been telling Sethur, the Nazarene carpenter has gotten out of hand. For nearly three years, he has spread his venom throughout Judea and Galilee. He has set up all kinds of fake acts of healing and even went so far as to pretend to raise someone from the dead. He constantly claims he is equal with God, which is outright blasphemy. He slanders us priests"—looking at Kore—"and you Pharisees."

Caiaphas paced, and his voice became shrill. "The man is undermining our religion. He violates the Sabbath, turning the common people against us. He has our nation in an uproar. He is tearing down our established laws and principles. If we let him continue, not only will Rome discipline us, but God Almighty will destroy us." Caiaphas caught a seething breath and spat out, "He is a convincing liar. Soon he will have the whole of Israel in his hand."

Kore was also burdened by Jesus' following among the people, but this discussion caused his heart to pound. His voice tense, he said, "You are absolutely right. It is reaching epidemic proportions. Just yesterday, some of my fellow Pharisees told me they have overheard discussions among the people. They were saying, 'When the Messiah comes, can He be expected to do more miracles than this man'?"

Caiaphas slammed his fist onto the palm of his other hand. "If we don't stop this, the people will begin to believe he is the Christ and declare him king. I'm sure that's just what he wants."

Sethur jumped up frowning. He was half again as old as Caiaphas, small in stature, and had a mousey appearance in a simple headdress and an unpretentious robe. "What can we do? We can't arrest him. The people think he is a great prophet, at the least. If we try to arrest him, his followers will riot. Who knows where that could lead?"

Caiaphas gave a smug smile. He motioned for Sethur to be calm. "I have a plan. If we discredit him in front of the people, he will lose their allegiance. They'll see him as a fanatic and the liar that he is. Gentlemen, what we need is a good old-fashioned scandal."

Kore exhaled a long sigh of relief. He'd feared Caiaphas would hold him responsible to stop Jesus, but now he understood the plan. His pulse quieted as he became emotionally engaged. "An excellent idea . . . a scandal. Do you know of something we can use to discredit him?"

"Not yet. However . . . maybe we won't need to. He's all the time talking, but he is not a learned man. All we need to do is trap him in his words."

Sethur plopped onto the bench. "I can get some of my lawyer friends to come up with some ideas."

A clear plan of action blossomed in Kore's imagination, causing his lips to twist a little. "I will have my fellow Pharisees set up some . . . situations. He is sure to become completely entangled."

Caiaphas bobbed his head. "I think we all have the idea. I'm sure he will be at the feast tomorrow, so let's start then." He addressed the two guards. "Brief your soldiers. When the carpenter shows up, have them get near him. After he's caught in our web, bring him to me. I'll make sure you are rewarded and . . . I'll announce that he has committed a mortal sin. Soon, his influence will be non-existent."

CHAPTER EIGHT

Three days had past since Malchus' near encounter in the catacombs. His master had instructed him to wait until this night to return, but to be extra careful to remain undiscovered.

Malchus leaned against the mud-brick wall, his large frame needing all the support an upside-down water barrel could provide. The silence of the room added to his feelings of despondency.

The windowless room was becoming dark. Malchus swallowed the last bits of crusty bread and salted lamb and picked up his cup. Downing the remainder of the wine, he stood, ambled to the door, and cracked it open. The aroma of roasting meat wafted over him.

He peered into the large courtyard. Beyond the open fire, two women were turning a lamb on a spit. His master, Caiaphas, had taken the office of high priest three days ago and moved into the palace in front and to the right of these nearly invisible servant quarters. Malchus was required to move into this single room which adjoined the servants' quarters but had no direct access to them.

As the sun slipped below the tall wall around Jerusalem, hopelessness invaded him. He felt as if he were in a vise. He had never been able to have a family or own anything. The chance he had been given could be lost forever if someone else found Melchizedek's Tomb first.

He tightened his outer coat, moved into the courtyard and stood, his reasoning retracing the possible tomb identifiers he had been given to search for. *Really . . . P and* R. *I wonder how Bukki comes up with ideas like this.*

> ▶ ▶ ▶

The first night watch had ended when Malchus stood in the location he had sprinted from three nights earlier. He tried to concentrate on the markings any of the tombs had, hoping to find one with a *P,* an *R,* or both. The experience of nearly being caught made him edgy, and he repeatedly looked up and down the corridor.

By the third watch, his lamp was burning low on oil. He had found nothing close to the two letters. Suddenly, he glimpsed a light far down the corridor. It took only a second for him to see it rapidly approached him. Caiaphas' warning about not being found in the catacombs rang loud, so again he sped back to the alley entrance.

As he turned the last corner which led to the stairs, he froze. Jehu, captain of the Temple guards, blocked his exit, a sword in one hand, a lamp in the other. Malchus took one step back.

Jehu's voice was commanding. "Stay where you are."

Malchus turned toward the sound of steps behind him and saw Attai jogging up the passageway. Remorse clutched him, and his stomach churned. He was trapped. He stood speechless.

Jehu moved to him, his voice scornful. "What is the lead servant of the high priest doing in the catacombs at this time of night?"

Malchus could not begin to imagine how he could lie his way out of this. The catacombs damp, cool air seemed colder, and he shivered. His gaze dropped to the floor, his voice a whisper, "Is it illegal to come here at night?"

Attai shoved Malchus' shoulder. "Not illegal, but strange. Are you searching for something?"

Malchus' heart raced, but he strove to appear dispassionate. "Searching? Searching for what?"

Jehu looked scornful, his voice a hiss. "Yes . . . for what?"

CHAPTER NINE

The boat pitched from side to side and rolled up and over the high waves. The third day of the fierce storm found the large passenger vessel tossed about by the angry sea like a twig. The crew had long since tied away all the sails, but still the ship was cruising over the foamy brine at speeds seldom possible. Lightening and thunder had been a constant companion of the passengers. During rare lulls, the creaks and pops of the twisting wooden hull were nearly as loud as the thunder.

The ship's interior design had railings along the cabin walls for times like these, and Justus sat in his cabin on his bunk and hung to one, barely able to keep from being dashed to the deck.

Claudius opened the door and was thrown into the room as the ship lurched to one side. "Ouch!" He sat on his bed, rubbing his leg with one hand and holding the bed tightly with the other. "I brought some dried meat from the galley. Do you want any?"

Justus shook his head. "Thanks. I don't get seasick, but it's too rough to deal with food now. Tell you what . . . give it to me anyway and I'll tie it to my bed for later." Justus edged his way to the end of his bed, took the pouch from Claudius, and secured it.

Claudius grabbed the railing to steady himself as concern clouded his expression. "One of the galley crew said the captain has ordered some sailors to sound the water. They are afraid we are near land."

Justus knew the common procedure. By constantly sending a heavy object tied to a repeatedly knotted rope into the sea, they could measure how far the ship was from the sea's bottom; the shorter the distance, the closer to shore. However, the futility of such action in a strong storm caused his lip to curl. "Fat chance they'll get a correct reading. Although we should be near Tyre by now, the storm could have propelled us anywhere."

"I'm sure the crew fears that, too."

Justus was slammed against the cabin wall, causing him to grimace. "We sure can't land in a storm like this."

Claudius clung to the railing and inched his way to the door, his brow creased with concern. "I will check on the prisoners. Please excuse me."

Justus glanced at him. "Of course." He handled the door after Claudius left, making sure it was tightly latched.

He worked his way back to his bed. As he rolled with the ship's movement, he thought of Michal. He had not seen her for two days and felt an unfamiliar emptiness.

> > >

Six hours later, night had claimed the cabin and the storm had waned enough for Justus to fall asleep. "What the . . .?" He propped himself up in bed on his elbows, trying to blink away the fog of sleep as water splashed onto his face. He instinctively grasped the railing as the ship lurched wildly to one side, marking the return of the storm's fury.

Are we sinking?

Claudius was poised directly over him, water running down his helmet and onto Justus, his make-up tense. "Honorable Justus, I'm sorry to wake you, but there is a problem."

Justus bolted upright. He had heard that tone of voice from soldiers before. "What's wrong?"

"The crew, sir. They are all gone. The lifeboats are gone. They tied the ship's rudder, but it has broken. We are at the mercy of the storm."

"Oh, no." Adrenaline shot though his system. "Go to Michal's cabin and tell them what has happened. Instruct them to meet me at the bow of the weather deck. Afterwards, get Cornelius and the prisoners."

"Done." As Claudius tried to go vertical, the ship lurched and sent him horizontal into the wall, amid the loud sound of tearing wood.

Gaining his footing, he used his rippling muscles to pull himself to the door. He glanced at Justus in confusion. "Shall we kill the prisoners?"

"No, cut them loose. We may all be dead soon anyway. Hurry . . . Go." Justus grabbed the pouch from his bed, tied it to his belt, and wrapped his coat around him. Leaving the cabin, he creeped along the corridor to the weather deck and used the railing to navigate the oscillating top-side to the bow. Wave after wave slammed into him. Between waves, the howling wind sprayed stinging water over him.

The ship's motion had changed from rolling to rapidly turning circles, like it was being sucked down a maelstrom. Every turn was dotted with tearing and cracking sounds.

Justus held his arm above his brow, shielding the spraying sea enough to see Michal, her two companions, and Claudius illuminated by repeated lighting bolts as they were creeping toward him on their bellies. Fearing for their safety more than his own, he put both hands to his mouth and yelled, "The ship is breaking up. Look for something that floats in case we must abandon . . ."

Before he could finish, the ship slammed into something solid and stopped dead, catapulting them into the water.

For an instant, Justus lost all orientation in the black sea. His air-filled lungs gave him enough buoyancy to move him slightly upward. He clawed at the water to reach the surface. Shaking salty liquid from his head, he searched left. The strobing lightening revealed just the ship. Bobbing like a cork in a waterfall, he peered right and only saw white caps shooting up and being blown off. He screamed with all his might, "Michal! Claudius!"

Since the ship was now grounded, every wave that slammed into its side accelerated its destruction.

Justus battled the water to stay afloat with long-cultivated muscles. His inability to find Michal caused his sanity to drown in panic. "Michal . . . Michal . . . Michal!"

The sound of thunder and breaking lumber gave a small reprieve, allowing Michal to give a shrill answer. "Here!"

Hope soared inside him as he looked behind him, away from the ship. He strained to identify her in the foaming inferno. *God . . . where is she?* A bolt of lightening flickered, and he caught a glimpse of her through the driving rain. Immediately, he swam for her, his muscles laboring against every wave, a moving wall to penetrate.

Justus' breathing sounded as if he were being tortured, but he glimpsed Michal's head illuminated by the lightening and drove toward her. He strained against the torrent, but could not reach her. Time was running out.

The very next wave covered Michal, and she did not come back up.

Justus panicked. *No, God, please . . . She's gone!*

A cross-current spun Justus sideways and the following wave threw Michal on top of him, pushing him under the water. He clutched her arm and swam to the top, sputtering. He pulled her limp body to him, lacing his arm under hers to keep her nose and mouth out of the water.

The boiling sea relentlessly pushed them in the direction of the ship-wreck. The harder he toiled, the larger it appeared. In seconds, they would be slammed against the side.

The next wave carried them within yards of the hull and broke the ship in half as it hit. The Twin Brothers figurehead twisted, wood splintering into a shower of shreds, and tore off the bow. It plummeted into the water, narrowly missing the struggling pair, but the force of its wake pushed them momentarily away from the wreckage.

Justus hooked the figurehead as it emerged from the water. Moving along its side, he pulled himself and Michal into the V-shape between the twin heads. "Michal, are you all right?"

She opened one eye halfway through wet, matted hair as she coughed and sputtered water.

Justus groaned with relief. "Here, let me set you on this small ledge on the neck of Castor." He helped her onto the rim.

Michal murmured, "What about you?"

Hearing her voice gave him a surge of strength. He took one of Michal's hands and placed it onto the twin brother, Pollux. "Hold on here."

She reached out her other hand, leaned forward, and weakly hugged as much as she could of the image.

Justus worked himself onto the neck, bent to the wood connecting Pollux's image, and effectively completed a triangle with Michal in the middle. Blood seeped down the back of her head. A sinking feeling erased much of his new-found hope. "You're injured."

She tried to nod, then winced.

They clutched the figurehead as it bobbed in the foaming water, and the waves pushed them far beyond the wreckage.

A new fear clamped Justus' mind. *That sound . . . rocks.* The sounds grew louder, while lightening continued to pulsate onto the sea. Justus searched ahead of them, frantically trying to devise a plan to avoid the new danger. *Oh no . . . There they are.*

A dark object appeared directly in front of them, silhouetted by long forks of light as a wave crashed the figurehead into it. The violent impact threw both of them back into the water.

Justus lost sight of Michal as his feet hit something. *Sand.*

"Michal . . . Michal." No response. Another strong wave threw him onto a sandy beach. He felt exhausted and laid on the sand as the surf bubbled around him on its way back into the sea. He rebelled against the idea that Michal was dead but lay in a feeling of defeat until the next wave threatened to drag him from the shore.

Stumbling, he got up on one knee and shook his head hard, flinging droplets everywhere. He made out the form of a white, ghostly image just yards from him. He slopped through the water and sand and dropped to his knees at her side. "Michal, are you all right? Michal?

He somehow managed to lift her limp form and struggle through the mushy sand away from the pounding surf. Several rocks jutted beyond the reach of high tide. *Maybe there is some shelter there.* He squeezed between two large rocks and found a cleft forming a slight canopy.

Justus laid her as far back under it as possible.

She was shivering.

If he could lie against her and drape his coat over the part of them not protected by the cleft . . . He sat down, pushing firmly against her body, wedging her between himself and the rock. He stared at Michal as he lay next to her and pulled the coat over them both, shutting out the worst of the rain and howling wind. His thoughts shifted between the exhilaration of having rescued her from the sea and the despair of knowing he could do no more to help her.

CHAPTER TEN

The dancing flames of many oil lamps made the walls of the upper Temple room appear to gyrate. The fanfare around Caiaphas being inducted as high priest for the coming year, coupled with his move into the palace of the high priest gave the scribes an excuse to deliver the eight large sheets of papyrus five days late. But, they were inscribed exactly as Asher had ordered. They were all three feet high by three feet wide, filled with letters: 100 across the top and 100 rows—10,000 letters in all—but not rolled into customary scrolls. Taken together, the eight sheets contained the entire first book of the Torah, Genesis.

Asher propped himself up on shaking legs as he bent over the third sheet. He had spent all of yesterday on the first sheet and all of today on the second sheet. Although late, he decided to continue, since this third matrix of letters contained the plaintext story about Melchizedek. Surely, the answer would be on it. Unless . . .

Asher straightened his back with the help of his hand, then forced his weary body to move to the pile of acacia-wood strips, where he gaped at them trance like. He had searched the first two sheets using all the board widths and found nothing.

His back ached from prolonged stooping. After hours of concentrated searching he tried to blink away a feeling like sand between bare toes after a day at the beach. The possibility that he might not find the proper designator caused his shoulders to sag. What if the sages in the Great Assembly were right? What if there must be a key?

During his training, they had brought that possibility up. Even his friend Mazis had warned him that some information in the Torah was so complex one needed to find a key before the answers would appear. What if he must find one?

The Mercy Gate night guard barked out the end of the first night watch and caused Asher to emerge from his thoughts. He replaced the boards from the last sheet, grabbed all of the 1-character strips and returned to the table with the third papyrus page. His method of searching had become routine: the first strip covered the second row of letters, the second covered the fourth row of letters and so on, until every other row of letters was covered. He duplicated the process, but this time covering columns. The result was very quickly obtained—a matrix of 50 x 50 visible letters.

The new set of visible letters seemed to energize Asher as he bent and examined them. *Yes, this is much quicker . . . Examining 2500 letters is much easier than looking at all 10,000 at one time.* He riveted the sheet, attempting to find words embedded in the visible letters, as his head weaved from time to time. No words were evident horizontally . . . none vertically. He squinted hard. Or, diagonally. Now the really difficult part . . . determining if a word was spelled backwards in those directions.

Asher spent a long while pouring over the 2500 exposed letters but found nothing. As was his method, he moved each column strip over one space and placed the last column strip onto the first column, uncovering the skipped column letters from before, but hiding the ones he had just examined. Still nothing!

He removed all the column strips and moved the row strips down one, followed by covering the columns as before. Still he found nothing. Asher's vision blurred. He stretched and rubbed his eyes with his knuckles.

I'll try the boards that skip 3 letters. If I find nothing, I'll retire for the night.

He put the first board on row 2 and it covered rows 2, 3, and 4. He skipped row 5 and placed the next board on row 6, covering rows 6, 7, and 8. He continued covering rows until the last board covered rows 98, 99, and 100. He repeated the process covering columns, resulting in a matrix of 25 x 25 letters. *This should go quite fast, since only 625 letters are in . . .* Asher jerked back in surprise. *Of course . . .* He rose upright, grinning. Six stood out clearly among the other 619:

T

T   O   L

M

B

Lot. Abram had rescued Lot. That must be the clue. Asher limped to a table holding writing materials. Selecting a very small sheet of papyrus, he wrote *L O T* on it and rolled it into a small scroll. To keep it rolled, he placed a large drop of melted wax at the seam, and pushed his ring into it, leaving a visible *A*.

First, he must return the wooden strips. No one need know about his methods. He removed them all from the large scroll and returned them to the pile, then replaced the large papyrus sheet on top of the others.

Asher shuffled to the door and pounded. "Perez, I have a clue. Perez? Perez?"

He continued pounding until he heard the door being unlocked. Perez edged through the door, his lids puffy and red. His hair was sticking up on one side. "Master, it's the middle of the night. What's wrong?"

"I have the clue."

"Are you sure?"

"Well, not sure. But, I have examined the Torah for a long time and what I have found is unlikely unless it is the clue we need. Please take this to those who are searching."

"I will, Master, first thing in the morning." Perez accepted the small scroll, rubbed his hand through his hair, then closed and latched the door.

The sound of the bolting action rang out loudly and caused anguish to flood Asher's thoughts. *This must be the sign . . . It simply must be.*

It was only the middle of the week of the Festival of the Tabernacles. He was well in front of the deadline. Heavy exhaustion swept over him, and his head began to spin. He extinguished the lamps and stumbled toward his bed in the corner. Still fully clothed, he crashed onto it. Now he could get back to searching for information about the Messiah. Now, he had . . . Suddenly, Asher felt excruciating pain. He grabbed his head with both hands.

➤ ➤ ➤

No clouds blocked the sun in the morning as Perez promenaded through the open Temple courtyard among several people carrying pigeons for offerings. Still others were empty-handed, certain to buy an offering in a side porch of the Temple. Perez greeted them with sincere warmness but continued to a nearby priest's residence. After leaving Asher's room, Perez had fallen into a deep sleep. He'd awakened late but fully refreshed. He crossed the priest's courtyard with a bouncy motion, clasping the pouch containing the small scroll. He knocked on a servant's door adjoining the larger residence.

A lean, muscular man with a long, well-trimmed beard and moustache opened the door and stood inside it, waiting. His dark, calculating features showed no warmth.

Although he had worked with the younger man for some time, his aura felt like having a damp blanket thrown over Perez's mood. He swallowed with difficulty. "Good morning, Bukki."

"And to you. Have you news?"

Perez retrieved the small scroll from his pouch and offered it to Bukki. "Master Asher gave this to me last night. He seemed very excited, and I think he believes this is the needed clue."

Bukki looked unconvinced but took the scroll from Perez. He rotated it back and forth with his hand, following the movement and shaking his head. He returned his gaze to Perez, his voice trimmed with impatience. "Well, let's hope so. This business must come to an end soon. I barely have time to get everything done."

Perez fidgeted. "Yes, I agree. Disaster is written all over it. I, too, hope that it will end quickly."

Bukki stepped back into his room and slammed the door.

Perez walked away. As the distance from Bukki's quarters increased, so did Perez's lighthearted mood. He smiled at several of the people he passed as he meandered to the Temple and climbed the long steps to the room where Asher was prisoner. He knocked mildly on the door, his voice upbeat. "Master Asher. Are you awake yet?" No answer. Perez raised his voice significantly and knocked louder, a little anxious. "Master Asher, may I come in?"

Quickly unlocking the door, Perez entered the room and found Asher, fully clothed and lying on his bed, unmoving. He darted to Asher and shook him hard. "Master Asher, wake up!"

The old man did not move.

Perez choked to the point that his next words were a squeal. "Master Asher, wake up!" Frantic, he grabbed the small knife he had given Asher some days earlier and held it under Asher's nose, pushing his white moustache down. *A moisture cloud . . . Thank God, he is still alive!*

Perez stood up, dazed. Finally, he bolted out the door. *I have to get a doctor. He must live. If he dies, all is lost.*

CHAPTER ELEVEN

Justus squinted as he pried open his stuck lids. The loss of two night's sleep from the storm and the intense struggle during the shipwreck had caused him to pass out lying against Michal. He managed to work them half open. The bright sun blinded him, but also basked him in peaceful warmth. Seagulls were arguing overhead and the surf was gently sounding in the distance. Blocking the sun with his hand, he pivoted his head. Michal lay next to him, dry and sleeping soundly. *She is beautiful.* Memories of the wreck deluged his consciousness. Thank God she was all right. He'd thought he'd lost her more than once.

Michal was alive, but Justus had no idea if she had suffered permanent damage. He was torn between waking her and letting her sleep. On impulse, he moved his hand from blocking the sun and gently traced one finger over her forehead, her cheek, and then her nose.

Michal wrinkled her nose, and a small slit appeared between her eyelids.

Justus moved his hand in the air to shield her from the glare.

She slowly focused on him, her voice scratchy. "Thanks."

"I know. The sun is bright."

"No . . . Thanks for saving me. I nearly drowned."

Justus felt pride knowing he did all he could to save her, but it was tempered with a humble knowledge they were more than lucky. "I think God was on our side."

Michal appeared to drift off to sleep again, her voice barely detectable. "Mmm."

Justus and Michal remained unmoving together under Justus' coat for several minutes.

Finally, she attempted to raise her arms above her head to stretch.

Justus heaved himself onto one elbow. "Are you all right?"

Michal lifted herself as much as possible under the rock ledge and rotated her head, for him to look. "How bad is it?" Close to her ear was a dark purple bruise with a small red cut. Blood was clotted around it.

"You really bumped into something. Looks painful but not severe."

"I think it happened when we were thrown overboard. I hit something and was dazed, but fortunately the cold water revived me." Michal touched the top of her head.

"Oh, that must be from hitting the rock near the shore."

Justus touched the bump.

Michal flinched. "Ouch!"

"Sorry. You're lucky it only knocked you unconscious. You could have been killed."

"Hmm . . ." Suddenly, Michal shoved on his chest with both hands. "Move over so I can get up. I need to see if anything else is injured."

Justus rolled onto his knees, made an effort to stand, but fell back as his knees made deep dents in the warm sand. He moaned. "Oh man . . . my legs. They feel like I've run a hundred miles."

Michal squeezed by him and jumped up with no apparent pain. "You're a baby. You couldn't run five miles, let alone a hundred."

"And . . . you could?"

"That's what I do, Justus. That's what I do."

Justus pondered her response, but it made no sense to him at all.

She looked right and left. "I'm thirsty. I wonder if there is any fresh water nearby."

Justus searched the beach and spied a clump of palm trees. Pointing, he said, "There's a chance fresh water will be there."

As they made their way to the trees, Justus dropped his hand to his belt and was surprised to discover the pouch of food Claudius had brought to him in the cabin. He undid the string as he peered down the shoreline. "We could be anywhere from Sidon to Egypt." He opened the pouch, dug out the meat, and stretched it towards Michal. "Here, I'll share some with you."

Michal glanced at it, then at Justus. "That's clever. How did you know to bring it?"

"Luck, I think."

As they ambled toward the palms, Michal's expression darkened. "Do you think anyone else survived?"

"We should look, but I doubt it. I think we were lucky the figurehead landed so close to us. Without it, I'm sure we would have been slammed into the side of the ship and killed."

Michal grimaced. "Poor Helen and Thorakis. Helen was excited about coming with me, but we almost had to drag Thorakis along."

The two arrived at the edge of a small pool of clear water surrounded by seven large palm trees. A small, sand-colored lizard took off for a nearby rock at their intrusion.

Michal gazed at the pool with a questioning look.

Justus dropped to his knees and used his cupped hands to sample the water. He glanced back at Michal and beamed. "It's fresh."

She joined him, and they satisfied their thirst.

The two walked to a nearby rock under a palm tree and sat. The breeze coming off the sea caused the branches of the palms to sway.

Michal pitched her head back and appeared to soak in the moment as the wind flowed through her black hair. After a few minutes, she gave Justus a pleased look, and tore the meat in half. She offered him some. Her gaze was penetrating and her voice almost normal. "So . . . what do you do when you are not saving someone? Serving as a centurion in the Roman army?"

Justus felt surprised at her straightforwardness. "My father is a Roman proconsul. He made me train with many of the soldiers under his command as I was growing up. You are merely seeing some of the habits I formed."

"Oh . . . You do have the bearing of a soldier. Well then, what do you do?"

Justus hesitated a moment while he attempted to guess at her reaction. "I'm an advocate."

She displayed a knowing look. "Ah . . . a Roman advocate."

"Do you need one?"

Michal suppressed a giggle. "No, and I hope I never do."

Justus made no reply. Over the course of his tenure as an advocate, he had been exposed to joke after joke. He took her comment as mild in comparison to others he'd heard.

Justus chewed slowly on a bite of meat. The repetitive sound of the surf was a soothing song, and he smiled at Michal. "Were Helen and Thorakis friends or servants?"

"More friends than anything. They were my trainers."

Justus bounced back. "Trainers . . . for what?"

"I'm a runner. They train me for races. In Athens, it's a big deal."

Justus looked mystified. "But I thought the Olympics were for men only."

"You're right. In fact, married women can't even watch the races. Although legend has it one woman, Callipateria, disguised herself as a trainer and did." Michal's look told him she expected him to be shocked. "The athletes are naked when they compete."

Justus' reaction was delayed. "I know." He felt miffed as he carelessly waved a hand at her. "I suppose you've watched?"

"Of course." She laughed.

"Hmm . . . So, where does your competing come in?"

Michal grabbed Justus' hand, and tugged him away from the rock. "Every fourth year, there are foot races held for maidens. The games are called Heraea. They are held in honor of a goddess called Hera, who, it's believed, in ancient times inaugurated the race to settle differences peaceably. They are held in the Olympic Stadium, but the course is only five-sixths the distance the men run."

Justus stopped, his gaze boring into Michal, bewildered.

Her eyebrows went high, her mouth forming a letter *O.* "Nooo . . . We don't run naked. Dreamer."

"Well, what do you run in?"

"The stadium."

Justus cocked his head and gave a pained look. "You know what I mean."

Michal touched her garment. "We wear tunicas colored after our hometown. The length comes to just above the knee." She stopped to measure the distance with her fingertips. "Our right shoulder must be bare down to here." She put her hand below her collarbone, angled her head, and looked at him, measuring his response.

Though wearing a torn, dirty garment stained with blood and mud, she captivated him. However, he carefully kept his face stoic as he asked, "What do you win?"

"A crown of olive leaves and a portion of a cow sacrificed to Hera. My mother never let's me accept the cow, though."

"Why not? I thought you were a liberal Jew."

Michal gave him an unbelieving look. "We are, but not even Hellenists are that liberal."

CHAPTER TWELVE

Miriam jolted awake. Where was she? The musky smell of the damp tomb brought everything back to her. How long had she been unconscious?

Lying on several blankets on the stone ledge, she picked at the dark, coarse wool. Where had they come from? She had been sick. She shook her head, struggling to organize the surreal bits and random visions shooting through her brain. The sound of a storm . . . someone covering her . . . someone feeding her soup. Who?

Miriam stared at the floor, barely visible in the faint light streaming through four cracks in the wall. Who had brought the blankets . . . and a bowl? She pushed back her matted hair with both hands, then rubbed the sides of her head, trying to clear it, and sat up. How long had she been here?

The cave twirled. For a moment, she leaned back on the ledge to regain her balance. After remaining only seconds, she wrapped a blanket around her and took a deliberate step towards the light. Was it morning or evening? When would that horrible man come back? Why would he have helped her?

Reaching one of the small openings, a spider shot through it and scurried up the tomb wall. Miriam blinked with little emotion at its brief obstruction, leaned to the hole, and scanned the outside terrain for a long while as she worked at lining up some of the details of her ordeal. She vaguely recalled shaking with chills and an old woman caring for her, forcing hot liquid down her throat. How long was she sick?

As she continued trying to piece together what had happened to her, she noted the light was now brighter. Morning. Nothing outside was recognizable. She could see a valley with some hills in the distance, but they could be anywhere.

The graveyard silence was punctured with a barely audible sound, causing Miriam to spin around. Someone was coming! She careened to the small opening not covered by the stone barricade.

The footsteps came closer and stopped. An old man peeked through the opening, his face uncovered. "You must be feeling better," he rasped.

"Please, help me get out. Someone forced me in here, and I don't know why."

"Take it easy. I've brought you food and water."

"Why? Please help me. I'm being held captive."

The old man said nothing but pushed a leg of roasted lamb through the hole. Its savory aroma made her stomach growl.

Miriam glanced at it, but with a sudden surge of understanding, her head drooped. "Why did you put me here?"

The old man frowned deeply. His voice sounded huffy. "I didn't put you in here. And I don't know who did. A man with a lot of money came to my village and hired me to feed you. I suspect he put you in here, but I don't know for sure. My job is simply to feed you once a day and keep my mouth shut. Now, take the lamb or I'll leave."

Miriam took the piece of meat and held it lamely at her side, as a feeling of defeat overtook her.

"Here is some water."

She took the small flask with her other hand. Her voice became a whisper. "How long have I been here?"

"Sorry, but I'm not allowed to say."

"Did you help me while I was sick?"

The old man continued looking at Miriam, and his expression softened. "No, my wife came. Between the two of us, we were able to move the stone enough for her to squeeze in. You were delirious . . . had a very high fever. You're lucky my wife is good with caring for the sick. She brought blankets and made her famous healing soup . . . got enough down you so you would recover. And, look at you. Almost as good as new."

Miriam put one hand on the stone to support her wobbling legs. The coldness of the tomb seemed to increase, and she gripped the blanket tighter as she shivered. "Sir, please let me out. My father is a very prominent man in Jerusalem. He will repay you greatly for setting me free."

"Your father?" The old man gave a short snort and pulled back to go.

"Wait. Please don't leave yet. Sir, please come back." Miriam felt light-headed. "Uh . . . I want you to take a message to your wife."

Miriam's comment caught the old man, and he returned to the small opening.

As he focused again on her, she could read his anticipation. One side of his mouth rose slightly, and his voice was quiet. "What do you want me to tell her?"

"I really, really am thankful you brought her. Tell her I am much better and it's because of her kindness. Tell her, I appreciate her efforts . . . and her soup."

The old man looked amused. "I shall tell her. She is one of a kind, she is. Always ready to help a stranger."

Miriam gazed at him unemotionally, and her voice became even softer. "Sir . . . Why am I here?"

A look of sympathy washed over the old man. He hesitated, then said, "Your father has a special knowledge. You are to remain a prisoner until he reveals it."

His words shocked her. Her little strength drained away, and she fell to the ground beside the door.

"Now, eat and rest. I'll be back tomorrow." The old man trudged away.

Miriam suddenly remembered she had not asked another important question. She shouted as loudly as she could muster, "How long do I have to stay here?"

The old man called back, "I was told to feed you until Hanukkah . . . but, I'm thinking you'll be here until your father gives him the information he wants.

"Sir . . . Where am I?"

The padding of the old man's sandals on the cave floor trailed off to silence, but he made no reply.

Miriam bit her lower lip as she mulled over why someone wanted her father's special knowledge. Still holding the leg of lamb and the flask of water, she stood, stumbled back to the stone ledge and flopped onto it, but her hunger had disappeared. Tears trickled down her cheeks, the weakness of despair making it hard for her to breathe.

I know what he wants. I'm as good as dead. There is only one thing my father would let me die for. He will never reveal the secrets of . . . Kabbala.

CHAPTER THIRTEEN

Justus and Michal ambled back to the oasis where they had shared the meat from Justus' pouch. Directly above them, large puffy clouds occasionally floated in front of the sun, causing shadows to move over the pair. They had spent the morning combing the beach for any survivors from the wrecked ship but had found none. They had also sifted through some of the debris, but the only things they found of any use were a couple of flasks.

The sun was directly overhead marking it the sixth hour, noon, as Michal mounted the same rock where she earlier sat eating breakfast. The wind was much calmer than during the morning, but the heavy salt smell from the sea was in every breath. "Do you think we should continue to look for people on the beach?" she asked.

Justus squatted to fill the two containers. He shrugged. "I don't think so. We've been up and down it all morning. I think the figurehead carried us pretty far from the wreckage."

Michal drew her feet up, wrapped her arms around her knees, and put her chin on them. "I'm glad we found no dead bodies."

Justus shot her a concerned glance as the clear oasis water gurgled into the flasks. "Yeah . . . me, too."

Michal looked inquisitive. "Since we don't know where we are, which direction do we walk to try and find civilization?"

Although unable to see far from his position on the sand, he glanced around, then nodded down the beach. "The wind first started blowing hard shortly after we left Cyprus. It was blowing somewhat north then, so I guess we should walk south and close to the shoreline. I think it more likely we'll find a village along the coast than just wandering out across the land."

Michal looked dismayed. "Looks like you may not be able to save your friend. Is he a Roman or Jew?"

Justus cast a glance at her, taken aback by her bringing up the topic. "He's a Jew."

"What's his name?"

He tugged on the jugs to gauge his progress. "Jesus. He's a childhood friend." Determining they were filled, he set the flasks on the ground near Michal and stared across the sea beyond the pounding surf. "He's totally unique. I thoroughly enjoyed doing things with him and his family." He turned to Michal. "Actually, he was a little more than a year older than me. His brother James and I were the same age and probably closer friends. But, Jesus was special. He understood me sometimes better than I understood myself."

Justus became transfixed, wonder in his voice. "He could pick up on the way I was feeling and say something that would invariably make me feel better. And his understanding of the Scriptures . . . next to none. It was unbelievable."

Michal raised her head and extended her hand. "How did you become such good friends?"

Her question brought his thoughts to the present. He smiled. "Remember? On the ship I said my family was not accepted very well by most Jews in Nazareth?"

"Yes."

"The family of Joseph, the carpenter, was the exception. They were very caring and visited us frequently."

Michal looked intrigued. "Why did they befriend your family when others didn't?"

"I think they accepted us because they had their own problems with the Jews at Nazareth."

"Really? What were their problems?"

The question caused Justus to stop for a moment. The innuendos rang in his head as loudly as they had twenty years before. He swallowed hard as he remembered the Jewish punishment for intimacy outside of marriage was death by stoning. "There was talk his mother,

Mary, had conceived Jesus before she married Joseph and that Joseph might not be his father."

Michal sat in stunned silence and shook her head in disbelief. "Was he?"

"I don't know. I never really talked to Jesus about it. However, my mother told me that during the census of Caesar Augustus, Joseph decided to take Mary with him to Bethlehem to be registered, even though she was almost ready to give birth to Jesus. He was afraid she would be stoned to death if he left her alone in Nazareth." He stepped close to the rock Michal rested on. "In fact, Jesus was actually born in Bethlehem."

Michal remained quiet for a few moments, as she ran her hand over the boulder's rough exterior. Her profile showed comprehension. "So you and Jesus grew up together?"

"Jesus, James, and I were often together until my father was promoted to tribune and called back to Rome."

"How old were you then?"

"Fifteen."

Michal shifted her position, totally caught up by the story. "You said earlier you were going to save Jesus from himself. Is he trying to commit suicide?"

Justus gazed at Michal, her hair fluttering in the light breeze. He felt a deep attraction for her. "Not long ago I received a letter from Mary. She said Jesus has been traveling about Galilee and Judea urging people to repent of their worldly lives, and teaching people what the Scriptures really mean."

Michal blinked, her voice hesitant. "What's so bad about that?"

"When he was twelve years old, Mary and Joseph lost Jesus in Jerusalem for three days. They finally found him in the Temple, surrounded by chief priests who were astounded at his knowledge. Unfortunately, their amazement eventually turned into jealousy." Justus focused on her. "Now that Jesus has a group of followers, the chief priests have become even more jealous. It's gotten to the point that Jesus now disputes their teachings and criticizes them harshly in front of large crowds."

Listening closely, she waited for him to go on. "Such as . . ."

Justus stared at the sky as he tried to remember Mary's entire letter. "Once, he described a number of the priests as a tomb: whitewashed on the outside to look good but filled with filthy dead-men bones inside."

"Ouch. I see what she means. He does need to tone things down." Palms up, Michal shrugged. "But . . . what can you do to help?"

Eyeing Michal, Justus paused a moment, his jaw set. After years of successfully defending innocent people, he could quickly get to the core of complex issues. "Mary is hoping I will be able to reason with him because of our close relationship."

"Do you think you can?"

Justus took a deep breath and expelled it in a long, low sigh. "No, Michal. You have to know him. When it comes to teaching the Scriptures, he has this ability to explain what they mean with . . . with . . . I don't know . . . authority. It's almost like he wrote them." He took two steps away and looked at the sea. "Added to that, he has always been impatient with people who pretend to be pious and better than everyone else. I think those parts of his personality are impossible to change."

He bent to pick up the flasks, but straightened instead. "Because of our friendship, though, I have to try to convince him to stop infuriating the priests and Pharisees."

Michal rose and stretched as she considered his story. She cocked her head. "Is he married?"

"No. I don't think he ever will."

"Why not?"

Justus' mother had drilled into him many subtleties of the Jewish faith as he was growing up. The memory caused him to hear her words again. "He is deeply involved in religion . . . and remember, Jews highly value the virtue of virginity. Moral purity is easier for a virgin."

Michal looked sheepish. "Something we Hellenists don't often think about."

Justus laughed and corralled the water flasks, glad Michal had quickly turned him from painful memories. "We had better start walking. Who knows how long it will take us to find civilization."

He moved ahead a short distance before Michal got up from the rock. Two seagulls landed in front of him and pattered on the sand. They kept the distance between Justus and themselves constant, although they weaved back and forth, warbling.

When Michal caught up to him, the gulls flew off, piping loudly. She asked, "How can you find Jesus?"

"I was certain he would be at the Feast of the Booths. Since it's a seven-day event, my plan was to search until I found him. However, here we are and the festival is half over. So, I guess I need to develop a new plan."

Michal matched his pace. She scratched the back of her head. "I'm sure you will." She stopped a step, then continued, "Hey . . . what about Hanukkah? It's only a few months away."

Justus slanted a glance at her. "That's a good idea. He'll likely be in Jerusalem for it. Maybe I'll get lucky . . . that is if we don't die out here."

Michal snagged his arm and tugged. She acted like she was poring over a baby, her voice sounding like she was talking to one. "I'll save you."

"How? Outrun a horse and catch him for a ride?"

She shoved Justus away, laughed, and took off. "Never underestimate a woman . . . especially a Greek runner," she called. The two sprinted a short way along the coastline.

Justus held the flasks away from his body to facilitate speed, but Michal easily outdistanced him, then suddenly she stopped dead in her tracks.

Justus loped up beside her, saw the chagrin on her face, and followed her gaze.

Pointing, Michal asked, "Is that dust rising from the desert?"

CHAPTER FOURTEEN

When Kore left the meeting with Caiaphas, he'd totally bought into the plan to catch Jesus in his own words and discredit him in front of the people. Despite the lateness of the hour, he had visited a fellow Pharisee, Chislon, briefed him on Caiaphas' plan, and told him to develop some questions that would trick Jesus when he showed up at the Festival of Booths.

That had been four days ago, and Jesus still had not appeared. Kore paced in the main hall of the synagogue. He pushed some fingers through his untrimmed, graying beard as feelings of hopelessness became a growing cancer. *If we don't trap Jesus soon, I'm sure to be held responsible. I'll never sit in the Sanhedrin.*

A loud knock caused Kore to freeze. "Who is it?" he asked.

"Jehu. He has finally shown up."

Kore slung the door open revealing a scowling Jehu with two other guards. "Are you sure it's the carpenter?"

Jehu's eyelids became slits. His voice was curt. "There is no doubt. A large crowd has already gathered around him."

"It's about time. The festival is half over. Where is he?"

"On the southwest porch of the Temple."

Kore's boldness intensified as he clutched his coat and slammed the door shut. "Tell Sethur to get some other scribes and also fetch some Pharisees. Make sure Chislon is one of them. Also, send a couple of Temple guards." Unable to contain his excitement, he jabbed a fist in the air. "Today, we're going to catch him."

It was a short walk from the synagogue to the Temple. More than a hundred people had gathered to hear Jesus. So many, the dusty pathways were hidden beneath their flowing robes and cloaks.

Kore muscled his way through the large crowd, causing some to trip over the many ornamental shrubs lining walkways. He didn't bother to apologize. He was silently rehearsing his trick questions.

Jesus was in plain view several steps above the crowd, his loud, firm voice blanketing the silent assembly. "You have heard it said you shall not commit adultery, but every one who so much as looks at a woman with evil desire for her has already committed adultery in his heart. Turn from your evil ways! If your right eye causes you to sin, pluck it out. It's better to lose just one eye than have your entire body cast into hell."

On the opposite side from Kore, Attai and Chislon threaded their way through the crowd to the porch where Jesus was teaching.

Chislon's large frame was prominent under the long robe of a Pharisee. He also was strong and easily pushed people aside as he followed Attai.

Jesus held an educational pose. "You have heard it said from men of old, you should not swear falsely but perform your oaths as a religious duty to God. Rather, you should not bind yourself by any oath at all, either by heaven, which is the throne of God, by the earth, since it is His footstool, or by Jerusalem which is the city of the great King. Don't swear by your head, for you can't make a single hair white or black. Just let your yes be a simple yes and your no a simple no. Anything more than that comes from the evil one."

Kore pursed his lips and caught Chislon's attention. He motioned Chislon to speak, but Jesus was already in mid-sentence.

"You have heard you should repay an eye for an eye and a tooth for a tooth, but instead, you should not resist an evil man if he injures you. If someone strikes you on the right cheek, turn to him your left. If someone sues you to take your tunic, let him have your coat, also. If someone forces you to go with them a mile, continue with him two miles. Show that you are children of your Father in heaven."

At that point, Chislon bellowed, "Is it lawful for a man to divorce his wife?"

Jesus spotted him and gave a look of interest. "What did Moses command you?"

"Moses allowed a man to write a bill of divorce and put her away."

Jesus' reply seemed to echo. "Moses wrote that precept in your Law because of the hardness of your hearts. But from the beginning, God made males and females. It was His intent they should leave their fathers and mothers with the specific purpose to become one flesh. They are no longer two, but one. Understand . . . what God has joined together, no man should separate."

Chislon's jaw dropped.

Jesus' answer stunned Kore until he heard a person behind him whisper to a companion. "Isn't this the man the authorities want out of the way? Here he is speaking openly. Can it be that they have discovered he actually is the Messiah?"

Kore's teeth clenched. Completely forgetting his question, his voice detonated in anger, "How is it you are so versed in the Scriptures and theology, seeing how you have never studied? You must be possessed by a demon."

Jesus looked stern, scouting the crowd and locating Kore. His speech became precise. "My teaching is not my own, but His who sent me. If you really desired to do His will, you would know I'm not speaking on my own accord. Otherwise, I would want glory for myself. But, I am eager to glorify Him who sent me. There is no unrighteousness or deception in me, and I teach against Satan. So how could I have a demon? That would divide Satan's house, and it is clear that no house divided can stand."

The rebuke cut through Kore like a two-edged sword. He retreated, pushing people right and left, his face obscenely distorted. At the back edge of the throng, he met Chislon and Attai and stomped the dust from his sandals.

He clutched Attai, pulling him within inches. "So, he wants to pluck out an evil eye. We'll see. Before dawn, you go to the house of Hazael. I'm sure you will find Bernice there. Bring her here."

Attai wrest himself free. He looked ready to retaliate, but instead he spat out, "As you wish."

Kore tramped away from the Temple, his fists clenched, his arms swinging, and his long robe billowing from his body.

> ❯ ❯ ❯

Sethur followed a guard across the Temple courtyard to the wall facing it. The guard methodically removed the torches strategically placed in the side to provide light at night and extinguished them. The artificial light was replaced by the soft dawning morning.

As people started their day, the scent of wood burning from nearby houses hovered over the Temple area. Sethur was amazed so many people had already assembled in the open area. *I guess Kore's plan might work. Surely these people have come expecting the carpenter to speak to them this early.*

He saw a wave of heads turn in the direction of the Mercy Gate. *That will be the Nazarene for certain.*

In minutes Jesus walked into the open courtyard and gave the crowd a pleasant smile. Rather than mounting the steps to the porch as he had the previous day, Jesus remained on the ground, several feet in front of the Temple proper and began to teach. "You have heard it said, you should love your neighbors and hate your enemies. Rather, you should love your enemies and pray for those who persecute you. By doing this, everyone will see you are children of God. What reward is it to love only those who love you? Even tax collectors and Gentiles do that. No, you must be perfect as your heavenly Father is perfect."

At that point, Attai dragged a completely nude woman around the corner of the Temple and yelled at the nearest listeners, "Move out of the way."

The crowd gawked at the display. They automatically formed a human circle as Attai towed the woman toward Jesus.

She struggled against the advance, but Attai was much stronger and dragged her forward. Having no way to cover herself, she held her chin against her chest, which caused her long brown hair to fall forward, providing a small screen.

Sethur positioned himself on the other side of Jesus.

Attai clutched the woman's arms with his beefy hands and stopped her near Jesus.

Sobbing loudly, the woman continued looking down.

All glared at her, except for Jesus who stooped to the ground. Rather than add his look to her humiliation, he focused on his finger as it pushed the dust to form words.

```
If   you   had   only   known   what   this   means
```

Attai assumed a pompous posture and showed a caddish grin. "Teacher, we have caught this woman in the very act of adultery. In the Law, Moses commanded such offenders be stoned to death. What is your sentence?"

Jesus was stoic. He watched his finger as he continued writing in the dust, but he said nothing:

```
I   want   mercy
```

Sethur drew near Jesus and stood on his tiptoes, trying to make his small stature as high above Jesus as he could. He knew the trap was set, but it would only work if Jesus took the bait. His voice dripped with contempt. "You presume to teach the truth, interpreting the Holy Scriptures as to what God really means so tell us, . . . should this woman be stoned to death for committing adultery, or not?"

Jesus raised himself up, glanced at Sethur, and slowly swept the entire crowd.

Everyone was frozen in anticipation.

The woman rose enough so she could peek through her hair at Jesus.

Sadness covered Jesus' expression. His words hung in the air. "Let him who is without sin among you be the first to throw a stone at her." After saying this, Jesus lowered himself and continued writing in the dust:

```
rather   than   sacrifice
```

The entire crowd became conscience stricken when they heard his words. Individually, they slowly slipped out of the courtyard. Sethur was the last to depart and stopped at the edge of the open area. He pivoted. Although several yards from Jesus and the woman, he could still hear them.

Jesus finished writing:

```
you would not have condemned the guiltless
```

The only sound now was two birds in the distance arguing over a worm. The lack of any human noise washed the area clean of the former hostility.

The woman straightened and stared at Jesus with a look of admiration.

Jesus returned her gaze, kindness flooding his face. "Where are your accusers? Has no one condemned you?"

The woman used her freed hands to cover her nudity as best she could, but she fixed her mesmerized attention on Jesus, rather than dropping in shame. "No one . . . Lord."

Jesus pulled off his outer coat, wrapped it around the woman to cover her completely, and gave her a tender smile.

"I do not condemn you either. Go on your way and from now on, sin no more."

❧ ❧ ❧

Sethur, Attai, and the guards barreled into the synagogue, their steps echoing in the large, empty room. It was far too early to hold any worshippers.

Hearing them enter, Kore tramped out to meet them, anger welling up. "Where's the carpenter?" he demanded.

Sethur looked astonished. "You should have been there. No mere man has ever spoken like this."

Kore cursed, kicked a bench, and shouted, "Are you also deluded? Have any of us believed in what he says? As for that multitude of rabble out there, what do they know about the Law and the Scriptures? They are all doomed anyway." He feinted a clenched fist at them. "Get out of here! I must report this to Caiaphas. There'll be hell to pay."

CHAPTER FIFTEEN

Justus bent over, panting as he tried to recover from his race with Michal along the beach. He dropped the flasks, rose, and became transfixed by a growing dust cloud in the distance.

Michal stared with him. "I'm sure that's caused by horses."

An uneasy feeling grew in Justus as the cloud drew closer. Though he'd never encountered bandits around Nazareth, he'd heard many stories about the ruthlessness of small bands.

He flashed the area for a place to hide, his voice tense. "They probably know about the pool of fresh water at the oasis we just left. Since we have no idea who they are, why don't we try to get to those rocky hills in the distance before they arrive? There we could hide and tell if they are friendly."

She pursed her lips. "That's a lot farther than you think. We're not going to outrun horses. Let's see if we can hide in the cleft of the rock where we were this morning."

They sprinted back up the beach past the oasis, but they were still several hundred yards from the rocky shoreline when hoofbeats sounded as if they were on their backs. In what seemed an instant, four riders surrounded Justus and Michal, swords drawn. All were filthy and wore dirty, ragged clothes. Three of the men—one short and fat, another tall and thin, and the third one of average build with a deep scar across his forehead—carried long, curved swords with a single-sided blade.

The fourth one held a Roman two-sided sword, his bearing showing he was their leader. He gave a near-toothless grin. "Men, the gods are smiling on us."

The scarred rider asked, "Shall we kill them?"

"No. That is money you see in front of us. I can get a good price for two slaves. And the woman will keep me warm tonight."

Justus bristled at the thought of Michal being abused by this loathsome scum, but he said nothing. He had trained to engage more than one man at a time and would wait for the opportunity to do just that.

The leader dismounted and ordered the tall one, "Water the horses and fill our flasks."

The other riders dismounted, swords still drawn.

The tall man led the horses away.

The others cautiously surrounded Justus and Michal.

The leader clutched a rope and crouched, ready to pounce as he inched his way toward Justus. "So, you are a Jew. What can you do?"

Justus returned a stony glare, but made no reply. If he could only get that short sword . . .

The leader didn't appear bothered by Justus' silence, his face arrogant. "It doesn't matter. I know one in Gerasa who will pay much for such a handsome, strong Jew, no matter what you can or can't do." He glanced sideways at Michal and grinned, unashamed of his missing teeth. "If I get enough for the Jew, I might keep you . . . if you are any good in bed."

Michal shivered.

The short, plump man approached Michal and placed the tip of his sword between her breasts, his body language showed he was wary.

The scarred man was almost as tall as Justus. He extended his arm with his sword about a foot from Justus' throat, making it easy to thrust Justus through if he made any effort to resist.

Other than seagulls in the distance and the rustling palm trees, the silence of the capture was punctuated only by the horses drinking from the oasis.

The leader sheathed his sword and advanced to Justus' back with the rope.

Justus squinted at the sword pointing at him, his muscles taut, anticipating the touch of the leader. His father had drilled offense in him for this situation, but he would only have one chance.

The leader grabbed Justus' right arm in order to tie his hand.

Justus exaggerated his move forward to make the arm available to the man in the rear, but the movement took him down and away from the pointed sword, giving him a split second of opportunity. Staying bent, he lunged under the sword, knowing the scarred man's sword was too long to do anything except hit his back with the handle.

The surprise attack caught the bandit completely off guard. He took the full weight of Justus slamming into him, knocking his sword away, and driving the breath from him.

The commotion caused the fat man to gape at the attack.

Michal used the break in his attention to fall backwards to the ground, roll away, and bounce up running at top speed.

The fat man realized his error and gave chase.

Justus grabbed the fallen sword, spun around, and swung violently at the leader, who by then had his sword drawn and parried the stroke.

Justus continued his onslaught. The sound of metal bouncing off metal was deafening. His skill allowed Justus to quickly gain the advantage. He was about to land a fatal blow when everything went black. Stunned, he fell to his knees and dropped his weapon.

The tall, thin bandit wrapped the rope around Justus, pinning his arms to his sides, and lifted him to his feet.

Justus shook his head, trying to clear his grogginess and succeeded in spotting the branch used to club him. Turning, he scanned the desert area away from the seaside and saw the fat bandit simply standing. Amazing. Michal was so far in front of him he'd never catch her . . . and she was still sprinting at top speed. What a runner.

The leader screamed at the man Justus had knocked down. "Take a horse and catch the woman before she reaches those hills. You will never find her if she gets to them."

Though not fully recovered from Justus' onslaught, Scarface managed to stumble to a horse. A moment later, he galloped off.

The leader marched to Justus and pummeled him.

Justus shook his head. His jaw clenched, he gave no other sign that the blows affected him.

The leader's nose nearly touched Justus', his scabrous jaws wrenched and his voice coarse. "Are you a Roman soldier?"

Justus turned his head slightly to avoid the stinking breath. "No, but my father was."

"Don't think your training will keep you from being a slave. There are ways to make you obey." The leader snarled at the remaining bandit, "Get the horses watered and make sure our water skins are full. We leave for Gerasa as soon as we get the woman."

CHAPTER SIXTEEN

Although clouds were heavy overhead, the dull morning light caused Malchus to feel uplifted. He was so intrigued by yesterday's possible tomb identifier, the word *LOT*, he'd spent almost the entire night searching the catacombs for it. His hopes were still high in spite of the fact he had three-fourths of the underground tombs yet to examine.

As he passed from the open courtyard of the palace of the high priest, he felt pleased, remembering four days ago when Jehu took him to the high priest the morning after Jehu discovered him in the catacombs. Caiaphas had defused the situation by informing Jehu that Malchus was in the catacombs at his direction. The assignment was secret, and he should leave Malchus alone. Of course, what could Jehu do? Though Caiaphas had only been high priest for four days, he was still Jehu's boss.

It took Malchus just minutes to traverse from the courtyard of the high priest to the lesser courtyard of Chief Priest Annas. As he entered it, he spied Bukki's quarters and his mood began to shift. While serving Caiaphas' father, he had never even met Bukki. But, Caiaphas' father died, Caiaphas married Chief Priest Annas' daughter, and Malchus was promoted to lead servant. The result was Malchus had to work with Bukki often. Bukki was ruthless and cared only about himself. Many times Malchus wondered why Annas had selected Bukki to be his lead servant.

This meeting was a first. Until now, he and Bukki had always come together with their masters. Annas and Caiaphas would not be attending today and that made him uneasy.

He drifted across the courtyard, hesitating twice. Both times, he inspected the people passing the house, expecting them to look suspiciously at him. However, the passers-by paid no attention to him at all. Attaining the front door, he remained frozen, and needed a surprising effort to knock.

❧ ❧ ❧

Inside his chambers, Bukki paced like a caged tiger. He had been directed by Annas to conduct this meeting but could not conjure up any sensible reason for doing it. His strengths had always been in managing those under him, but now he was told to handle two other lead servants.

He glanced at Perez and gave a bleak sigh. The room was stuffy and carried the heavy odor of sweat.

Perez sat quietly on the only bench in the spartan room. He jumped as a loud knock sounded on the door.

Bukki stopped and looked at the door, agitated. "Who is it?" he called.

A nervous voice replied, "It is I, Malchus."

"Come in. The door is open."

Malchus crept into the small servant quarters.

Bukki stood between Malchus and Perez. Detecting Malchus' lack of recognition, he made introductions. He wanted to get this meeting over as quickly as possible. "Please, sit down. We need to talk."

Malchus slumped onto the bench next to Perez, apprehension sweeping his face. "Is it about the Tomb?"

"Yes and no." Bukki remained silent for a long moment, feeling anger and frustration. He had been involved in the passing of clues from Perez to Malchus from the beginning. The whole effort appeared to be a waste of time and effort, but being the obedient servant he was, he fulfilled every request of his master as well as he was able. Still, his heart wasn't in it. When his master wasn't around, he was open with his feelings.

Searching for the right words to begin, he said, "As you know, my master and yours are close relatives. They are secretly directing this search. I don't know what it is all about, but I'm sure money is involved."

Bukki's comment caused Malchus to leap to his feet. "Money? I thought this was a religious quest."

"Hmm . . . perhaps. Perez, do you know?"

Perez tugged nervously at his yellowish-brown beard. "No, I'm not certain. Master Asher seldom talks about his work. Only once, about three years ago, he did tell me something because he was so excited. A cousin of his, a man named John—I think it was his father's brother's only child—started baptizing people in the Jordan." Perez stood and turned away. "Master Asher was convinced John's baptizing in some way predicted the coming of the Messiah and told me he had substantiated it in the Torah."

A flood of disgust washed over Bukki. "You mean that lunatic who lived out in the deserts near Qumran?"

"Yes, that's the one. After his parents died—you know they were very old when he was born—he disappeared into the desert rather than going into the priesthood, which he should have done to follow his father's profession."

Bukki grimaced. "Herod cut his head off a couple of years ago."

"I know, but that didn't stop Master Asher from searching the Torah for the Messiah."

Malchus clamped his lower lip as he settled again on the bench. He shook his head, his voice hinting impatience. "What's all this to do with the Tomb?"

"Yes, of course." Perez continued, "A few months ago, Chief Priest Annas came to visit Master Asher. I was not privy to the meeting, but several strange events happened immediately after that."

Malchus riveted Perez. "Strange events . . . like what?"

Bukki felt caught up by Perez' dialogue, but remained silent.

"First, Master Asher was moved from his house to a room in the Temple. I was instructed to go also to assure he remained there."

Malchus appeared interested. "How did you do that?"

"I locked the door from the outside every time I left. Of course, you know, Master Asher occasionally gave me small scrolls to have delivered to you by Bukki."

Malchus stared in astonishment. "The clues were from Asher? No, I only knew they were coming from Bukki."

Bukki's voice was gruff. "Asher came up with them after searching the Torah."

Malchus tossed his head, looking incredulous. "From the Torah . . . then, certainly the search is for religious reasons, not money." His face betrayed his inability to put the puzzle together. "You said several strange things happened. What else happened?"

Perez waved a hand. "Recently, two scribes visited him. They brought several large papyrus sheets filled with writing. But, the really strange part is . . . Five days before the scribes brought the new sheets, I was instructed to obtain many large, but very thin, acacia-wood boards and a sharp knife."

Bukki felt baffled. "Acacia boards, why?"

"I don't know, but Master Asher cut the thin boards into many strips of various widths. I have no idea what he used them for."

Malchus' brows creased, his voice strained. "I find this discussion very interesting, but what does all this have to do with the Tomb?"

Perez gazed impassively at Malchus and blinked several times. "There may be no more clues."

Malchus froze. "What has happened?" he asked, through dry lips.

"Master Asher is in a coma, and the physicians do not know why."

Malchus' shoulders slumped. He looked like he had just learned his mother had died.

Bukki was amazed how hard Malchus was taking the news. "Have you finished searching using the last clue?"

Malchus' voice was little more than a whisper. "No, but I am close." He bolted upright, his words suddenly exploding, "I still don't understand why I can't just start opening the oldest tombs!"

Bukki's nostrils flared, taking the attack personally. "How would you know if you have found the right one, since you don't know what you're looking for?"

Malchus began to pace, then paused and gave him a meditative squint. "Of course, we need to be told what he's hunting for."

Bukki sighed, "If it's money, he will never tell you. If it's for some religious answer, he probably doesn't know what's in the Tomb, anyway."

Bukki studied Malchus' despair and straightened his frame. He grimaced and extended his hand toward Malchus, his voice strained. "What's in this for you, anyway?"

"Caiaphas has promised my freedom as soon as I find the Tomb."

Bukki relaxed. "Ah . . . a great prize," he said, nodding.

"What are we going to do?" Malchus burst out. It was a cry for help.

Perez placed his hand on Malchus' arm, sympathy in his voice. "We have moved Asher back to his house. Perhaps when his daughter returns, she will know enough about his methods to continue searching the Torah."

Malchus stared, his voice filled with disgust. "His daughter? What could she know?"

"They are very close. After her husband died, she spent considerable time with Asher. It's likely he shared much with her."

Malchus shot a glance at Perez. "When will she return?"

Bukki turned his back to the other two men. "Master Annas has ordered me to get her. I leave first thing in the morning."

Malchus looked perplexed. "To go where?"

"To Greece. She is visiting a close cousin."

CHAPTER SEVENTEEN

In a panic, Justus startled awake from a deep sleep. A hand covered his mouth. He had been forced to jog and occasionally to run in front of a bandit's horse for much of the afternoon. And after eating what little food the thieves had leftover from their supper, he had nearly passed out from fatigue. They'd bound his hands and feet, preventing all but small movements.

He blinked repeatedly, trying to shrug away sleep-generated confusion. Finally, he remembered. He was a prisoner of four hooligans. He attempted to move his head, but the hand over his mouth kept it immobile. He caught sight of the glowing orange embers of the dying campfire and slanted toward the owner of the hand. Michal.

She put her finger to her mouth. When she realized he recognized her, she brought out a long curved sword and cut the ropes binding him.

Justus was dazed. Where did she get that? He noticed a form lying in an awkward position next to the fire. The night guard. His admiration for this beautiful woman multiplied.

The other desperados were under covers and showed no evidence they were awake.

Justus rubbed the circulation back into his arms and hands as Michal helped him upright. Within seconds, they crept from the camp.

After picking their way through the rocks and bushes for about a hundred yards, Michal leaned close to whisper, "Can you run?"

He nodded. "Some."

"Well, we had better. Who knows when they will wake up?"

Justus grabbed the sword from Michal with a questioning glance as they started jogging. "How did you find us?"

Michal matched his speed. "After I lost the horseman in the mountains, I hid for a few hours assuming they would head toward Gerasa. Later, I walked back to the oasis and followed the tracks from there."

Justus felt delighted. Michal continued to amaze him with talent after talent. He glanced at her, mentally applauding her. "So, you're not only a good runner, but you can track people, too."

She grinned. "It really isn't hard to follow the trail of four horses."

After they got started, he found energy he didn't know he had. In the distance, the pig-like squeal of a tree hyrax broke the silence of the night.

They jogged for a long while. The terrain was primarily flat desert, but dotted with scrubby bushes and occasional rocks. A half moon hanging in a star-filled sky gave them enough light to avoid large, dark obstacles. However, both regularly stumbled on the uneven, sandy ground.

Although they only jogged, Justus' breathing became labored and his pace slowed to a trot. "I have to catch my breath. Let's walk awhile." He noted that her flowing stride slowed in concert with his. "You are in shape, aren't you?"

Michal's breathing was heavy but not labored. Her voice sounded joyful. "Helen and Thorakis were good trainers. They have been hard on me recently, but you can see, it's worked."

"That's for certain. I couldn't believe how far you had outrun the short guy."

"Next year, I will win the race in Athens."

Justus grinned at her, thinking, *And I'll be there to congratulate you.*

They alternated jogging and walking the rest of the night. As morning dawned, they reached the slopes of a mountainous area.

Suddenly, Justus stopped. He bent over, clutching his chest, trying to hide his pain. He knew he was near his limit and spoke with a ragged voice. "This is a good area to find a hiding place and rest."

She surveyed him a moment with a worried look. "I agree. Do you have enough reserves to make it up the hill to those trees?"

He estimated the distance to the tree line at about a half mile. He'd be lucky to get half that far. He pushed himself to straighten his body and took a deep breath. "Of course." He tried to keep his voice light, but it still sounded strained. "I'll beat you there."

"Ha!" Michal sprinted up the mountain slope, sidestepping rocks as she went, eager to win the challenge.

Shaking his head, Justus watched her run. Didn't she ever get tired? He let out a *woof* of air and ascended the hill at his best attempt at a fast walk. The breaking dawn provided ample light to weave through the boulders and bushes hindering his ascent.

In minutes Michal attained the trees halfway up the slope. She turned and yelled down to him, "Walk the rest of the way! Take a look at the plain. No one's following us."

Justus stopped, gasping for air. After a few moments of panting, he continued to thread his way up the slope, even pulling on tree limbs and bushes to work with his legs. Finally reaching Michal, he collapsed.

A mischievous look covered her face. "I thought you were going to beat me here."

Justus managed to roll his head toward her. "I would have, but you cheated."

"Cheated, how?"

He gave a teasing smile. "I got lost in watching you run and forgot to run myself."

She pushed him, grinning. "Right."

She helped him to a nearby tree, and they sat in its shade, for by then the sun had completely risen.

Justus took her hand. "Thanks."

"For what?"

"For saving me."

Michal leaned against his arm. "Guess we're even."

"I guess."

They sat quietly together as they looked out over the desert floor until his breathing became normal. The heavy smell of olives from nearby trees encompassed them as birds chirped, welcoming the new morning.

Michal broke their silence. "When was the last time you saw him?"

"Who?"

"Jesus, of course. How long ago has it been?"

Justus peered at her. "Why do you ask that now?"

"Even with the little I know about you, it's obvious you don't give up on things easily. I'm sure we will soon be heading toward Jerusalem."

Justus reveled in her quickness. "We are headed for Jerusalem right now."

"I thought as much. When we started jogging last night, I noticed you didn't ask for directions."

"No, I knew we were heading east towards Gerasa . . . Jerusalem is south."

Michal looked relaxed and leaned more against Justus, using him as a support for her body. "So . . . When did you see him last?"

Justus gazed over the open country, but he saw none of it as a flood of memories swept through him. "Two years ago last spring," he began, "my mother and I went to the wedding of her friend, Tirzah, in Cana . . ."

❧ ❧ ❧

Justus and his mother, Leah, had heard laughter and music as they approached the open door of Tirzah's new home. Both had been dressed in their finest clothes, fitting for a wedding.

Excited about returning to Galilee and attending the wedding of a dear friend, Leah had organized the entire trip and insisted Justus go with her.

Justus wasn't really enthused about the wedding, but he relished the chance to see his friends again. He had arranged his caseload so he could join her.

Leah, a well-shaped older woman, bustled through Tirzah's front door, yielding to her delight. "Tirzah, congratulations! You finally did it."

The smell of roasted meat was mixed with the sweet smell of charoset.

Very little hair showed under either woman's shawl. Tirzah was only a few years younger than Leah, but the lack of significant age differences was overshadowed by their contrasting physical appearance. Tirzah was short and plump with gray hair; Leah, taller, thin, and brown hair.

Tirzah and Leah hugged. Tirzah said, "Thanks for coming. Remember how we used to talk about waiting to find the right man? Well, it took a bunch of years, but I finally found him."

Justus squeezed by them and surveyed the area. An open courtyard was aesthetically placed in the middle of the house, the result of the common Jewish custom of continually building additional rooms to an existing house as sons brought their brides back to their father's house to live. A number of guests were present.

Justus peered into the courtyard, his heart pounding. Was that?

Jesus stood in the courtyard near two men. Both were intently listening to him.

Justus darted toward him and called his name.

Jesus turned. His pearly white teeth separated a well-trimmed moustache and beard. His olive eyes filled with glee. "Justus. My friend."

They embraced long, tears close to falling.

Still holding Justus by his arms, Jesus studied him. "It's been too long, but you are looking well. How's your life as an advocate?"

This was the last thing Justus had expected Jesus to say. Incredulous, he asked, "How did you know?"

Jesus grinned as he changed the subject. "It's been almost fifteen years since I last saw you. You look the same, just older and wiser."

"Well . . . older anyway," Justus retorted with a broad grin.

"Here, I want you to meet a couple of my new friends." Jesus said, turning to the two strangers behind him.

Although they were attending a wedding, both men wore simple clothes. One had a full beard but his head was balding. The other had long, wavy light brown hair and a short beard. He was much younger. "This is Simon . . . I call him Peter. And this is John."

Justus soaked in Jesus' presence, the memories of good times flooding him. He felt a joy he hadn't felt for years. "Are these new employees in your carpentry business?"

Jesus beamed. "No, they are fishermen."

Justus chuckled. "Are you going into the fishing business?"

Peter put his hand on Justus' arm, with a look of awe. "We are fishers of men."

Justus perceived the deeper meaning and shot a questioning look at Jesus.

Jesus' eyes were deep pools of expectancy. "Justus, I'm thirty years old. Now the people will listen to my teaching without dismissing me as being too young. It's time to tell them about the Kingdom of God. They need to understand the Scriptures."

Touched, Justus nodded. "No one can do a better job of that than you can. But who will carry on your father's carpentry business?"

Jesus replied, "James. He's already managing it."

"A good choice. He was good in the shop even when we were kids. Where is he now?"

John pointed toward the front door. "He's just arrived."

At that moment Jesus' mother, Mary, came in and greeted Tirzah. She had very few wrinkles expected of a woman in her mid-forties with eight children. Her appearance exuded health and happiness. Her movement was surprisingly agile. She hugged Tirzah, then Leah. "Leah, it has been so long . . . I'm glad you were able to come."

James followed Mary through the door. He sported a short beard, trimmed as Jesus' was to avoid accidents during carpentry work. His rugged body and thick forearms gave testimony of hard labor, but today he wore a fine linen robe.

A new wave of emotions overwhelmed Justus. Again tears gathered as he hurried toward his friend.

They embraced and laughed.

Justus was much taller than James, so he looked down at him as he said, "You are looking great, but where did the beard come from?"

James laughed. "From the same place you got your height."

Justus settled down. "Where are Joses, Judas, and Simon and your sisters, Sarah, Ruth, and Hannah?" As he questioned James, out of the side of his eye he caught Mary whispering to Jesus.

"Joses will be here shortly," James replied. "Judas and Simon stayed to work at the carpentry shop. Sarah, Ruth, and Hannah are all married. Sarah is about to give birth to her third child, so she didn't come."

James skimmed the courtyard. "Hannah and Ruth are here somewhere with their husbands and children."

Mary traversed the courtyard and hugged Justus.

Before she could speak to him, a servant passed nearby and Mary grasped his arm. "Go over to Jesus and do whatever he tells you to do."

The servant nodded and headed for Jesus.

Mary looked annoyed and said to Justus, "Tirzah may have found a good man, but he didn't plan the guests' wine consumption very well. They have already run out." Her expression softened. "But look at you, Justus. You have really grown up." They stood talking for several minutes, catching up with the recent news.

A few minutes later, two servants made several trips to pour water into the six large water pots used for ceremonial purification.

Casually watching them, Justus asked James, "Do you know these two new friends of Jesus?"

James glanced at John and Peter and shrugged. "No, but they are just common fellows. He has others, also. Actually, one named Nathaniel is from here. They intend to be disciples and listen as Jesus teaches. I think they want to learn, so they can tell others the things Jesus teaches here."

Justus asked, "Is there anyone better to learn from than your brother?"

"No, I agree. However, these men seem to be slow. They definitely aren't scholars."

Justus watched one of the servants draw a pitcher of water from the now-filled ceremonial pots, pour it into a cup, and take it to the manager of the wedding feast.

Amid the loud talking and laughing of the guests, James began to speak.

Justus held up his hand to stop him. "Wait a minute," he said. "What is going on there?"

While Justus and James looked on, the manager tasted from the cup, and laughed loudly. "Beriah, what have you done? Everyone else serves their best wine at the beginning of the feast. Then after the people have drunk freely, they serve what's not so good, but you have kept back the best wine until now. Everyone, try this. It is excellent."

Justus turned away from James to search out Jesus. He spotted him at the edge of the courtyard, alone. Jesus was watching the manager, with an expression Justus had never seen on him before—not cold . . . but determined . . . and very distant.

James asked, "Justus, what's wrong?"

Not answering, Justus marched to one of the water pots and looked inside. It was dark purple. Bewildered, he had filled a cup and tasted it. Shock delayed his faculties. It took a few seconds for him to process the flavor of the finest wine he had ever tasted.

❧ ❧ ❧

Michal appeared concerned and shook Justus. "Are you all right?"

Her shaking jostled him back from the far-off thoughts. Still, he held a look of doubt. "Yes. But Michal . . . I don't know where the wine came from. It was like . . . like . . . a miracle."

Michal looked unconvinced. She used both hands to shake him again. "Silly, wine comes from grapes."

"Of course it does." Her playful response completely dissolved his trance-like mood. He surveyed the flatland from their hill perch. "Surprising, but we still are not followed. Did you kill the guard last night?"

"No, I waited until he went to sleep, then made sure he stayed asleep a while longer by hitting him with a rock."

Justus laughed and scouted the hillside they were on. He furled his eyes as he looked to the left. Then he cocked his head as he glanced to the right, leaned forward, and looked over Michal at the mountain slope on her side. "Well, I'll be," he said.

"What is it? What's wrong?"

He pursed his lips and nodded. "I've been here before. I know where we are."

CHAPTER EIGHTEEN

Annas strutted through the courtyard of the high priest. He was dressed in a finely woven robe of an off-white color. His headdress was burgundy and flowed far down his back. The darkness of his long, untrimmed beard masked his seniority, but did not hide the haughty expression. He felt uneasy. It was time. He must know today. Annas barely glanced at the remnants of autumn flowers dotting the fringe of the walkway as he knocked on a door.

A female servant opened it and bowed. "Most Honorable Annas. My Lord Caiaphas is expecting you. Please follow me."

"Never mind," he said harshly, "I know where to find him."

The maid cowered. "As you wish, my lord."

Annas had been in the palace so many times he knew every crook and cranny. He was next in line to become the high priest, so his familiarity would serve him well. He climbed the three steps at the end of the foyer and hastened through the hall. It was lined with small ledges, each holding a piece of religious artwork. He made sure his robe didn't brush the artwork, but other than that, paid no attention to them. The hall ended at a large balcony facing the greater part of Jerusalem.

Annas had been a chief priest many more years than Caiaphas, who had come to rely on him heavily. Their close kinship added to their professional relationship, resulting in a solid bond between the two.

That connection had not only resulted in power to control the Sanhedrin more than any before them, but it also enabled them to devise and implement various schemes to increase their wealth. The most recent—to find Melchizedek's Tomb.

Caiaphas leaned on the balcony railing, looking over the city. The balcony was a perfect place to view the open courtyard of the Temple and inspect people coming and going from the Temple area. The distant chattering of people performing their daily tasks did not drown out Annas' approaching footsteps. Caiaphas' average frame looked even smaller without the public robes of a high priest, as he turned in a nonchalant manner. "Father-in-law . . . it's good to see you. Please sit down."

"Thank you." Annas propped against the balcony railing and appeared grim. "We have a new problem," he said.

Caiaphas' expression looked perplexed. "Not with the Nazarene, I hope. He already has been occupying most of my time. In fact, I had a trap set recently to catch him, but it failed."

Annas sneered. "No, we do need to talk about him sometime, but this is something else. I've been putting off telling you about it." His face clouded as he shifted his weight. He thoughtfully ran his hand through his beard. "It's about Asher."

Caiaphas drew up. "What about Asher?"

"He's in a coma."

Caiaphas stiffened and tried to swallow. "For how long?"

"A couple of days now."

Caiaphas' shoulders bowed. "How did it happen?"

"The physicians are not sure. And they have no idea how to treat him."

Caiaphas gave Annas a furtive glance. "Has Malchus completed searching the catacombs with the last clue?"

"No, he has a few more nights to go."

With a hint of desperation in his voice, Caiaphas said, "If he doesn't find the Tomb, we can't just give up. Is there another kabbalist we can force to continue the search?"

"You know Asher was the only one we could coerce. However, I have an idea." He paused and narrowed his brows. "I'm bringing Miriam back."

"You mean, she's still alive?"

"Actually, I'm not really sure. Bukki hired a man to feed her, but never checked up on him."

Caiaphas looked perplexed and shook his head. "What good would it do to bring her back?"

"Two things . . . first Asher and Miriam developed a close relationship over the past two years and she may know something of his techniques for searching the Torah. Secondly, maybe she understands the significance of the acacia-wood strips."

Caiaphas' reaction was delayed. "What acacia-wood strips?"

Annas told him of the strips Bukki had found in Asher's room.

Caiaphas mulled over the new information as he pushed himself from the railing and moved across the balcony's polished stone floor to the hall entrance. "Won't she tell everyone she was abducted?"

"Yes, but she doesn't know why or by whom. Bukki concealed himself from her."

"Can she connect anything to us?"

"No, only Bukki and Asher know. Perez knows something has changed with Asher, for I directed him to keep Asher locked in the Temple. But, as far as he knows, Miriam has been visiting a cousin in Greece."

Caiaphas tugged at his beard. "What will he think when he finds out she was abducted?"

Annas became impatient. "What would it matter? Who is Perez that we should be afraid of him?"

"But what if Asher regains consciousness?"

Annas scowled. "Then we'll have them both killed."

The flat statement cut through the air like a lightening bolt. And as ozone after a thunderstorm, it freshened both of their moods. They remained silent for a long moment.

Caiaphas strolled back to the balcony railing and bent forward to rest on his forearms as he mulled over the plan. Slowly, his expression softened. "How long until Miriam returns?"

"Bukki left yesterday to go to Greece. I think his idea is to learn from her cousin that she never arrived, then investigate areas through which she would have traveled, and supposedly find clues leading to where she is imprisoned. Lastly, he will pretend to search for her and finally find her. He intends to return, claiming he saved her life."

Caiaphas grinned, suddenly delighted. "It will take time, but that just might work."

"He guessed he would be back by Hanukkah."

Caiaphas winked as a smug smile grew. "I'll inform Malchus he will have to wait awhile before continuing the search for the Tomb . . . and gaining his freedom."

CHAPTER NINETEEN

Still sitting beside Justus, Michal mimicked his scanning of the hillside, including leaning in front of him and examining the slope on his other side. A skeptical look covered her. She stared at him with dark eyes, head reared back. "You know where we are?"

"Sure," Justus replied and stretched his legs out. His back rested against a tree trunk.

"Where?" she demanded. Her sandals crunched the coarse ground as she stood to get a better view.

He hopped up beside her and brightened. "We're near the border of the field Jacob bought from the sons of Hamor."

Michal looked unconvinced. "You mean where Joshua buried the bones of the twelve patriarchs?"

Abraham's grandson Jacob later became known as Israel. His twelve sons became the fathers of the twelve tribes of Israel. All of them lived nearby, so Jacob bought a large cave to be the burial spot for his family. When a severe famine forced them to move to Egypt, their descendants saved the bones of the twelve brothers, so they could one day bury them on their home property.

Justus began scaling the steep slope. "Yes . . . one and the same. Shechem is a short walk from here, but first, let me show you the cave." It had been twenty years since he had been on this mountain, but the changes in the foliage made little difference.

Michal mounted the slope behind Justus. At the top, she scoured the wide, flat expanse.

No evidence of a field remained as several trees dotted the area with bushes haphazardly growing between them. A few birds lazily floated on wind drafts rising up the slope of the mountain. No cave was in sight.

"Are you sure this is the place?" she asked.

Justus skimmed the terrain with a casual look. "Quite sure."

"I don't see a cave."

"I came here two years before we moved to Rome. Jesus' family decided to pilgrimage here to visit the tombs of our ancestors, and I came along. Actually, this is not all that far from Nazareth."

That had been his first long trip. Memories of fun days and his friendship with Jesus made him grin broadly. "Jesus' father was still alive then," he told her. "His family asked my family if we would like to accompany them. My father couldn't because he had centurion duties, but my mother, I, and even my grandfather came."

"Your grandfather? I thought you said he was against your mother marrying your father and nearly disowned her."

Justus took Michal's hand and escorted her to a slope on the hill that rose higher than the open field, swinging her arm like a kid. "There's something about my grandfather that may shock you. He was a very unusual man."

She pulled away from him. "In what way?"

Justus snickered. "He hewed tombs . . . as did his father, his father's father and back as far as they know. He craved seeing these catacombs where many believe his profession began." Visions of the kindly old man and the wonder he experienced during their pilgrimage made the intervening twenty years evaporate. He beamed.

"After touring here, I think Grandfather realized the chain would be broken, since he had no son. There was only my mother and me, so when we returned to Nazareth, he spent considerably more time with me than he ever had, mostly imparting information about catacombs." Justus puffed out his chest. "I can tell you more about tombs, graves, and catacombs than you would ever want to know."

Michal's voice became saucy. "If that's true, where is this cave you're so sure is here?"

Justus held his right palm upward and moved it in pretended honor in the direction of the slope a short distance in front of them. "This way, my lady."

Michal headed out, deftly avoiding the bushes. "The path looks worn," she called over her shoulder. "Do many people come here?"

"Quite a few."

"Is this the only opening?"

"No, there are several. This entrance is closest to the tombs of the Patriarchs."

Justus bent and entered the cave. The opening was narrow and low, but the corridor inside was high enough that Justus could almost stand straight. The coolness of the cave and its dank odor caused long-forgotten feelings to swamp his memory.

Michal barely needed to stoop as she followed him inside.

They walked only minutes before all sounds of the outside wind and singing birds were hushed. The interior became so dark, they could barely see.

Justus stopped, crouched near the wall, and located several unlit torches leaning against it. Next to them was a pile of small twigs and dried grass held down by several pieces of flint.

Michal raised her eyebrows. "Who put those here?"

"Often people come bringing something—a torch, flint, or dried leaves—knowing some people will come without light."

Piling some kindling, he expertly struck the stones, which sparked into the fine brush causing smoke to float up. He lightly blew on the heap, and a flame danced up. He picked up two torches, lit one, and stomped out the fire in the mound.

"Stay close to me," he said. "I'll give you a guided tour." Justus glided deeper into the cave.

Michal moved close to Justus and grabbed the back of his robe.

They descended deeper into the cavern. Presently, the torch's light lost the walls of the tunnel. They had entered a large area, almost a room. The torch barely provided sufficient light to see large stones regularly spaced along the walls. One nearby had a faintly visible drawing carved into it.

In reverence for the place, she whispered, "Is this it?"

"Yes."

Justus led her to the other side of the room where the walls narrowed. He felt again the amazement he'd experienced his first time in the catacomb. His grandfather had become the tour guide. Still hearing his grandfather's deep, confident voice, Justus repeated the words received so long ago. "This is Rueben's tomb." He held the torch close to the stone. "You can barely see a pot boiling over."

"What's that got to do with Rueben?"

Justus shivered as he heard Michal ask the exact question he had asked his grandfather. He grinned as his grandfather's explanation streamed through his memory. "Before Jacob died, he gathered his twelve sons around him and predicted their character, their future, and the outcome of their lives and their children's lives. Each prediction could be summarized by a specific picture. Jacob even stated the image when he invoked his blessings."

Michal traced the drawing with one finger. She looked cross as she murmured, "Some blessing."

He moved on. "Here is Judah's tomb. See the lion? Remember, Israel's kings were to come from his tribe. David was in his lineage, as is the coming Messiah. Here is Dan's . . . with a serpent." Justus continued through the eleven sons of Israel by interpreting the tombstone's pictures for Michal. The tunnel grew smaller with each tomb.

At the end of the eleven descriptions, Michal peered into the gloom surrounding them. "Where's the twelfth tomb?"

Justus inhaled the musky staleness. "That's a long story. You're referring to Joseph's tomb. He was ruler over Egypt, second only to Pharaoh. Tradition has it Joseph sent some Egyptians to hew out twelve tombs, believing God would one day return the nation of Israel to their homeland. Four hundred years later, the Israelites finally came to this cave with the bones of the Patriarchs." Justus bent closer to her and waved at the walls. "They found the Egyptians had constructed the tombs too close to the surface. Some were even damaged and useless, so Joshua had these new ones made. Since Joseph held such a high position, Joshua decided to make his crypt larger and in a different place. Come, I'll show you the most likely place."

Justus took Michal's hand and guided her deeper into the cave to an unusually large stone. "This is thought to be Joseph's tomb."

Michal squinted as she studied it. "There are no markings, so how do you know?"

"My grandfather claimed Joseph's stone had the traditional symbol, probably a branch or a bow, but so many people over the years touched the image, they wore it completely off."

"I guess that's logical."

Justus enjoyed playing the part his grandfather had played twenty years earlier. "Let me show you where my grandfather thinks the original tombs were made by the Egyptians. It's some distance from here, but there's another opening by them, so we can leave that way and go on to Shechem."

Michal meandered after Justus. The large roomy area with the eleven tombs narrowed to a tight corridor, better lit by the torch. "Where are Abraham's and Sarah's tombs?" she asked.

Justus glanced back at Michal, smiling at her sincere interest. "There's a big controversy about that. The Torah states Abraham bought a cave from the Hittites located near Hebron. Grandfather believed that cave and this are one and the same. No one really knows, but check this out."

Justus took a few more steps and turned down a separate, more spacious corridor. On opposite sides of the tunnel were two massive stones, both with a smooth depression located at Michal's shoulder height. "Those depressions are likely where people continually touched the markings. My grandfather said the deepness of the depressions suggests many, many people have touched the stone over the years. The people entombed here were quite important. He believes they are Abraham and Sarah."

Michal nodded, looking convinced.

Justus returned to the original corridor. His speed increased as his excitement mounted. "We're not far from where Grandfather believed the original catacombs for the Patriarchs are located. Come, I'll show you."

They had been in the cave for over an hour. The longest distance in the cave was from the Hamor's field entrance to an opening on the slope of the mountain exactly opposite of where Justus and Michal had ascended that morning. They had almost completed the course when Justus pulled up. The sound of their sandals scraping over the cave had become a standard interruption of the catacomb's silence, but now he heard something different.

Michal stopped near his back, her voice anxious. "What was that?"

"That's a scream. Someone's in trouble." Justus trotted toward the sound. His steps were awkward since he was bent over and carrying the torch.

Michal remained close behind him.

He stood still, concentrating on the screams.

Michal squeezed past him. "It's a woman," she gasped. "She's crying." When the cries became defined, Michal bolted to the stone covering a low tomb.

A woman babbled, "I heard you talking. Please help me. I can't get out of here." Michal bent slightly and peered into the small opening. "It's OK . . . We'll get you out in a second. Hold on. We won't leave you."

Michal's voice calmed the woman, but she continued sobbing.

Justus ran up and surveyed the situation, formulating a plan. He was all business. "Stand back," he told Michal as he wedged the torch in a crack in the wall of the cavern. He grabbed a large pole leaning against the wall next to the stone and handed it to Michal. "Hold this for me, please."

Michal grabbed the pole as Justus moved a rock onto the cave floor, sighting its position, then adjusting its location. He hooked the pole, rammed it under the stone covering the tomb door and laid it on the rock, making it a fulcrum. As he pushed on the pole, the leverage gained from the fulcrum moved the tombstone up two feet. His voice was commanding. "Try to squeeze through."

The girl twisted her body and slithered through the opening. As she tried to stand, she tripped over the pole and collapsed into Michal's arms. She clutched Michal, her chest heaving, her voice barely a gasp. "Thank you. Thank you. Thank you."

Michal squeezed the girl tightly and guided her up the cave tunnel toward the opening. "You're safe now," she murmured again and again.

Justus watched as the two women stumbled out of the cave and disappeared. He moved the pole, letting the heavy stone again cover the tomb opening. He snatched the torch and sprinted to the cave opening. The brilliant sun was like a wall, its brightness blinding him. He used his hand as an awning to give time to adjust. In seconds, he was able to locate a tree where Michal had led the woman.

Justus stepped close enough to examine the freed prisoner. She was about Michal's height, but very frail-looking. Her tunica was filthy and her long hair matted. Her facial features were pleasing, but her face was dirt smeared and muddy from tears.

Swelling anger took over his thoughts. Whoever had put her in the tomb must be held accountable. Justus moved toward the women.

Suddenly, Michal stiffened. She lifted the chin of the weeping girl to look into her eyes, then gasped, "Miriam?"

The girl squealed. "Michal?"

CHAPTER TWENTY

The Temple guard's station was a small set of rooms attached to the Temple proper, but somewhat set back from the central courtyard. Although inconspicuous, it housed all the guards who were responsible to protect both the Temple property and the priests. They were, in effect, the Jewish providers of law and order. Roman authorities allowed them much latitude, since they knew peace was easier to maintain if conquered people handled most of their own police actions.

Kore's dark beard dotted with white looked distorted as a strong wind whistled through the open area in front of the Temple and blew it far to one side. He marched toward the attached buildings, his headdress flapping in the wind. His stern look was of one on a mission.

Jehu stood with Attai near the entrance. Both were in full uniform, except Jehu held his black helmet under one arm, letting the wind toss his long hair. Apprehension grew as he marked Kore's progress toward them. He spoke low from the side of his short, brown beard. "This looks like bad news."

Kore came to an abrupt stop an arm's length from Jehu. "Just the person I was looking for."

Jehu's expression was stony. He nodded slightly. "Honorable Kore, what can I do for you?"

Kore glanced at a group of people passing by them from the Temple. "Please accompany me into the courtyard. I need your help." Kore spun and paraded through the quadrangle.

Jehu and Attai exchanged glances of disgust.

Jehu had come to expect abnormal assignments from the Pharisee, but he didn't like it. He sulked after Kore, motioning Attai to tag along.

Attai scowled as he fisted his spear with muscles bulging and followed the two men.

Kore tarried at the side of the garden area where it was impossible for the uninvited ear to hear. Still, he kept his voice low. "Caiaphas has a new plan to discredit the Nazarene."

Jehu grimaced. "New plan? What kind of plan?"

Kore swallowed hard. His voice sounded like he was reciting a learned script. "Rather than trapping him with his words, Caiaphas wants to expose his 'healings' as the fakes they are. You and Attai are to circulate around the city outside the Temple enclosure until you find someone who claims they were healed by this liar."

A gust of wind blew a small dust devil from the courtyard, pushing their robes about wildly.

Jehu took a step toward Kore. He held a deep conviction the carpenter was receiving too much time and attention. The whole affair was merely a fad. The best approach was to simply ignore him. "But how do we know where he will be?" he demanded.

"Spend a few days walking around," Kore replied. "Rumors about healings are rampant. If Caiaphas' idea is correct, someone will soon claim he has been healed."

Jehu had dealt with Pharisees and chief priests for many years. Although he would rather have teeth pulled than spend time hunting for people pretending to be healed, he knew resistance to orders led to events worse than wasting time. He swallowed his disdain. "As you wish."

Kore added, "If you don't find anyone in two or three days, report back to me. However, if you do, bring them to me at once."

❧ ❧ ❧

Two days later, Jehu and Attai concluded a tour of the city near the pool of Siloam. The air was stagnant, and the smell of perspiration hung in the atmosphere over those waiting for the pool water to show movement, so they would know when to enter.

Jehu scoured the area and sulked. This was the second time they had visited this site, and this day had proven to be as worthless as the first one. Jehu tried to imagine how someone would pretend to be healed, but merely shook his head as he glanced at Attai. "The Sabbath certainly brings a large number of them out," he said.

Attai nodded with an icy demeanor. "Yes. It's amazing how many people have some type of infirmity and actually believe the water will heal them."

"Incredible . . . but as every other Sabbath, they all simply sit and wait for the water to ripple." Jehu glanced at the sun sinking over the west wall. "This one is nearly over. Let's go back. We've wasted another day."

Attai stepped aside to avoid a dirty-faced, blind beggar trudging to the pool. He pretended the man was invisible. "I agree. You know, I'm not sure about this plan of Caiaphas. I mean, really. Who is going to allege to be healed right in front of us?"

Jehu gazed disconcertedly. "I don't know. People are funny, but I can't comprehend it, either. However, when the high priest orders us to do something, we have to do it. In a few days, they'll come up with some other harebrained idea."

The two guards pivoted to leave.

As they did, the beggar ran into a man on crutches, nearly knocking him down. "Excuse me, sir," the blind man said. "Please help me to the pool. I must wash in it."

The man on crutches was not bothered by the mild accident. He regained his balance, put one hand on the beggar's shoulder, and physically pushed him in the correct direction. "You are nearly there. Walk straight ahead about seven steps."

The beggar gingerly inched his way along, allowing people in his path to move until he found the edge of the pool. He fell to his knees and cupped both hands together to bring water to his eyes. He repeated this two more times, washing the mud completely away. He hopped to his feet and shook his head, liquid from his hair sprinkling those at the edge of the pool. "Praise God! I can see . . . I can see!"

Jehu and Attai whirled and gaped at the beggar who was dancing about, his face clean, his wet hair sticking to it.

Attai shook his head in disbelief. "You've gotta be kidding me."

Jehu scampered to the beggar and collared him. "What do you mean, you can see?"

The beggar broke off dancing for a second. "I can see! I can see!"

Jehu faked a punch to the beggar's head. When he flinched, Jehu's jaw dropped.

Attai bellowed at the others near the pool. "Does anyone know this man?"

One near the street called out, "Attai, I think this man is a beggar who frequently sits by the Dung gate."

Attai looked up. "Ah, Kemuel. I'm glad you are here. Please come closer. Tell me if this is the man."

Kemuel was a dark-skinned man with a bony frame. He was short, so he kept moving his head around people to maintain eye contact with the beggar as he worked through the crowd toward Attai.

Kemuel examined the man suspiciously. "He looks very much like him, but the man who sat at the Dung gate was blind. This man can obviously see."

Jehu leaned into the beggar. "Are you the blind man who frequently sits at the Dung gate?"

The crowd by the pool grew quiet, entranced by the unfolding drama. Four people close to Jehu and the beggar retreated from the pool's edge to avoid being part of the exchange.

The beggar continued to bounce and sway in Jehu's meaty grip, his voice a loud song. "I am he. But now I can see." The beggar clapped his hands and laughed.

Jehu pulled him close. "How did you get your sight?"

The beggar's lips went from ear to ear as he kicked one foot, then the other. "The man called Jesus smeared mud on my eyes and told me to wash in this pool." The beggar grabbed both of Jehu's upper arms. "So, I did! Praise be to God! I can see!"

Attai grabbed the beggar's other arm. He yanked the man away from Jehu and anchored him, disgust evident. "Where is he?"

"I don't know." The beggar oscillated his head as he checked the people around the pool area.

Jehu swallowed hard. He was sure this would lead in a direction he didn't care to go, but he had no alternatives. "OK . . . you must come with us and tell your story to a Pharisee." Jehu glowered. "It's still the Sabbath."

▸ ▸ ▸

Kore breezed into the large area in the synagogue used for formal meetings. Since the Sabbath had almost ended, all services were complete. Only two days had passed since he had forwarded Caiaphas' command to Jehu and here he stood holding a filthy man wearing rags, who was surveying the room as if he had never seen it. He smelled victory, sure he was facing a liar and certain he would soon prove Jesus a fraud.

Jehu clutched the beggar with one hand. "Honorable Kore. We found this man at the pool of Siloam. He claims he was born blind, but the Nazarene cured him. We have sent for his parents. They should be able to tell us if the man is lying to us."

Kore assumed a regal posture as he drew close to the beggar. "How do you think you received your sight?"

The beggar's look of awe was replaced by excitement. "He smeared mud on my eyes. I washed and now I can see."

"What do you say about this man who *you think* restored your sight?"

The beggar beamed. "He is . . . He must be a prophet."

Kore gave a seething exhale. "He can't be a man of God, because he does not observe the Sabbath."

Two guards burst into the synagogue leading an old man and woman. Both cowered as the guards thrust them forward. The old man's thick white beard did not hide his fear. The old woman pulled her shawl farther over her head as her shoulders slumped forward; she gazed at the floor.

Kore confronted them with contempt. "Is this your son?"

The old man peeked at the beggar. "Yes."

"Was he born blind?"

"Yes, he has been blind until this day."

Kore's anger infiltrated his voice. "If this is your son and he was born blind, how is it he now sees?"

The old man studied Kore, then Jehu. His voice became little more than a whisper. "His mother and I know this is our son, and we know he was born blind. But as to how he now sees, we do not know. Who has cured him, we do not know. He is of age. Let him speak for himself and give his own account of it."

Kore twisted back to the beggar. "Now give God the praise. The fellow you credit is nothing but a sinner."

The beggar became somber. "I don't know if he is a sinner or not. Yet, one thing I do know. I was blind before, but now I can see."

Kore's pulse thundered and stared daggers at the beggar. He held out his open hands and gave two forceful thrusts from bent elbows, his voice dripping with vexation. "What did he exactly do to you? How did he give you vision?"

The beggar's words were tinged with impatience. "I already told you, but you wouldn't listen. Why do you want to hear it again? Can it be that you wish to become his disciple also?"

Kore stomped his foot and held his clenched fist in front of the beggar's nose. "You are his disciple! I am a disciple of Moses. I know God spoke with Moses, but this fellow you talk about—I don't know where he comes from."

Frowning, the beggar ripped his arm from Jehu's grasp and glared at Kore beyond the fist. His back arched. "Well, if this isn't astonishing. Here a man cured my blindness, and yet you say you don't know where he comes from. That is amazing. Since the beginning of time, no one has opened the eyes of a man born blind. If that man were not from God, he would not be able to do anything like this."

Kore shook his threatening fist as he screamed at the beggar, "You were wholly born in sin . . . from head to foot! And you presume to teach me? Throw him out of the synagogue and never let him come in again!"

CHAPTER TWENTY-ONE

The darkness of the tomb was forgotten as the two women huddled together under the tree, shaded from the brilliant sunlight.

The surprising revelation that they knew each other stopped Justus dead in his tracks. He stared in wonderment as a reunion of sorts unfolded in front of him.

The women hugged each other. They laughed and cried at the same time. Both rapid-fired their sentences, but neither listened for answers.

Justus deduced the women knew each other, but their connection mystified him. Unsuccessfully, he strained to understand their words.

Presently, the prisoner began sobbing so hard, she was unable to talk.

Michal seemed to feel the source of emotion and held her tight. She moved the woman's head to her shoulder, rocked her and chanted, "It's OK. Everything is all right. You're safe now."

Justus moved closer but stayed back far enough to not intrude on them.

The frail woman's chest stopped pitching, and she looked long at Michal. She appeared relieved as she heaved a big sigh and said, "Oh, Michal . . . Thank you."

Justus moved to the women and touched Michal's shoulder. "I think introductions are in order."

Michal rose, gently pulling the girl with her. She glowed. "Of course. This is Miriam, my cousin . . . who I was intending to visit in Jerusalem. Miriam, this is a good friend, Justus."

Justus grinned. "What a pleasure."

Miriam hugged Justus, her voice filled with joy. "Believe me, the pleasure really is mine. I thought I would die in that tomb. Thank you so much for moving the stone so I could escape."

Justus chuckled. "I'm glad I could help."

Miriam let him go and turned to Michal with an incredulous look. "What on earth are you doing here?"

"Me? What are you doing here?"

The two hugged again and laughed even louder.

Michal's expression darkened. "Who put you in there?" she demanded.

Miriam looked confounded. "I have no idea."

Michal's rage erupted. "Why did they?"

Miriam broke down again. Between gasping sobs, she struggled for the correct words. "They wanted infor . . . mation . . . from my father."

Justus came alert, his advocate gift kicking into high gear. "What information?" he asked.

Miriam squirmed, slanted a glance at the ground, and her voice was hushed. "About what my father does."

"What does he do?"

She gulped and studied her filthy fingernails. "He's a priest."

Justus would have no part of her evasion. He pressed her with an authoritative voice. "Why would someone be held hostage to get information from a priest?

"He's a kabbalist."

Justus sent Michal a perplexed look. He had never heard the word *kabbalist*.

Miriam whispered something in Michal's ear.

Michal's brows scrunched into an unsatisfied look. "We have talked about this in the past," she told her cousin firmly, "especially how confidential it is. But you have been kidnapped, and who knows what has happened to your father. You must tell us everything you know. Justus is a Roman advocate. He may be able to help you."

Miriam lowered her head, hopelessness oozing from her words. "I can't. The secrets of Kabbala are closely guarded."

Michal became brusque. "Miriam, someone has been holding you hostage to get information from your father. As soon as they get it, they will kill you. Don't you see? The only way to help your father is to tell us everything you know. Besides, your father may tell them all they want to know to save you . . . in fact, he may already have."

Miriam withdrew a step. "But . . . if my father did tell them, why have they not come to kill me?"

Justus touched her shoulder. He could see the turmoil in her expression, so he tried to be gentle. "Miriam, maybe they don't need to come. How long have you been imprisoned here?"

"I don't know . . . Probably weeks."

"And how have you stayed alive?"

"An old man brings me food."

"When is the last time he came?"

Miriam's shoulders slumped, recognition showing on her.

Michal's expression softened as she laid her hand on Miriam's arm.

Miriam looked defeated. "OK . . . I'll explain, but first, I just want to get away from here. Then I'll tell you everything." She glanced at Justus. "Do you know where we are?"

Justus pointed south. He wanted to hear Miriam's story now, but acquiesced to her desire to get away. "Shechem is just a short walk over that ridge."

"Good, let's go there." For the first time, she took note of Justus and Michal. "Why were you in the cave?" She glanced from one to the other. "Your clothes are dirty and torn. Were you in a fight?"

Michal put her arm around Miriam, and they set off for the ridge. She chuckled softly. "How about a shipwreck and a brawl?"

CHAPTER TWENTY-TWO

The journey from the catacombs to Shechem had taken nearly two hours, primarily because Miriam was so weak from her captivity that she needed frequent rest stops. A pleasant surprise occurred, however, upon their arrival. The commandant of the Roman garrison was a friend of Justus' father. A quick summary of their story led to food, water, baths, and new clothes for the three of them, in addition to paid rooms at the inn.

Justus stepped onto the inn's wood-covered porch facing an open courtyard, now dark by the long shadows from the inn veiling it. He was dressed in the clothes of a centurion, minus the breastplate, helmet and weapons. As he looked at the courtyard and the town beyond, the quaint picture of a few people doing their last chores of the day at a relaxed pace erased most of the recent day's calamities. The aroma of baking bread filled his nostrils, as quiet peace seeped into his soul.

It had felt so good to eat, get cleaned up, and change clothes. The next time he saw his father, he was going to thank him for being a prominent Roman soldier with lots of friends.

Several empty benches lined the porch. Justus eyed one and moved to sit down. He was interrupted by Miriam and Michal coming out the inn door. He drew up at the sight of Michal. *God, she's gorgeous.* Being around her for the last several days with both of them a dirty mess, he'd forgotten how beautiful she was.

Michal and Miriam quickly joined him.

Michal's black hair was uncovered, and she was dressed in a fine linen white robe with delicate red trimmings. The designs were uniquely

Roman, the dress of royalty. A golden braided-rope belt drew in the robe, accentuating her slim waist. She rubbed her hands down the sides of her hips, and gave a teasing look. "Do you like it?"

Justus caught her double meaning. "You look stunning," he said with a grin.

Michal raised her eyebrows, soaking in the compliment. "Thanks."

Justus glanced at Miriam, who also was wearing a fine linen, off-white robe and scarf. Its designs were Roman but a subtle grey with no belt. Miriam was from a priestly family, not a royal one. Even their body language was distinct. Miriam wasn't stunning like Michal, but her long, light-brown hair framed her petite face as it peeked out from the head scarf and made her attractive.

Michal interrupted Justus' thoughts, her demeanor gracious. "Thank you for finding these. I'm glad you knew the commandant. "

"Actually, he knew my father."

"Well I'm glad you are your father's son," she said, smiling. "The clothes are great, the food superb, and the room perfect."

The cloak of night faded into nothingness. All he saw was the curve of her cheek, the fullness of her lips, the . . .

Michal's chin lowered as her lips curved up. "Miriam is ready to tell you her story." She showed she was laughing at him.

"Uh . . . yes . . ." He cleared his throat as he glanced at Miriam. "Now would be a good time for your long story." He held his arm out toward the bench. "How about if we sit here?"

Miriam's expression became resigned. She barely nodded. They sat for a long pause before she said, "Over the years I've told Michal bits and pieces of information relating to Kabbala." Reluctance caused her to squirm on the bench, but she managed to continue, "I didn't know all that much myself until after my husband, Ira, died a couple of years ago. My father and I spent many hours together. He taught me several things about Kabbala, even though it is forbidden for him to instruct anyone not selected."

Justus took over, his expression questioning. "What is Kabbala, anyway?"

This time she replied without hesitating. "Kabbala is the truth of the Torah. A person must believe this in his heart totally, or he should not study it. If he tries, but does not believe in the pure truth of the Torah, he will end in frustration and with falsehoods."

Miriam's words amazed Justus. "But why have I never heard of this before? I'm from a Jewish family. We were friends with some deeply religious people."

Michal patted Miriam's arm and expressed tenderness. "Start from the very beginning. I think Justus will be able to answer his own question."

"Yes, you're right . . . the beginning." Miriam took a deep breath and went on. "Kabbala means to receive. Moses 'received' the first five Books of the Torah directly from God, letter by letter. It is believed Moses understood those five books perfectly. Moses transmitted them to Joshua in that spirit of understanding. Joshua transmitted them to the elders who continued the process with select disciples—ones who believed in the pure truth of the Torah and demonstrated an ability to find specific meaning in it.

"After the period of the prophets ended, Kabbala was entrusted to 120 sages: the Great Assembly. These sages are now sprinkled throughout Israel. They allow the transmitting of Kabbala to individual students, one at a time. This process insures transmission to the smallest possible circle of masters."

Justus immediately understood the concept, and a feeling of respect swept over him. "So . . . outside the circle, their practices would remain almost totally unknown."

"Exactly. My father was one of those few students, and now he has become one of the sages."

Even as he questioned her, Justus filed his ideas and bits of Miriam's explanation, organizing them for later use. He pushed ahead. "Why would someone hold you hostage?"

Michal gave a look of surprise, her hands in front of her, palms up. "Isn't it obvious? To force her father to teach them about Kabbala."

Justus looked doubtful. "Hmm . . . let's think about this a minute. If he forces Miriam's father to teach him Kabbala, he still could not enter the inner circle of the Great Assembly. So, what would be his gain?"

Michal sighed. "To learn truths from the Torah?"

Justus shook his head. "Miriam just said, if they don't believe in their hearts about the pure truth of the Torah and demonstrate some specific ability to understand on their own, they will only be frustrated and arrive at falsehoods."

The two women sat and said nothing for a long time.

Michal nodded appreciatively. "I see now why you're an advocate."

Miriam gave a perplexed frown. "If their goal isn't to learn Kabbala, why was I held hostage?"

Justus shrugged. He pursed his lips, deep in thought. He knew the answer to her question before she had even asked, but still took time to mentally flip through his internal files. This woman was in grave danger. He weighed his words carefully before he said, "Someone wants your father to get some information from the Torah. Whoever it is wants that information badly enough to use you to force your father to find it."

CHAPTER TWENTY-THREE

Malchus warmed himself by a blazing fire in the open courtyard of the high priest as night hid nearby houses. Several other servants were around the same fire, talking to one another and laughing, but none spoke to him. He was the lead servant. Consequently, a natural barrier existed between him and the others.

He had learned to perform his duties efficiently to give himself time to search the catacombs for Melchizedek's Tomb. Since Asher's coma had stopped the flow of clues, Malchus now had considerable free time.

He stared into the fire, wallowing in his frustrated thoughts as the smoke rose around his head. Weeks ago, Caiaphas had ordered him to stop searching the catacombs. He was no closer to freedom now than he was when he'd first started. He turned his large body to warm his back. Asher *would* have to slip into a coma now. Why wouldn't Caiaphas just tell him what was in the Tomb, so he could start opening them? And he thought he was so close. He peered into the dark, night sky and held out his hand. Raindrops. Great.

Malchus chose a nearby lamp, lit it in the fire, and tramped to his room. Inside, he remained standing, fingering a cup, and slowly turned it around, a melancholy feeling possessing him. He had looked at thousands of tombs . . . probably every tomb under Jerusalem. It's likely he'd walked by the correct tomb many times. *Wait.*

He parked the lamp on the old water-barrel chair and spoke out loud. "I have seen all the tomb markings. I have seen the tomb I am looking for, but I haven't recognized it." He mulled that over for a while. *I'm not a kabbalist, but maybe I can figure out the direction of Asher's search. I still have all his clues.*

He strode to his trunk and fished out a large cloth bag. Moving the lamp to the floor, he sat the bag on the barrel-chair, pulled out ten small scrolls, and laid them on the barrel. If he could work out the direction Asher was heading, maybe he'd be able to tell where Asher's search of the Torah was leading him.

He unrolled the first, revealing an *S* and a *G*. What did he remember about the Scriptures and Melchizedek? Hmm . . . the kings of Sodom and Gomorrah battled some kings. Sodom and Gomorrah . . . that's the *S* and *G*.

He selected a second scroll. Three letters: *A, Z,* and *B*. *I remember . . . the kings were from Shinar, Elam and some other places . . . Admah, Zeboiim and Bela. Of course,* A, Z *and* B.

Malchus picked two more. These both had pictures rather than words or letters. The first was a picture of a priest, the second a picture of a valley.

He studied the two pictures for a long time, a feeling of hope rising in him. The battle was in the Valley of Siddim, so that could be the reason for a picture of a valley. But what would be . . . *Oh, yeah, Melchizedek was a priest.*

Malchus continued through all the small scrolls until only two remained. The *P* and *R* . . . Salem means peace and Melchizedek means righteousness. And lastly, the word *Lot*. After the kings of Sodom and Gomorrah lost the battle, all the wealth and all the people of Sodom and Gomorrah were taken by the victors. Abram's brother's son, Lot, lived in Sodom and was among the captives. So Abram assembled some allies, rescued Lot, and brought back all the wealth. Hmm . . . what's Lot have to do with Melchizedek's Tomb?

Malchus pitched the scrolls back onto the barrel. The room felt damp as wet outside air filtered its way in. He paced, frustration squeezing his thoughts. Why didn't Asher have more clues with pictures? All the very old tombs had pictures instead of words or letters.

He stopped pacing, stuffed the scrolls back into the bag and dropped it into the chest, slamming it closed. He changed into his sleeping clothes and lay on the pallet in the corner, his anger suffocating the sound of the rain on the roof. The old man had no idea what clues to provide. There was absolutely no pattern or direction. *I'll be glad when his daughter gets back. Maybe she can find something.*

CHAPTER TWENTY-FOUR

The sun was shining brightly, causing Justus to squint as he exited the inn. He had caught up on the sleep he had missed during the shipwreck and capture over the last several days in Shechem. Uncharacteristically, he'd slept late this morning, a victim of lack of sleep the previous night. His thoughts rolled as he had lain awake late into the night, trying to come up with something worthy of a ransom that might be in the Torah. He felt angry with himself for not remembering more about what it described. He knew he needed more information.

The Roman commandant, Julius, stood in the open courtyard. He wore no insignia of leadership, but his stance showed he was in charge. He was a few years older than Justus, with short black hair, now invisible under his helmet. He wore the breastplate of a high-ranking officer and the short sword of a common foot soldier, all the while exuding the confidence of a lethal warrior. Behind him were ten horsemen, twenty-five spearman and foot soldiers, and a single centurion.

"Honorable Justus, good morning," he said, as he slammed his right fist onto his breastplate above the heart. "I trust your stay has been pleasant."

Justus easily moved into the station of nobility, his true environment for several years. "Julius, it has been great. Of course, the last several days of rain were restricting, but the land needs the rain."

"You are quite right."

Michal and Miriam emerged from the inn, both dressed to travel.

Michal smiled at Julius. "Commandant, I'm so glad you came to see us off. We are all very thankful for your generosity and hospitality."

Julius gave a respectful nod. "It has been a pleasure to have you visit us, even though the circumstances could have been better." Looking at Justus, he offered, "And for the opportunity to serve the son of a good friend." Julius pivoted and motioned the centurion to come forward. "This is Gaius, one of my most trusted men. He will be in charge of the force escorting you to Jerusalem."

Justus grasped Gaius' forearm with his hand and, with a surprised look, Gaius grasped Justus' forearm in return.

"It's good for you to be in command."

"Thank you, Honorable Justus."

Julius became less formal as he turned to Miriam. "My lady, I pledge to you your safe return to Jerusalem. However, I personally invite you back to Shechem any time. You are very welcome here." He held her gaze a couple of extra beats, clasped her hand, and guided her to a wagon with a wide seat immediately behind the horses. "I have selected this wagon for your trip. I hope it will be comfortable."

Miriam looked teary, but expressed friendliness. "Thank you."

He swiveled to Justus. "Honorable Justus, would you prefer to ride with the ladies or on a horse?"

"I'll ride with Miriam and Michal. I'm still full of questions, and it'll be easier for us to talk."

"As you wish. Please give my regards to your father."

"Of course. And I, too, thank you deeply for your assistance."

Julius helped Miriam into the wagon while Justus assisted Michal on the other side and climbed aboard after her.

Gaius' horse was in the lead as he bellowed, "Move out."

Michal watched Julius wave as they left the inn's courtyard, then nudged Miriam and gave her a telling look. "It appears you made quite the impression on the commandant."

Miriam flushed and glanced at Michal in surprise. "Julius is very nice."

"Julius?" Michal demanded. "Who's fallen for whom?"

Miriam pushed Michal's arm in mock anger.

Michal laughed but addressed Justus. "When will we arrive at Jerusalem?"

Justus assessed the sun and glanced sideways. "We could probably make it by late tonight, but Julius had supplies put into the wagon to take to his troops detached in Ephraim. So, we will spend the night at the inn there. We should be in Jerusalem by lunch tomorrow."

The wagon groaned as the horses pulled it forward. Miriam's expression seemed to tighten. "I can hardly wait to ask Father why I've been held hostage."

❥ ❥ ❥

The trip to Ephraim was uneventful. Although Justus, Miriam, and Michal had talked during the trip, Justus felt the timing was wrong to push Miriam for further details about Kabbala.

They arrived as darkness was falling and right before the officers reclined to supper, so Gaius arranged to eat with them. The barracks were much smaller than Shechem's—basically one large building with only two windows on the front.

While they ate, Gaius had a soldier orchestrate rooms at the only inn. Afterward, Miriam, Michal, and Justus hiked the short distance there. Conventional mud bricks made up its exterior, but it extended back twice the distance of a normal house. As they entered the small room at the front of the inn, they encountered the surprising aroma of burnt incense.

Justus surveyed the area while the innkeeper told them what rooms were theirs. Miriam and Michal had to share one. Justus stepped through an opening just off the innkeeper's cubicle, which had no door. He noted it was a long, narrow chamber for serving guests. The space was empty, an excellent opportunity for a private talk. He lightly touched Miriam's arm. "Tomorrow we arrive in Jerusalem. You'll talk to your father and find out what's been going on. Gaius told me Julius has ordered him and the troop to remain with you until you are convinced you're safe. So, things look good . . ."

Miriam looked distressed. "But, I have a bad feeling."

Michal came closer, showing her concern. "Why?"

"I don't know. I just feel something is very wrong." Miriam stifled a sob.

Justus pointed to two benches in the corner. "Let's sit a minute. I have been thinking about what you told us the first night at the Shechem Inn. You said the assembly of sages only picks students to receive Kabbala who believe the pure truth of the Torah and demonstrate a specific wisdom and ability to understand the Torah on their own." Justus guided the women to the benches. "I'm sure you could tell me all kinds of things that would convince me your father believes in the truth of the Torah. But, what was your father's specific ability that led the sages to accept him?"

The change of subject was effective. Miriam settled on the bench and her tears vanished. "It will sound strange." She glanced at Michal. "To both of you."

Justus was quick to pick up on her change of demeanor and knew he had opened the correct door. "Michal and I have been exposed to a bunch of strange things these last several weeks, so please . . ."

Michal rested beside her and chimed in, "That's the truth."

Miriam looked from Michal up to Justus. "OK. My father has always loved working with numbers. So much so, he developed a technique to use numbers to find deeper meanings in the Torah."

Justus' eyes were wide saucers as her statement crumbled all his preconceived notions of Asher's gift. So complete was the nonsensical answer, Justus lost his advocate demeanor. "What? What have numbers to do with finding truths in the Torah?"

"See, I told you it's strange."

Her answer put him completely off balance logically, and he placed his hand on the wall. "Strange? It's ridiculous."

Surprised, Michal said, "Justus, you're an advocate. Let her finish before entering judgment."

Michal's words deflated Justus' pompous bubble, and he turned sheepish. "Of course, Michal, you are absolutely right. I am sorry, Miriam. I really do want to understand. Please continue."

Miriam shrugged and turned one corner of her mouth down. "Well, that's really all there is. The Great Assembly saw how my father was able to use numbers to find truths hidden in the Torah, so they selected him as a student . . . and, as they say, the rest is history."

Justus blinked several times and rubbed his forehead back and forth with his hand, unable to fathom a connection between numbers and Torah truths. He crumpled onto the bench perpendicular with the one supporting the two friends. His intuition raced down a few credible paths, but he arrived at nothing and felt a clueless wonder. "OK, I'm really slow on the uptake this evening. But, I see no way to use numbers to get truths from the Torah. Can you give me an example?"

Miriam shook her head, and her expression lightened. "Not really. But I can tell you how it works . . . I just can't remember any specific examples."

Eager for any clue, Justus leaned toward her. "OK, tell me how it works."

Miriam cleared her throat, paused a moment, then beamed. "Remember, I told you the Torah is believed to have been directly given to Moses by God, letter by letter?"

"Yes."

"I neglected to tell you a small detail. It is believed the Torah was dictated to Moses letter by letter, with no spaces or punctuation marks. If you will, one very, very long word of approximately 305,000 letters."

Justus attempted to discern if Miriam was toying with him. "That's a really big word. Wonder if God took a breath . . ."

Michal interrupted, "Justus, please."

The excitement of encountering a new mystery began to seize him. "If there are no punctuation marks or spaces, how does one read it?"

"Actually, easier than what you might think," Miriam went on. "Remember, Moses completely understood it when God gave it to him. It is believed He transmitted the true meaning to Joshua, and so forth."

Justus sat transfixed, his intellect an open sponge. "This sounds intriguing, but how do your father and his love of numbers figure into this?"

"In order to handle 305,000 letters in any meaningful way, one must inscribe them onto several scrolls. However, once they are put on scrolls, the result is a matrix of letters with as many columns as room to write across the top and as many rows of letters as there is room to write down the side."

Justus propped his chin on his elbow and pictured a scroll filled with a matrix of letters. A sensation of expectancy took hold of him.

Michal broke the silence with a frustrated expression. "I think I follow you, but I still don't see how your father uses numbers to get deeper meaning."

Miriam leaned close, and whispered, "What he does is skip letters, equidistantly, to see if he can find different words not easy to see embedded in the plaintext."

Michal jaw dropped. "Ah . . . I think you lost me."

Suddenly, the concept mushroomed in Justus, causing him to become animated. "I'm getting it! You mean he might choose to skip, say . . . every third letter in the entire Torah, write that third letter down, along with every third letter after it, and see if a message comes out."

Miriam grimaced. "Well, almost."

Justus' forehead wrinkled. "What do you mean, almost?"

"You're missing a specific point. Because the scroll makes a matrix, it is possible to find new words of truth vertically, horizontally, diagonally, or all those directions backwards."

The concept exploded in Justus, but the next moment his elation gave way to a frown. "Amazing . . . however all those combinations would be nearly impossible to see."

"Not impossible, but very difficult. It takes such a long time to perform a single examination. However, my father did say he had an idea that would make it faster."

Justus gave a look of interest. "What is it?"

Miriam threw her hands up. "He's never told me."

Justus leaned against the wall, perplexed. "I get the idea totally, but there are an almost infinite number of combinations of letters when you consider different sizes of scrolls and reading in all directions. Can't you eventually find anything? How does Asher know he has arrived at a new truth?"

Admiration covered Miriam's features. "You really are quick. Well . . . he has one other mechanism. He only accepts the new information if associated words occur in close proximity to one another. He believes it's too unlikely for two or more words related to the same topic to be found close together just by chance. In fact, the closer they occur, the surer he is of the new truth's authenticity."

Justus shook his head, the disbelief a few minutes earlier replaced by the awe of this profound knowledge. He looked at Miriam with new concern. She had just given the basis for her abduction, though he still didn't know the reason behind it. Asher was being forced to use his gift to find something embedded in the Torah. It was so important, someone would resort to holding Miriam ransom for it. *What's going to happen tomorrow when the culprit sees us eliminate his leverage over Asher by delivering Miriam? They will both be in severe danger.*

Miriam appeared excited. "Wait. I just remembered an example. Once, my father was very interested in knowing if one of our relatives named John was a prophet. He spent weeks skipping various numbers of letters in just the book of Genesis. Finally, he found the word *John* with the word *prophet* nearby. Come outside and I'll write in the dirt what it looked like."

Justus grabbed Michal's hand, an eerie feeling taking hold of him as the three moved outside.

Miriam crouched and used her finger to write in the dust. "Here's what it looked like eliminating the skipped letters and the letters not making words."

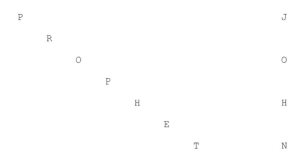

CHAPTER TWENTY-FIVE

Although winter is the rainy time of year in Jerusalem, the trip from Ephraim had been under partly sunny skies. It was cool, with a brisk wind causing the three passengers to cover their legs with blankets and wrap their coats tightly about them.

Justus clasped the wagon seat as the wagon lurched when a wheel hit a hole in the road. Before the small caravan embarked, he had detailed the ransom plot to Gaius as well as he knew it and warned him of the danger Asher and Miriam may be in when they arrived at her house.

As they weaved along the narrow road, he focused on the undulating hills and the Jerusalem skyline, the cold air tickling the hairs in his nose. The city walls loomed larger with their approach as did Justus' rising impression of peril. Asher must be extremely worried about Miriam. It was probably easy to make him use his gift to search the Torah, given the threat that his only child might be killed. Kidnapping was a dark part of human nature. Though he normally defended people, this time he would find the guilty one.

Gaius led the troop opposite the Antonia Fortress area and entered through the Herod Gate.

Justus felt a surge of uncertainty. Had Asher found what he was being blackmailed to find? What could possibly be so valuable that someone would resort to such extreme measures? He shuddered with a haunting thought just out of his reach. He rolled the possibilities in his head again and again, but they had no logical connection.

As Gaius stopped the company at Herod's gate, a watchman strolled to them, appearing bored. "What's your business?"

"I'm escorting three people to Jerusalem on order of the commandant of the garrison located at Shechem."

The guard stood aside and picked at food lodged in his teeth. "Very well. You may enter."

As the troop moved through the gate and turned south towards Asher and Miriam's house, Michal laid her hand on Justus' arm. "How long has it been since you were in Jerusalem?"

Justus came back from distant thoughts. "Not since I was a kid. What about you?"

"I was not that young."

He glanced at both sides of the street. "It doesn't look all that different to me inside the city walls, but there are a lot more houses outside."

"I noticed that, also."

Justus set aside his mental search for saneness in the kidnapping plot, and processed the moving-city show. "I guess when I was a kid, the smallness of the houses and how close they are together in the city didn't make an impression on me. However, it's pretty cramped in here. When were you last here?"

Michal grinned. "Miriam visited me last about four years ago. It was probably three years before when my mother and I came here. It really does look the same to me, though."

Justus waved his hand in the general direction of the house to the right side of the wagon. "Is Miriam's house the same as those?"

"Somewhat. Most of the courtyards you see are not covered, but Miriam's house has a small covered courtyard in front."

"Because Asher is a priest?"

"Yes. He is wealthier than the common people. Also, remember, most Jewish houses have a wide front room with three individual rooms at the back, each having a private door. When two people become engaged, the groom adds a room to the house, opening into the front room or to the courtyard, depending on space available. When he's finished, he brings his bride there to live."

Justus ignored the lesson on Jewish life he already knew and nodded in the direction of a large building. "What about those two-story houses on the wall?"

"In cities, there often is too little space to add to the side of an existing house or courtyard, so many times people simply build up." She shoved him hard. "You know all about housing anyway."

He laughed.

Michal suddenly grew sober. "Hanukkah begins day after tomorrow. Are you going to start hunting for Jesus?"

Justus noted coldness in Michal's tone, but her question reminded him of his quest, all but forgotten because of the mystery surrounding Miriam. He heaved a perplexed sigh. "Yes. First, I want to hear what Miriam's father has to say about her abduction, then I'll start hunting."

Miriam fidgeted on the wagon seat. Her expression was austere as she yelled from the wagon to Gaius, whose horse had moved several feet in front of them. "Turn at the next street. It's the last house on the right before the city wall."

The troop turned. As they neared the dwelling, the covered courtyard stood out among the other houses, but it also made the house appear smaller. The courtyard was empty. Smoke from a smoldering fire carried the pleasant smell of burning cedar. Justus spotted two Temple guards stationed at the door and bristled. Were they protecting Asher? Had they found out about the plot?

Before the wagon could fully stop, Miriam lighted onto the ground and sprinted through the covered courtyard. The guards crossed spears, physically blocking Miriam. "Halt. No one can enter."

"But I'm Miriam, Asher's daughter."

The guards exchanged looks of unbelief, and the older of the two squinted under bushy eyebrows. "Where's Bukki?"

"Who?"

"Bukki. He was sent to Greece to get you."

Justus slanted a quizzical glance at Michal, which she returned, her head shaking.

Miriam fell to her knees and sobbed. "I was not in Greece. I was abducted and held hostage. My friends helped me escape. Please let me in! I must talk to my father."

Justus bounded from the wagon to Miriam's side, all his faculties on full alert. "I demand you allow this woman entrance to see her father."

Gaius backed up Justus with five swordsmen and five spearmen, his voice stern. "I suggest you do as he says."

The guard's attitude changed instantly. "Of course. As you wish. But please let me inform them you are here."

"Hurry."

The guard disappeared inside.

Michal reached Miriam and helped her stand. She glared through slits and her teeth clenched as she guided Miriam to a point next to Justus.

Perez ran out the door, the guards close behind him.

Miriam disengaged herself from Michal and grabbed the sleeve of his robe. "Oh, Perez. Take me to Father."

Perez pored over those gathered about the door. He seemed to be in a quandary. He craned his neck around Justus and searched the area behind him. "Where's Bukki?"

Justus was on the verge of losing all emotional control. His gaze burned into Perez. "Who in the name of common sense is Bukki?"

At that outburst, Perez seemed to gather his wits. He hugged Miriam. "My dear, I'm sorry. Master Asher has been in a coma for weeks. We can barely feed him. He is very weak. When I first noticed you were gone, he told me you went to Greece to visit your cousin."

Justus felt the jigsaw puzzle was receiving new pieces.

"As soon as he fell into the coma, Chief Priest Annas ordered his lead servant, Bukki, to go to your cousin in Greece, inform you of what happened, and bring you home."

Miriam fainted in Perez's arms.

Michal and Justus took Miriam from Perez and laid her gently on the ground.

Michal flushed crimson as she bore in on Perez. "I am her cousin from Greece, and I was coming to visit *her*. She had never planned to visit me."

Perez retreated from the onslaught.

Michal stayed in his face. "She was abducted. We found her and brought her back. Now, we want to know, what in the name of Caesar is going on?"

Perez blinked several times. "Abducted?"

CHAPTER TWENTY-SIX

The Temple receiving room was small and set off from the Temple worship area and expressly designed as a place the high priest could have private meetings. A table with benches comprised the furniture, and the walls were black with inlaid gold designs which made the room seem even smaller.

Kore had been sitting in the receiving room for more than an hour. His stomach was knotted and his face wrenched with frustration under his beard. Jesus had developed into a deep thorn in his side. He knew this summons had something to do with him. He stood up and paced. *I have done everything asked of me. The Nazarene is simply impossible to handle. What does he expect . . .?*

Caiaphas surged into the room, interrupting Kore's thoughts. He wore royal robes and hoisted his average frame with feigned superiority as he ignored the civility of a greeting. "I've received multiple reports that the carpenter's influence is growing steadily. He is totally undermining our religion. Do you know where that will lead?"

Sweat broke across Kore's brow. "The people will no longer follow us."

"Precisely. We will lose all our power, all our money, all our prestige, and all our influence over the Romans."

Kore felt his future seat on the Sanhedrin slipping away. His throat narrowed. "We have tried repeatedly to discredit him, trap him, and show his healings to be false, but our plans always backfire and he gains greater credibility."

Without answering, Caiaphas gave Kore an icy stare.

The high priest's silence became unbearable, and Kore swallowed hard. "Chief Priest Caiaphas, I really have attempted to follow your orders . . ."

Caiaphas brandished anger and waved a hand. "Now is not the time for apologies. It's time for more desperate action."

Kore could barely breathe. "What do you mean?"

"The Nazarene must be killed."

Kore reeled. "But many of the rabble views him as a great prophet, or more. If we kill him, the people will revolt. They may turn on us and kill us."

Caiaphas was unable to completely hide his disgust. "Take it easy. I didn't say we kill him . . . I said he must be killed."

Kore's brow crinkled. "If not us, who?"

"The people themselves."

⁊ ⁊ ⁊

Chislon hurried into the large room in the synagogue where weekly services were held. As most Pharisees, he was dressed in a large, finely woven, flowing robe and a long headdress tied with an elegant, soft rope. His beard was untrimmed and was a rusty brown, matching what little hair was visible. He had known Kore for years and had assisted him with numerous difficulties. However, he did not see Kore as a friend, but a benefactor.

A synagogue attendant recognized him. "Master Chislon, may I help you?"

"Yes, Kore has sent for me."

"Please follow me." The attendant led him through a door that had a cloth covering which gave it the illusion they were passing from one room to another in a tent. The attendant bustled down a narrow hall to a room at the back of the synagogue. He held a similar cloth covering back for Chislon. "Please wait here, and I will inform Master Kore you have arrived."

Chislon gave the room a look-see as he inhaled the heavy scent of very old papyrus and animal skins processed so they could hold writing and be rolled up. A wooden rack holding multiple scrolls leaned against one wall. A large shelf protruded from the opposite wall with an ornate design above it. On the shelf was a beautifully embroidered cloth wrapped around what certainly must be a Torah. A single table was positioned in a corner so only two sides could be reached. One side had a backless chair beside it. Although a large room, so many objects were crammed in it that it appeared quite small.

This was an honor. Kore was one of the few Pharisees in line to be selected to the Sadducee-dominated Sanhedrin, and Chislon suspected he needed his help again. *When he gets the nod, I'll take his place as head of this synagogue.*

Kore rushed into the library, grinning broadly. "Chislon, my friend. Thank you for coming."

Chislon gave a courteous bow. "I'm pleased you asked for me. How may I serve you?"

Kore closed in on Chislon, an air of secrecy in his manner. "Do you have any friends who have not become bewitched by this Nazarene called Jesus?"

Chislon softly nodded and half smiled. "Of course. I have many friends who do not believe what he says. Do you have plans for another trap? The last was not very successful."

Kore's teeth clenched. "Well, more than a trap."

"How much more?"

"An execution."

Chislon stepped back, nearly stumbling. He had observed Kore do some repulsive acts in the past, but never murder. "Sir, I've overseen necessary executions, but none who were high profile."

Kore set his jaw. "No, no. I'm not asking you to kill him. Let me explain."

Chislon intentionally diverted his gaze and said nothing.

"The Nazarene continually says inflammatory things. And you're a Pharisee . . . you know the Law. If he blasphemes, death by stoning is required."

Chislon pulse hammered. "Yes, the Law is clear. Blasphemy is punishable by stoning to death. Has he blasphemed?"

Kore cocked himself up tall and gave a smug grin. "Of course. Frequently. The injustice, however, is no one who understands the definition of blasphemy has been around to evaluate what he's said. All I want you to do is get some of your people to stay around the Temple area during Hanukkah and question him. Once he blasphemes, it's the solemn duty of all people present to stone him to death, not just you. You know the Law."

Chislon's imagination conjured up the scene, his face smutty. "Of course, but how do you know he'll be there?"

"Oh, he will be there. He never passes up a chance to try to teach a crowd."

"OK, I'll line up some experts in the Law who can test this Jesus. I'll make sure they are at the Temple day after tomorrow. If he gives us the wrong answer, he will be dead before the feast's end."

CHAPTER TWENTY-SEVEN

Gaius and Justus sat silently in Asher's front room. The room had a large area on the floor on one side, with a finely woven table cover and several cushions which would accommodate several people reclining for a meal. The other side of the room held a couple of benches and two shelves holding lamps, leaving the larger part of the middle area open and unfurnished.

Considerable time was required for Gaius, Justus, and Michal to restore order to Asher's house, but now Roman guards manned the door, troops were stationed along the city wall near the house, the servants were ordered to their quarters, and Miriam was in her room.

Michal slipped into the front room from Miriam's bedroom. She held an old blanket and closed the door quietly. Her voice was soft. "Miriam is asleep. She's been through too much lately and is simply drained. After she sleeps, I'm sure she'll be better. She's in her own bed now, so I'll bet she sleeps long and well."

Gaius rose, looking at Michal as if she were his commander. "My lady Michal, I have posted two guards at the door and directed the Temple guards to leave. The rest of the troop is encamped next to the wall at the end of the street. If anything happens at all, you will have enough men at your disposal to prevent anyone from hurting you or Miriam."

Michal's voice was faint. "Thank you."

Gaius turned to Justus. "Honorable Justus, I must report to the procurator, Pontius Pilate. I'm sure you understand, a company of soldiers from a different legion must check in with the highest in command."

"Yes, I know. But, Gaius, I would prefer you not tell Pilate I am here. If you do, I won't be able to investigate why someone made Miriam a hostage."

Gaius looked grim. "As you wish, but my silence could be my death."

Justus offered a sympathetic smile. "I know the risks, and I appreciate your courage. Thank you."

Justus had forgotten the search for Jesus and the mystery of the Torah while they attended to Miriam. As the sound of the closed door faded, he was captivated by Michal's natural beauty. His look betrayed his emotions. "Are you staying tonight?"

"Yes. I don't want Miriam to wake up and have no one to comfort her."

"I understand, but the lady Perez hired . . . What was her name?" he asked.

"Abigail."

"Right . . . Abigail. She's in the next room. She can care for Miriam and Asher."

A kind look captured Michal's face. "I know . . . Miriam's really dear to me, though. I want to stay." She spread out the cover onto the floor in the middle of the room. "I'll use this as a pallet and sleep here tonight. If Miriam awakes, I'll be right here to comfort her."

Justus picked up his coat and fumbled with it, his body language screaming he didn't want to leave. "I'll stay at one of the inns tonight."

Michal expressed tenderness. "Please . . . don't go yet. Let's talk for a while."

Justus stopped fingering his coat and laid it on a bench, his stomach churning the same as the first time he had defended a client. "OK, I'd like that."

Michal tapped her hand on the makeshift pallet. "Sit here."

Justus lay in the spot indicated by Michal, but propped himself up on one elbow and smiled. "What do you want to talk about?"

"Well . . . since Asher is in a coma, are you still going to hunt for him?"

"Jesus?"

"Yes."

Justus contemplated a nearby wall, a lump forming in his throat. Simply thinking about Michal had blocked out thoughts of his mission, but her question brought it all back. "The feast starts day after tomorrow, so I'll hunt then. Before I do, I want to first see how Miriam is doing and question Perez about Asher."

"Good." Michal placed her hand on his. "You know, we have been through a lot."

"I know. My simple trip to Jerusalem has turned into quite an adventure."

Michal looked flustered. "There's no one I would rather have gone through what we have, other than you."

He leaned closer, and his body trembled imperceptibly. "Me too." He lightly traced the lines of Michal's cheek with one finger, soaking in the softness of her skin.

Her eyes half closed, but her lips half opened.

Justus faintly kissed her and traced her lips with the tip of his tongue. *God, she's a beautiful woman.*

Michal's chest rose with a deep inhale, and she flushed. "Hmm . . ." She kissed Justus' lips firmly.

The stillness of the room was shattered by a loud knock on the door.

Justus cringed and froze.

Michal had a pained look.

The knocking continued. "Honorable Justus? Honorable Justus?"

Justus' chin fell onto his chest.

She shook her head and whispered, "Answer the door."

The guard knocked again and called, "Honorable Justus."

Justus bounced up, his disappointment replaced by anger. "What is it?"

The guard stepped into the room, his appearance shaded with concern. "Sir, I'm sorry to bother you, but a man is here who says it is urgent he speaks to you."

Justus leaned his head past the guard to see the man. "Let him in."

As the guard stepped aside, a large man crowded in. He spoke directly to Justus with a look of authority. "Peace to you, Justus."

Justus squinted. The man looked familiar, but he couldn't retrieve his name. He quickly filed through his memory for a match. Finally the man's uncovered baldness gave him the clue. Recognition swept across him. "I remember you . . . You're Peter. I met you with Jesus at the wedding in Cana a couple of years ago." His anger was replaced with swelling hope. If Peter was here, Jesus was close by.

"Yes, that's right."

Justus motioned to Michal. "This is Michal. She is a good friend of mine from Greece. Michal, this is Peter, a friend of Jesus."

"Welcome. I've heard about you."

"And peace to you." He took Justus' arm and pulled in an impatient manner. "Jesus has sent me to bring you to him."

The unexpected summons caused excitement to blossom in Justus. "Jesus? Where is he?"

"In the Garden of Gethsemane. He wants you to come now."

Justus looked at Michal in disbelief, elation battling disappointment. "But how did he know I was here?"

Peter was stoic. "Jesus knows many things other people don't. Now, please come. He is waiting." Peter spun and dove through the door.

Justus didn't move. He grimaced at Michal, suspecting a moment was lost that might never be recovered.

She appeared to read his conflict, stood, and touched his arm, her look encouraging. "Justus, this is why you came. Go with Peter."

"Will you be all right?"

"Silly . . . How many Roman soldiers did Gaius say were outside?"

Peter pushed his head back into the doorway. "Come on, it's late."

Dismay disappeared, as jubilation swept Justus. "Don't wait up. I don't know when I'll be back."

"I understand." Before Justus could shut the door, she yelled, "Save him."

CHAPTER TWENTY-EIGHT

Although darkness was upon them, Peter and Justus didn't slow down as they burst through the Mercy Gate, exiting the city. In moments they were beyond the light of the gatekeeper's fire.

Justus had little difficulty matching Peter's long strides. However, as they hustled from the city a feeling of apprehension filled him. He had rehearsed over and over what to say to Jesus, but—uncharacteristic for Justus—his thoughts began to turn into pea soup.

The cold, damp night gave Justus a chill, and he pulled his outer coat tight. "Why the Garden of Gethsemane?"

They slowed as a moonless darkness caused both men to stumble on the well-worn road to Bethany.

Peter continued the new pace with an air of urgency. "Our party often stays at Bethany, usually Lazarus' house, when Jesus wants to teach in Jerusalem. Since we all have different things we must do in and around the city, we've formed the habit of using the Garden of Gethsemane as a place to rendezvous."

Justus' curiosity was piqued. "What are the different things everyone does?"

"Sometimes we listen to Jesus teach. Sometimes we buy food or clothes. Several of us have family and friends here, so often we visit with them. In addition, many people have come to depend on us, so we frequently help them. You know . . . just normal things."

"Hmm . . . helping needy people isn't all that normal."

"It's who we are."

A faint glow in the sky became brighter as they veered off the road and jumped over a small creek at the edge of the garden.

Although difficult to see clearly, enough campfires were burning in different locations to detect a wide area of sparsely scattered fig and mulberry trees and several aesthetically placed large stones amid various sized, leafless bushes.

Justus shivered in anticipation as he passed from one encampment to another. Twenty to thirty people were spread out in different places. Some were huddling around the flames warming their hands. Most were exchanging the details of what the day had brought, occasionally punctuated with laughter. There was very little breeze, so the smoke spiraled straight up into the darkness above, filling the air with the pungent odor of burning mulberry branches.

Peter pointed toward the opposite edge of the Garden where a large sycamore tree stood, surrounded by several shrubs. "Jesus is near that blaze," he said.

A sudden, powerful thrill seized Justus as he followed Peter to the area.

Jesus was standing close to the flames, talking to another standing figure, but Justus didn't catch any of the words.

When Justus entered the circle of light, Jesus interrupted himself and immediately embraced him, his expression delighted. "I'm glad to see you again!" Jesus disengaged, but held Justus' right arm as he half turned toward the fire. "Come. Sit with me."

Justus eyed Jesus. He had expected a tired, worn-out, maybe defeated evangelist, but was astonished at the vibrant figure in front of him. His expression and body language displayed calm assurance, peace, and joy.

The distant happiness Justus had experienced with Jesus in childhood enveloped him again and caused a feeling of safeness to press on him. "It's good to see you again, too," he said, crossing his legs as he joined Jesus in sitting by the fire.

Peter and the young man with wavy brown hair who had been talking with Jesus joined them on the ground.

Jesus glanced at them, then asked Justus, "Do you remember John?"

Justus smiled and nodded at John. "Yes, I do. Peace to you, John."

John leaned sideways and gave Justus' arm a single pat. "And to you, Justus."

Jesus expectantly scrutinized Justus. "What is it you wanted to tell me?"

Justus became flustered. "Well . . . I . . . How did you know I was in Jerusalem? And how do you know I want to talk to you?"

Jesus held a mirthful expression. "Justus, remember when we were kids and we played together?"

"Of course."

"You used to say I could tell things were going to happen, almost before they did."

Justus grinned broadly, happy memories flooding his mind. "I remember."

"You were right."

The starkness of Jesus' conclusion chilled Justus. He shifted uncomfortably. Jesus had the same ease and softness of expression as when they were growing up together. But clearly something was happening that Justus did not understand. Remembering his mission, Justus asked, "Is it all right to speak freely among these men?"

John stood. "Lord, do you want to be alone with Justus?"

Justus felt puzzled. *Lord?*

Jesus nodded, his smile pleasant. "Please. I think Justus would feel more comfortable if we were alone." Peter rose, joined John, and they strolled to another campfire.

Jesus focused on Justus. "You have come a long way. I know you would only have done that if you loved me very much. Though that fact alone makes me feel good, please tell me your concerns."

Powerful remorse flooded Justus, and his well-planned words dissolved in an unknown vapor. Tremors coursed through his body as he fumbled with his message. "Your mother wrote me a long letter. She's extremely worried about you. She's afraid your teachings will get you in trouble with the Jewish authorities. She told me your brothers, sisters, and she have wanted to talk with you, but you will not listen. So, she asked me if I would reason with you."

Jesus beamed. "Then, by all means . . . let's reason together."

The comment shocked Justus. *He knows exactly why I'm here.* Justus hesitated, waiting for his composure to settle in. "You must stop inciting the priests, Pharisees, scribes, and the Sadducees. If you antagonize them too much, well . . . who knows what they might do?"

Something in the coals snapped and an ember flew to the ground near Justus as sparks danced up through the smoke, only to disappear into the night.

Jesus shook his head, an expression of calm dismissal on his face. "I know exactly what they will do. Don't worry about them. They are blind guides leading the blind."

Justus sensed he was losing the case. "Why not tone your message down for a while? If not for me, then for your family?"

Jesus took on the determined expression Justus had seen at the wedding in Cana. "There comes a time when one must understand that the correct definition of *family* is all those who obey."

The words were empty to Justus. Still, he didn't want to be sidetracked. "Listen, I am trying to get you to understand. You may be in a very dangerous situation, and I don't want to see you get hurt."

Jesus grinned and displayed eagerness. He leaned toward Justus. "Do you remember our last discussion together as fifteen-year-old boys before we parted?"

The vivid memory blocked out everything. Justus, Jesus, and James had hugged for the last time. Justus' mother had issued her final plea for him to get in the wagon for the trip to the coast. Tears were close to falling, so to prevent them, he had tried a new bravado. "Hmm . . . I remember exactly what James told me. I had just predicted to you both that as soon as I arrived in Rome, I was going to become an advocate. James pointed toward the sky and announced, 'Excellent! Finally, the common man will get justice from Justus'." He laughed out loud.

Jesus laughed with him, "And . . . look at you now . . . You're the Chief Advocate of Rome."

Jesus' declaration crashed Justus back to the present reality, stunned. "How did you know I was chief advocate? I was promoted only a short time ago. The news isn't even widespread in Rome."

"My Father tells me many things." Jesus picked up a stick and pushed a charred log into the hot spot from which it had fallen. It instantly erupted. "Back to our discussion before you left for Rome. After you made your prediction and James gave his jingle, I told you I believed in you, but suggested you do what?"

Justus felt the old emotions wash back over him as if they were again in Nazareth, some eighteen years earlier, as he recited Jesus' exact words. "To stay on the narrow path, and do not deviate to the right or the left. People who took the broad road failed to arrive at their goal and usually ended up in destruction."

Jesus turned to put his hands on each of Justus' shoulders and peered at him, his countenance aglow. "Yes. My goal is clear and it is near. I, too, cannot deviate to the right or to the left. I must complete the course. I know where your heart is . . . but understand . . . it must be finished!"

CHAPTER TWENTY-NINE

At the home of Chief Priest Annas, Bukki threaded his way through the courtyard. A dying fire gave up wispy white smoke and a burning wood smell. Patchy lighting from two flickering torches allowed him to avoid the many dormant flowerbeds and ornamental shrubs. He gave a sigh as he shot a yearning glance at his quarters, knowing home must wait until after his report.

He had modified his original plan by fabricating an encounter with a wharf rat who had told him of hearing a drunk brag about helping abduct a woman and imprisoning her in the catacombs near Shechem.

When he had arrived at the catacombs, the stone was in place, but the tomb was empty. During the remainder of his day in Shechem, his investigation resulted in learning old man Abihu had vanished and that Miriam had been found by two strangers. They had taken her to Jerusalem with a Roman escort. Bukki had realized that the conspiracy was ended and his master in grave danger, so he had raced back to Jerusalem.

Bukki had risen through the ranks of the chief priest's servants by being tough, resourceful, and successful. He rarely failed. As he approached the chief priest's door, all the possible consequences of the intrigue deluged his reasoning. Trepidation squeezed him as he knocked on the door and peered into the dark courtyard. He flexed his muscular arms, though no one was around. The start of the new day had sent everyone to prepare for supper or for bed.

A maid in charge of the door opened it and greeted him, "Bukki. You have been gone a long time."

"I must see Chief Priest Annas . . . now."

"He has retired for the evening."

"He will want to hear me. I have very important news."

The maid weighed Bukki's words for a few seconds. "Come in. Wait here in the foyer. I'll tell the master you're here."

The foyer was six-feet square and employed as a buffer for Annas. Visitors seldom came to a chief priest's house unannounced, but when they did, Annas wanted a place for them while he donned his stately apparel.

The maid had barely left the foyer when Bukki began pacing. The room was so small he could only step twice before spinning in the opposite direction. He still couldn't believe the tomb holding Miriam was empty. Pilgrims visited the catacombs all the time, but no one visited those old, worthless tombs. The opening was unmarked, inconvenient, and—if one didn't know the catacombs well—one could get lost trying to find the tombs of the Patriarchs from there.

Bukki stopped, leaned against one wall, and rubbed his fingers through his well-trimmed beard. The weight of the unraveled plan added to the exhaustion of his long journey. A vision of his nearby bed drifted across his consciousness.

Annas rushed into the foyer wearing a simple robe wrapped around night clothes. He gave Bukki an uneasy nod. "What is wrong? Where is the daughter?"

Though he had been alone in the room the entire time, Bukki glanced right and left, making sure no one could overhear. He stepped closer and lowered his voice. "Asher's daughter was not in the tomb. She had not been there for several days." He detailed his new fabrication and his trip to Shechem, but omitted information about the three strangers.

Annas appeared tense. "What about the person you hired to feed her?"

"Abihu?" Bukki felt ice cold, knowing he was balancing on the pinnacle of Annas' disposition. "I went to his house. He had left, taking all he owned."

Annas spun his back to Bukki as he weighed the information. Turning suddenly, he asked, "Is there anything else?"

Bukki gulped, knowing the last was worse than the first. He felt like a trapped rabbit. "I went into Shechem and inquired around. It appears three strangers had stayed at the inn for about a week. One was Miriam. One was a man who knew the Roman commandant. The third was a woman. The commandant sent Miriam and the strangers here under armed guard."

Annas' lips formed an evil curl. Before he could speak, someone knocked on the door. With a frustrated gasp, Annas snatched the door open.

Standing just outside, Jehu jumped to attention. He looked surprised at seeing Annas before him, rather than the door maid. He gave a short glance at Annas' robe, regained his composure, and bowed. Behind him, the two Temple guards assigned to Asher's house looked embarrassed.

"Chief Priest Annas, I am sorry to barge in on you like this, but I have news . . ." Jehu glimpsed Bukki over Annas' shoulder and stopped short, his confusion apparent. "Bukki . . . why did the Romans bring Miriam instead of you?"

Annas stepped back, his expression rigid. "Please come in. I think an explanation is in order."

Jehu crowded in, but the two guards remained outside.

Annas' posture became pompous as he gave an earnest expression. "Bukki has just returned from his intended trip to Greece to inform Miriam about Asher and escort her back to Jerusalem. As he was waiting in Tyre for a ship to take him to Greece, he overheard stories about a young woman being abducted and held in a tomb in the cave of our forefathers, near Shechem." He went to Bukki and placed his hand on his shoulder. "After further investigation, he was convinced the woman was Miriam. He went to the catacombs and found a tomb with evidence suggesting it had been a prison, but it was empty. Going into Shechem, he learned the prisoner was indeed Miriam and had been freed by a man and a woman familiar with the Roman commandant, who sent an escort to return them here."

Jehu stared at him unblinking, saying nothing.

Annas stepped away and asked Bukki, "Is there anything you want to add?"

The story sounded authentic and washed all apprehension from Bukki. He kept his face down to hide any evidence of his relief. "No, Master."

Annas focused on Jehu. "Is there a problem at the house of Asher?"

Jehu gave a empty air of unconcern. "No, but the Romans basically took over and told my two men to leave."

"I'm sure they will protect Miriam and Asher from any further mischief. You may go."

Annas stared at Jehu's back as he closed the door, gave a long satisfied sigh, and turned to Bukki. "What a fortunate turn of events. Now we only have to deal with why Asher told people Miriam went to Greece, instead of calling for help because she'd been abducted."

❧ ❧ ❧

The day before the start of the eight-day Hanukkah feast was cold, and the sky held more clouds than sun. Annas and Caiaphas ambled about the empty courtyard of the high priest's palace as Annas updated him on the new story about Miriam's absence.

Caiaphas felt a renewed confidence as he half smiled and rubbed his palms together. "So . . . our plan to bring Miriam back didn't work, but she has been returned anyway."

Annas stepped over the remains of dead flowers not yet cleaned up by the gardener. "Yes, it appears we are quite fortunate. All she knows is she was abducted, though she will wonder why Asher told Perez she was going to Greece, rather than admitting she'd been kidnapped."

Caiaphas knew the question was rhetorical, but answering it was soothing. "She was held hostage and her captors were holding her safety over Asher's head, so he told a lie to protect her." A new concern began to gnaw at him. "The problem is the other two people. What do we know about them?"

"Nothing yet. I have instructed Bukki to get details about them."

"Good." Caiaphas focused on an old man and a boy meandering down the street near his courtyard, as his thoughts returned to the old problem. "Do you think she knows enough to help?"

"I don't know, but I think the chances are good. I will summon her during the feast and question her myself. If she does, I'll make sure she helps us."

Annas' answer made Caiaphas spin toward him with an incredulous look. "You can't tell her what we're looking for."

"I know, I know. Take it easy. I'll simply devise a way for her to teach Bukki the methods without knowing she's doing it."

Caiaphas glowered, unconvinced. He knew Annas was very good at deceit, but he knew nothing about Miriam. "Sounds easier to say than do."

"Just watch, Son-in-law. Just watch."

CHAPTER THIRTY

Sethur ascended the narrow staircase directly behind Perez. Although he was only a scribe and did not have a great deal of power or own servants, he did command significant authority. At the direction of Annas, he had been the one to organize and preside over the scribes who had generated the large papyrus sheets from the Book of Genesis with the letters in fixed rows and columns for Asher.

From Sethur's habitual probing, he'd learned that Asher's coma had caused a complete termination in the search for Melchizedek's Tomb. Being a scribe, he was fully aware of the possible contents of the tomb and had kept his thumb on Malchus' quest. However, the weeks of inactivity, sprinkled with a large measure of greed, compelled him to conduct his own research. The first step was to explore Asher's workroom. Perez was easily convinced of his trumped-up need to be allowed in.

The top of the stairs gave way to a small landing large enough to have the doors on the right, left, and middle be open at the same time, yet not touch each other.

Perez showed no apprehension and was visibly bored as he unlocked the door to Asher's room.

Sethur needed a minute to settle the excitement in his puny frame. "Who else has a key to this room?"

"Only Bukki."

Sethur barely allowed Perez time to open the door before he pushed by him and hotfooted it to the table stacked with the large papyrus sheets. He studied them as his thoughts spun, ignoring the stale smell of a room unopened for weeks. They had followed Asher's specifications exactly, but why would he want the sheets to be so large with so many letters crammed onto them? The old man examined letters after skipping equidistant numbers of letters, but the larger the scroll, the more difficult it was to search that way.

Perez leaned against the doorframe and picked the dirt from under his fingernails as Sethur examined the scrolls.

Sethur fingered the top sheet, feeling the coarseness of the pressed plant pith, and lifted the corner of each one in the pile. "These are in the same order as when I delivered them. Didn't he examine them?"

Perez hurriedly completed a wide yawn. "I'm sorry, sir. Master Asher never worked in front of me. I have no idea what he has done with them."

Sethur felt a growing uneasiness. He was sure Asher had the ability to find truths in the Torah, but had his age impaired him? "Do you know if he searched anything at all?"

"Yes, sir. I replaced the oil in the lamps frequently, so I know he often stayed awake late. And, the night before he slipped into a coma, he woke me in the middle of the night."

"For what? Another clue?"

"A clue, sir?"

"Come now. Do you think Annas would pay me to have the Book of Genesis written on these sheets and not tell me he needed Asher to find a tomb of great religious importance?"

"I'm sorry . . ." Perez stammered. "I wasn't sure . . ."

Sethur scowled as he waved off Perez in disgust and shoved the sheets away from him. He eyed the table with the wooden strips. "What did Asher use those for?"

Perez shrugged. "I have no idea. He requested thin, acacia-wood boards the day after he instructed me to tell Chief Priest Annas about the large scrolls."

"Did you cut the boards into strips?"

Perez rubbed his bony chin through his well-trimmed beard. "No, Master Asher cut them right before you brought the sheets."

"I didn't see them when I came."

Perez straightened, and his voice became tense. "I'm sorry. I only know he asked for the knife, and the wood had been cut when he went into a coma."

Sethur fanned out the wooden strips, noting they were organized by narrow widths, progressing to very wide ones, and their numbers varied. Not being able to think of any sensible explanation, he became more perplexed. Somehow he must solve this mystery and soon.

Sethur browsed the room, but nothing else caught his eye. "Thank you for letting me examine the room. I'm finished . . . at least for the time being."

"As you wish, sir." Perez opened the door for Sethur and locked it after they stood again on the landing. "If you want to come again, just contact me."

Sethur did not wait for Perez, but bounced his small frame down the stairs. He avoided worshippers on the main path by angling across the Temple courtyard to the guard's station, a feeling of determination enclosing him. He was convinced the wooden strips were a key to finding the location of the Tomb and felt the powerful urge to share the information. He addressed the guard on duty. "Is Jehu in?"

"Yes, sir. Come this way, and I'll take you to his office."

The guard marched through a hall and knocked on an unmarked door. "Captain Jehu," he called, "you have a visitor."

"Send him in."

Sethur opened the door to a cramped room. Four spears leaned together in a far corner with a leather helmet on its side in front of them. A short sword hung on a wall peg next to a breastplate near the spears. A leather-covered bench used up most of one adjoining wall. Opposite it, Jehu sat on a backless chair, repairing a sandal.

Jehu's eyebrows ridged as Sethur trekked in.

Sethur felt a momentary pang of regret. "I know you said we shouldn't meet here, but I just came from Asher's searching room and have discovered an assortment of wooden strips."

Jehu scowled. "Look, we have a system in place to exchange information. Use it and don't come here anymore. I don't want people to see you and become suspicious."

"Yes. Of course . . . I won't from now on, but we must obtain more information about the wooden strips."

"What wood strips are you talking about?"

Sethur detailed the information to Jehu.

Jehu half turned, interwove his fingers, and put them against his nose and mouth. A few moments passed. "Let me think on this matter further," he said finally. "Maybe Miriam knows something about them."

"And if she does, how will we find out?"

Jehu grinned. "Perez hired Abigail."

CHAPTER THIRTY-ONE

The sun was high in the sky as Justus approached Asher's covered courtyard. He had spent several hours talking to Jesus before retiring with his followers at the town of Bethany. The morning was filled with activity as everyone broke camp and headed out in their different directions. Jesus was preparing to teach in Jerusalem, so he spent very little time with Justus. However, the short time with Jesus the night before had reenergized him. He felt like a man without a care in the world.

A servant-woman was busy cooking over the fire. Justus remembered her from the day before, but could not recall her name. He could almost taste the birds she was roasting as the savory aroma filtered across the breeze as he passed.

At the door of Asher's house, two Roman soldiers saluted and stood aside as Justus bounded up the steps. Justus knocked and burst into the room.

Michal was leaning back on a small, cylindrical pillow beside the elaborately designed dining carpet, which was thickly woven to rise from the floor about two inches. She faked a frown and pitched her head, tossing her short, black hair. "It's lunchtime. You've been out all night. Was she pretty?"

"Beautiful . . . but not close to you."

The compliment brought a wide, toothy grin. She bounded to Justus and wrapped her arms around him. Releasing him, she stuck her head out the door and held her voice down. "Abigail, I'm sorry, but we have one more for lunch."

Abigail glanced up from her preparations and replied, "Yes, Lady Michal."

Miriam appeared from her room. She was nicely dressed, her features taut but not as much as from the preceding day's tension. Uncharacteristically, her long, brown hair was completely uncovered and flowed over her shoulders.

Justus studied Miriam, his mood still bright. "Miriam, you look rested and much more composed than yesterday. Guess you slept well last night."

Miriam blushed and bowed. "Thank you. I did sleep very well. Also, Michal and I talked this morning and that helped a lot."

Abigail trudged through the door, holding a plate piled with food in one hand and a round loaf of bread in the other. She was a middle-aged woman with red hair, green eyes, and a dark brown mole under her left eye. Her frame was slight, and her face gaunt.

Justus took a long inhale of the scent of freshly baked bread, and reclined by the dining rug. "Where is Perez?" he asked.

As Michal joined Justus, Abigail set the plate and loaf on the carpet, having a slight smile. "He has a meeting with some other servants I think. He won't be back today."

Miriam tore off a piece of bread and a pigeon leg, tension again showing. "Please excuse me. I want to be with Father."

After Miriam left and Abigail had returned to the courtyard, Michal leaned forward. "How did your meeting with Jesus go? Did you convince him to change his tactics?"

Justus tore a chunk of bread from the loaf, chewed slowly, then swallowed. He sighed. He understood Michal's interest, but knew he didn't have adequate words to describe the emotions of their meeting. "It was as I had predicted," he said. "His teaching about the Kingdom of God and the Scriptures are so important to him that he doesn't care if the authorities are upset or not. He made it clear to me that he must get his message out, so as many people as possible can understand it."

"Then, you were unsuccessful?"

Justus contemplated her question, a glimmer of contentment in his voice. "No, I don't think I was unsuccessful. I believe now I would have done an injustice if I had used my friendship to change what he is doing. Besides . . ." He stopped.

"Besides, what?"

Justus' expression was meditative. "Well . . . I have the distinct feeling he is in perfect control of what is going on."

Michal looked stymied. "You mean he wants the authorities to be disturbed with him?"

He thought about her question as he prodded a couple of the six dates on the plate, before selecting one. He pressed his lips tight, nodded, and replied, "You know, I think he does."

"But, that's not logical."

Justus decided to tell her of the conclusions that came to him before going to sleep the previous night. He wasn't sure he had convinced himself, but admiration began to overwhelm him as he said, "What if he is intentionally setting up situations so the authorities react in a way that leads toward his ultimate goal?"

"Hmm . . . that can be very dangerous. People are not all that predictable. It's too easy to misjudge a response."

"For most people, I agree. But Jesus has an uncanny ability to understand what's going on inside someone. It's like . . . hmm . . . like he knows their hearts."

"You mean he can read their emotions and see what they are going to do?"

Justus took a bite of the date and chewed it, nodding. "Yeah."

Michal was unconvinced. "I want to meet this guy. He sounds like something else." She bent forward and placed her hand on his. "Now that you have found Jesus . . . well, actually, he found you . . . are you still going to the Hanukkah Festival?"

He shook his head. "No, I must go to Nazareth and tell Mary and James the outcome. Do you want to come with me?"

A pregnant silence followed. Michal's expression grew soft. She almost glowed. But she shook her head, earnestness in her voice. "You know I would love to, but I need to stay with Miriam. She is going through a lot right now. On top of that, you saw Asher yesterday . . . he's not long for this world."

CHAPTER THIRTY-TWO

Sethur's house was built on a slope within the city walls. The sloping ground enabled the house's front door to be on the same plane as the surrounding houses, but the main part of the house was one story lower, creating an odd formation. Sethur had only one hired servant, so he was often interrupted from his work in the lower part of the house to greet people who visited.

Today was no exception. As he heard knocking, he sulked up the stairs and looked up at the large, muscular man standing in the doorway. The man's brown beard and hair were trimmed short, branding him as a servant of someone well-to-do or a foreigner. However, he was sure he should recognize the man, but he couldn't. "Do I know you?"

"Master Sethur, my name is Malchus. I am the lead servant of the high priest, Caiaphas."

"Ah, yes, Malchus. Please come in. Are you on an errand for the high priest?"

Malchus looked decisive. "No, I come because of a recommendation."

"A recommendation?"

Head bowed, Malchus stationed himself in the foyer as Sethur closed the door. He shot Sethur an uneasy glance and resumed staring at the floor. "Yes, Master. I went to the synagogue to ask the Pharisee, Master Kore, some questions. When he heard what I desired, he sent me here to you."

Sethur's interest was piqued. "Please. Sit."

The foyer was small with just enough room for two under-sized wooden benches against opposite walls.

Malchus parked his large frame on one as best he could, while Sethur settled onto the other. Muffled voices from a neighbor's courtyard could be heard.

Though Sethur was iffy about this unplanned visit, he detected a conflict waging inside Malchus, so he broke the silence. "Why don't you tell me what's on your mind?"

Malchus looked troubled. "Master Sethur, I have recently become interested in our ancestor, Abraham."

"Why?"

He shrugged. "Jesus has been talking about him. I want to know more, so I can make my own judgment."

Sethur felt utter disgust. Another person bewitched by the Nazarene. *Will it never end?* "Well, I'm glad you have decided to search out the truth rather than just believe what people claim the carpenter is doing and saying. What specifics do you want?"

Malchus took a deep breath. "I'm sorry, but I don't know what I don't know."

Sethur felt a feeling of favor. He shifted his small body and crossed his legs. This man wasn't bewitched. Finally, someone wanted to conduct research, rather than have an itinerant preacher dictate it. "Your words are true of many people, but most don't have the wisdom to realize it. Why don't I summarize Abraham's life, and you ask me for specifics as you think of them? I will start before God changed his name from Abram to Abraham."

"That would be perfect."

Sethur relished instructing people about the Scriptures. He had studied hard in his youth and his learning helped him compensate for the feelings of inadequacy caused by his small stature. He never used his knowledge to help people. It merely puffed him up with feelings of superiority. He stretched his seated frame as tall as he could and began to describe how God had called Abram to a new land and continued through a summary of Abram's life.

"When the herds of Abram and his nephew Lot became too large, they were forced to separate from one another. Lot chose Sodom, and Abram remained in the hill country. During that period, there was a war. Five kings fought against four in the Valley of Siddim. The valley was full of slime pits . . ."

Malchus looked befuddled. "Slime pits?"

"Yes. They prevented the Kings of Sodom and Gomorrah from moving their armies effectively, so the four kings defeated the five."

Malchus sloped his head, but remained intent. "Please go on."

Sethur inhaled deeply. "The four kings took all the wealth and people from Sodom and Gomorrah. Lot was among them. When Abram heard about what had happened, he obtained some local allies, split the forces at night, and defeated the four kings. He brought back Lot, along with all the people and all the wealth. Upon returning, Abram met the kings of Sodom and Gomorrah at the Valley of Shaveh to return everything. While there, Melchizedek, the King of Salem, which as I'm sure you know is now Jerusalem . . ."

"Yes, I know."

". . . went to Abram and blessed him."

Malchus' shoulders slumped as a dubious expression covered his face. "Did Melchizedek do anything more than bless him?"

"No, why?"

"Just interested. Did he say anything else to Abram?"

Sethur's internal alarms registered as he concluded Malchus was more interested in learning about Melchizedek. "Why are you so interested in what Melchizedek might have said to Abram?"

Malchus straightened. His expression became abstract, and he spoke hurriedly, "Ah . . . nothing really. It just seems interesting. What happened then?"

Sethur thoughts churned. He pretended to regain the story line. He securitized Malchus' physiognomy as an uneasy feeling grew. "The King of Sodom told Abram he only wanted the people returned, that Abram could keep all the goods. Abram was very firm, however, and told the King of Sodom he would take nothing, lest the king would boast about making him rich." Sethur detected no interest on Malchus' part, so he asked, "Is there more detail you want here, though I have no clue what this story has to do with the Nazarene?"

An expression of failure oozed over Malchus, and he shook his head. "I don't know how it relates either. In fact, it probably doesn't. Please, instruct me, though. Did Abram's refusal to take anything from the King of Sodom affect any part of our religion?"

"No, not really." Sethur sized up Malchus, trying to ascertain what he really knew. He was surprised that Malchus appeared to discern there was more to the story, so Sethur instantly decided to redirect him. "I think the incident is recorded in the Torah only to show us the deep character of Abram. He swore to God he would take nothing from the five kings, if God would help him defeat the four kings. God helped him, so Abram kept his end of the bargain."

Malchus stood and bowed, his voice controlled. "Master Sethur, I appreciate your time. Unfortunately, I believe I am wasting it. Surely there is no connection between the Nazarene and Abraham."

"I, too, am sure there is no connection between them. But if you have questions later, please contact me."

Malchus looked vexed as he shoved through the door.

Sethur felt a surge of suspicion as the door clunked shut. *I wonder if he came to me of his own accord, or if someone knows . . .*

▸ ▸ ▸

Although Malchus' quarters were halfway across Jerusalem from Sethur's house, he made the jaunt in less than an hour.

Malchus slammed his door shut. The room was cold inside, so he left his outer coat on and sat on his barrel-chair in the dark, his mind pressed between anger and frustration. That visit had gotten him nowhere. He already knew what Sethur had told him, except the part about Abram declining the spoils and the slime pits. How would that lead to a Tomb? He leaned his back against the wall.

Suddenly the chair crashed to the floor as he leapt to his feet. *Caiaphas wants Melchizedek's Tomb!* He pressed his clenched fist to his chin. *But why? What religious significance could it have? What clue will find it?*

Malchus threw his outer coat over the barrel as it lay on its side. He needed help, but he didn't know where to get it. Had Bukki found Asher's daughter? She may know something about Asher's ways.

He began to pace. As he neared the barrel, he kicked it with his foot, spinning his coat onto the floor. Suddenly he froze, tingling with anticipation. Wait . . . Salem is now Jerusalem, but what if the two cities were located in slightly different places? What if there were catacombs he'd never seen?

CHAPTER THIRTY-THREE

Two days had passed since Chislon received his new assignment for stoning Jesus. He had barely enough time to set the trap, but now everyone was in place.

Hanukkah was not one of the seven mandatory feasts described in the Torah, but for almost two hundred years it had been celebrated as a festival of Jewish freedom. The only part of the celebration at the Temple involved the lighting of eight candles in the Temple's outer sanctuary, one additional candle each day.

Late in the afternoon, Chislon had arrived with four friends who were definitely not Jesus sympathizers. They came well before anyone else arrived to await the new day and the lighting of that day's candle. He positioned each of them in the general area of the corners of the Temple proper with instructions to mingle with worshippers entering the courtyard and to notify him as soon as they spotted Jesus.

Although it was cold with a misty rain, several clusters of men formed throughout the courtyard, talking softly and waiting for dusk. When the new day started, they would enter the Temple for the lighting of the second candle.

The winter season had caused most of the courtyard's decorative vegetation to be dormant, and only stones for flowerbed borders and pathways stood out as adornments with an occasional larger stone in an aesthetic location.

The weather was generally depressing, but laughter was heard from most of the clusters, since this was the anniversary of a great Jewish victory and re-dedication of the Temple. A few of the clusters had young adults who looked about twelve years old mixed with older men. The men related the miraculous story about the Temple having only enough consecrated olive oil for one day's burning but that it actually lasted the eight days needed to rededicate more.

Though a large man, Chislon meandered incognito between various small groups and heard a few of the men debating whether Jesus would come to the festival. So, the reason for a larger-than-normal attendance was the possibility of Jesus' presence.

Suddenly, a young man sprinted across the courtyard in his direction. "He's walking in Solomon's Porch," he called out. He wore the coarse clothing of those who do menial labor. His outer coat was much worn, but a burgundy shawl over his head was finely woven and clashed with the commonness of the rest of his attire.

Chislon motioned to some of his men nearby, his heart thumping and his profile tense. "Let's go."

It took only moments to reach a long stone porch raised four steps above ground level. The raised floor had no covered sides except the outer Temple wall from which a low, angled roof protruded.

Jesus' arrival was noted by more people than Chislon's young friend. The open area in front of Solomon's Porch swelled with humanity, as the clusters of people converged in front of the porch area. Laughter ceased, replaced by hushed whispers and an occasional cough.

Chislon and his gang muscled their way through different sections of the people. They arrived at the same time and surrounded Jesus, who stood with another man.

Chislon's voice rang out, "How long are you going to keep us in suspense? If you really are Christ the Messiah, tell us openly."

The crowd fell silent. The front ones took a couple of steps closer and those behind compressed the available space.

Jesus' look held firm assurance. "I have already told you, but you did not believe me."

Chislon spat. "When did you tell us?"

"Have you not heard of the works I have done? All were by the power of my Father. They are my credentials."

Since Jesus always won a debate, Chislon avoided answering the question. "I don't believe any of them."

Jesus countered, "You do not believe, for you are no sheep of mine. I know the sheep that are mine. They listen to me and obey me. Because they are mine, I give them eternal life, and no one can take them from me."

Chislon scoffed. "How can you give anyone eternal life?"

Two strident voices at the back of the large group echoed his question.

"My Father, who has given them to me, is greater and mightier than all else. No one is able to snatch them out of His hand, to all eternity. Know . . . my Father and I are One."

A man in the front let out a low *Ohhh*. The man next to him glanced sideways at the sound, then fixed back on Jesus.

The congregation had grown to over a hundred men, young and old. Voices from several places sounded: "All eternity . . .?" "He's one with the Father?" "What did he say?"

Sensing triumph, Chislon waved at the crowd. "Did you hear that? This man just claimed to be God. That's blasphemy! Stone him!"

Several gasps sounded. The people began to resemble a herd, pushing each other as multiple individuals shouted, "He can't say he's God."

The man with the burgundy shawl was the first to push Jesus away from the porch and toward the crowd.

He was joined by a burly fellow whose head was bare, his hair grimy. He pushed Jesus' companion to the ground and, with knit brows shouted, "No mere man can claim to be God."

Jesus stumbled as the four men herded him away from the Temple porch and into the misting rain.

The crowd parted to make room, as several shook their fists at Jesus and yelled, "You're just a man . . . not God." "Blasphemer!" "You're crazy."

Watching with an evil smile, Chislon remained on the ground at the edge of the porch steps.

Once away from the porch, Chislon's henchmen backed into the mass of people, mixing with them and chanting, "Stone him. Stone him."

Jesus' friend darted to his side and screamed, "No!"

Mob mentality exploded, and people shoved others away, so they could find any rock or stone nearby.

Jesus extended a hand and shouted, "Wait. I have shown many acts of mercy in your presence. For which one of these do you stone me?"

The multitude quieted.

Smelling blood, Chislon bent and pulled a large stone from the central path. He raised it threateningly and gloated as he yelled, "We're not going to stone you for doing good, but for blasphemy; because you, a mere man, make yourself out to be God."

Jesus bore into Chislon. "Is it not written in your Law, 'I said, Ye are gods?' So men are called gods by your Law, men to whom God's message came." Jesus' voice reverberated. "The Scriptures can not be set aside."

Silenced filled the courtyard.

Sweat broke out on Chislon's forehead as he heard stones hitting the ground. He was speechless.

The mist condensed and ran down Jesus' face as he looked toward heaven. He spread his arms wide toward the crowd and spoke with a firm tone. "Since that is true, how can you say I am blaspheming, because I say I'm the Son of God?"

Chislon's peripheral vision caught an older man shake his head, water showering from his hair. The man grabbed the arm of one much younger beside him and pulled him from the courtyard.

Chislon was frozen, his thoughts swirling in a haze of ignorance. His crew looked at him for guidance.

Entreating, Jesus concluded, "Understand, my Father has set me apart for Himself and has sent me to the world. If I'm not doing the works of My Father, then do not believe in Me. But if I do them, even though you don't believe in Me, believe the works, in order to understand clearly that the Father and I are One."

His words were like salve. The misguided righteous anger vanished and just as suddenly as they had turned into a mob, the company reverted back into simple spectators who now only wanted to get out of the rain.

Jesus held the arm of his associate. Both merged into the bulk of the people leaving the porch area as the skies opened and rain poured onto them.

Chislon's despair grew as the assembly drained from the courtyard, but all he could muster was a feeble, "Arrest him."

Chislon's burly friend motioned to the man in the burgundy shawl to come along. They pushed into the crowd to detain Jesus.

Yet somehow he glided untouched through the rain away from the Temple area and vanished from their sight.

CHAPTER THIRTY-FOUR

As Michal and Miriam marched through the Temple courtyard, they wrapped their coats tightly around them against the chilly winter afternoon. The celebration of Hanukkah was half over. Even though the primary service at the Temple was the daily lighting of an additional candle, this day two rivers of humanity flowed through the courtyard, one entering the Temple, the other filing out.

Michal was glad Miriam had insisted she accompany her when summoned by Chief Priest Annas. She dearly loved Miriam, but knowing her personality, she was sure Miriam would not do well in what was sure to be an inquisition. Since Justus was still in Nazareth, Michal easily slipped into the lead role, feeling completely capable of meeting any challenge they might encounter.

The city sounds faded away as they went through one of four doors on the west side of the Temple enclosure. Colonnades lined the enclosure wall, breaking up the starkness of its expanse.

Michal glanced at Miriam and noticed her pale color. "Are you all right?"

Miriam started wringing her hands, her voice a whimper. "Why does Chief Priest Annas want to talk to me? I don't know anything."

Michal gave a pleasant smile and patted Miriam's arm. "Hey, don't worry. You and I together can deal with anyone."

As they crossed the large, open courtyard on the west side of the Temple, the ascent became steeper than in front of the Temple. Wind funneled through the porches around the Temple's inner court and tousled Michal's black hair.

Miriam pulled her shawl tighter. "Thank you for coming with me. You have always been more outgoing than I am. And more confident."

Michal guided Miriam to a small door on the Temple's west side, which was relatively empty of other people, and knocked eagerly. "Here we are. Let's see what this mystery is all about."

The door was opened by a muscular Temple guard in full uniform. He harshly demanded, "What do you want?"

Miriam jumped back in shock.

Michal surmised the guard had likely been bothered during the entire feast by pilgrims attempting to enter the Temple incorrectly. However, his tone raised her ire, so her voice was brittle. "We were told Chief Priest Annas wanted to speak with us."

The guard eyed the two women with suspicion. "I see. Come with me." After filing through a narrow corridor that bordered the ladies court in front of the Temple proper, the guard led them into a large room annexed to the court. The ceiling was unusually high. The walls were made from crude mud bricks, revealing the temporary nature of the structure. No Temple hardware was in the annex, only multiple backless chairs.

"You may sit. I will inform the chief priest you are here."

Before the women could reach any chair, two men breezed into the room. One wore a finely woven robe with broad borders, the sign of a priest. His untrimmed beard did not hide the bird-feet wrinkles near his eyes.

The other was dressed in servant's clothes. He was thin, much younger, and his pulled-back cloak showed rippling muscles on each arm.

The priest held a haughty expression. "Welcome. I am Annas." He looked first at Michal and then Miriam. "I'm sorry, but which of you is Miriam, Asher's daughter?"

Miriam looked down. "I'm Miriam."

"Good . . . welcome. But, who is this?"

"My name is Michal. I'm from Greece, and I am Miriam's cousin."

Annas stiffened, but his voice remained pleasant. "And why did you come with Miriam? I only want to talk to her."

Miriam glanced up at him. "I asked her to come."

"And . . . I wanted to come," Michal added. She tuned her emotional radar as high as she could, wanting to gather every ounce of information from this meeting. She was suspicious from the moment Miriam had received the original summons.

"I see." He waved toward the man behind him. "This is Bukki, my lead servant."

Michal went rigid. "I thought you were going to Greece to get Miriam from my house."

Bukki remained silent and appeared frozen, his expression devoid.

Annas motioned with an upward palm toward two chairs. "Please sit. There is much we must talk about."

Miriam sat facing Annas, but Michal moved to her side and remained standing. Annas was only a little taller than Michal, so she refused to give him the height advantage by sitting.

Annas took a small step toward Miriam. He scrutinized Michal for a moment, then concentrated on her cousin. His voice softened. "I'm sure all of this is confusing. Let me try to make some sense of . . ."

Michal interrupted, "Please do."

A tinge of impatience crept into Annas' tone as he looked at Michal. "When Perez told us Asher had slipped into a coma, he suggested we notify Miriam. I sent Bukki, my most trusted servant, to Greece to tell her and accompany her home."

Michal placed her hand on Miriam's shoulder. Her eyebrows raised, and her voice was cold. "But she wasn't in Greece."

Annas gave Michal a narrow stare. "I know that now." He turned his head to Bukki and slowly rotated back to the women as he continued, "At Tyre, while waiting for a ship, Bukki heard 'dock talk' about a young woman fitting Miriam's description being abducted and held prisoner in a tomb in the cave of our forefathers, near Shechem. He went there and indeed found a tomb that appeared to have been a prison cell. Upon going to Shechem, he learned three strangers had been sent to Jerusalem under armed Roman guard. Believing one to be Miriam, he came back to Jerusalem and found, indeed, she was safely returned."

Michal held Annas' gaze and knew he was rehearsing a prerecorded story. "Miriam was abducted from her home here in Jerusalem," she said between terse lips.

"That's what the guards told me when they were relieved by the Romans. I have no idea who or why someone would abduct Miriam, but we will have the Temple guards investigate it thoroughly."

Michal realized she was losing her advantage. "Why would Asher tell Perez that Miriam had gone to Greece to visit me?"

Annas' expression became condescending. "Likely whoever abducted her threatened Asher with Miriam's safety, so he lied."

"Why?"

"I have no idea."

Miriam had remained silent, her gaze fixed on the floor, but when she heard Annas' answer, she glanced at Michal. "But the old man . . ."

Michal moved her hand from Miriam's shoulder and used it to break off her sentence.

Annas showed no emotion. "What old man?"

"One we met in Shechem. He has nothing to do with what we are talking about."

Miriam's head drooped.

Annas looked long at Michal, as if trying to read her thoughts.

Michal took advantage of his silence. "So . . . you wanted Miriam to come here just to tell her Bukki was supposed to bring her back to Jerusalem?"

Annas pursed his lips. His voice took on a formal quality. "We were very concerned about Miriam's safety. First and foremost, we wanted her to know the truth and assure her the authorities will do whatever is necessary to find out who abducted her. Also, Asher is a dear friend and a member of the priesthood. We wanted to show her our sympathy for his condition." After several beats, Annas raised his head higher. "And . . . there is one other thing."

Comprehension swept Michal like a gust of fresh air. *Of course that's why she's here.* She remained silent.

Miriam's head shot up, her expression quizzical.

Smelling the kill, Michal feigned a look of innocence. "And what is that?"

Annas attempted a nonchalant look, but one hand clenched into a fist. His voice tensed. "Asher was in the middle of something very important, and I was wondering if Miriam could help us."

CHAPTER THIRTY-FOUR

She glanced at Miriam then slowly back to Annas. "In the middle of what?"

"I am sorry, but we can only reveal that to Miriam."

Michal hesitated for a long moment. "So you want me to leave?"

"Yes, please."

Miriam jumped up in a panic. "No! If Michal leaves, I go with her."

Annas held both hands up, his expression stern. "Please sit." He looked at Michal. "You may stay, but please treat what I'm about to say with the utmost confidence."

Michal held a stony look.

Annas turned, walked a few steps, and rotated back. As he did this, he spoke in a hushed voice. "We have a situation with a certain Nazarene carpenter. He has been going around most of Israel for the last . . . hmm . . . almost three years teaching doctrine that is opposed to our understanding of the sacred Scriptures and the Law of Moses."

Michal was pleased as the pieces of the puzzle were complete, yet she remained silent.

"Not long before Miriam was abducted, we asked Asher to search the Torah to learn whether this man called Jesus is a prophet or not."

Michal still said nothing but maintained a look of interest.

"We knew Asher had somehow found from the Torah that Jesus' cousin—known as John the Baptist—was a prophet. I hoped he could do the same with this Jesus." He turned full to Miriam, his expression humble. "So, Miriam, since Asher went into a coma before he could complete his search, we were hoping you might know enough about Asher's techniques to continue the search."

"Oh no, I could not . . ."

Michal interrupted her, her voice conciliatory. "Now Miriam, you and I have talked some about Asher's techniques. You know a few things. Nothing would be harmed if you try to find out something about Jesus."

Miriam gaped.

Annas' countenance became pleasant. "Good, then it's settled. After the Hanukkah celebration is over, I'll have Bukki take you to the room where Asher was working when he became ill."

CHAPTER THIRTY-FIVE

Jerusalem's streets seemed barren the day after Hanukkah ended. However, Justus was impervious to them as he hurried through the city. He replayed over and over his recent meeting with Mary and her family in Nazareth. He had described his failure to change Jesus' mind, but he'd also assured them he felt Jesus was in control of the events surrounding him.

Asher's house with its covered courtyard came into view. His thoughts detoured to Michal, and a warm feeling wrapped around him. He felt like he was returning home.

The guards greeted Justus and stepped aside as he bounded up the steps and through the door, calling, "Hi!"

Michal was already crossing the room as he entered and hugged him. She laughed. "I'm glad you're back. I really missed you."

Justus lingered in the embrace. "You look great," he said, soaking in her beauty. Her tan had lessened, but the finely woven, white tunica still accentuated it. She wore a black necklace matching her hair.

Michal had a dreamy look with a brilliant smile. "How was Nazareth?"

The question clouded Justus' mood slightly, and he stepped back, letting his hands slowly slide down Michal's smooth arms. "I suppose things went as well as possible. I think Jesus' family has resigned themselves to his activities."

"That's good . . . I guess. So, they won't try to intervene anymore?"

"No, not anymore."

Miriam entered the front room from Asher's quarters, displaying a pleasant expression. "Hi, Justus."

Justus turned to Miriam and nodded, his guise playful. "Julius sends his *heartfelt regards*."

Miriam stepped toward him, her hand extended and her complexion aglow. "Was he in Nazareth?"

"No, but I stopped in Shechem on my return."

Her lips turned down as she cast a glance at Asher's door.

Justus noted her pensive features. "Is your father worse?"

Miriam clouded up and seemed to sag. "I've not been able to get any food into him for a couple of days. He's much weaker."

"I'm sorry. Have the doctors been here?"

Michal put her arms around Miriam and answered, "Yes, but they can do nothing more than what Miriam is already doing."

Michal quickly changed the subject. "Ah . . . there's been a development."

Justus slanted his head. "A development?"

Michal released Miriam and walked away from Asher's door. "Yes, we were 'invited' to a meeting with Chief Priest Annas."

A chill coursed down Justus' back. "A meeting about what?"

Miriam blurted, "To learn about Jesus."

Justus looked from Miriam to Michal, feeling a rising uncertainty. He put his left fist on his hip and his right hand on his chin. "Hmm . . . start from the beginning."

Michal and Justus sat on a bench near the outside door, and Miriam selected one across the corner.

Michal summarized their meeting with Annas. Miriam sat intently, nodding occasionally.

When Michal finished, Justus asked, "Do you think he is telling the truth?"

"No, I think it's all hogwash."

Miriam chimed in, "It sounded true to me, but why would they think I knew enough about Kabbala to help find out about Jesus?"

Justus glanced at Miriam, surprised she didn't pick up on what was really happening. Although Michal hadn't said Annas was using Jesus as a diversion, it was clear to him. Annas was hiding the truth about what he wanted from Asher.

Michal patted Miriam's arm. "They don't care about Jesus."

A puzzled look transfigured Miriam's face. "But, if they don't care about Jesus, why do they want me to . . .?" Miriam interrupted herself, her confused expression lifting, and her teeth clenched. "They only want to know what I know about Dad's methods. But why?"

Justus maintained a matter-of-fact attitude. "They were expecting Asher to give them some answer from the Torah. He went into a coma before giving it to them. Now they are trying to learn enough from you to find it themselves."

"What answer?"

Justus shook his head and sighed heavily. "I have no clue. Do you, Michal?"

"No . . . none. But that's the whole reason I pushed Miriam to say she would help. We need to pretend to know more than we do, to find out what they're really after."

Miriam sat stunned. "Did Annas have me abducted?"

Michal and Justus exchanged glances.

Michal answered, her voice metered. "I don't know. But, one thing I'm sure. Annas knows more than he told us. And that cock-and-bull story about Bukki hearing of your abduction at a dock in Tyre . . ." She stopped and made a wry smile.

Justus shook his head. "It's hard to imagine what Asher could find in the Torah so valuable Annas would risk a kidnapping. Still, we must be very careful. There is some reason he hasn't simply contacted another kabbalist."

A knock at the door interrupted their discussion, and a guard leaned in. "Excuse me, Honorable Justus, but Miriam has a visitor."

The trio exchanged mystified glances.

Justus looked tantalized. "Thank you. Let him in."

A well-built man with a long, neatly trimmed beard and moustache entered. "Chief Priest Annas arranged to have me bring Miriam to Asher's working room in the Temple. I am here to escort her."

Justus marked Michal, his expression inquisitive. "Is this the man you said was with Chief Priest Annas?"

"It's him, Bukki."

Bukki fidgeted and wouldn't look directly at Miriam. "My lady, we must go now."

Miriam became stern. "I will not go unless both of my friends can come also."

Bukki recoiled. "But Master Annas directed me to bring only you."

Miriam stepped to Michal and intertwined her hand through her friend's arm. She scrunched her eyebrows and held her jaw tight before saying, "You heard me. Both come or I stay here."

Michal gave Miriam a wide-eyed look.

Bukki weighed the demand and gave a long sigh. "All right . . ."

❯ ❯ ❯

An hour later, Miriam crept into the large room in the upper part of the Temple.

Michal and Justus filed in after her.

Bukki stalled in the door opening, tracking the others' movements.

Even though the sun was setting, the three large windows allowed considerable light to flood the room.

The trio felt the reverence of the stale-smelling room and acted as if they were in a mausoleum. Miriam went to Asher's bed in the corner, contemplated it, and lightly traced her fingers over its wool cover.

Justus' muscles were taut, a surreal feeling overtaking him as he surveyed the large room. He was sure Asher was accomplishing things here on the border of the unexplainable and the hair on the nape of his neck stood in ranks. However, the advocate part of him took over as he scrutinized the area. His attention was first caught by four large, level-topped stands supported by four legs reaching to Justus' waist. He had seen similar small ones in homes of Roman royalty, but never this high from the floor. Scrolls were everywhere, but one stand held a stack of several large papyrus sheets, laid flat.

He moved closer. Why were these left flat instead of being rolled? Hmm . . . this one was filled with letters. Were they all the same? Justus fingered the corners of the stack of sheets, moving them enough to validate that they all were, indeed, filled with letters.

Michal joined him as he examined them. She gave an incredulous look, her voice a whisper. "No spaces or punctuations."

Justus nodded, his brows knotted.

Miriam migrated to the table with piles of thin strips of acacia wood. She grasped one and brought it close to her with a bewildered expression.

Bukki's voice boomed. "What are those for?"

Miriam jumped and dropped the stick. "I've never seen anything like these," she gasped. Shivering, she pulled her coat more closely about her.

The new mystery captured Justus. Relocating, he examined the wooden strips by selecting several and fanning them out in his hand. Some were different widths, but not all that many different widths. Most were simply duplicates. Justus returned the strips to the table and pivoted to Miriam. "Which ones of these do you want to take back to your house?"

Bukki stiffened. "Oh, no. I'm sorry. All things in this room must stay in this room."

Michal shot him an angry look. "How do you expect Miriam to examine them?"

"She must come here to do her work."

Miriam gave Bukki a pleading look. "I can't come here. I have to stay with my father. He needs me."

Bukki shook his head repeatedly. "Master Annas was specific. The scrolls must stay here."

Miriam glinted Michal a tortured look.

Michal strode to Miriam like an angry tigress. She grabbed her hand and guided her to Bukki as she commanded Justus, "Come. It's clear they don't really want Miriam's help." Shoving past Bukki with her head tilted back and her eyebrows high, she said, "You tell your master, if he wants Miriam's help, he'll deliver the scrolls and the wooden strips to her house. Otherwise, good luck finding out who the carpenter really is."

CHAPTER THIRTY-SIX

Malchus' even strides carried him quickly along the dirt path. It had taken little time to learn who the best tomb hewer in Jerusalem was. Though he was forced to wait several days for the man to return from a job near Mount Carmel, the hewer was to arrive the following day. Beside himself with excitement, Malchus decided to spend the night near the man's house, so he could meet with him the instant he came.

Malchus carried an unlit torch. Although it was dusk, he could still make out his destination, an old, dirt-walled house with a single goat tied to a nearby stump. Turning, he glimpsed the Antonia Fortress and the upper part of the Temple jutting above the northern Jerusalem wall. Though hated by the Jews, the Roman occupation had created a peaceful life over the years, which led many people to live outside the city walls.

Malchus harbored no hopes that the hewer would be home early, but still automatically knocked on the door. No one answered, so he sought a place of partial protection to spend the night. Spying a mustard bush nearby, he stumped toward it. He flinched as a startled covey of quail shot up from the grass. Their multiple wing-beats broke the stillness of the evening but soon disappeared in the sky behind a mulberry tree, restoring quietness.

Suddenly a twig cracked, and Malchus whirled.

Caked with dirt, a short, bald man confronted Malchus. He was muscular. His eyes glared over an unkempt beard. He held a stake and mallet, his voice harsh. "What do you want?"

"Are you Heber, the hewer?"

"That would be me. Who are you?"

"Malchus, servant of the high priest."

Heber stared icily at Malchus and remained unmoving. "And what would a servant of the high priest want from me? His tomb was constructed years ago."

"I'm not here on behalf of the high priest. I'm here because many people in the city claim you are the best tomb constructor. They say many citizens of other cities come and ask you to build tombs for them. In fact, didn't you build one recently near the hill of Golgotha for a man from Arimathea?"

Heber relaxed. He tossed the mallet and stake against the house wall, making a dull thud. "Do you want me to make one for you?"

"No, No. I'm not here for that. But is it true your family has been building tombs for years and that your forefathers built much of the catacombs under Jerusalem?"

Heber showed confusion. "Yes, so what?"

Malchus cleared his throat while he weighed his words carefully. The goat gave a soft *nanny*. "I have asked several people this question, but none have any idea about its answer."

"What question?"

"Is Jerusalem built on the exact location of the ancient town of Salem?"

Heber snorted and shook his head, contempt in his voice. "Why do you think I would know that? You should ask a scribe. They're the ones who look into ancient records."

Malchus shook off Heber's question, but a sinking sensation gnawed at his gut. "I have. Their records do not go back that far. They tell me the only reference to it in the Holy Scriptures has no geographic information." Malchus felt defeat constricting his throat. His voice sounded raspy. "I'm sorry to have bothered you."

"Why are you so interested?"

Malchus' head rose with the obvious question and hope washed away his former feelings. "Well . . . ah . . . I can't tell you all the details. Let's just say my master would be very impressed if I learned the answer."

Heber didn't blink as one corner of his mouth twisted up. "I'm a poor man. What would the answer be worth to you?"

Malchus shivered with excitement. "I'm far from rich, but I can pay you a little."

"How much?"

Malchus fished a small pouch from his belt and dumped several coins into his hand. They made a soft clinking sound.

Heber leaned forward and examined them by pushing one, then another with a single finger to ascertain the value of the coins covered.

The sweaty smell from Heber's body caused Malchus to slightly turn his head to one side for fresher air.

"I'll tell you what I know for all of those, but you may not like the information."

Malchus snatched Heber's hand, pulled it to him palm upward, and transferred all the coins to him.

Heber clenched the bounty and stifled a laugh. "My forefathers indeed built much of the Jerusalem catacombs, although Salem goes back farther than my family. However, stories about it have been passed down from generation to generation."

Malchus was absorbed. "Were there any stories about the location of Salem?"

"Yes, several. I paid little attention to them, for they do not benefit me. However, my father—who has been dead these last fifteen years— loved those old stories. He had an uncle who dabbled in history, so I think some of it rubbed off. He talked about it far too much for me."

Malchus' thoughts swirled with possibilities too good to be true. "So, where did your father claim Salem was located?"

"He said the bulk of Salem lies under the current Jerusalem. A small part, he claimed, was north of the city wall."

Malchus quivered, but steadied himself. It took a couple of moments before he was able to speak. "Did your father believe people in Salem used tombs to bury their dead?"

Heber glanced up at the stars and grinned, his voice jocular. "You and my father would have gotten along fine."

"I'm sure . . . but . . . did he think they did?"

"Actually, not at all. He was sure our profession started when Abraham bought a cave from some Hittite and started burying relatives in tombs there."

Malchus held his breath, his darkest fears beginning to be confirmed.

"However, I told you his uncle loved history. He would argue with my father every time they got together—which thank God was seldom—that Abraham got the idea from the people at Salem."

Malchus gasped, optimism reborn. "Where did your father's uncle think they were located?"

Heber blinked twice. "The northern part . . . not under Jerusalem."

CHAPTER THIRTY-SEVEN

In the foyer of Annas' house Bukki hunkered on a bench, his back against the white-washed wall. He mentally reviewed his aborted attempt to get Miriam to work in the Temple so she might disclose some of Asher's techniques for searching the Torah. Frustration wrinkled his brow. This whole episode was consuming his life, yet he didn't know how to get out from under it.

Annas burst through the door. A loud thud echoed as the heavy wood crashed against the wall. He paused a moment to peer at Bukki with a calculating gaze. "Tell me what happened."

Bukki bolted from the bench, anger boiling over. "I went to get Miriam as you directed, but she would not go without her two friends."

"And you let them go, right?"

"Of course."

"What did they do in Asher's workroom?"

The fresh memories coursed through Bukki, and disgust snagged him. He took half a step away from Annas, leaned on his hand extended high up the wall, and stared at the polished stone floor. "Nothing. Miriam showed no signs of recognizing anything."

"What about the wooden strips?"

Bukki glanced up. "She claimed she'd never seen anything like them before."

Annas put his hand to his mouth. He moved close to the bench by the wall. "What about the other two?"

"The other two appeared to be interested, but it didn't look like they had any idea why Asher wanted the wooden strips, either. I heard the woman whisper to the man something about the absence of spaces and punctuations when they were examining the large papyrus sheets. But that's all I have to report."

"Spaces and punctuation?" Annas chewed this new information, his words dreamy. "Did you know that was one of Asher's directions for constructing the sheets—no spaces or punctuations?"

Bukki looked confounded as he straightened and stepped from the wall. "Why did the old man request that?"

"I don't know. Obviously, it has something to do with his methods . . . which means, the two know something about them we don't."

Bukki appeared dazed. "But how can they know . . .?"

"You heard the Grecian woman. She said Miriam had talked to her about Asher's technique. It appears one of them has also talked to the man."

Bukki stood silently, unable to comprehend how Michal and Justus could learn vital information so quickly.

Annas' bearing softened. "This Michal is obviously royalty. She's much too bold and self-confident. But since I have not met the man, I cannot guess. What have you found out about him?"

The question shook Bukki from his thoughts. "Not much, yet. He acts Roman but looks Jewish. The soldiers address him with honor, so either he was a high-ranking officer, or he has family who was."

Annas held a far-off expression as he processed these tidbits.

Bukki felt awkward. Sweat formed on his brow as Annas' silence clocked on. "I think we are not going to get anywhere with Miriam while the other two are around."

Annas looked devilish. "You may be right, but they might be the key."

"How"

"Miriam is too meek to aggressively try any of Asher's methods. The other woman, and maybe even the man, certainly have the personality to utilize the kabbalist's techniques to their limits. Who knows, they may even improve on them."

"Maybe . . . but I doubt it. I think they will just remain a big problem."

Annas didn't respond for a second or two as his expression turned icy. "If they get in the way, they will be eliminated."

"With pleasure." Bukki brooded over the fact he had not revealed all the information about the visit. Although he half-turned and put his hand on the door latch, he knew he could not leave without doing so. He'd stalled as long as he could. He turned full front to Annas. Gathering up a final bit of courage, he said, "Master Annas, there's one more thing."

Annas inspected Bukki with a scowl. "And what is that?"

"Miriam refused to come to the Temple to work on the scrolls. She said she had to be with Asher. Her friend demanded we take the scrolls and wooden strips to her house, or they would do nothing."

Annas stared at him and didn't answer for a moment. Finally, his shoulders slumped and he whispered, "Take the scrolls and the wood to Miriam's house."

CHAPTER THIRTY-EIGHT

Though it was still in the middle of the afternoon, the covered court-yard was somewhat darkened by thick clouds. A rare light snow was falling, but not enough to provide much reflected light.

Although Justus wore his outer cloak, the chilly air caused him to move closer to the fire. He chuckled, remembering how Michal cast Bukki aside when she towed Miriam from Asher's Temple workroom the previous day. He was frequently surprised how she took control of difficult situations, but dismissing Bukki's demands was his favorite.

Abigail was kneading bread dough in preparation of baking it in the small oven near the fire. She was too preoccupied to converse with Justus.

He turned his backside to the fire to warm it and caught the image of a man approaching, quickly recognizing him as the Shechem com-mandant. "Julius," he said, "this is a welcome surprise. Come by the fire."

Grinning, Julius ambled into the covered courtyard in full uniform and stomped snow off his knobby-soled boots. "Honorable Justus, it's good to see you, also."

Abigail looked up from her work but said nothing. A Jewish woman was supposed to be invisible around a Gentile man.

"What brings you to Jerusalem?"

Julius was unable to hide his excitement. "Pontius Pilate has offered to provide Miriam protection and relieve my men. I decided to assess the situation myself before executing that decision."

Justus gave a knowing smile. "I'm sure you will be assessing Miriam first."

Julius looked like he had been caught stealing. "Well . . ." He glanced at the door of Asher's house, and his expression became worried. "How is Miriam dealing with her father's illness?"

Justus gazed at Julius. "Let's go see. I'm sure she will be excited to see you."

Julius glanced back with consternation on his face. "I hope so."

When they reached the front room, Justus helped Julius remove his cloak, hung it on a peg near the door, and added his own. He called softly, "Miriam, you have a visitor."

Miriam slipped from Asher's room. She wore a long, purple tunica with no belt. Her hair was covered with a pale white shawl. When she saw Julius, her demeanor became brighter than the lamp on the shelf beside her. She clasped her hands behind her back. "Julius . . . Why are you here?"

As Miriam entered the room, Julius pulled off his plumed battle helmet, releasing his short, black hair. He held the leather helmet close to his breastplate, his rippling bicep in plain view. His gaze lingered as he extended the other hand. "I wanted to see . . . I mean, I was told my men were being relieved by Pilate's soldiers, and I wanted to make sure you were all right before I agreed."

She looked delighted. "I'm glad you came. I am fine."

"And your father?"

Miriam issued a bleak sigh, half turned, and waved toward the door. "He's becoming weaker every day."

"Have the doctors been able to do anything?"

"No . . . nothing."

"I'm sorry. Can I help in anyway?"

As he spoke, Michal exited Miriam's bedroom. She heard Julius' offer and grinned. "I think your being here has already helped." She had a white, thickly woven wool robe wrapped around her slim waist and drawn tight with a thin golden belt.

Julius turned red as he broke the look with Miriam.

In an attempt to divert his embarrassment, Justus stepped to Michal's side, brushing her arm with his, and said, "Let's all sit. We need to catch up on recent happenings."

The four settled on benches at right angles in the corner—Miriam and Julius on one, Michal and Justus on the opposite. They talked for some time, each telling about different things from the previous few weeks. As they shared, some laughter was heard, mixed with occasional quiet periods, but the bond they had formed in Shechem was quickly renewed.

At a lull in the conversation, Julius asked Justus, "Have you any news about who may have abducted Miriam?"

Justus looked perplexed and shook his head. "No. The Temple guards are supposed to be conducting an investigation, but I'm not sure they could find their way out of Jerusalem, let alone discover who kidnapped Miriam. I have met with Jehu the captain four different times in the past few weeks, but I've learned nothing."

"Do you personally have any suspects?"

Michal spoke up, "A chief priest."

Julius flinched. "Are you serious?"

"No. I was kidding . . . Well, partially. He's the only one who seems to know anything about it. That is, he and his lead servant. I don't trust either one of them."

Hoofbeats and the grinding of wagon wheels on the uneven stone pavement outside interrupted their conversation. Julius shot to attention, opened the door, and commanded a soldier, "Find out who that is and what they are doing here." His wide shoulders blocked the door as he stood with one hand on his sword, one on his waist.

The other three crowded behind him, and the women tried to see around his frame.

Justus was taller than Julius and watched as two soldiers, spears in thrusting position, approached the unmoving wagon. Two men climbed down.

Julius stepped through the doorway and down one step. He drew his sword, giving the trio behind him clear view of the courtyard.

Abigail moved several yards away from the oven and the men.

A guard demanded in a loud voice, "What business do you have here?"

Bukki's tone was dangerously defiant. "Lady Miriam told me she needed Master Asher's materials delivered here. I was ordered to do it today."

Michal quirked in one side of her mouth. "Really bright . . . bringing scrolls when it's snowing."

Julius glanced back at Miriam, then turning toward the men his voice became authoritarian and loud. "Bring them in now."

Julius pivoted and stepped back into the front room as Justus, Michal, and Miriam retreated. He gave an incredulous look and his voice became softer as he raised his palm and asked Miriam, "Why scrolls?"

Miriam's lips crinkled in delight. "I'll explain later."

Bukki carried the large papyrus sheets to a corner while a very young servant carried the wooden strips, placing them at the side of the pages. Two soldiers carted in the remaining scrolls and added them to the pile.

Bukki seemed hesitant when he addressed Miriam and avoided looking directly at her. "Master Annas thought a tall stand might help you. We brought one."

They soon assembled a single stand in the vacant area of the front room. The guards escorted Bukki and the servant out, closing the door softly behind them.

Julius stared with wonder at the wide, level expanse of the stand, and rubbed his forehead. He glanced at Miriam and said, "I've never seen furniture like this. What is it for?"

CHAPTER THIRTY-NINE

Waiting in the foyer of the high priest's palace, Malchus paced between the door and the stairs to the side hall. He had been angry with himself since leaving Heber the night before, but now his anger was transformed into trembling anticipation. Would he be allowed to search the Salem catacombs?

After less than five minutes, Caiaphas approached the top of the steps, his eyes testing Malchus. "What is wrong?"

Malchus swallowed hard, his voice barely controlled. "Has Asher regained consciousness?" he asked.

Caiaphas glided down the stairs. "No. In fact, it doesn't look good. Bukki says they are able to get little food into him, but he is fading fast. Is that why you came?"

Malchus stammered. "Master . . . the catacombs . . . I found . . . I've not been in all of them."

Caiaphas grimaced. "What? You told me you have extensively searched them all."

"I know, but I recently visited a tomb hewer. He told me some believe Salem's catacombs lie north of the Jerusalem city wall."

Caiaphas staggered. "Could it be true?"

"It's information handed down father to son for many years, so it may be only a legend. Still, what if it is true?"

Caiaphas rubbed his mouth with his thumb and forefinger as he made a slow circle around the room. His sandals moving on the polished stone barely made a sound. Finally he said, "Do you remember all of Asher's clues?"

Malchus bent forward, and his whisper was tinted with excitement. "Not only do I remember them, I kept all the small scrolls they were written on."

"Excellent." Caiaphas took two steps toward the staircase, then spun back with questioning eyes. "If the Salem catacombs exist, how will you find where they are located?"

Malchus' face darkened. "As you know, the city wall does not extend perfectly east to west, but angles from the south to the northeast. So the potential area is very large. I intend to initially search above ground from the wall out to find a cave or opening in the ground anywhere north of the wall." He shrugged. "I hold little hope of finding anything. By now the ancient catacombs would be very deep below the ground."

A lamp placed on a head-high shelf began to sputter as though running out of oil. Caiaphas glanced at it. His voice sounded as if he were thinking out loud. "Could they be somehow connected to the catacombs under Jerusalem?"

Malchus leaned his leg against a bench positioned by the foyer wall. "Maybe at one time, but now all the corridors of the catacombs on the north side stop at the foundation of the city wall."

Caiaphas asked, "You mean the foundation is deeper than the catacombs?"

Malchus scanned his memory of the corridors blocked by the city's north wall foundation. He had spent hours down there, but usually tombs were not next to it. "I've always assumed the foundation was in place before the catacomb's corridors were constructed. However, it is possible the laying of the foundation actually cut through existing corridors, and they continue on the other side of the wall."

A bewildering fact he had merely filed away as interesting pierced his memory. His voice became thoughtful. "There are a few corridors that appear deeper than the wall, but they just descend to a solid dirt barrier, like a pit."

Cold-sober, Caiaphas came close to Malchus. "Why?"

"I guess whoever was hewing them had no need to go further." A new idea formed in Malchus, and his pulse increased. "With your direction, I could get a few men to start digging on the outside of the north wall, hoping we could uncover a tunnel."

Caiaphas turned away and stared down the side hall for a few beats. He spoke with studied indifference. "No . . . I don't want to answer continual questions. If digging is to be done, do it in one of the pathways that stop at the wall's foundation."

The idea titillated Malchus. He tapped the bench with his leg, forcing it to make a thumping sound on the wall. "That's a thought. It's already deep there, and surely the catacombs under the old city would be even deeper. But where would I put the dirt?"

Caiaphas looked back at Malchus and gave a sigh, his voice crisp. "You said there are some pits. Put the dirt in those."

"But what about any tombs in them? How would people go there?"

Caiaphas turned full to Malchus and shook his head. "From your description, those are some of the oldest areas in the catacombs. Surely no next of kin are still alive." He swiveled and climbed the steps as he spoke in harsh tone. "Now get going. I want to find Melchizedek's Tomb before Passover."

❦ ❦ ❦

Three lamps were burning in the front room, giving Justus and Michal ample light to examine the scrolls. The burning olive oil gave a sweet smell throughout the room.

After Bukki had left, they immediately began searching the scrolls.

Julius had gone to the Antonia Fortress. Miriam had little interest in their quest and remained in Asher's room. Perez retired to his attached quarters and Abigail to her room which was connected to the front room.

Michal pored over a scroll, her frown pronounced. She still wore the wool robe around her.

Opposite her, Justus examined one of the large, flat papyrus sheets on the edge of the stand. The silence in the room was heavy as both were immersed in the searching process.

Michal shot a glance across the table. "This is really tedious. I see why Asher wanted to find something to make his examinations go quicker.

It takes forever to keep track of letters you don't skip and see if they say anything."

Justus didn't look up but nodded. "And then to try to find another near-by word if you do happen to find something."

The room again was filled with silence for almost an hour. The white-washed walls seemed to move as light flickered from the three lamps.

Presently, Justus sank onto a bench and heaved a tired sigh. "This could drive you insane if you worked at it long enough. I wonder if it's even possible to find anything."

"At least once. Remember—John and Prophet."

Justus grimaced and leaned back. His clothing didn't soften the un-even texture of the mud brick walls. His gaze fell to the pile of wooden strips, still lying on the floor. Focusing on them, he soon became transfixed by a couple of different widths jutting out from the main pile. He sat straight, then stood and moved to the pile. He squatted down for a closer look.

Michal flashed him a puzzled look. "What?"

Justus made no indication he'd heard her question, his face mesmer-ized. Suddenly, he gasped. "Of course. He's a genius."

Justus snatched a handful of wooden strips and bounded back to the large sheet he was examining. "Watch."

He sorted through the strips, selected one, and laid it on columns 2, 3, and 4. The 3-character-wide strip completely covered them. Skipping the 5th column, he laid down the same width strip covering columns 6, 7, and 8.

Michal's jaw dropped, and she sucked a deep breath. "I see it. By continuing with the same-size strips on the columns, we can conduct a 3-letter skip in a matter of minutes."

Justus looked up with awe. "No wonder he could find things in the Torah."

CHAPTER FORTY

Jehu paced his small, sparsely furnished office. He had been the head of the Temple guards for years, but the high priest's demands for him to do something about Jesus, coupled with Miriam's kidnapping, had caused him to spend long hours away from his normal duties. More than anything, he wanted to resolve both problems. However, every time he plugged one hole in the dilemma, another appeared.

Attai scurried into the small room. Although Jehu was officially his boss, they had risen through the guard ranks together and were close friends.

Jehu stopped and gave a grim sigh. "I need you to do something."

"What is it?"

"The man who came back with Miriam has been here several times."

Attai held Jehu's gaze and nodded. "Yes, I've seen him. What does he want?"

Jehu's distress intensified, and he waved his hand though the air. "He wants us to spend more time investigating Miriam's abduction. Chief Priest Annas sent word that we must assist him, but not at the expense of our dealings with the Nazarene carpenter. So I really haven't done much."

Attai appeared to relax. However, his voice sounded tense. "I understand. The rumor is the Nazarene has gone back to the other side of the Jordan River. Are you thinking he won't be back for a while, so now would be a good time to start the investigation on the abduction?"

Jehu's facial muscles stretched tight. He pulled his short sword from its peg in the wall. He studied the leather sheath and slowly felt the soft exterior. "Actually, the carpenter's location has nothing to do with it. I know who the Roman is." His gaze shot up to Attai. "He is the Chief Advocate of Rome."

Attai went rigid. "The Chief Advocate of Rome? This is not good. What if he . . .?"

Jehu shrugged and interrupted. "There are a lot of 'what if's' but one thing is certain. We must do a thorough job on this investigation. I don't want the whole affair turned over to some type of Roman tribunal."

"I understand."

He placed the sword on a chair against the wall and gave Attai a purposeful expression. "I need you to lead the investigation."

Attai stood straighter and bowed his head slightly. "As you wish."

"Interview all the guards of the city gates. Try to find out if anything suspicious happened between Yom Kippur and the Feast of the Booths. I will personally interview Miriam and Perez. After you report back to me, I want you to go to Shechem and try to find something about the old man who brought Miriam food. Before returning, check out the tomb and the nearby areas in the catacombs to see if you can find any clues that would lead us to her captor."

Attai waited to be excused, his expression perplexed.

Jehu's jaw was clenched as he said, "Debrief me on what you find out, then journey to Shechem as quickly as you can arrange it."

Attai hesitated and raised both hands waist high, palms up. He gave Jehu a skeptical squint. "But we know what happened."

Jehu returned a cagey look. "Of course. However, the Roman doesn't know it. We must convince him we are thorough."

▸ ▸ ▸

Bukki warmed himself by the fire in the open courtyard. He had been summoned by Annas' door servant. Although the flames were jumping high with very little smoke present, no one was around it. He had stopped to shake off the chill of the cold afternoon before reporting for duty. As he warmed himself, he glimpsed Annas hurrying out the door.

Annas carried himself toward Bukki like a hungry fox and spoke while he was still in stride. "Have you completed your inquiries about the Roman staying at Asher's house?"

Bukki waited until Annas was near, and spoke in a mild voice. "Yes. It's not good."

Annas shivered as he pulled up near the fire. "Tell me."

Bukki scowled and heaved a dismal sigh. "The Roman's name is Joseph Justus. He's the Chief Advocate of Rome."

Annas blanched and stumbled half a step back. "Chief Advocate of Rome? But I thought you said he looks Jewish."

No longer cold, Bukki stepped away from the fire. He looked from one street along the courtyard to the other. "As it turns out his father, Marcus, is Roman and his mother is Jewish. He was born and raised in Nazareth while his father was a centurion there." Bukki paused as he observed two men quickly passing by the open area on the street nearest them. He lowered his voice. "They returned to Rome when his father was selected to be a tribune. Marcus is now a proconsul. And because of his distinguished career, not only does the Senate know him, but many Roman soldiers do, too."

Annas glowered. He rotated to face the fire. "Is there more?"

The faint sound of a neighbor practicing a lyre floated across the courtyard.

Bukki was disquieted. He had provided Annas disturbing information before and was never accosted for it, but these were perilous times. He looked away from Annas. "Yes. Justus was trained as a soldier, but was never officially in the Roman army. Instead, he was given the best education one can get in Rome. His early attempts at being an advocate were unbelievably successful. He is said to have an uncanny ability to put facts together to arrive at truth."

Bukki detected someone approaching from the street farthest from them. He finished with rapid bursts. "As success came, his fame grew and he became more and more prestigious. He even defended two cases in front of Caesar himself, with Caesar judging in his client's favor both times. Recently, Caesar directed he be given chief advocate duties."

Annas stared into the fire.

Only a moment passed before Perez padded to the fire, his prominent cheek bones red from the cold air, his hood pulled tight around his ears. He loudly cleared his throat. "Master Annas, you requested to see me?"

Annas slanted a displeased look at Perez. A long beat passed before he replied, "Yes, I need your help."

Perez looked uneasy. He turned slightly and extended his hands toward the blaze, his voice shaky. "How may I be of service?"

Annas assumed an instructional pose. "Not too long ago, the high priest and I were informed there was a link between the coming of the Messiah and the Tomb of Melchizedek. And, as you know, for the last three years this Nazarene carpenter has been teaching people that he has a 'special' relationship with God. The Sanhedrin Council fears people will believe he is the Messiah, so they want to carefully weigh the information in the Tomb before making a judgment."

Bukki risked an interruption. "But isn't there clear evidence he cannot be the Messiah?"

"Like what?"

"The Messiah is supposed to come from Bethlehem, not Nazareth."

Annas looked impatient and gave a single, sharp headshake. "I didn't say the Sanhedrin thinks he *is* the Messiah; I said they were afraid the *people* would think it. The council wants all available information before guiding the people. Besides, the Torah contains many secrets. It is often very difficult to fully interpret, especially how God will ultimately send the Messiah."

His speech was interrupted by a loud snap in the fire, and sparks jumped at the trio. All three stepped back, but Annas continued as if nothing happened. "It's for this very reason, when we heard about the connection between the Messiah and Melchizedek's Tomb, we went to Asher to have him search for it. Right before he slipped into a coma, Asher informed me he was very close to finding the Tomb."

Sweat beaded Perez's brow. He coughed. "I'm . . . at your service, Master. What exactly do you want me to do?"

Annas had a pugnacious expression and spoke with a loud whisper, "I want you to watch Miriam and her two new friends as they search the

Torah. Try to understand their techniques. I'm sure Miriam has some ideas the other two will improve on. If they need anything, offer my help in providing it for them. But the essence of what I want is for you to figure out how we can ultimately find Melchizedek's Tomb."

Perez looked down and pulled his hood farther over his head. "I will do my best."

A sly smile pulled up Annas' lips. "I'm sure you will." He glanced from one servant to the other. "And both of you, remember . . . no one is to know about this. You may go."

Perez charged from the courtyard.

Bukki stared at Perez until he was out of earshot. He swallowed his apprehension and gave Annas a sideways glance. "Ah . . . there is one more fact about the chief advocate you should know."

Annas slowly swiveled his head. "What is that?"

"He is a childhood friend of the Nazarene."

CHAPTER FORTY-ONE

The loud noises of the busy market began to wane as Justus and Michal walked away from it. They had worked late into the previous night, using the wooden strips to examine the scrolls and some of the large papyrus sheets, but had found nothing. They had chosen to not search during the day, for too many trafficked through the front room. In order to bide time until the evening's quiet hours, they had decided to visit street vendors to purchase supplies.

Justus held several bolts of cloth over his arms.

Michal carried a basket of dried meat with two loaves of bread on top of it, the fresh baked smell washing over her and Justus as they strolled. Even holding the basket with both hands, she moved with fluid strides. She had a broad grin. "This has been a fun afternoon. I love helping Miriam, but it is so depressing. It's good to be away a while." She glanced at Justus. "Didn't you have fun?"

Justus caught Michal from the corner of his eye, and his tone held a hint of sarcasm. "Yes, it was fun . . . especially paying for all this material."

Michal continued her easy walk, but leaned her shoulder into Justus with a seductive grin. "You wait. It will be worth it."

Justus again felt his feelings gravitate to unexplored ground. He changed to a more comfortable subject. "You know, the strips are perplexing when you try to use them."

"Aha. I knew something was bothering you." With a nod, Michal motioned to a street intersection ahead. "Let's stop there and rest for a few moments, so you can tell me what you mean."

Justus was glad for the offer. He needed to clear the inconsistencies from his thoughts. He didn't wait until they reached the intersection. He looked baffled. "Not all the strips work."

"Don't work? But we did a skip of three, and it worked perfectly."

"Well . . . think about it a minute. When one uses 2-letter skips, column 1 remains uncovered, as does column 100. So, dropping down a row and looking at column 1 destroys the 2-letter skip, for letters 100 and 101 are both uncovered."

Reaching the intersection, confusion covered Michal's appearance, as she set the basket down.

Two women hurried past them, one carrying a flask of olive oil, the other a small basket of eggs.

Justus paused for a second. However, before Michal could say anything, he continued, "Besides that, there are twice as many wooden strips as he'd need for a page."

"Maybe he did two sheets at a time."

Unconvinced, Justus said, "Perhaps."

Michal picked up the basket and started walking again. "We aren't solving anything here. Let's get back to Asher's house."

Their tempo increased, and they covered the remaining distance in silence.

As they neared the house, the courtyard scene brought Justus from his far-off thoughts. He felt goose bumps climb his back. No one was in the courtyard, and no guards stood at the door.

Michal gauged the same scene instantly and gasped, "Something's wrong."

Justus crossed the courtyard with three giant steps and slammed open the door. Michal was on his heels. A woman's sobs came from the back of the house.

Justus stopped at Miriam's door and whispered to Michal, "Check to see if she's decent."

Michal set the basket by the door and slipped through, closing it behind her. A heartbeat later she opened the door and motioned for Justus to enter. She led him to Miriam's bedside.

Miriam buried her face in her pillow as she sobbed, "Daddy's dead."

Michal and Justus exchanged knowing looks.

Michal bent and hugged Miriam, her voice soft. "We're here. We'll help you." Justus perched on the side of her bed and laid the bolts of cloth beside Miriam. He had no skill at consoling people, but he touched her shaking shoulder and said, "Miriam, I'm sorry."

Miriam rolled over, rose halfway, and hugged Justus. Her lids were puffy, red, and tear-drenched. Her breathing came in gasps. "Why did this have to happen? Why now?"

Justus hugged Miriam and gazed at Michal, his shaking head revealing he had no idea what to say.

Miriam continued sobbing in Justus' arms.

Michal watched her friend vent her anguish, and softly petted her hair. "Miriam, your father was a great man of God. You know he will be with God in the resurrection."

"I know, but I don't want him to go."

"Your father knew you loved him . . . even though it is a shame you didn't get to tell him one more time."

Miriam's head shot up. Sniffling, she said, "But I did."

Michal's chin dropped. "What?"

"I did tell him I loved him."

Justus bent back to look into her eyes. "How did you do that?"

"He came out of the coma right before he passed away."

CHAPTER FORTY-TWO

Bukki opened his apartment door and the setting sun silhouetted Malchus standing in the doorway. Only that morning Annas had informed him of the possibility of a virgin set of catacombs beyond the north wall of Jerusalem and directed him to assist Malchus in any way. Bukki had remained silent when receiving the order, but his gut churned in rebellion. Annas' quest to find Melchizedek's Tomb had consumed Bukki's time, and he was sure the entire episode was nonsense.

He gave Malchus an ominous look since he now symbolized the futile search. "I assume you are here because you found no entrance to the catacomb."

Malchus stiffened. "I see our masters have talked."

"They do all the time. Tell me what you know." Bukki pushed the larger Malchus backward into the courtyard as he shut his door behind him.

Two women were preparing food by the fire, so Bukki curled a finger at Malchus and led him to a far corner of the courtyard, away from them.

Malchus positioned himself with his back to the women and in a soft voice gave a detailed report of his search of the entire area north of the city wall.

Bukki glanced to both sides to verify they were alone. "And you looked closely at the hillside where the new, unused tomb has just been completed? If it is good for tombs today, maybe it was good a thousand years ago."

"The one for Joseph of Arimathea?"

"I think that's the one."

Malchus glanced back at the women and answered, his voice hinting impatience. "Yes, I looked closely in that area. Other used tombs are nearby, but I could find no hole or cave that might be the entrance to the old Salem catacombs."

Bukki's lips curved downward. "So, I guess you and I start digging."

"Yes, it appears that is the only way."

"What's your strategy?"

The women placed a small, prepared lamb on a spit over the open flame. Immediately, the sweet smell of roasting meat filled the courtyard.

Malchus let his nose sample the savory air, but his appearance remained grim and his voice subdued. "The corridors are very narrow, so I suggest we work in shifts. I have been spending many nights searching the catacombs already, so why don't I work at night, and you can work during the day?"

Bukki drew a short breath as a powerful feeling of disgust swept him. "You know, we can't get all of our other responsibilities completed if we work every day."

Malchus nodded. "We will just have to work as much as we can."

Bukki had an abandoned expression and swallowed hard. "When do we start?"

Malchus met Bukki's gaze. "Let's meet at the entrance to the catacombs near the Dung Gate tomorrow at dusk. I will search my maps and find the corridors which most likely end at the northern wall. Then I can show you how to get to the dig site."

"Done."

➤ ➤ ➤

Perez sat on the steps leading to Solomon's Porch. The day was nearly over, but he had intentionally delayed his return to his quarters. He wanted to talk to Abigail freely. Perez positioned himself on the Temple porch giving him a wide view of the courtyard to be sure he didn't miss her, for it was quite busy during the afternoons with many people bringing offerings. A crowd was often the best place for servants to meet and be ignored.

He surveyed the people. He watched with bored interest as a man and a woman purchased doves for their sacrifice from a Temple vendor. As they moved to the Temple entrance, he glanced at a priest and a scribe in deep debate, but the distance and multiple discussions between Temple visitors prevented him from hearing the disagreement. His survey continued until he glimpsed a small patch of red hair jutting from under a light blue shawl. He leaped from the steps, weaved his way around people, and grabbed her arm from behind. "I need to talk to you."

She squealed and tried to pull away. "Let go of . . . Oh . . . it's you. You frightened me."

Perez grinned. He glanced at a man and woman brushing by him and winked at Abigail. "I need to tell you something . . . in private."

Perez continued to hold Abigail's arm as he guided her to the edge of the courtyard where traffic was less. He felt light-headed and laughed. "Annas has commanded me to spy on Miriam's two friends."

Abigail covered her mouth and snorted. "You have got to be kidding me."

"No . . . really. Amazing isn't it?"

Abigail's face held an expression of hilarity, her voice merry. "I'm doing it for Jehu . . . you for Annas."

Perez couldn't believe their good fortune, a smug smile drawing up his lips. "Between the two of us, we will learn where the Tomb is and control who finds it first."

CHAPTER FORTY-THREE

Michal lay asleep on a pallet at the foot of Miriam's bed. She had consoled her late into the night, before Miriam had finally cried herself to sleep. Fearful Miriam would awaken distraught in the middle of the night, Michal had slept on this improvised pallet. Not knowing what the night would bring, she had asked Justus to sleep in the front room. She also left a lamp burning in that main room and cracked the door open, so Miriam's room was softly lit.

Michal jerked awake. A moment later, she realized Miriam's faint crying had awakened her. Michal sat up.

Miriam whispered, "Have you been there all night?"

"Yes, I wanted to make sure you were all right."

Miriam shook her head hard, then used her fingers to comb back her hair. "Thanks, but you shouldn't have."

"What are friends for?"

Miriam pushed away the covers and got out of bed, some composure returning. "I'm not going back to sleep."

Michal climbed to her feet and pushed the door open inches more, allowing the women to easily see each other.

Miriam's face took on resolve. "Although my father talked mostly nonsense when he came out of the coma, I want to share with you what he said."

Michal was proud of her cousin, knowing this was sure to be painful. "Let's wake Justus so he can hear."

Miriam looked confused. "I guess . . . but why?"

Michal swallowed hard. "Your safety may depend on what Asher said."

"My safety?"

Michal did not answer Miriam's question, but took her hand and led her into the main part of the house. She gently shook Justus.

❧ ❧ ❧

Justus blinked several times, then bolted to his feet. "Is something wrong?"

Michal smiled softly and put her hand up. "No. We are both fine. Miriam wants to tell us what Asher said before he passed."

Miriam seemed a little embarrassed and more than a little scared. "How would Dad's last words affect my safety? I don't understand."

Justus straightened his robe as he moved in the direction of the outside door. Glancing at Miriam, he replied with a worried voice. "Whoever kidnapped you was forcing Asher to give them information hidden within the scrolls. If that person finds out Asher revealed his identity to you, he will kill you to protect himself."

Miriam looked distressed. "But Dad didn't tell me who abducted me."

Justus opened the door for a moment and asked the guard, "What time is it?"

The guard replied, "It's nearly the end of the fourth watch."

Michal could see a slight light through the open door, indicating a new day was dawning.

Justus shut the door and motioned to a bench with a look of intent. "Why don't you tell us exactly what he did say."

Miriam sat, and Michal joined her. A single tear rolled down one cheek. She said, "OK, but there really wasn't much that had any meaning."

"Let Michal and I decide that."

Miriam inhaled deeply and she looked settled. "I heard Dad coughing, and I ran into his room. When he saw me, he looked surprised, then happy. He said my name. I hugged him and told him I loved him.

He started to faint, but he regained consciousness again. He said 'not equal skips,' some words I couldn't understand followed by 'matrix' and 'wood strips'."

Miriam brushed away another tear and used her hand to wipe her runny nose. "He fainted. I held him, stroking his hair, saying, 'Daddy, I love you, come back.' He woke up and mumbled something ending with the name *Annas*."

Miriam moved off the bench and took two steps from it, her head down. When she turned, her struggle to keep her emotions in check was evident. "He kept mumbling. I couldn't understand him. He said, 'measly dock' and 'tomb,' and 'messiah.' After that he went to sleep." Miriam began to sob into both hands. "And . . . stopped . . . breathing."

Justus leaned against the wall, transfixed as he tried to interpret what she had told them.

Michal went to Miriam and held her tight.

Deep in thought, Justus became all advocate. Pushing away from the wall, he began to slowly circle the large stand in the middle of the room, occasionally lifting his index finger and making a stabbing motion, as if making a silent point.

Michal petted Miriam's hair, while she followed Justus' movements.

After a time, Justus pulled up and wheeled about, facing the two women. "Is it possible what you heard as *measly dock* could have been *Melchizedek*?"

Michal gave Justus a questioning look and released Miriam.

Miriam dropped her hands, her sobs stopping. She rocked back and forth, sniffling but weighing his question. "I suppose so."

Justus clapped his hands together and arched his neck back. "Yes! That's it." He punched his fist into empty air. "Of course . . . Melchizedek's Tomb." He darted to the women and bent forward, his face glowing. "It's Abram's Tithe . . . They're searching for Abram's Tithe."

Michal and Miriam exchanged puzzled looks.

Justus spun around and laughed out loud. "Abram's Tithe."

Michal bounced to him, grabbed his head in both hands, and pulled him inches from her. "What are you talking about?"

Justus grinned, swept Michal off her feet, and spun her around.

Miriam was frozen, gaping at them.

"It's Abram's Tithe. Someone kidnapped Miriam to get her father to find Abram's Tithe."

As Justus released her, Michal's bewilderment showed. "Take a breath. We don't know anything about Abram's Tithe. What is it?"

Justus regained some composure, but he was still beaming. "Of course. I'm sorry. Let me explain. In ancient times, the kings of Sodom and Gomorrah, plus a few others, got into a war with some other kings and lost. The other kings took all the wealth from Sodom and Gomorrah, along with all the people. Abram's nephew, Lot, was captured, also."

Justus paused as if someone was silently talking to him. "Well, when Abram learned that Lot was a prisoner, he enlisted some allies, defeated the kings, and regained all the people and all the wealth. On his way back, the king of Salem—whose name was Melchizedek—went out to bless Abram on God's behalf, since he was not only a king but the high priest of God. Abram responded by giving ten percent of all the recovered wealth to Melchizedek. You know . . . that's the foundation of our Jewish belief in tithing our increase."

Michal caught Justus' excitement. "But what does that have to do with Miriam?"

Miriam added with enthusiasm, "Yeah, what's that got to do with me?"

Justus beamed, stepped to the stand, and used one hand to lean on it, his voice at a normal pitch. "You see, Melchizedek has no recorded beginning, and scholars believe he never died. You know, like Enoch. And, he was a very wealthy king, so he didn't need the tithe Abram gave him. The legend is, Melchizedek put the tithe in his tomb. He knew he wouldn't need a tomb anyway."

The idea began to grow in Michal, along with a feeling of exhilaration. "OK, I understand ten percent of the wealth of two cities may have been hidden away in an unneeded tomb, but still . . ."

Justus stood tall, his expression festive. "Don't you see? Someone thinks Asher had a way to find out where the Tomb with the treasure is, but the only way they could make him find it was to hold Miriam for ransom."

Miriam cocked her head, moved to the bench, and settled on it. She appeared to be processing Justus' explanation. Glancing at Justus with a look of wonder, she exhaled loudly. "Wow. How do you know all that?"

Justus glided to Michal and wrapped his arm around her waist. "I heard about this for almost an entire year before my family moved to Rome. My grandfather talked about it all the time. He would joke that his brother down in Jerusalem was dirt poor because he looked for Abram's Tithe more than he hewed tombs." He gazed at Michal for a long second. "And . . . as I've already told Michal, I can tell you more about tombs, graves, and catacombs than you would ever care to know."

A warm feeling spread over Michal. She looked with new admiration at Justus, and her voice grew soft. "That was a thousand years ago. Surely the treasure has been found by someone by now."

Justus laughed out loud. "If there even was a tomb with the riches."

"What do you mean?"

"My grandfather said it was all legend."

Michal asked, "What do you think?"

Justus inclined his head, moved his arm from Michal. "These events—including Abram giving Melchizedek the tithe—are recorded in the Holy Scriptures, so that part is definitely true. Most learned religious leaders agree that Melchizedek had no recorded beginning or end, hence likely didn't need a tomb."

He stepped again to the high stand in the middle of the room and stared absently at the large sheet with the matrix of letters. "My grandfather said it was common practice to obtain a tomb or a spot in a catacomb long before you die." He glanced at Miriam. "That's still done. Asher has had one for years. Right, Miriam?"

"Yes. His was finished years ago."

"So, Melchizedek probably had one. It's likely a tomb would have provided an immediately available place to seal in the tithe. It's reasonable Melchizedek didn't need any more wealth and also to assume when Melchizedek left Salem, he was so revered no one would touch the Tomb." Focusing on Michal, he said flatly, "I think it's likely true.

And I doubt if anyone has found the Tomb. In fact, I think the real question is, how could anyone ever find it?"

Miriam appeared to be absorbing the full implication of Justus' explanations and her brows knotted. "But Justus, isn't Jerusalem built on top on the city of Salem?"

"Most of it."

Michal glared. "What do you mean most of it?"

Justus took one step towards the outer door and waved at it. "My grandfather was certain that a part of Salem lies beyond Jerusalem's northern wall."

"Where were the Salem catacombs?"

Justus pretended to smirk. "What makes you think Salem has catacombs?"

"Didn't it?"

"Most tomb hewers believe their profession started when Jacob bought the cave where Miriam was imprisoned."

"What did your grandfather think about that?"

His voice became quiet. "He thought Abram got the idea from the people of Salem."

Miriam repeated Michal's question, her voice regulated. "Where did he think the catacombs were?"

"Under the part of Salem not covered by the current Jerusalem."

A loud knock on the front room door punctuated Justus' conclusion. A guard's rough voice said, "Honorable Justus, a man is here to see you."

Justus looked incredulous. "All right. I'll be out in a moment." He gave Miriam a questioning look. "Won't Perez be the one who prepares Asher's body for burial?"

She nodded and answered, "Of course."

Justus thrust open the door as he spoke, "Then . . . I wonder . . ." He stopped in mid-sentence and blinked in surprise. "Peter, please come in."

Peter shook his head. "Jesus wants you to be with him today at Bethany."

Justus glanced at Michal. "Bethany? Why?"

"His good friend Lazarus has died. Do you remember him? We all went to his house after you met with Jesus in the Garden of Gethsemane."

"Yes, I remember. Of course, I will be there. But what does Jesus want to talk to me about?"

Peter tilted his head and looked confused. "I didn't say Jesus wanted to talk to you . . . I said he wants you to be with him."

CHAPTER FORTY-FOUR

From the balcony of his palace, Caiaphas gazed at the long shadows of the houses bordering the outer enclosure of the Temple courtyard below. The sun had barely cleared the city's east wall across from him. A strong breeze whipped across him and billowed the head covering rustling his long black hair, but he didn't take note of it. Annas had wanted to see him yesterday, but there was no way he could squeeze him in. He hoped there was new information about the Tomb and not more trouble with the Nazarene carpenter. He needed some good news for a change.

Annas bustled through the hall to the balcony. He paused halfway from the door to the railing, breathing hard and saying nothing.

Caiaphas' desire for good news was swallowed by foreboding. He half sat on the railing. "Well?"

Annas looked withdrawn. "Perez has agreed to watch Miriam and her friends to see what they know and how to search the Torah."

Caiaphas gave a dubious look, surprised that Annas would look so worried about such a trivial matter. "Do you think he is capable of it?" Caiaphas remembered Annas was the one who had placed Perez with Asher years ago. Caiaphas had seen nothing noteworthy in the servant. "He looks to me to be quite timid."

"Of course, you are right. There is a risk, but since Bukki cannot watch, Perez is our only chance."

Caiaphas heaved a disgruntled sigh. "OK, but make sure Bukki gives him some direct training." He was convinced Annas had come to tell him something of importance and began to feel agitated at the delay.

Annas scooted his sandals over the polished stone floor as he slowly moved to the railing. He gazed at the Temple courtyard, his expression stony. He spoke through a clenched jaw. "Our bigger problem is the Roman."

Caiaphas' pulse quickened. He stood up. "The Roman? How so?"

"Caesar recently appointed him Chief Advocate of Rome."

Caiaphas reeled under the weight of Annas' words. "Chief advocate?"

Annas' nostrils flared, as he turned his head to Caiaphas. "Yes, but worse . . . he was a childhood friend of the Nazarene carpenter."

Caiaphas bowed his head and put his left hand on his forehead. A few beats passed before he dropped his hand and stared at Annas with a grim expression. "This is going to make things tenfold harder."

"I know. We must be very careful what he learns."

A maid shuffled through the hall and took one step onto the balcony. With bowed head, she interrupted. "Excuse me, Masters, but Kore the Pharisee said you asked him to come."

Caiaphas flashed Annas a frown. Even though he had designed a new plot against Jesus, he felt perturbed by the interruption. Caiaphas harshly replied, "Send him in."

As the maid hurried to obey, Caiaphas questioned Annas. "What if the advocate finds out about the Tomb?"

Annas raised both palms up as he gave a half shrug. "I don't know."

Both priests assumed a lofty pose.

Kore approached them with a jerky gait. He stopped in the middle of the balcony floor, his robe nearly touching it. He remained silent a long moment. He cleared his throat, but his voice still broke. "You wanted . . . to see me?"

Annas sounded gruff. "Kore, the Nazarene carpenter's friend, Lazarus of Bethany, died a few days ago, but Jesus did not attend the burial ceremony."

Sweat beaded on Kore's forehead. "What does that mean?"

Caiaphas answered flatly, "It means he will surely show up soon at Bethany."

Kore swallowed hard, and held out a hand. "But the last time he was in Jerusalem, he was almost stoned to death. What makes you think he will go to Bethany?"

Annas gave a jabbing point. "After three years of watching this guy, do you not understand that he has little fear of us?"

Kore abruptly asked, "What is it you want me to do?"

Caiaphas drew in an irritated breath and said, "We need to know what happens in Bethany. Probably he will simply visit the tomb and leave. However, we need to know if he again says blasphemous things. If he does, you must incite the people to respond according to the Law and stone him."

Kore gave a short nod. "As you wish."

The maid again interrupted. "A man named Perez has requested an audience. He said it is urgent."

Caiaphas and Annas exchanged a puzzled look.

Caiaphas felt a tinge of impatience. "Send him in." He glowered at Kore. "Go at once."

Kore spun around and charged down the hall, brushing past Perez without acknowledging his existence.

Perez stopped in the doorway of the balcony, gave a slight nod, and absently pulled on his earlobe. "Masters Annas and Caiaphas, I have bad news."

Caiaphas blurted out. "What is the bad news?"

"Master Asher died late yesterday evening."

Annas looked worried. "Did he come out of his coma before he died?"

"I don't think so, but I was not there when he died. Miriam was."

Caiaphas rubbed his chin with his fingers. He swallowed his foreboding. "Were her two friends there as well?"

"They were at the market when he died, or so the guard told me. However, they returned afterwards. They were the ones who gave me the news since Miriam was asleep when I arrived. She took the death very hard."

Caiaphas gave Annas a stony gaze. "I will notify the council. We must have a burial procession and ceremony today."

Annas broke the gaze by focusing on Perez. "Prepare his tomb in the catacombs for internment."

"Right away."

Before Perez could turn, Annas added. "And . . . ask Miriam if Asher regained consciousness so we may make any of his last-minute wishes part of the ceremony."

CHAPTER FORTY-FIVE

Rays from the early morning sun illuminated several spring flowers budding near the well-worn path from Jerusalem to Bethany. Spring was Justus' favorite season and though the buds had not totally opened, he knew it was a short time before the endless cycle of life would blossom in fullness anew.

Justus matched Peter's long strides until Peter slowed and pointed toward a barely distinguishable path. "We are not going into the city, but bypass it to the north side. Jesus will be waiting for us there."

Justus filed after Peter in the new direction. He glanced up and noted two hawks in the deep blue sky lazily circling one another on air drafts unknown to those close to the ground. Justus was excited about seeing Jesus again, but dread began to darken his thoughts. "Why is Jesus waiting there for us?"

Peter shot an impatient sideways glance at Justus. "Because the tomb of Lazarus is not far from where we will meet."

Justus wondered if Peter was being intentionally vague but said no more. He heard voices and muffled sobs long before anyone came into view. As he approached the back of the crowd, he came alert at seeing Jesus. Most of the disciples were there, but who were all the other people surrounding him?

Justus was too far from Jesus to greet him, but close enough to notice a distraught woman run up to him and cling to him, talking.

Peter explained, "That's Martha."

Peter's comment caused Justus to search his memory, and he felt uneasy. "Thank you. I remember." Justus politely worked his way through the assembly and came close enough to hear the exchange.

Martha spoke through sobs, ". . . even now I know whatever you ask of God, He will grant you."

Jesus' lips pressed together. He looked disturbed, but his voice soothing. "Your brother will rise again."

"I know he will rise at the resurrection in the last day."

Jesus looked patient, his voice firm. "I am the Resurrection and the Life. Whoever believes in Me, although he may die, yet he shall live. And whoever continues to live and believes on Me shall never actually die at all. Do you believe this?"

Justus was paralyzed.

Martha cried, "I do believe that You are the Messiah, the Son of God, the Anointed One Who was to come into the world." She whirled and dashed back to her house.

Jesus deliberately turned toward Justus and gazed at him with a pleasant smile. "I'm glad you came, dear friend."

Justus frantically tried to process Martha's words. Jesus hadn't denied anything she had said. He asked, "What's happening here?"

"I know the gifts My Father has given you. Stay and observe. Put together all you see and arrive at your own conclusion."

Leading several other people, Martha's sister, Mary, bolted to Jesus and flung herself at his feet, sobbing, amid a hushed crowd. "Lord, if You had been here my brother would not have died."

Justus reeled back, bumping into people, his logic repelling the impossible as he observed the effect of the emotional volcano.

Jesus sighed loudly, "Where have you laid him?"

A nearby person helped Mary to her feet.

Tears streamed down her cheeks as she forced out the answer, "Lord, come and see."

As they marched to a small hillside, Justus focused on a large stone covering a tomb while those around him left him standing alone. With a few steps, the procession stopped beside the stone.

Justus maneuvered through them to be near Jesus, but at the rear of the crowd. Since he was tall, it was easy for him to see over those in front of him. The unfolding scene hypnotized him.

Jesus wept.

A woman immediately in front of Justus leaned to the person next to her and whispered, "See how tenderly He loved him."

Her friend responded, "Could not He, Who made a blind man see, have prevented this man from dying?"

Justus sidled away from the two women and closed in on Jesus. He could hear Jesus sighing deeply over and over.

Suddenly Jesus' countenance became authoritarian as he pointed to a group of three men. His voice sounded as an officer giving troops a command. "Take away the stone."

Justus felt a tight knot in his stomach.

Martha pleaded, "But Lord, he is decaying and by this time has an offensive odor. He has been dead for four days."

Jesus' stern appearance melted into tender patience. "Did I not promise you that if you would believe and rely on Me, you should see the glory of God?"

Justus was paralyzed as he watched the three men lumbering to the tomb. When they pushed the stone aside, Justus instantly put his hand over his mouth and nose to protect against the putrid smell. But it didn't come.

Jesus raised his head and both hands to the sky, his words echoing as it broke the complete silence. "Father, I thank You that You have heard Me." Pausing a second, he continued, "Yes, I know You always listen to Me, but I have said this for the benefit of the people standing around, so they may believe You did send Me."

Justus felt he was in a dream.

Jesus fixed a strong gaze on the open tomb and his voice reverberated. "Lazarus, come out."

Justus' heart pounded as he stared at the tomb door, not willing to even blink. He teetered back and gasped along with the crowd as a man shuffled out, his hands and feet still encased with the linen strips of his burial clothes. A napkin formed from smaller linen strips remained rolled around his head.

Jesus glowed. "Free him of the burial wrappings and let him go."

Justus remained captivated as he watched several people undo the cloth around Lazarus. His sisters were crying with joy. They alternately hugged Lazarus, then Jesus. The crowd joined in the celebration, and Jesus, Lazarus, and his sisters were nearly carried to the house by the joyous crowd.

Mystified, Justus didn't move. *What just happened? Jesus raised a dead man to life! It is not possible, but I clearly saw it. He did it, but how could he? Martha called him the Messiah. Could she be right? I wonder how far Asher got in his searching for the Messiah. I wonder if he looked for Jesus' name.* Justus' peripheral vision caught two men approaching him.

It was Peter and John, but Justus still didn't move.

Peter surveyed Justus' astonishment, and his lips turned up slightly. "It was good you were here."

"Did Jesus just raise a man from the dead?"

John held his gaze. "Do you believe he did?"

Justus shook his head in an attempt to shed his dream-like feeling. "I want to talk to Jesus about this. However, it will have to wait until another time. I must return and attend Asher's funeral."

"We know."

"Please tell Jesus I will try to see him soon. Where will you be going?"

Peter looked at Justus, amused. "To Ephraim."

CHAPTER FORTY-SIX

The day was nearly over as Malchus stationed himself at the entrance to the catacombs near the Dung Gate. Knowing of the night's meeting, Caiaphas had allowed Malchus to not participate in Asher's burial. So, after the funeral service at the Temple, he rushed here.

Although it was still early spring, the evening was quite warm. After spending the bulk of the day perusing the catacombs, Malchus felt confident he had found the correct corridor and was eager to begin digging. However, as he observed Bukki tramping through the alley in his direction, all of the previous day's feelings about Bukki being of little help came back to him.

Bukki carried himself with a confident step. His voice showed his impatience. "Have you found the north wall?"

"Yes, I'm sure of it. It took longer than I thought, but let's go in. I will show you where it is." Malchus' muscles flexed as he plucked a few torches and handed them to Bukki. "We may need these." He held a lighted lamp and a flask of spare oil as he descended into the subterranean caverns. His excitement warded off the usual shiver caused by the initial coolness. "Follow me."

Malchus hustled down the corridor to an intersection of three other passageways. He heard Bukki stop behind him and felt surprisingly in control. His voice sounded like a schoolmaster as it broke the catacomb's silence. "The tunnel angling back to the right continues parallel underneath the west Temple wall to the tombs of the minor priests. The one to the left continues curving around and ultimately goes under the east wall to the Kidron Valley, where the well-to-do often build tombs. Very close to it is the underground river that flows through the city."

Bukki's bored expression changed to disgust, but he remained silent.

"This middle one is the main corridor to the many tunnels under Jerusalem proper. Come . . . I'll show you how to get to the northern wall." Malchus glided along the middle corridor.

Bukki trailed him. "How do you keep from getting lost down here?"

Malchus dipped his head back, his voice still instructional. "I'll show you, but first remember to count the side tunnels on both sides. You will turn into the seventeenth one."

Bukki scowled.

Malchus continued his speed, pointing to each side tunnel and silently counting. "This is the seventeenth passage off the main tunnel," he said finally. "Even though this intersection is not a perfect right angle, it will be closer than any you will see after this. Immediately to the left is the way to the main catacomb entrance near the Herod Gate. You are to take the one to our right."

Turning, Malchus padded down the corridor. "Four times I stepped off the distance above where we are now, and I think I have the right place. Also, I marked the journey to this spot with whitewash. Notice, I placed the marking at the bottom of the corridor on the right. This is to make it less noticeable if someone comes in to visit a tomb, for most people hold torches and look up."

Bukki suddenly became interested. "Have you often seen others down here?"

"No. However, I most often come after dark. When people do come, it's usually only in the day. Rarely, someone will be entombed late, as Asher is today." Malchus stopped where the corridor had a Y-shaped intersection with the one they were on and another opening just a short way in front of the Y. He held the lamp low and pointed. "Do you see the marks?"

Bukki bent and examined the mark. "Why is one end smaller than the other?"

"It's a help. As you go toward the area in which we will be digging, proceed in the direction of the little side of the mark. When finished, proceed in the direction of the big side of the mark."

Bukki sighed, but seemed to relax. "I see. That way you don't just go in circles down here."

"Exactly."

The two men continued to weave their way through the catacombs, changing direction several times. Finally, they walked to a point where the hall abruptly stopped at a solid wall.

Malchus held his light close to the wall and rubbed his hand over the rough expanse, almost lovingly. As dirt fell away, large stones stacked on one another became visible. "See, this is the foundation. When they laid it, they apparently cut through the tunnel, sealing it off. I believe directly on the other side of these stones, the passageway continues for some distance. In fact, I hope, it connects to the catacombs originally under the ancient town of Salem."

Bukki perked up. He seemed pleased. "You know, until seeing this, I thought we had no chance of accidentally burrowing into a catacomb on the other side. Now I think it reasonable to assume the tunnel really does continue beyond the wall. We may have a chance at this. How deep do the city walls go down?"

Malchus' complexion darkened. The sweet smell of burning oil filled the stagnant air as he hesitated. "I don't know. I went to the scribes to see if they have a record and, of course, they have nothing. If you noticed, however, as we moved from corridor to corridor, we were usually moving down, so we are considerably lower than when we first entered."

Bukki stood in silent wonder. "When do we start digging?"

"I will start tomorrow night. You can begin tomorrow or whenever you have time."

Bukki gave a bleak sigh. "I must finish some things tomorrow. I'll start the following day. Where do we put the dirt?"

Malchus motioned Bukki to follow as he retraced several steps to an opening branching off. "This tunnel is actually a hole. It descends a short distance and stops. It has stairs, but whoever was extending the catacombs downward quit for some reason, so we will dump the dirt into it."

▸ ▸ ▸

Darkness punctuated by several lamps framed the processional as they snaked toward the Herod Gate from the Temple. Perez and several other servants held Asher's body high on a pallet of sticks covered with purple cloth. The night was filled with singing of dirges and wailing from professional mourners.

Michal held Miriam tightly, occasionally needing to almost lift her to keep her from falling as she poured out her grief.

Justus and Julius held stern features as they marched immediately behind them, followed by a large number of mourners, priests, Pharisees and scribes.

Justus had hurried from Bethany to Jerusalem for the funeral and now mechanically kept his place in line. His thoughts swirled around the events in Bethany. Clearly, Jesus was more than a preacher . . . but, the Messiah? When he had told Michal what Jesus did, she accepted it . . . almost as if she expected it.

Miriam's grief appeared to cause Julius pain. He glanced at Justus, his voice low. "Is his tomb outside the city or in the catacombs?"

Justus came out of his fog to reply, "In the catacombs. The entrance is near the gate."

As the processional neared the Herod Gate, they turned left to the main opening. Perez and three other servants took one purple cloth, laid it on the ground, and placed Asher's frail body on it. He and one servant went to one side, the other two men lined up opposite them. All stooped at the same time to grab the purple cloth and lift the body.

Perez turned to Justus and, with a look of regret, spoke firmly, "Only you four may follow to the tomb."

Two servants treaded the stairs with large torches as the four pallbearers easily maneuvered Asher's rigid body downward.

Julius held his strong arm around Miriam's waist in case she needed support. Justus and Michal trailed them closely. They wove their way through the corridors to two young men holding burial cloths positioned on either side of Asher's tomb. Identical large pots of spices sat on the floor beside them.

A pair of pallbearers jockeyed Asher's thin body onto a small shelf hewn out of stone in the tomb. Soon, they exited.

Shaking, Miriam stumbled in alone, her voice breaking. "Good-bye, Daddy. I love you. I know you will be with God in the resurrection." Miriam coughed as she tried to hold back her sobs. She whimpered twice, turned and tried one step, but fell forward.

Julius lunged to catch her. He sent Justus an anguished look, his jaw tight as he held back emotion. "I'm taking Miriam home."

"Of course. We will be there soon."

Perez stepped into the tomb. He draped one edge of the purple cloth over Asher's corpse and pivoted to the servants with the spices. "Wrap the body with spices, and the burial cloths, and seal the tomb." Perez turned to Justus and Michal. "You should go now."

Justus gave a curt nod. "Yes. Of course."

One of the torch-carrying servants took the lead and weaved through the passages, lighting the way back.

Justus allowed Michal to follow the servant, but as they turned a corner, he grabbed her arm to stop her. "Look, down this tunnel," he whispered. "It looks like someone is coming toward us."

Michal studied a faint light bouncing on the irregular, hewed walls of the corridor. "Who would be down here this time of night?"

"Maybe someone hunting for Melchizedek's Tomb."

Michal pulled her arm away. "We had better go. If they are down here for that reason, it may be better they don't know we know."

As they exited the catacombs, one servant handed Justus a torch, then followed his counterparts into the city proper, leaving them alone.

Michal looked disconcerted. "Do you think the person . . ."

". . . or persons . . ."

". . . yes, or persons, really are looking for Melchizedek's Tomb?"

Justus' thoughts churned as he shook his head. "I don't know. I was kidding more than anything, but it is strange someone would be in the catacombs at this time of night, unless they were burying someone."

Michal reached for Justus' hand. "Too many mysteries for one night."

Justus was amused at the dismissal of the topic, but said nothing.

Michal pulled his hand and gave him a coy expression. "Walk me home."

"My pleasure."

As they embarked to Miriam's house, she exaggerated the swing of Justus' arm. "If there are catacombs outside the city walls, how could we ever find them?"

He grinned at her. "Actually . . . it's quite simple."

CHAPTER FORTY-SEVEN

Justus rose from the blanket he used as a bed in Asher's front room. Although it was early, light was streaming into the front window. After returning from Asher's burial, Miriam and Michal had gone to bed in Miriam's room. Abigail had already retired in the spare room. Justus had no idea when or if Perez had returned, for the only door to his quarters opened directly into the courtyard.

For most of the night Justus' thoughts had wallowed through the bits of disjointed facts and information. He had reached no conclusion and thirsted for more information. As he saw the scroll and wooden strips, random ideas bounced through his brain. Did Asher find clues to the Tomb's location? Did he use Jesus' name in any searches? Who had used his clues to search?

Justus spent an hour attempting to find words using the 2-letter-wide strips. He heard but didn't react to muffled voices coming from Miriam's room. Finding nothing on the sheets, he went to the corner where the wooden strips were still heaped and sorted through them, collecting those that covered 3 letters.

Michal slipped into the room, followed by Miriam. The three exchanged morning greetings.

Miriam went to the outside door, grabbed her outer cloak, and wrapped it around her tightly. She smiled brightly. "Julius has some free time this morning, so I'm going to show him Jerusalem."

Justus gave Michal a knowing look.

Michal grinned at Miriam. "Good. You need to get out of the house."

Miriam closed the door behind her.

Michal turned her attention to Justus. "Have you found anything?"

Still squatting and sorting strips on the floor, Justus held her gaze, his face showing his frustration. "I used the 2-letter-wide wooden strips on every scroll. I'd hoped to find the word *tomb* or *Abram* or *tithe*, but have found no word relating to anything about Melchizedek." He threw the handful of wooden strips back onto the pile. "I know this is difficult, but I'm certain there is something we still don't understand."

Michal went to him and placed her hand on his shoulder, her voice soft. "You may be right, but we have no way of finding out anything else."

As Justus gazed at her, calm settled inside. "Yeah. Let's keep trying."

They sorted through the wooden strips and moved to opposite sides of the large stand. Both used them to search—Michal on a regular scroll and Justus on a large papyrus sheet.

After two hours, Michal loudly tapped the stand next to the scroll. She stood straight, her voice crisp, and pointed to the array of wooden strips covering parts of the scroll. "You were certainly right yesterday. Few of the board widths result in equidistant skips. I wonder if Asher's *not-equal-skips* comment to Miriam had something to do with that fact."

Hearing the irritation in her voice, Justus shot her an uneasy glance. He rubbed his lips with his index finger before answering. "I'm not really sure, but he wouldn't have made all the wooden strips if he didn't intend to use them."

Before Michal could answer him, Miriam breezed into the front room from the courtyard, her face aglow. "Julius is really a nice man. We spent all morning walking around Jerusalem and talking."

Michal grinned. "So you were tour guide?"

"Yes, it was fun."

Justus' smile dissolved in a shiver of apprehension. "Has anyone asked you if Asher awoke from his coma?"

"Yes . . . Perez and Julius."

"What did you tell them?"

Miriam looked dismayed. "I recited to Julius what I told you two, but I reported to Perez that Dad did not regain consciousness." She took a deep breath. "Hey . . . I know what you guys said . . . I'm not stupid."

Justus gave a calm look of apology. "I'm sorry. I was simply worried about what might happen to you."

Michal glanced from Justus to Miriam with a look of frustration. "Miriam, I have spent hours trying to find something in this scroll. Is there anything you know about how Asher conducted searches that you have not told us?"

The comment successfully diverted Miriam. Thinking, she looked upward at the ceiling of clay-covered sticks for a moment, then said, "Hmm . . . I told you how to skip the same number of letters . . . about no spaces or punctuations . . . about looking around a 'found word' to see if there was another word in close proximity . . ." She looked at Michal and shook her head. "Nope. That's all."

Michal looked disappointed and shrugged.

Miriam took a step for her room, stopped abruptly, and pivoted. "Dad did talk about keys."

Justus' head lurched up. It took him a second to process her words. "Keys? What kind of keys?"

Miriam pursed her lips and tapped them several times with two fingers. "Dad once told me some of the sages said the Torah was so complex, keys were sometimes needed before specific concepts could be understood. He said he expected one day to need one."

Michal appeared exasperated. "That's it? He never gave you an example of a key?"

"Not only did he never give me an example, I don't think he ever tried to find one."

Justus simply stared at her.

Miriam entered her room and closed the door.

Michal looked puzzled. "A key. This gets harder and harder."

"That's for certain."

At that moment, Perez barged through the front door, looking apologetically at Justus. "Miriam stopped at my quarters a few minutes ago and suggested I clean Asher's room for you."

Justus was only partially aware of the interruption as he scrutinized the wooden strips on the large sheet, but his voice was pleasant. "I would appreciate it. I slept on the floor last night, but it would be nice to move out Asher's things and put new bedclothes on the bed."

Michal had a questioning look. "But where's Abigail?"

He hesitated a moment, a smile almost forming. "She's gone to market." He looked long at the wooden strips on Michal's scroll before closing Asher's door behind him.

Justus' wrinkled forehead revealed his deep concentration as he sat in silence. He slowly turned and absently gazed at Michal, his voice thoughtful. "I know how I would like to search the Torah."

"How?"

He leaned forward, his expression piercing. "Suppose we could look at the entire string of 305,000 letters until we could find the specific, equidistant skip length that yielded a word, say *messiah*. Then, if we divided the string of letters into the exact number of rows of that skip length and have a scribe write it on multiple sheets of papyrus, sewn together to make it big enough for all those columns, we would have the word *messiah* perfectly spelled down vertically, with no skips."

He straightened and firmly patted the stand. "Then, it would be possible to roll the papyrus into a large tube and look all around, you know: to the right, left, above and below the word *messiah* for other words, maybe even names of people."

Michal stared at him as if he had grown another head. "You need to get more sleep. You've been thinking about this way too much"

Justus returned from the clouds. "I know, I know. It's a neat idea, but can't be done." He shrugged and placed a 6-letter wooden strip on columns 2 through 7.

Michal pondered his placement. "What if Asher meant that we should do orderly skips instead of equidistant skips?"

Justus was stunned for only a second before realizing the extent of Michal's idea. "Of course. There are only twenty-eight 6-letter-wide strips, so . . ." He quickly covered the columns, then laid a 6-letter strip on rows 2 through 7, skipped row 8 and continued until all the strips had been used.

Michal's jaw dropped. "There are only 15 columns and 15 rows of letters visible."

Justus' pulse thundered. "It's a lot easier to examine 225 letters to find words than the entire matrix of 10,000 letters." He bent to examine the visible letters for a few moments before saying, "You know, it still bothers me that Asher had sheets of papyrus filled with rows and columns of 100 letters. Why not some other number?"

"I don't know. But if you were going to have the Book of Genesis written into specific matrices, what would you have selected?"

Justus studied Michal. "Well, you saw how the 6-letter strips didn't fit well at the end of the search."

"You mean that the strips extended beyond the sheet as the final columns and rows were covered?"

"Yes. It seems to me if you want to search for a specific word, you should have even multiples of the number of letters in the target word, so as a minimum, one letter of your word would have a chance to be in each row or column."

Michal gave a dubious look. "I'm not following you. Give me an example."

"Take the word *messiah*. It has 7 letters. An equal skip of 7 letters would require 49 letters to get a minimum of one uncovered letter for each letter in the word to be on a single row or column. You know . . . 7 sevens."

Michal's lips formed a circle. "Oh . . . but we don't have a matrix of letters 49 x 49."

Justus shivered as he felt someone's presence and wheeled.

Perez stood in the open door of Asher's room, gaping at Justus.

Justus tried to conceal his alarm. "Yes, what is it?"

"I can get you Genesis written in matrices of 49 x 49," Perez said.

Startled, Michal and Justus looked at each other.

Justus turned to Perez and said, "OK . . . What about an additional set with matrices of 121 x 121?"

CHAPTER FORTY-EIGHT

Kore fidgeted as he bided time in the large meeting room of the synagogue, now highly decorated for the coming of the high priest. He was well aware that Pharisees seldom were placed on the Sanhedrin, but until a few months ago he was on a fast track to be selected. Now every failure to deliver the carpenter put another stone in the wall preventing him from being chosen. *How am I going to tell Caiaphas this? I know he wants to hear that the crowd stoned the carpenter to death, but when he hears what I have to . . .*

Kore's thoughts were interrupted by the noisy entrance of Caiaphas and his entourage.

Caiaphas marched up close to Kore. "And what is the health of the Nazarene?"

Powerful guilt gripped Kore. "He is alive . . . and worse."

Caiaphas gave a guttural roar of rage. "What!"

Kore's stomach knotted and his throat barely allowed sound to come through. "As you directed, I sent men knowledgeable in the Law to Bethany."

Caiaphas' glare bore into Kore as he leaned even closer.

Kore's discomfort from Caiaphas' violation of his body space forced him to lean back slightly. "He was not there at first. However, on the fourth day after the burial, he and his disciples came."

"And?"

Kore blanched and trembled as he blurted out, "The carpenter went to the tomb, told some men to roll away the stone, and commanded

Lazarus to come out." His voice trembled. "Lazarus walked out of the tomb *alive*!"

A look of unbelief covered Caiaphas. "That's crazy. Dead men don't walk out of tombs." Caiaphas took a half step back. "He said nothing about being God?"

Kore shook so violently he was barely able to remain standing. "Only that he was the resurrection and the life and anyone believing in him would live forever."

Caiaphas grabbed Kore's arm and tugged. "Come with me to the Temple. You must tell this to the Sanhedrin, now."

Kore's chin fell mashing his long beard into his chest. "Sir, there is one other thing."

"What's that?"

"The Roman chief advocate was there."

▶ ▶ ▶

The Temple room called the Hall of Hewn Stones held visages of ancient ornamental artifacts arranged to enhance the aurora of position and power. It was a separate room, half in the Temple sanctuary, allowing Temple access and half out of the Temple proper, allowing access to the outside.

Inside was a semi-circle of large stone benches which could comfortably accommodate the seventy members of Israel's Supreme Court, the Great Sanhedrin, who were predominately Sadducees, with the balance being Pharisees. The bulk of the members were elderly, as new members were only added when existing members died.

A small wing extended from each end of the semi-circle straight towards each other. Caiaphas sat alone on one wing, the place designated for the high priest.

Kore left the presenter's dais in the center of the semi-circle after telling them all the events at Bethany. He was sure his fate was in the hands of others. His dreams of becoming part of this august body had been flushed into an abyss. He stumbled as he moved to the wing opposite Caiaphas.

Only little more than half of the council members were in attendance, but they sat quietly with fixed expressions until Kore sat.

A white-haired, white bearded member near Caiaphas boosted his body upright. His feeble voice was tainted with desperation. "What are we to do? This man has been performing many miracles. Soon, crowds of people will go out to see Lazarus alive again, and then believe on this Jesus."

A brown-bearded man several positions away thrust both hands in the air, frustration evident. "If we let him alone to go on like this, everyone will believe in him."

A third man directly across the semi-circle stood, his voice very loud. "Yes, and when that happens, the Romans will destroy us and our way of life."

As they spoke, Caiaphas strode to the center, raised platform, his chest puffed. He made a contemptible face while he waited for them to give him their undivided attention. When they were quiet, he thundered, "You know nothing at all. Don't you understand, it is more expedient and better for your welfare that one man should die on behalf of the people than that the whole nation should be destroyed and ruined?"

The elderly councilman still standing countered, "But we do not have the authority to kill anyone. Only the Romans can do that."

Caiaphas sneered. "Then we will get the Romans to kill him."

"But how?"

"We will tell them the carpenter is setting himself up as a king against Caesar. They can't—and won't—tolerate that."

The brown-bearded councilman nodded with an evil tightening of his lips. "When are you going to do it?"

"As soon as we can find out exactly where he is. Certainly before Passover."

CHAPTER FORTY-NINE

After Perez had charged off to fetch Justus more matrices, Michal and Justus decided to take a break from their searching.

Michal watched Justus as she settled onto a bench near the oven Abigail used to bake their bread in the covered courtyard. The afternoon air held a chill, so she leaned toward the oven's warmth. She smiled, remembering Justus' story of what had happened at Bethany. It had sounded farfetched, but she had come to respect Justus' honesty and attention to details so much she accepted the incredible idea Jesus could bring a dead man back to life. Clearly, Justus was having a hard time believing something he did not understand.

Justus joined her opposite the oven. As he sat, he asked, "Were you surprised when Perez offered to get the new matrices for us?"

Michal shook the hair from her face and gave him an unemotional glance. "Not really. He's the one who was told to get the others for Asher."

"I think we need to be careful around him. I'm unsure who is involved in this intrigue, and . . ."

Justus was interrupted by Jehu and Attai invading the courtyard. Jehu nodded tersely and removed his helmet. "Honorable Justus . . ."

Justus grimaced. "So . . . you've learned I'm a Roman advocate."

"Yes, Chief Advocate."

Justus gave a grim sigh. "Why have you come?"

Attai stood behind Jehu at attention, his spear anchored on the ground by a clenched fist with the point toward the courtyard's roof.

Jehu motioned toward Attai. "This is one of my best men, Attai."

Justus mocked by swinging his hand at Michal. "And this is my best friend, Michal."

Michal was pleased with Justus' parody, but maintained a stony glare.

Jehu didn't seem to notice Justus' insolence. "I thought it time to give you the status of our investigation."

"It's about time. What have you learned?"

"I asked Attai to interview all the gate guards to determine if they remembered anything strange between Yom Kippur and Hanukkah." Jehu turned to Attai and motioned for him to speak.

Attai's voice was firm, his look frosty. "During that period, only three reported anything mildly unusual."

Justus asked, "What was unusual?"

"In the middle of the Festival of Tabernacles, a hooded man entered the Mercy Gate, trying to not be noticed. Shortly after Yom Kippur, a veiled man left the Dung Gate in a wagon late at night."

Michal showed interest. "What was in the wagon?"

"Only a large tent cloth."

Michal eyed him with a determination. "Was anything under the tent cloth?"

"Our gate guards do not search wagons leaving and seldom those coming in." Attai hesitated momentarily and inhaled deeply when no one asked further questions. "The same guard saw the lead servant of the newly appointed high priest stop by the guard's fire to light a torch several nights in a row after Yom Kippur. And lastly, the guard of the Water Gate observed a servant of a chief priest riding into the city on a horse."

Michal was angry. "Which priest?"

"Chief Priest Annas," Attai replied.

Michal and Justus swapped questioning looks.

Justus asked, "Why is that so unusual?"

"Although it occasionally happens, servants aren't usually allowed to ride their masters' horses."

Michal bit the inside of her cheek. *That's probably when he was returning from Greece without Miriam.*

Justus glanced at Michal, then turned to Attai. "What about the hooded man?"

"We think it was the Nazarene carpenter."

Michal murmured to Justus, "The middle of the festival is too late, for we found Miriam near the festival's end."

Justus nodded. "Of course, you are right." He eyed Jehu. "What do you intend to do next?"

A bird flew near the four, carrying grass to a corner under the courtyard roof where it was building a nest.

Jehu nonchalantly raised his eyebrows. "Well, that's why we came. We do not think the information obtained from our gate guards leads anywhere. So Attai is going to Shechem to examine the tomb in which Miriam was held captive and search for the old man who fed her."

"And?"

"We thought you might want to go."

Justus looked surprised. He shook his head. "Umm . . . no . . . I couldn't possibly go."

Michal marveled at his words and touched his arm, the feeling of adventure seizing her. "I think it's a wonderful idea. It would be fun to conduct the investigation ourselves."

"But you know we have research here."

Michal playfully shook his arm. "Silly, Perez said it would be a couple of weeks before the scribes finished with your request."

Jehu's eyes half closed.

Justus looked excited and put his hand to his chin. "I have been involved in numerous investigations . . . and this one is in Shechem, not Jerusalem." He shrugged. "Why not?"

Jehu leaned in, curiosity showing. "Do you think you could talk Miriam into going? If we find the old man, she could identify him."

Michal didn't think twice. "Of course."

"Good. Attai will meet you at the Herod gate shortly after dawn tomorrow."

Jehu put on his helmet and led Attai from the courtyard.

Justus stared at them until they disappeared, and turned to Michal. "You committed Miriam pretty quickly. How do you know she will want to go?"

Michal gave a sly grin. "Julius is leaving for Shechem first thing in the morning. I'm sure she will jump at a reason to accompany him."

❯ ❯ ❯

Attai and Jehu trooped side by side, neither speaking for fifteen minutes. When the Temple came into sight, they were still alone. Attai grew an impish grin. He slanted a glance toward Jehu and spoke in a low voice. "They took the bait."

CHAPTER FIFTY

Deep within the catacombs, Malchus had two dirt-filled buckets tied to a pole across his shoulders. His muscles bulged, but he groaned as the pole bent under the load and hit first one wall of the tunnel then the other. In the flickering light of torches on the walls, he shuffled down the corridor to the pit where he dumped his excavations. He had been down here every night for two weeks. Bukki almost never came down here. Only twice had the size of the hole changed from when he had left it.

Malchus propped himself against the corridor wall to catch his breath. The silence of the catacombs engulfed him, and the musky smell was stronger with each breath. He wiped away sweat with the back of his hand. Maybe it was a good thing Bukki didn't come often. Malchus wanted to search the new catacombs himself. He had the clues, but if there were only a few tombs behind the wall, Bukki might accidentally find Melchizedek's Tomb first . . . then what about his freedom?

▸ ▸ ▸

With a large bag slung over his shoulder, Jehu followed the maid through the foyer to the stairs of the odd-shaped house that was Sethur's home.

She stopped and pointed down the stairs. "Master Sethur is in the main part of the house. He is expecting you."

This was the first time Jehu had visited Sethur's home. He looked in wonder at the stairs made from hewn stone that descended five steps to a room below. The walls and ceiling around the staircase were like a short chute from the upper rooms to the lower ones.

The maid exited through a side door to an open courtyard outside. *And I thought it looked strange from the outside.* Jehu shook his head in disbelief and hurried down.

The large room at the bottom had two doors on either side of the opposite wall, but no windows. Several lamps were strategically placed around the room. Two were on shelves, head-high. Two were along the wall opposite from the stairs, and one was on an inverted barrel close to where Sethur was working. All were burning, which filled the closed room with considerable light and a heavy aroma of combusted oil.

Sethur looked up from examining a scroll, his pointed nose even more prominent when knotted by intense study. His brown hair was matted from wearing a head covering, which had been carelessly discarded onto the floor by the barrel. The scroll lay on a large, flat stand, a duplicate of one of the four Asher had used in the Temple. Sethur's small stature worked to his advantage, as he could study the scroll without bending over.

Recognizing Jehu, his expression became pleasant. "Welcome Jehu. Do you have the strips?"

Jehu lifted the bag from his shoulder, causing his cloak to fall over his leather breastplate. He had a look of victory. "Where do you want them?"

"Here, on the table."

Jehu opened the bag and poured out many long, thin strips of various widths of acacia wood onto the table. "The exact sizes Asher cut."

Sethur's lips thinned as he scrutinized the pile. "And the same number."

"Exactly."

Sethur clutched a few and studied them, visibly excited. "I wonder how Asher came up with this ingenious way to reduce the time it takes to search the scrolls."

"I have no idea."

Sethur began to sort the wooden strips by width. "When will Attai and the Roman return?"

Smug, Jehu replied, "Probably in about four days. But, it doesn't matter. I'm finished going through Asher's house. We have all the information we need . . ."

"Except how they will examine the new matrices," Sethur interrupted.

"Yes, of course. But we have Abigail."

Sethur nodded, said nothing, and continued to finger the wooden strips.

Jehu's nearly black hair fell around his shoulders as he pulled off his helmet. He asked, "How soon will those matrices be finished?"

Sethur waved at the large stack of papyrus on the stand between them. "All the 49 x 49 ones are done, including my copy. The 121 x 121 sheets are taking longer. We had to stitch the membranes together to make them big enough to accommodate the large number of rows and columns. My copy should be completed right before the Roman gets back; his shortly afterwards."

Jehu scanned the pile of panels and looked puzzled. "How many pages are there?"

"Thirty-two for me and thirty-two for the Roman."

"And the large ones?"

"Only six each."

Jehu wrapped one arm around his helmet as he converged on the sixty-four sheets, his expression one of confusion. "How is it a scribe takes a year to create a Torah scroll, but can do these so quickly?"

Sethur beamed at the inquiry. "There are extreme requirements when generating a Torah, but none of them apply to this exercise. An error in a Torah scroll invalidates the entire text, but these are merely working copies, so errors can be corrected at the point where they occur. I have gathered three scribes to do the copying and they are working in shifts. Besides, we are only copying Genesis, not the entire Torah."

CHAPTER FIFTY-ONE

Justus felt depressed as he and Michal relaxed on a bench under the covered porch of the same inn at Shechem where they had stayed after rescuing Miriam. The gentle rain and dark skies didn't help his mood.

They'd learned nothing since arriving eight days ago. Every lead had turned into a dead end. They couldn't find the old man. Only three houses were empty, and none had anything suggesting their former occupants had anything to do with the kidnapping. A complete search of the tomb revealed no clues. Nobody in the area of the cave saw anything out of the ordinary. The tracks of the wagon and footprints were both nondescript.

Justus glanced at Michal, looking gloomy. "We've wasted a week."

Michal leaned against the wall behind her and gave a half-smile. "Not totally. You see how close Julius and Miriam are now."

Justus caught the fact she was being soft on him, so he tried to shake off the influence of melancholy. He watched water trickle from the slanted porch roof and nodded. "You're right. Julius has helped Miriam through her grief, so the trip is not totally wasted."

A man with a young boy darted across the street to the shelter of the porch. They wiped away excess rain and crossed in front of Justus and Michal on their way to the inn's entrance.

Michal waited until the two were inside before asking, "Do you think the sheets are finished with the matrices?"

Justus glanced at her. "They should be by the time we get back to Jerusalem."

"When are we leaving?"

He shifted in his seat and focused on her question. "Tomorrow."

"Good. Explain this business about reinforcements to me."

Justus gave a loud exhale. "Pilate is afraid there may be problems in Jerusalem because of the large influx of pilgrims and the dissension caused by Jesus' followers. So he has directed Julius to bring additional troops during Passover. Julius told me he is bringing some from Shechem and Ephraim."

"So he and Miriam are returning with us to Jerusalem?"

"Yes."

Michal hopped up, grabbed one of his hands, and pulled. Grinning, she said, "Let's go find the two lovebirds."

❡ ❡ ❡

In the covered courtyard, Abigail held a steaming piece of lamb on a spit she had just removed from over the fire. The smell of the simmering meat could almost be tasted as she offered it to Perez.

Her forty-five-year-old face appeared years older because of its drawn features and the mole under her left eye. She had enjoyed the time she was able to spend with Perez. Happiness enveloped her as she watched him eat. "Did you finish the hole through the wall after Jehu left?"

Perez sat on a bench, his feet stretched toward the open fire. "Yes. Now I'll be able to overhear everything said in Asher's front room. I'm glad Jehu tricked everyone into going to Shechem for a few days."

Abigail moved to Perez's back and began kneading his shoulder muscles. "Hadn't you almost finished anyway?"

"No, I could only work on it when the house was empty. Even then, I had to be very quiet so the door guards wouldn't overhear me. But with everyone gone to Shechem, it was simple."

Abigail leaned her cheek close to Perez's, a few locks of red hair falling from her shawl onto his neck. "Won't they see it?"

Perez glanced sideways and gave a soft snort. "My calculations were perfect. The hole is right above a shelf with a lamp and a Star of David ornament behind it. It is concealed very well."

Abigail sat beside Perez and looked lovingly at him. "I'm proud of you. You are so resourceful." A gust of wind blew through the covered courtyard and fanned the flames near her. She brushed ash away and smiled at Perez.

He stood, traced a line with two fingers down the side of Abigail's cheek, and picked a small branch from the ground near the fire. "Did Jehu obtain copies of all the wooden pieces?"

Abigail rose and stood close to Perez, but glanced toward the closed front door. "I know he measured them all. I assume he made the copies."

Perez used the branch to stir the fire and push burning sticks together. He dropped the branch into the flames. The two focused on the blaze for some time, lost in their thoughts.

Abigail held one of Perez's hands and whispered, "Once we hear the location, who do we tell first?"

Perez scratched the back of his head with his free hand. "Jehu, I guess."

"Why?"

"He will involve fewer people than Annas will."

CHAPTER FIFTY-TWO

The courtyard in front of the chief priest's palace was spacious and well maintained. Its beauty accentuated the palace. In addition, it offered a somewhat private area for the chief priest to contemplate religious matters or to hold small meetings with other priests and city elders. This day it would hold an informal meeting of the Sanhedrin, the first since Kore revealed Jesus' activities at Bethany.

As Annas made his way through the numerous plants, trees, and budding flowers, Caiaphas watched his progress. They had spent a week perfecting their plan, but Caiaphas was not taking a chance the Sanhedrin wouldn't buy into it. He had arranged this impromptu meeting at a time when his most vocal opponents could not come. In addition, he had made certain three of his strongest allies attended: Elon, Machir, and Zerah. The net effect was that only forty members were present, but they formed an agreeable majority.

The courtyard was easily large enough to accommodate the assembly; however, only enough benches were sprinkled about the garden to allow seating for half of the attendees. The oldest chose to sit. A few younger men leaned against larger ornamental stones, but the remainder simply stood. A nearby mustard bush was showing the start of multiple green leafs.

Caiaphas was poised at the top of the stairs to his palace, magnifying his average height and easily seen by all. He gave a grim sigh, as Annas' arrival was their prearranged cue to begin. He loudly cleared his throat for everyone's attention and held the bearing of a king. "Thank you for coming," he said. "Not long ago, you agreed the Nazarene carpenter, named Jesus, should be killed. I asked you all to come today so we could discuss and finalize plans to accomplish this."

Annas had intentionally taken a spot behind most of the group, effectively bounding them between him and Caiaphas. He placed his hand on a tree next to him and began the script. "The Passover Festival starts in six days. I think we must do it before then."

Machir stood one person from Annas. He was tall, and his massive frame was not concealed by the long robe of a priest. He appeared surprised. "Why?"

Annas stood straight and swept both hands from his midriff out. "I don't think we should do it during the feast. Many pilgrims will be here. You know how mobs react. Who knows where a riot might lead."

Caiaphas was pleased with the initial interchange, but faked a deep frown. "Annas is right. We must do it before the feast starts."

Standing to the left of Annas, Elon took a half step forward and countered, "Six days is not much time." Elon was always finding problems where there were none.

Caiaphas scowled at him.

Annas shrugged. "Of course, you are right. However, if we finalize the plan today, we only need to find the Nazarene when there are few people around."

One of the oldest and most pliable members of the Sanhedrin, Zerah, gave Caiaphas a startled look from his perch on a bench directly in front of the stairs. "How do you intend to find him like that?"

Caiaphas wrestled against showing a smug expression, but lost. "Actually, I think I have a way. Let's not dwell on finding him, but on what we'll do afterward."

All attention moved to Annas as he spoke quickly to prevent interruptions. "At the Sanhedrin meeting we decided to convince Pontius Pilate the Nazarene is trying to become king. If we can prove this, Pilate will have to kill him or incur the wrath of Caesar. We must interrogate everyone we know to find his specific words which imply he wants to be king."

Caiaphas pointed above their heads, his voice authoritative. "After collecting evidence and obtaining witnesses, you must be prepared to assemble the council at a moment's notice. Remember . . . the testimonies must be sufficient to convince Pilate to kill the Nazarene."

Zerah looked back at Annas from under bushy white eyebrows, his voice devious. "I know of two who say the Nazarene claims he'll destroy the Temple and raise it up in three days. I'll make sure they're ready to testify."

Machir took an exaggerated step in Caiaphas' direction, his sandal crushing a fallen sparrow's nest. His voice was loud. "This is a great plan. It's sure to work." He glanced around to draw confirmation from the rest of the crowd. Machir had a gift for bringing people into agreement. Caiaphas had brought him here for that very purpose. "The Romans will conclude if a carpenter is crazy enough to think he can build a temple in three days, he is crazy enough to attempt to be a king."

Some whispered to friends, and others stroked their beards. Many of them nodded.

Caiaphas desired to end the meeting with no opposition, so his voice became authoritative. "Now go. The hour may be soon. Hurry."

The priests haphazardly filtered from the courtyard.

Machir drifted toward Caiaphas. He paused and smiled vilely. "I think you have found a permanent solution," he said, then picked up his pace to join Elon.

Caiaphas nodded to Machir and descended the stairs as Machir left.

During their exchange, Zerah had worked his way to Annas. He straightened his bent frame as much as possible. "Make sure those testimonies agree."

"Of course."

Zerah shuffled off.

In only minutes, Zerah, the last to depart, had disappeared.

Alone, Caiaphas moved to Annas.

Annas exhaled long and loud. "That went better than I expected."

"Nicodemus and Joseph weren't here. That helped."

"How true."

An evil grin pulled up one side of Caiaphas' lips, and he clenched Annas' arm. "I want you to meet someone."

Annas looked dubious but went along. They arced around a palm tree to a small room in the back, of the palace.

Although the room was dimly lit, inside was a thin, rugged man. He wore coarse clothing and had black, curly hair with a matching beard. The man's muscles were taut. Like a caged animal, his eyes darted from window to door as though judging the best escape.

Annas shot a questioning look at Caiaphas. "Am I supposed to know this man?"

"On the contrary, I doubt you have ever seen him. His name is Judas. He is a disciple of Jesus."

Annas looked shocked. "What does he want?"

Caiaphas paused for effect, enjoying the loss of his father-in-law's composure. "He wants to take us to Jesus."

Annas' jaw yawned opened. He stared at the man.

Now Judas flashed from Annas to Caiaphas. "What will you pay me if I take you to him?"

Annas glanced at Caiaphas with a look of stark disbelief.

Caiaphas slanted his head, gauging the offer. His voice was condescending. "I think we would be willing to give you thirty pieces of silver."

Judas' head bowed as he looked at the ground. "That will be enough."

Annas stepped forward, menacingly. "We only want you to do this when there are few people around. Preferably not in the city."

Judas stole a glance and nodded. "I'll wait until the timing appears right, then come and tell you."

Annas radiated a new concern. "OK . . . but before the Passover feast begins."

Judas fidgeted and looked distressed. "All right . . . before the feast. May I go now?"

"Yes."

Judas bolted to the door. In his haste, he bumped a bench and knocked it to the floor with a loud thump. He slammed the door hard, and dust shot away from the door jam.

Annas stared at the entrance and spoke as though sleepwalking. "Who would have thought of this turn of events?"

"Amazing, isn't it?" Caiaphas beamed as he rubbed his palms together. "Nearly perfect timing. Judas tells us the Nazarene's location; we capture him, try him, and turn him over to Pilate for execution."

Annas' lips crinkled. "And without disrupting the Passover Festival. Hmm . . . who will lead the capture?"

"Malchus, of course."

Annas' thoughts crashed back to the Tomb search, accompanied by a look of consternation. "Has he found the Salem catacombs yet?"

"No, but he will be under the wall by tomorrow." Caiaphas' mood changed as he leaned close. "However, we have a more pressing problem to address."

Annas finally came fully awake. "What kind of problem?" he asked.

Grim, Caiaphas spoke in a metered tone. "The Roman chief advocate must not be around when we arrest Jesus. All we need is for the procurator to tap the services of Rome's finest advocate to defend the carpenter."

CHAPTER FIFTY-THREE

Michal, Justus, Miriam, and Julius dismounted their horses at the stables near the Roman garrison's quarters at Jerusalem. The one hundred soldiers they had led from Shechem and Ephraim remained mounted. The sun was directly above them, eliminating all shadows except for slivers here and there.

Julius' tone sounded gruff and official. "Honorable Justus, I must notify the procurator we have arrived and obtain his deployment instructions. Please accompany Miriam to her house. I will send a guard detail as soon as I understand plans for our reinforcements."

"As you wish," Justus formally responded.

Giving Miriam a slight wave, Julius remounted and proceeded toward the Antonia Fortress, his entire troop following two by two. The snorts of two horses sounded above the clomping hoofs.

Miriam grinned and waved back. She stared at the processional until the last soldier passed by and the hoofbeats had died down, appearing ready to burst from excitement. "Do you know what Julius asked me?"

A strong breeze whipped Michal's hair back as she gave a pleasant laugh. "No what?"

Miriam appeared close to floating. "Since all the soldiers will be on duty the entire week of the Passover festival, Pilate has invited his top troop commanders to a dinner tomorrow night with him and his wife. Julius invited me to go."

Michal squeezed Miriam's arm, beaming. "That sounds like fun."

Justus contemplated their exchange, nostalgia sweeping over him. "Miriam, you'll have a great time." He took Michal's hand in his with perfect ease. "Let's go to Miriam's house and start searching scrolls."

The trio moved at a brisk pace along the familiar streets, weaving through uncommonly heavy pedestrian traffic. In fifteen minutes they entered the covered courtyard where Abigail was kneading bread.

Perez was stacking small logs of firewood. He saw them first and expressed friendliness. "Welcome back. Did you find out anything?"

Justus approached the fire and grimaced. "That part of the trip was a total waste."

Miriam went directly to Abigail, her manner showing excitement. "I know you have been working on a new tunica. Is it nearly finished? I'm going to a dinner with Julius at the fortress tomorrow night, and it would be nice to wear it."

Perez looked in wonder.

Abigail rose, wiping her hands on a coarse cloth towel. "My lady, that is exciting news. Not only have I finished the tunica, I've almost finished a new robe. I can complete it by tomorrow. Come and see if they are acceptable."

The three women went into the house, Abigail still holding an earthenware bowl with the bread dough inside it.

Justus watched the door close. He glanced at four men treading the street by the house as he spoke to Perez. "Have the scrolls been delivered?"

Perez focused again on the woodpile. "No, they won't be here until tomorrow."

Justus couldn't believe his ears. "Why haven't they been finished?"

Perez balked and assumed a more formal appearance. "Sir, the scribes needed to stitch sheets of papyrus together for the matrices of 121 x 121 letters. That required a little extra time. I have been told they are laboring night and day."

Justus wasn't even vaguely convinced. "But they were supposed to be done two days ago."

Perez looked away. "I'm sorry, sir."

Justus glared into the fire, his disappointment playing out in anger simmering below the surface. Smoke curled up a short distance, then hit the brisk flow of air through the open area and disappeared.

Perez remained upright with no eye contact for a long time until the silence became deafening. "I guess you didn't hear about your friend?"

Justus felt disgusted as he slanted a glance at Perez. "What friend?"

"Jesus."

Justus' stomach tightened. "What about Jesus?"

"Day before yesterday, a vast crowd of the Passover pilgrims heard Jesus was coming into the city. So, they went out to meet him."

A shiver coursed up Justus' back, his countenance guarded. "And . . . he spoke to them there?"

"He wasn't teaching this time. He was riding on the back of a donkey colt."

Justus looked incredulous. "Why was he riding a donkey?"

"I'm not sure, but the people cut palm branches and laid them in the path of the colt. As he rode over them the people kept shouting over and over, 'Blessed is He and praise be to Him Who comes in the name of the Lord, even the King of Israel'!"

Justus felt nauseated. "Were you there?"

Perez was surprisingly engaged. "Actually, I did go."

"Were any Jewish authorities there?"

"Many. A Pharisee near me yelled at Jesus to instruct his disciples to stop saying the chant."

Justus felt a deeper chill. "And how did Jesus answer?"

"He answered, 'If my disciples remained silent, the very stones would cry out'."

Justus moved to a nearby bench and slumped onto it. "What happened then?"

"I'm sorry. The crowd was so large I really couldn't see much after Jesus continued toward the city. I later heard he stopped before entering the gate and wept over Jerusalem, but I have no idea why." Perez canted his head. "Why are you so worried?"

Justus said, "This will make the Pharisees and Sadducees desperate . . . and . . . desperate men do desperate things."

Michal bounded out of the house, her concern evident. "I see the sheets are not yet here."

Justus grimaced. "Perez has informed me they will not be delivered until tomorrow."

"That stinks."

"Umm."

Michal tilted her head, her expression confused. "What's wrong?"

Justus stood and stepped close to the fire. "I'll tell you later."

She was unsmiling. "Well, I've got a question."

Justus glanced at Michal, surprised by the harshness in her voice. "And what would that be?"

She stared at him for a few moments trying not to smile. "You told me a little while back it would be easy to find the Salem catacombs."

"Yes . . . it likely will be."

Michal raised her frame to a faked haughty position. "How could it be so easy . . . Mr. Catacomb?"

Justus laughed out loud, her playfulness washing away his depressed mood. "Instead of telling you, why don't I just show you?"

Michal swung her fist down across her body, unable to resist a grin. "Done."

Justus twisted to Perez, who had returned to stacking logs and was about finished. "Is there a mallet and a long rod somewhere around this house?"

In his best servant's tone, he replied, "Yes, I have a mallet. The Roman detachment left some tent pegs at the back of the house." He paused his work to look at Justus. "But why do you want them?"

Justus wrapped his arm around Michal's waist and looked deep. "I'm going to demonstrate the finer points of catacomb construction."

CHAPTER FIFTY-FOUR

Two hours had passed while Justus collected lamps, extra oil, the mallet, and a tent peg. The hike from Miriam's house had taken little time, but the afternoon had nearly slipped away.

Justus and Michal were poised in the subterranean foyer of the Jerusalem catacombs, their lamps causing light to dance on the rough walls leading into the caverns. The city wall blocked all but a faint glimmer of daylight down the entry shaft. A dank, musky smell wafted by them on the cool breeze rushing from the caverns up the stairs to the entrance above.

Miriam had chosen to remain with Abigail and finish the robe she would wear when accompanying Julius to Pilate's dinner.

Michal moved close to Justus and gazed at him, her voice eager. "Will it really be easy to find the Salem catacombs?"

Justus grinned as he returned her look. "Actually . . . very."

Michal took his hand and pulled him. "Then let's go."

Justus moved with her, but resisted her speed. "Hey . . . we need to be deliberate."

Michal whirled back. "What do you mean?"

"When you explore catacombs, you need to take certain measures so you won't get lost."

Michal angled her head toward her right shoulder and gave a slight frown. "Oh . . . like what?"

Justus moved in front of her, still holding her hand. He drew her to him. "Come on . . . I'll show you the Lazy V technique."

"The Lazy V?"

Holding his lamp high, Justus led Michal along the passageway to an intersection. Using the tent pole, he marked > on the wall at eye level.

Michal inspected it, still showing no understanding.

Justus gave a cheery smile, but his soft tone was explanatory. "The small part denotes the direction you are going into the catacombs. The open part denotes the direction to go out. Even if you get turned around, when you find a > mark, you'll always know which way to go."

Recognition swept Michal, but quickly gave way to a teasing look. "What if someone follows you and reverses the mark?"

Justus laughed. He shook his head but said nothing.

Michal's expression changed again to determination. "We're deliberate now. Let's find the Salem catacombs." She pushed Justus forward. "How will you know when we have found it?"

Justus advanced slowly. "When hewers connect newer catacombs to the ancient ones, the difference in ceiling height is significant. We merely need to find a vertical shaft near the northern wall."

They threaded their way through five corridors, Justus marking each one. Coming to an intersection resembling a Y, Justus glanced back at Michal. "I think this way is north. Let's see how far we can go."

❧ ❧ ❧

Malchus' hole was ten feet deep. He had brought a ladder with him a week earlier, suspecting he would need to burrow farther down than he was tall.

His excitement had him digging earlier and earlier each day. Today he had been able to start long before the sun set, but he struggled against fatigue as he worked the dirt-filled pail up the ladder he'd braced opposite the city wall's foundation.

Reaching the floor of the corridor, he pushed the wooden pail next to the one he had taken from the hole a few minutes earlier. He sat catching his breath, sweat beading on his brow. He must be close to the base of the foundation. His worst fear was that it was set on solid rock.

He flinched as he heard a sound. What was that? He jumped up, his heart pounding. He took two short steps from the wall and froze, his ears straining. A faint murmur floated through the tunnel. Malchus' pulse raced as he snatched the lamp, plunged into an adjoining tunnel, and extinguished it. He hugged the wall, trying to quiet his heaving chest. Although he couldn't see it, he could smell the curling smoke from the wick. He fanned the air.

The footsteps became louder and a man's voice said, "Would you look at this?"

A woman answered. "That's fresh. Someone is filling this hole with dirt and rocks."

"Just the type of vertical hole a hewer would use to connect ancient catacombs to this one."

Malchus couldn't believe the words. *No . . . I have been filling in the entrance to the Salem catacombs.*

The lady spoke again, "I think I see something farther down."

Malchus watched as the intersecting tunnel became brighter. He only had a glimpse of the two intruders as they passed, but immediately recognized Justus. Perez had pointed him out one day when Justus visited Jehu at the Temple guard's station. He inched his way to the opening and peeked after them. He was sure the woman was with Justus at Asher's funeral, but had not caught her name.

The maiden commented, "Hmm . . . what is that?"

Justus replied, "Here's where the dirt in the pit came from. Looks like someone is trying to get to the corridor on the other side of the wall. Apparently, he thinks this corridor goes to the Salem catacombs and won't let the wall stop him."

Malchus stifled a gasp. They knew of the Salem catacombs. He ducked back from the opening as the woman turned and spoke. "I wonder if he . . . or they . . . are still here."

"I doubt it," was Justus' reply.

Malchus moved his head as close to the opening as possible without being seen and angled his ear to hear better. His fear of being caught was being replaced by thirst for information Justus might have about the Salem catacombs.

Justus' companion spoke. "Shall we use the shovel here to empty the pit?"

Justus laughed. "If this is the only place people are digging and filling in holes, it won't be a problem."

Malchus leaned far from the wall, straining to hear.

"Why not?" the female voice asked.

"My grandfather told me hewers always had more than one connection to old catacombs—usually several. They never knew when one might collapse, so they had to make more than one way out."

Malchus' jaw dropped. His grandfather?

"Well . . . let's try to find another one."

Malchus was too close to the intersection to hide, so he risked making noise and tiptoed deeper into the adjoining tunnel as he heard sandals slapping the tunnel floor approaching him. Again, he froze back against the damp wall and watched the light get brighter, then blink by as the duo passed his hiding place.

After only seconds, he stealthily trailed them, back far enough so they wouldn't hear him but close enough so he could see where they went.

After only two turns he heard Justus' voice. "Aha. Here's another pit."

The woman answered. "There is nothing down there. The hole just stops . . . It doesn't connect anything."

Malchus pulled up closer than he should, but his craving to learn if Justus knew the secret of finding the Salem catacombs made him reckless. He watched as Justus began to disappear down the hole and heard him speak to the woman.

"Follow me down these steps, and I'll show you why we have a hammer and tent stake."

Justus' head completely disappeared, and his partner began to follow. As she did, Malchus worked his way closer to the pit, little by little. The light beaming up from the hole guided him. He stopped at the edge where he could just barely watch them at the bottom and remain nearly hidden.

Justus held the mallet and tent pole inches from the girl. "Observe." Pivoting to the wall, he placed the pole onto it and pounded hard with the mallet. The pole bounced back off solid rock.

CHAPTER FIFTY-FOUR

His companion moved back to a safer distance.

Justus moved the pole to another location about a foot from his original placement, and hammered hard. Again, the pole bounced off solid rock.

The lady sighed with impatience.

He moved the tent peg to a third place and struck it again. This time the pole went deeply into the side of the pit.

The lass gasped. "What does that mean?" she asked.

Justus turned his head and grinned. "It means we've found a sealed off entrance to the Salem catacombs."

Malchus labored to remain absolutely silent and gawked at Justus, who continued moving and hitting the pole until he had outlined a stone. He pushed heavily and the stone fell in, landing on the other side. Justus repeated the procedure until he had an opening just big enough to squeeze through.

Malchus struggled to keep his breathing quiet as he watched Justus disappear through the newly formed entrance. He clearly heard a muffled voice drift back.

"Wow . . . the Salem catacombs are even further down."

CHAPTER FIFTY-FIVE

Unable to sleep, Malchus paced the palace courtyard in the light of a blazing fire another servant had built. He played Justus' words over and over. He couldn't believe Justus had so easily found the Salem catacombs and then so nonchalantly led the woman away without exploring them. What a fool. Had Malchus known how to find an entrance to the older catacombs, he could have searched the entire Salem catacombs by now.

The sun finally topped the eastern city wall, making it an acceptable time to call on the high priest. He bolted to the palace door.

Beulah, the maid, opened the door. She was short, the same age as Malchus, but graying hair visible in the front of her shawl. They had served Caiaphas' father together until he died. She smiled. "I will notify Master Caiaphas you are here. Wait in the courtyard."

Malchus returned the smile, nodded, and circled back into the open area, burning to talk to Caiaphas.

The morning was beautiful with no clouds. Though the night had been very cool, Malchus felt warm as he sat on a stone in the garden with the sun beaming on him. The warmness, however, did little to thaw his thoughts or warm his emotions.

Caiaphas approached Malchus, pompousness in his stride.

Malchus shot to attention.

"Have you found the Salem catacombs?" Caiaphas demanded.

Malchus swallowed hard, a rising feeling of frustration slowly gripped him. He had so much to say that he was having difficulty knowing where to start. "In a way."

"What do you mean by that?"

"I was working in the catacombs late yesterday afternoon when the Roman and his girlfriend came down."

Caiaphas appeared grim. "What were they doing there?"

"Hunting for the Salem catacomb connection."

Caiaphas reeled back. "How do they know?"

Malchus blurted out, "The Roman told the woman his grandfather was a tomb hewer."

Caiaphas blinked several times. "A tomb hewer?" he hissed.

"Yes, and that's just the beginning. They found the hole I was digging and where I was putting the dirt."

Appearing entranced, Caiaphas waited.

"The Roman said I was filling in the entrance to the Salem catacombs."

Caiaphas took an ominous step toward Malchus. "What?"

"Yes, he said the dumping pit is a connection to the Salem catacombs. But, he didn't appear concerned about it. They merely found another one."

Caiaphas jaw dropped as he pondered Malchus' words.

Malchus waited a courteous moment, but couldn't contain his excitement. He rapid-fired the rest. "He descended to the bottom of the pit and beat around on the wall. He traced a stone and pushed it in. He did several more the same way until a small opening was formed." Malchus took a deep inhale. "I saw him enter, but as he came back out, I rushed to a hiding place. After they left, I went through the opening the Roman made." Malchus' complexion radiated. "I was in the Salem catacombs!"

Caiaphas bore in on him. "So they really exist?"

"I went in far enough to tell they are ancient. A thick layer of very fine dust covers everything." Malchus kicked a stone. "If I had just asked Heber, the hewer, how people connected catacombs, I might have been able to save weeks in the search. I might have found the Tomb by now."

Caiaphas held up his hands. "Quiet. I don't want all of Jerusalem to hear you."

Malchus realized he had nearly crossed the line and bowed his head, assuming a servant's demeanor. He needed support from his master more now than ever before.

Caiaphas continued in a calmer tone, "When will you start searching?"

"Tonight and every night until I find the Tomb."

Caiaphas frowned, squinted, and turned away. "No."

Malchus' head shot up. "Why not?"

Even though no one was in the courtyard, Caiaphas looked over it and pivoted back. He took on a crafty look. "I want you to wait until the Passover."

Malchus couldn't believe his ears. "But why?"

"I have something very important for you to do." Caiaphas placed a hand to his chin and held it there. "I'm just not exactly sure when you are to do it."

➤ ➤ ➤

Jehu had been warned about Justus' return as soon as he arrived at the Temple guard's station that morning. He immediately ventured to Sethur's home to get a report of his success with the matrices. As he cleared the stairs to the main room, he demanded, "Have you been searching?"

His voice testy, Sethur replied, "My copies of the matrices were finished late night before last. I started examining them yesterday morning and I have worked on them non-stop. The other copy will be delivered to Miriam's house this morning."

"Have you found anything?"

Sethur gave a shrug of dissatisfaction. "No." He waved his palm in the direction of the wooden strips. "I have run across something puzzling, though."

Jehu stepped closer. "What is that?"

Sethur seemed hesitant. "Are you sure you made copies of every width of the acacia-wood strips?"

"Absolutely, why?"

"When the Roman was deciding on the 49 x 49 sized matrix his premise was hunting for a 7-letter word required 7 times 7 or 49 columns or rows. It's easy to see how a matrix such a size could be quickly searched using wooden strips with a width of 7."

"So?"

"Well, for the 121 x 121 sized matrices, I would expect he intended to search with wooden strips 11 letters wide, but the largest is 10."

Jehu nodded. "I see what you mean. However, I personally determined the exact size of all the wooden strips."

Sethur gazed into the middle distance. "I wonder why the Roman asked for the large matrices."

"I don't know, but he knows more than I have given him credit for."

Sethur looked interested. "What do you mean?"

"The Roman went to the catacombs yesterday with the woman. He took a mallet and a stake with him."

Sethur's expression tightened and he leaned on the large stand with one hand. "Then they know how catacomb connections are sealed."

CHAPTER FIFTY-SIX

Michal bent over one of the small matrices at the end of the large table. She had considered the idea of finding hidden truths in the Torah quaint at best, but finding the Salem catacombs the previous day had turned her thinking 180 degrees. She began to believe it truly was possible. Since Perez had delivered the papyrus sheets that morning, she actually identified several words, although she found no other words near them. It was beginning to resemble a treasure hunt to her, and a feeling of excitement simmered within her.

She turned to Justus on the other end of the table. "When did you realize the name *Melchizedek* had eleven letters in it?"

Justus stretched with one hand supporting his back. His tallness was working against him in this endeavor. He gazed at Michal and grinned. "Not until Perez was standing in the doorway eavesdropping and offered to get the 49 x 49 sized matrices."

"Quick math."

"I did count quickly in my head. I'm just glad I wasn't wrong. I'm sure quite a bit of work went into making these matrices."

As Michal relived the surprising scene, she became uneasy. "Did you notice he didn't even ask why you wanted the big ones?"

"Yes, I did. I'm certain he knows more than he's letting on. And isn't it interesting scribes were standing by on orders of a priest to fulfill a request from us?"

Michal nodded, and showed a knowing look. "Which says to me, the abduction could also have been ordered by a chief priest?"

Miriam flowed into the room wearing the new robe and tunic Abigail had made for her. Her uncovered hair was pulled back in a tight bun. Her eyes were lined with a popular Roman black accent. She wore a gold necklace, bracelets, and belt.

Michal moved her right hand up and down, like she was waving to her stomach, sideways. "Whoooooa . . . my, my, my, my my. Aren't we dressed for the kill?"

Miriam reddened. "Do you really think I look all right?"

"Spectacular."

A loud knock at the door was followed by Julius' voice. "Miriam, may I come in?"

"Please, do," Miriam responded.

Stepping through the door, Julius drew up abruptly with a look of wonder. "Miriam, you are beautiful."

She reddened more, as she glanced down then gave him an up-from-under look. "Thank you, Julius."

Julius bowed slightly and held his hand out. "Shall we go to Pilate's dinner?"

Miriam stepped forward and took his hand. Her smiling features were all the answer he got.

After they left, Justus gave the closed door a long, far-off look. "I'll bet I'm seeing a replay of my mother and father."

Michal chuckled. "I won't bet against that."

Justus bent over the large papyrus sheet and methodically moved several of the wooden strips.

Michal contemplated him for several moments, as she listened to the sounds of the door guards following Julius and Miriam. In only moments, the only sound was the click of wood as Justus laid strips on the sheet. She marveled at how quickly he could search the uncovered letters. "Have you found anything yet?"

Justus flashed her a displeased glance. "I find words every once in a while, but they have nothing to do with Melchizedek's Tomb. Even then, I haven't found any other words close by. What about you?"

"Same thing. How many of the sheets have you examined?"

"All but one."

Michal exhaled loudly through open lips. "You're fast. How do you do it?"

Justus replied, "I would be finished by now, but using a 10-letter strip plus a 1-letter strip to skip 11 letters slows things down."

Michal stared at the pile of 49 x 49 matrices with a sinking feeling. "I've spent the entire day and have only searched five sheets. There must be thirty here."

"Hmm . . . thirty-two to be exact."

Michal grimaced, but went back to the sheet in front of her. She pushed a strip over the rough lines of pressed pith. Having placed it in sequence, she stared, her fingers tapping.

A half hour passed, and Justus completed his search of the last large sheet. He trudged to a bench and slumped onto it, appearing dejected. "There's nothing. I guess my theory was wrong."

Michal looked up as she heard the defeat in his voice. "Maybe we will find something in the other matrices." She joined him on the bench and sat a little closer than usual.

They lounged quietly a few moments, gazing dreamily at the items on the stand.

Justus gave a bleak sigh. "Maybe I'm losing the ability to piece to-gether puzzles."

Michal turned to him, measuring the depth of his defeat. Her voice was soft. "Have you really examined all possible combinations of the letters?"

Justus gaped at her as if she had gone mad. "You saw me work on them the entire day."

"I know you examined them all day, but did you look at all combinations?"

Justus' voice was edgy. "I used all the wooden strips like Asher did. I found nothing."

One hand came to her mouth. She placed a finger across to her lips with her thumb under her chin. "Do you remember when you told me how you really wanted to search the Torah?"

Justus shook his head. He spread his hands out palm up. "There aren't enough scribes in the world to keep changing the row size based on how many equal distant skips it takes to find a given . . ."

Michal placed her hand in front of Justus mouth. "No, not that part. The other part."

Justus' teeth clenched. "What other part?"

"The part about rolling the sheet to form a tube."

Justus roughly pushed Michal's hand away. "But we can't roll the sheets into a tube with wooden strips . . ." Suddenly, he stopped. He leaped to the tall stand. His hands were trembling. "I'll start with the second one. It has the plaintext story about Melchizedek on it."

Justus covered columns 2 through12, left the next column uncovered, covered 11 more columns, left the next column uncovered, and continued until the last 11 columns were covered. He performed the same procedure on the rows, resulting in an 11 x 11 matrix of visible letters. A few seconds later, he froze.

From his expression, Michal suspected Justus had found something, but search as hard as she could, she saw nothing in the visible letters.

Finally, he breathed, "It's under the hill of Golgotha."

Michal frantically scrutinized the uncovered letters but saw only:

```
G O


        T                                              L


        H                                                  O


            A                                          G


I T H E                                                T I
```

Her frustration mounted. "Point to it."

Justus laid his fingertip on the *G* on the left side of the papyrus, his voice a whisper. "Wrap it around into a tube in your head."

Michal concentrated, wrapping one side to the other and saw:

```
            G O

        L       T

    O               H

G                       A

    T I I T H E
```

CHAPTER FIFTY-SIX

She gasped, "Why two *I's?*"

Justus shrugged. "I don't know." He didn't move and appeared as if he were staring through the covered sheet. He twitched his head and snapped his fingers. "But it must be the answer." He stepped toward the door. "I'm going to go walk off the distance from the city's north wall to the hill of Golgotha. Tomorrow we'll travel the same distance in the Salem catacombs. Want to come?"

Michal shook her head, hooked by Justus' solution. "No, now I see how to look at all combinations. I want to search for *messiah* and find what words are around it. Besides, it won't take you long to count the steps to the hill."

Justus kissed Michal lightly on the lips. "I'll be back in no time."

▶ ▶ ▶

In his quarters, Perez staggered away from the opening in the wall and sank to a bench near the window. He caught a glimpse of Abigail's brown veil flapping as she dashed across the covered courtyard toward the street. His back was killing him from having his ear glued to the hole in the wall for the past three hours. He knew he must report Justus' discovery to Annas, but allowing Abigail time was not the only thing that held him back.

He had never really accepted the idea that Abram's Tithe was in Melchizedek's Tomb. Now he sat awe-struck. *The Roman has found it. The Tomb is in the Salem catacombs underneath the hill of Golgotha.*

CHAPTER FIFTY-SEVEN

Inside an abandoned house about a hundred yards away from the covered courtyard, Bukki grimly peered at Miriam's front door through a small window. The Roman guards had escorted Miriam and Julius, so the courtyard was empty. Bukki had hated Annas' command to help Malchus dig in the catacombs and masterfully came up with multiple reasons to avoid it. He didn't like this latest command from Annas either, but he knew he could get some personal benefit from this one. Besides, he didn't like Justus and liked Michal even less.

He shifted his weight and gave a disgusted sigh. He'd been here all day and no one else had left the house. It was a waste of time. The chances of Michal being alone were one in a million. He was going to have to . . .

Suddenly, Abigail bolted through the courtyard, interrupting Bukki's musings. She held her robe tightly around her body and her reddish hair shown as the scarf was inflated by the wind. She appeared driven.

Bukki came alert and stared at the front door with renewed interest. A breeze blew leaves across the street towards Miriam's house. Two pigeons chased each other, riding the breeze to the courtyard's covering.

Ten minutes later, Justus slammed the front door shut and approached Bukki's hideout with smooth strides.

Bukki ducked back and froze as Justus passed the house.

What luck. The only one left was Perez. Bukki moved like a tiger stalking his prey, and the muscles on his lean body rippled. Outside in the alley stood a wagon a couple of steps from the window, but before he could climb inside it, footsteps made him go rigid. He slid behind the wagon, his senses on high alert. He pored over the small part of the street visible from the alley.

Jogging, Perez burst into Bukki's constrained visual window and quickly disappeared.

Michal was alone. For only a second, he was paralyzed by the revelation. Resisting the impulse to hurry, he jumped into the wagon and urged the horses in a slow approach to the house. Seconds later he was ten feet from the front step.

Jumping down from the wagon, Bukki leaped to the door and pounded. "Honorable Justus, are you there?" he bellowed.

Michal's quavering voice replied, "No, he is not. Is there a message I can give him?"

There was a pregnant pause as Bukki grinned inside, but stammered. "N-No message . . . but . . . you must let me in."

"Why?"

"The chief priest is in need of the high stand. He has sent me to get it."

After a moment, Michal cracked the door open. "Why does he need it this instant?"

Bukki acted confused and meekly inched forward. "I'm not always told reasons, Lady Michal."

Michal left open the door, spun, and approached the stand used for searching, her head shaking. "Let me clear . . ."

Bukki lunged in like an angry bear and delivered a crushing blow to the back of Michal's head with his right forearm.

Michal stumbled, but didn't fall, and half turned her face back at him.

Bukki slammed his closed fist into her left jaw. Blood squirted from her splayed mouth and she fell hard onto the floor, unconscious.

He had to hurry before the Roman came back. He fished in a pouch hanging from his belt, removed a small scroll, and tossed it onto the papyrus sheet.

Picking Michal up, he peeped out the still-open door just enough to discover if anyone was present. Seeing no one, he carried her to the wagon and laid her in the back. Lifting the tent cover, he retrieved some rope and two long cloths. He bound and gagged her.

Last, he blindfolded her and covered her still form with the tent canvas. He looked at his handiwork, followed by a fugitive glance down the street. Climbing onto the wagon seat, he pulled his scarf up and moved the horses at a leisurely pace toward the Water Gate.

➤ ➤ ➤

An hour after leaving Michal, Justus strolled through the Herod Gate into the city. The wall cast long shadows in the setting sun. The mystery had completely captured his imagination. He had walked off the distance from several points along the northern city wall figuring that the routes in the Salem catacombs would not be as direct as his path above them. Tomorrow he'd see how easy the catacombs were to negotiate.

As he meandered down the street to Miriam's house, his thoughts strayed back to the puzzle. Why would the word *tithe* be spelled with two *i*'s? Justus stopped dead. The house door was wide open. He dashed through the courtyard, but drew up at the entrance.

What's this?

A red spot lay on the stoop. His neck muscles knotted. He prodded the spot and raised it for a better look. What he saw caused his stomach to roll.

He exploded through the opening. "Michal, Michal!" He only needed a moment to process the empty room, and focus on a pool of blood a few steps from the doorway.

Justus let a guttural roar of rage as he bolted from room to room, confirming the house was empty. He returned to the small pool of blood, his voice ragged as he asked the empty air, "What has happened? Is she dead?"

He shot out the entrance and leaped to the isolated entrance to Perez' apartment. He slammed his fist repeatedly on the door. "Perez . . . Perez! Are you in there?" He cocked his ear, but heard nothing. *If he hurt her, I'll kill him!* He forced the door open and peered in. The room was dark, but empty.

Justus pivoted, scoured the courtyard, and returned to Miriam's front room. He breathed hard and a sickening feeling came over him. Immediately, he noticed the small scroll lying on the table, now looking as large as a camel. He plucked it up and unrolled it, squinting to read the inscription:

```
Bring the location of the tomb to the Ephraim catacombs
before Passover. Come alone or she dies.
```

Justus' blood boiled as he darted through the door and slammed it shut. He raced to the Roman garrison quarters, but a new guard stopped him. Though gasping for air, he managed to identify himself. "My name is . . . Joseph Justus. I am Chief Advocate . . . of Rome."

The announcement caused fear to sweep across the guard's face.

Justus' breathing became easier. "I need a horse and a short sword."

The guard gazed hollowly at him. "You must tell this to my centurion."

"As you wish."

The guard stiffly went to the barracks, motioning Justus to follow him.

Gaius was a muscular man, shorter than Justus. He sat on a bench using a whetstone to sharpen his sword. He wore the dress of a centurion, but his helmet lay at his feet.

"Sir, we have this . . ."

Gaius looked up and broke into a broad grin. "Welcome, Honorable Justus."

"Gaius, I need to borrow a horse and a short sword."

Gaius jumped up and asked, "Do you need soldiers, also? I will accompany you myself."

Justus shook his head. "I know you would, but I need you to do something more important." He extended his arm. "I need you to give this to Julius as soon as he returns." Justus handed the small scroll to Gaius.

Gaius nodded once. "As you command, sir." Gaius pointed at the door as he looked at the guard who stood behind Justus. "Take this man to the armory, then to the stables. Report to me afterwards."

Justus and Gaius exchanged a handshake, each clutching the forearm of the other.

Gaius looked troubled. "May the gods be with you."

"I'm sure He will be."

CHAPTER FIFTY-EIGHT

Sethur straightened as he heard footsteps on the stairs to his workroom. He had searched the sheets the entire day and found nothing, so he welcomed the interruption.

The color of Abigail's cheeks matched her red hair. Her shawl covered only the back part of her head. Her breathing was deep, as she studied the large sheet in front of Sethur, holding multiple wooden strips.

"It's good to see you, Abigail. Since it is apparent you have hurried here, what information do you have?"

Abigail tugged nervously at her sleeve. "The Roman has found something."

"What?"

"I couldn't quite hear it all, but something is located under the hill of Golgotha."

"Golgotha?" Sethur felt a rising uncertainty. "That's all you have?"

She went on with more confidence, "I know a secret about how the Roman is searching. He rolls the sheets into a tube."

Sethur looked incredulous. "How does he do that with the wooden strips? They will fall off."

Abigail leaned forward to whisper, "He does it in his head."

Sethur's chin came up. "Of course. That opens up a whole new set of combinations."

› › ›

Malchus stationed himself at the door of the high priest, knocked, and shuddered—not only from the cold night but also with anticipation. He would soon find out what task was so important, it restricted him from searching the catacombs for Melchizedek's Tomb.

Beulah opened the door, her normal pleasant manner rigid. She shivered as the cold air washed over her.

She had given Malchus multiple instructions on the habits of Caiaphas since becoming high priest, allowing him to visit at convenient times. This day, however, Malchus had been summoned. "Beulah. I see you are still on duty as even am I."

Her expression softened. She was quite short and, though Malchus was not tall, Beulah looked up at him. "My day ends when the high priest retires." She turned her head towards the stairs and sighed. "And sometimes . . . not that soon. He awaits you on the balcony."

"Of course." Malchus scurried through the foyer and up the stairs. Although he rushed through the hall to the balcony, he was careful to not brush against the ornate religious relics on shelves lining the hall. He stopped short of moving onto the balcony's polished floor. "Sir, you wanted to see me?"

Caiaphas slowly turned from facing the city, his voice having the undertone of victory. "We are going to arrest the Nazarene carpenter, and I need you to lead the arresting party."

Malchus stepped back in shock. "Arrest him? Arrest him for what?"

"That is not your concern."

Malchus looked skeptical. Jesus was constantly going to different places to teach. Malchus was sure he'd left the immediate vicinity after entering Jerusalem on a donkey three days ago. "Do you know where he is?" he asked.

"I will know shortly."

Malchus had a sinking feeling. He only wanted to secure his own freedom. He had nothing against Jesus. His voice sounded sad. "When do you want me to lead them?"

"I will tell you soon. Early in the morning, notify the Temple guards and several of my other servants. Tell them to be ready at a moment's notice and to be prepared to be heavily armed. We don't know what his disciples might do." Caiaphas turned back toward the city. His voice became low, but precise. "Afterwards, stay in your quarters. I'll send someone to you who will show you the Nazarene's location. At that time, assembly your party and arrest him."

Feeling he was dismissed, Malchus took a step to leave.

Caiaphas cleared his throat, his voice louder and tinted with mirth. "After you have delivered the Nazarene to me, you may go back into the catacombs, but concentrate your search only under the hill of Golgotha."

Malchus felt a surge of adrenaline. "Why there?"

With a lopsided grin and an evil squint, Caiaphas replied, "The Roman found a clue suggesting the Tomb is under the hill of Golgotha."

CHAPTER FIFTY-NINE

Justus had journeyed from Jerusalem the entire night. Since it was moonless most of the time, he was footing it so he could lead his horse and prevent it from stepping in a hole and becoming lame. It had been a slow trip and the remorse dominating him had been powerful, causing the trip to feel even longer than it was.

As dawn brought sufficient light, Justus returned to riding. By the time the sun was about to peek over the eastern hills, Justus spotted the opening to the Ephraim catacombs halfway up the slope of a small hill. He pulled his horse to a stop and dismounted. The intense darkness had made the trip a lot longer than he'd hoped, but at least he had some light to make sure it was safe to approach the cave.

Justus slowly drew the short sword from its sheath as he studied the entrance and the surrounding rocks. Seeing nothing, he moved stealthily toward the opening, thinking he should have brought a shield. The closer he climbed to the opening, the more uncomfortable he felt. Rage pushed him on. Michal was hurt and he had to find her.

He worked his sandals from boulder to boulder, but twice slipped onto the coarse-dirt slope, causing him to momentarily lose his footing. At those times, he drew up and surveyed every inch of the large hillside before him.

The sun cleared the mountains and bathed him in bright light as he arrived a stone's throw from the opening. There was no cover from here to the opening. It would take awhile for his sight to adjust to the darkness once inside. Although sheer folly, he couldn't hesitate. Every second could be Michal's last.

He looked around one final time and darted to the wall at the side of the cave opening, hugging the rocks. He strained to hear sounds coming from the cave, but heard only a few birds in the distance.

A cold sweat broke across his forehead as he twisted slightly, trying to examine the cave while protecting his body from being exposed. He saw nothing but thick blackness.

Justus took a deep breath, jumped one sidestep from the wall, and plunged into the pitch-darkness. A loud *twang* greeted him and a searing pain shot through his left shoulder, spinning him out of the entrance with such violence that he lost his footing and rolled several feet below, his sword clanging as it bounced from rock to rock.

He lay gasping for breath, skirting the edge of consciousness. He squinted and riveted the cave opening. With his jaw clenched, he held pressure on the wound to soften the burning pain. *An arrow from a crossbow.* It had passed completely through.

He began to faint, but pebbles showering him brought him around. Unable to formulate any kind of a plan, Justus played dead and ignored the pumping pain in his shoulder. Footsteps stopped beside him.

Finally, the suspense became unbearable. He eased open one eye.

Above him, Bukki plunged a death blow with a long sword.

Justus dodged enough so the sword merely cut his tunic and made a shallow wound on his left side. As he evaded the thrust, he hit the back of Bukki's knees.

They buckled and Bukki tumbled a few feet farther down the slope, dropping his sword.

Justus hopped up and dived the short distance between them, crashing into Bukki's chest. Blood from his shoulder and his side splattered his opponent's tunic. The force of the collision caused both men to roll onto a plateau, legs and arms thrashing the air.

Bukki hooked Justus and hammered his shoulder wound with his iron fist.

The pain was so intense Justus almost fainted.

Bukki scrambled up the slope after his fallen sword.

Justus' muscles tightened. Unarmed, he was easy prey. He wobbled to his feet and managed a stumbling run along the side of the hill.

Justus' thoughts raced as Bukki grabbed the sword and tried to intersect his path by angling down the mountain. He wheeled and ran away from the mountainside across a grassy knoll.

Justus sprinted through the grass, his blood pumping. Pain hammered through his shoulder wound. Suddenly, he stopped short, tottering on the edge of a wide crevice in the plateau. It was too wide to jump. Terror seized him. He spied the bottom of the crack more than a thousand feet below. He was trapped.

He turned to Bukki.

Bukki pulled up in front of Justus. He paused to catch his breath only to snarl, "Prepare to die, you Roman scum."

Every nerve in Justus' body was wired. "I thought you wanted the Tomb's location. You intend to kill me before I give it to you?"

Bukki gave a scowl. "Why should I care about the Tomb? I'll get my reward one way or another."

"Where's Michal?" he demanded.

"She'll follow you, after I kill you and rape her."

Justus burned with rage, but he made no move.

Bukki seemed reluctant to get too close to him. "Jump or you'll taste the sword."

Justus remained silent, boring into Bukki.

"Jump!"

Justus froze.

Instantly, Bukki pointed the sword at Justus' heart and lunged.

Justus flinched left and the sword slid past him. In the same move, his right hand hit solid in Bukki's back.

Bukki screamed as he fell into the chasm.

The maneuver also threw Justus off balance. His feet began to slide down the cliff edge. Frantically, he lashed out with both arms to grab anything to stop his fall. His left hand caught a root, but the pain from his wounded shoulder was so intense, he couldn't hold on. It did slow him enough so he could grasp a jutting rock with his right hand and work his body onto a narrow ledge. Secure on the ledge, he slumped in pain and exhaustion, as his body shook uncontrollably.

CHAPTER SIXTY

Though the Passover Festival did not start officially until dark, a large number of people had arrived in Jerusalem and as always, the Temple area was the focal point of activity.

The early morning sun basked the visiting pilgrims in the open Temple courtyards with warmth, fueling their excitement about being there for Passover. Mixed smells of roasting meat and baking bread from nearby private courtyards floated over the Temple area.

Jesus strode with certainty as he crossed the open court to a Temple porch. However, before he was able to ascend the steps he was intercepted by his disciples Andrew and Philip, who were followed by several other people.

Andrew was the same height as Jesus, but his frame was thicker. He still wore the short tunic of a fisherman, and his robe was pulled back, revealing bulging biceps.

Andrew knew several Grecian Jews, so it hadn't surprised him to be approached by some of them. In fact, he was actually glad they had requested to talk to Jesus. With high hopes, he indicated four people nearby. "Lord, here are some people from Greece who have come to Jerusalem to worship. They have asked to see and hear you."

A young man stood close to a woman appearing to be his age. His face was ruddy. Behind them was an older couple. Both men wore short tunics and short robes, but the cloth was finely woven. The women had uncovered heads—the younger with jet black, mid-length hair, the older one with long dark-brown hair. They wore long robes, drawn at the waist with leather belts.

Jesus looked at the visitors as he placed a firm hand on Andrew's shoulder. His voice was energized. "The time has come for the Son of man to be exalted." Turning to the Greeks, he smiled broadly. "Peace to you. So, you have come to Jerusalem to worship. Let me direct you to the correct object of your worship."

All four focused on Jesus with a look of hope. Several Jewish bystanders shuffled beside them and stood in silence.

Jesus mounted the porch and confronted the four newcomers with a look of assurance, his voice reverberating from the Temple walls. "I have come into the world as a light, so that whoever cleaves to, trusts in, and relies on Me may not have to continue in darkness. My light shines through My teachings. And My teachings disclose the wicked ways of this world and denounce its evil, for My teachings are about love. However, if any of you hear My teachings and fail to observe them, I will not judge you, for I came not to condemn the world, but to save it."

The young Greek man looked perplexed. "But we came to worship the God of the Jews."

Jesus stared at the questioner, his voice firm. "If you believe on Me, you not only believe on, trust in, and rely on Me, but on Him who sent Me. And, whoever sees Me sees Him who sent Me. However, anyone who rejects Me and persistently sets Me aside, refusing to accept My teachings, has his judge, for the very messages I have spoken will themselves judge and convict him on the last day."

Jesus took one step from the Greeks and surveyed the Jews. "This is because I have never spoken on My own authority, but the Father who has sent Me has Himself given Me orders of what to say. I know His commandments mean eternal life. So all that I say is just what the Father has told Me to say."

The Greek stared in wonderment, a look of understanding growing. His voice was strong. "So, if I believe on You and accept Your teachings, which really originate with God, I will have eternal life. But how will you accomplish it?"

Jesus focused on him. "I assure you most solemnly, unless a grain of wheat falls into the earth and dies, it remains by itself alone. But if it dies, it produces many others and yields a rich harvest." Jesus' voice softened. "Try to understand. Sentence is being passed on the world, and its ruler shall be cast out. When I am lifted from this earth, I will draw all men, Gentiles and Jews alike, to Myself. In like manner, though you continue to live in it, you must die to this world."

A voice rang out from the Jewish side. "How do we die to this world?"

Jesus showed a triumphant look. "Whoever has no regard for his present life here on earth but despises it, preserves his real life forever and ever. Turn from your present life and serve Me." He spread both arms. "If anyone would serve Me, he must cleave steadfastly to Me, conforming wholly to My example in living and—if need be—in dying. Then, wherever I am, there will My servant be also. Know that if anyone serves Me, the Father will honor him."

Both elder Greeks nodded, comprehension visible.

Several of the Jewish people in the crowd murmured among themselves and whispered their lack of belief. A voice from the back of the crowd sounded. "We serve God, not him."

Andrew climbed two steps toward Jesus, ready to repel any who might approach the porch.

Vexation held Jesus' face. "You will have the Light only a little while longer. Keep on living by the Light, so darkness may not overtake and overcome you. He who walks in the dark doesn't know where he's going. While you have the Light, have faith in it, hold to it, and rely on it, so that you may become sons of the Light and be filled with it."

CHAPTER SIXTY-ONE

Justus lay safely on the ledge until his breathing became natural. The mid-morning sun was bright in a cloudless sky. His short brown hair barely moved in the strong updraft along the cliff wall from the floor below.

His shoulder pain numbed somewhat, allowing the threat of certain death to be replaced with the urgency of Michal's situation. He sized up his predicament and evaluated the projection he was on. It narrowed, but did rise eventually to the top of the cliff. He balanced himself as he stood and began snailing along the shelf.

Even though his left shoulder had calmed to a dull ache, it made his left arm almost useless. He pressed his chest against the rough stone and tried to spot handholds, but his poor visual angle forced him to use his right hand to see. He slid it slowly over the coarse rock wall, his fingers searching for something to clasp. When they found an indentation or protrusion, he hooked it to balance his body as he slid his sandals over the narrow path.

He repeated this five times before his hand found a large, solid jutting stone. He clutched it, but before he could move his feet, the narrow sill crumbled, suspending him above the chasm. Pumping both feet in all directions, one hit a solid area on the ridge. He used it to position his second foot and gain his equilibrium. Only his chest heaved as he strained to recover composure.

In a minute, Justus swallowed his fear and shifted one foot after the other until he felt the dew-wet grass at the top of the cliff. Straining to see overhead, he paused to assess his final movements. He may just make it after all.

He continued, slowly sliding his feet along the rim until he was able to roll onto the grassy plateau. Panting and trembling, he lay on the green carpet for a moment, savoring the sensation of solid ground beneath his back. A rustling breeze added to the peaceful feeling sweeping over him.

He opened his lids wide and stared at the bright blue sky. Michal needed him. He shrugged off his longing to rest on the grass and got to his feet. After a final glance at the crevice, he jogged across the grassy plateau and threaded his way through the rocks to the catacomb entrance.

He stared at the gaping black hole and hesitated. Surely if Bukki had an accomplice, he would have helped him in the skirmish. Still . . .

Justus stepped to one side of the opening and snaked along the wall, tingling with expectation of another attack. As he slithered against the irregular stone area deeper into the cave, a cool breeze washed over him and revived his strength.

The sun dimmed as Justus worked his way from the entrance, stooping lower the deeper he went. An opening on the left side of the cave caught his attention. A prime place to hold Michal . . . not far enough to require a torch, but deep enough to easily defend.

Justus took a half step into it and scanned the small area. It was empty, but a musky, tent odor overpowered the common, dank smell of a tomb. He stood in stunned silence. Was this just a trap? Was she . . .?

He felt more than saw a slight movement above his head. His head snapped up and his blood went cold.

My God, what has he done to her?

He gaped at an object wrapped in chains latched to the roof of the tomb. It was completely encased in coarse cloth.

Justus whispered, "Michal, is that you?" He saw a slight movement, but there was no answer. He stretched upward and pulled at the chains, only to find they were threaded through large rings embedded in the ceiling, their ends held together with a lock.

Justus was suddenly paralyzed. Bukki had the keys at the bottom of the cliff.

His voice became firm. "Michal, I'm going to try to find something to break the chains holding you. I'm not leaving, just searching. I'll be back soon."

Michal made a muffled noise.

Justus gave a bleak sigh. He darted out of the catacombs and stopped short. Dust was swirling on the desert floor, and he heard the hoofbeats of several horses. *Julius . . . God, what a great sight.*

He waited until the large company of soldiers stopped at the base of the hill with Julius at the head. He yelled, "Julius, thank God you are here."

All looked up at him.

Julius queried, "Are you all right?"

"Michal is bound in chains, and I don't have a key. Have you any bars or hammers to free her?"

Julius barked at the man next to him, "Get those, soldier!"

Justus couldn't stand still. He paced in front of the entrance, willing them to hurry. How long would she be able to breathe wrapped up like that?

In short order, Julius, Gaius, and Miriam climbed the rocky slope, followed by five soldiers. They dislodged several stones on the ascent, which made loud thumps as they bounced their way down the bank.

Before they reached Justus, Miriam cried out, "You're wounded."

His voice was ragged. "We've got to hurry. She's going to suffocate."

Justus led Julius, Miriam, and Gaius into the catacombs and squeezed into the tomb with them. They stared overhead.

Julius looked stern. "This space is too small for everyone, so all of you wait outside."

Miriam and Gaius instantly obeyed, but Justus remained.

Julius marked Justus' bloody left side. "I know you want to help, but you must wait outside. My troops are fresh, and you aren't going to do much with that arm."

"I've got to help!"

Michal made a muffled sound and jiggled her cocoon slightly.

Both men inspected Michal's wrappings.

Julius took Justus' good arm in a fatherly fashion, his voice gentle. "See, she agrees with me. Now go outside."

As Justus exited the cave, two soldiers entered, carrying grappling hooks, a few iron bars, and a mallet.

Miriam approached Justus with concern. She wrapped a scarf over his shoulder wound. "This will help stop the bleeding."

Still staring at the cave opening, Justus gave a brief nod. After several minutes of pounding and grunts from the soldiers, the two men carried Michal out, still wrapped in the tent covering and chains.

Julius emerged behind them, a grim expression showing. "We pried out the rings holding the chains from the roof ceiling, but they were too tightly wrapped to get Michal out without hurting her. We must break them."

The two soldiers laid mummified Michal onto the ground. One slipped a stone next to her body and pulled what little slack was in the chain over the stone, holding it with his hands on either side. The other soldier began beating on it with a hammer. The strikes and subsequent echoes filled the air making discussion impossible. Finally, the chain severed.

Miriam and Julius tore the chains away as Justus gently pulled the canvas from Michal's head, revealing a bloody gag and a filthy blindfold. He gasped. "I'm glad I killed him." He untied the blindfold to reveal her tightly squinted eyes, one of which was swollen and blackish blue.

He shook as he undid the gag. Her upper lip was split and framed with dried blood. He carefully removed the cloth. Dried blood also had pooled on her bruised chin.

"Michal . . . I'm so sorry. It's all my fault. If I had stayed with you . . ." Justus stopped, overcome with emotion.

Michal opened her good eye to peer at him. Through stiff lips, she murmured, "Not . . . your fault."

Julius and Miriam pulled the tarp completely away from Michal's body. One breast was nearly exposed, blood had stained her clothes, and deep blue bruises were present everywhere the rope had bound her.

A warm feeling swept over Justus. He touched her sweaty dirt-matted hair, as he barked to a nearby soldier, "She needs water!"

CHAPTER SIXTY-ONE

Miriam softly massaged Michal's mottled arms and legs to restore circulation.

Justus took the water flask from the soldier and helped Michal drink. He bathed her face and hair, removing the dried blood and some dirt.

After an hour of attention, Michal sat up and held the back her head, grimacing. "Oh . . . umm . . . God, what a headache."

Justus examined it. "At least the skin is not broken."

Relief washed over him as he realized she was not severely hurt. Resisting the urge to kiss her bruised and bloody mouth, he blurted out, "God, you're beautiful."

Michal squinted at him. "Bukki hit you on the head one time too many."

CHAPTER SIXTY-TWO

Malchus was reluctant about leading a posse to arrest Jesus, so he had used every excuse he could to delay going to see Jehu. He busied himself the entire morning, mostly directing the duties of other servants from his own quarters. Occasionally, he would tour the courtyard to check on the efforts to prepare it for its spring splendor and add his huge muscles to the repositioning of large, decorative stones.

During a short break after giving a particularly difficult assignment to four other servants about how to repair a colonnade at the entrance of the palace, he slumped on the barrel chair in his room. His thoughts immediately flew back to searching the catacombs and he thought about Caiaphas' comment about Justus' discovery. Golgotha was a large area. Knowing the Tomb was located there was good, but not precise information. *I wonder if Caiaphas is telling me everything the Roman knows.*

Finally at the fifth hour, he forced himself to set aside all his remaining duties and trudge to the headquarters of the Temple guards. This Nazarene's popularity might lead to a riot during his arrest. *I hope we can contain them, so they won't kill us.* He shook his head as he approached the Temple guard's station. He was so close to becoming a free man.

Encountering the duty guard of the day, he fought the reflex to wheel about and head for home. "Is Jehu available?" he asked. "The high priest has sent me with a message."

"I am not sure if he's back yet," the guard replied. "The Nazarene was teaching at the Temple early this morning, and the captain led some soldiers there. If you wait here a few minutes, I'll see."

As the guard disappeared into the complex, a knot formed in Malchus' gut. One hand repeatedly rubbed his well-trimmed brown beard. Caiaphas had better be careful about arresting the carpenter in front of all these people. It had been a mere four days since many of them laid palm branches on the road as he rode in Jerusalem, proclaiming him King of Israel. Surely an uprising would develop if Caiaphas captured him here.

Two swallows dived by Malchus and shot up to one of the Temple gables.

Jehu strode from the guardhouse in full uniform, his black helmet shining. The two rows of polished silver studs traced both sides from front down the long, curved protective back. They glistened in the sun. He was not able to disguise the distaste in his voice. "What does the high priest want this time?"

Malchus turned his attention from the birds to Jehu, his voice sounding official. "He has ordered me to gather and lead a band of loyal Jews to arrest the Nazarene."

Jehu cringed. "Here? Now? What's he thinking? There'll be a riot."

Malchus shrugged. "I don't know when. He only told me to select a large group, including armed guards, who will be ready to assemble at a moment's notice." Malchus glanced about the Temple enclosure and swallowed hard. "I don't think he will have us do it in front of these crowds. That would be near suicide."

Expressionless, Jehu stared at Malchus for a moment. "Did he specifically ask for me?"

"No, just armed Temple guards. He also wants anyone we can find who has not been seduced by the carpenter's teachings."

Jehu gave an uneasy nod, his voice bland. "I see. I will have Attai ready some soldiers. Contact him when you know the details."

"As you wish."

▸ ▸ ▸

Jehu's expression remained grim as he focused on Malchus disappearing into the crowds. He directed the duty guard, "Get Attai and have him meet me at Sethur's house."

"Yes, sir."

Jehu gave a bleak sigh and stepped into the crowds, most of whom were entering the Temple enclosure. The only good thing about having the chief priest's attention centered on the carpenter was it allowed Sethur time to search.

It took a full ten minutes to reach Sethur's house, moving against the stream of humanity going to the Temple to prepare themselves for the Passover Festival. Twice he was stopped by a lost pilgrim in need of directions. Finally, he was in front of Sethur at the bottom of the stairs in the workroom, his thoughts churning. "Have you made any progress?"

Sethur's small, sharp facial features twisted in a grin. "Come look at this."

Jehu looked doubtful, but followed closely behind him. The room held a stagnant odor of moldy plant paper, mixed with the sweet smell of pressed olive oil burning in multiple lamps.

Sethur stopped at his work area and waved his hand over the large matrix with wooden strips covering most of the letters. His voice sounded egotistical. "The answer."

Jehu gawked at the letters for a moment, followed by a mistrustful glance at Sethur. "I don't see words at all, let alone an answer."

Sethur placed his finger on a *G* on the right side of the papyrus sheet and chuckled. "Wrap the sheet into a tube in your mind."

Jehu studied the letters indexed by Sethur's finger and felt a surprising feeling of recognition. "Amazing. It's under the hill of Golgotha."

"Exactly. It's in the Salem catacombs below the hill."

Jehu's countenance darkened. "Why is the word *tithe* spelled with two *i*'s?"

Sethur shook his head slowly, his voice soft. "I don't know."

Sethur's maid tromped down the stairs and interrupted the men pondering the two *i*'s. She stopped with her head bowed, silently waiting.

Sulking, Sethur slowly moved his gaze to her. "What is the problem?"

"Attai is at the door. Shall I show him in?"

Sethur shot an inquisitive glance at Jehu, but said nothing.

Jehu gave a slight nod and winked. "Send him in." He waited until the maid reached the top of the stairs. "I was hoping you had found something, so I asked Attai to come. Besides, he and I must talk about the Nazarene."

Sethur looked surprised. "What about him?"

"Caiaphas wants him arrested."

Sethur sucked air. "That's crazy. With his popularity, the people will go berserk."

"I know, but orders are orders."

❧ ❧ ❧

Peter had remained outside the city, helping a man finish the repair of a large fishing net while Jesus went to the Temple to teach. He was surprised to see Jesus leaving the city at the sixth hour of the day. However, since he was finished with the net, he fell in behind Jesus' entourage and followed them. Andrew walked beside him and filled him in on the Greek's morning dialogue with Jesus.

The sun was at its peak as Jesus motioned his disciples to stop at the edge of the Garden of Gethsemane. Peter and Andrew were farthest back. Although this location near the Mount of Olives was a common place for the group to congregate, they seldom used it during the day.

Peter had unexpected apprehension. He threaded between the other disciples, so he could get close to Jesus. He stopped and scratched his balding head through the loosely bound headdress.

Jesus looked almost excited as he skimmed the area. "Let's rest here for a while before we return to Jerusalem." Jesus turned to Peter, his voice happy. "Take John and go prepare the Passover meal that we may eat it."

Peter pondered Jesus' words and was unable to hide how surprised he was. "Where do You want us to prepare it?"

Jesus smiled and held his hand toward the city. "Go into Jerusalem and walk until you encounter a man carrying an earthenware pitcher of water. Follow him to the house he enters. Ask the master of the house where I may eat the Passover with my disciples."

Peter grabbed John's arm with a large calloused hand. He recognized the orders to be as fanciful on the surface as many others they had received from Jesus, but he also knew preparation of the Passover meal was time consuming. Even if they started now, it would be difficult to have it ready by nightfall when Passover began. "As You wish, Lord," Peter replied.

The two disciples scurried off to the Mercy Gate and passed through it into Jerusalem. They talked very little as they aimlessly roamed street after street. The city bulged with visitors come for the festival. Both disciples surveyed the clusters of people for someone carrying water.

The pavement was well worn on the popular route from the Temple, past the palace of the high priest, and on to the Herod Gate. They made poor time as they tussled through the crowds. Suddenly a man cornered a building in front of them with a large pitcher of water on his shoulder.

John and Peter exchanged unbelieving looks.

John relaxed as he shook his head. "And again, it's just as He said."

Peter returned a look of astonishment. "Yes. Again. I wonder when it won't seem so incredible. Come, let's follow our guide."

The two trailed after the pitcher-carrier as he turned into an alley and proceeded to a large house attached to the city wall.

As the man started to enter, Peter called out in a firm voice, "Excuse me, sir, but could we speak with the master of the house?"

The servant glanced back, his expression changing from startled to puzzled. "I will summon him for you."

Peter and John silently waited outside, both of their countenances merry.

In less than five minutes, an old man came out, looking expectant. "How may I help you?"

Peter's routine boldness poured out. "The Teacher has sent us. He asks where the guest room is, where He may eat the Passover meal with His disciples."

The old man looked incredulous. "The Rabbi?" He glowed as he motioned the two disciples to follow him. "Come, I'll show you." He bustled in front of them, led them up some stairs into a large room, and closed the door behind them. His hand trembled as he pointed. "See, here are dining couches on the carpet and it is properly spread. I'm sure it's large enough for you all. You are welcome to make your preparations here."

CHAPTER SIXTY-THREE

Justus sat up on the floor of a small room in the building housing the Ephraim Roman garrison as its physician treated him. Although the trip from the catacombs had taken until dark, it had been uneventful. He was exhausted but felt a humble pride at Michal's successful rescue.

The physician was a muscular man, shorter than the average Roman soldier, but showed the common training of one. He wore no body armor and bore no weapon.

A strong smell of an unidentified ointment hung in the air as the physician commenced packing his instruments and materials. "All in all, you were very lucky," he said. "The arrow hit the fleshy part of your shoulder and passed through it cleanly. Although it will be painful for a while, it isn't life threatening, and it should heal quickly. The other two cuts are just superficial wounds. By tomorrow, they will be simply a nuisance."

Grimacing, Justus climbed to his feet with some difficulty. "What about the woman? Did you treat her?"

The physician looked bright, and he gave a pleasant laugh. "Yes, she'll be fine. Nothing is serious. Most of her wounds will heal nicely in a few days. Ah . . . she's one tough lady."

Justus grinned. "You're telling me? It would take more than a couple of bruises to keep her down."

The physician laughed. "I'll bet you are right there." He handed Justus some bandages. "Here, make sure you change your shoulder dressings daily."

"I will. Thank you for your prompt care."

"My pleasure." The physician grabbed his gear and strode from the room.

Justus followed him out. He knocked on Michal's door. "May I come in?"

Michal's voice was strong, but her words were slurred. "Of course."

Justus opened the door. Miriam sat with her legs crossed on the pallet next to Michal. Michal leaned against a wall, her legs stretched forward. They were covered with a coarse, gray, Roman soldier blanket. Neither her black eye nor lip was swollen.

Justus asked, "Am I interrupting something?"

Miriam smiled. "Just girl talk."

Justus focused on Michal. "The physician told me you would recover quickly."

Michal mumbled, not moving her upper lip, a hint of fire in her voice. "Did you have any doubts?"

Justus smiled broadly, stepped into the room, and closed the door. "Not even one."

Miriam hopped up with a knowing look. "I'm going to leave you alone for a while. Julius has arranged for us to eat in this building tonight." A troubled expression quickly crossed her face. "He was worried about not being able to prepare a Passover meal."

Michal looked concerned and managed the words, "How did you tell him we couldn't eat it anyway? Because of him?"

The Mosaic Law considered a Jew who entered the dwellings of Gentiles to be ceremonially unclean and not fit to eat the Passover meal. And even though they could eat it anytime from when darkness fell until dark the next day, the required period of purification exceeded the complete twenty-four hour period available.

Miriam shifted her feet and looked muddled. "Justus, how did your mother handle all the Jewish ceremonial regulations with your father being a Roman?"

Justus remembered his father and mother agonizing over the regulatory impossibilities created by Gentile-Jew marriages. He hesitated, uncertain if he should offer any advice and shot a questioning glance at Michal.

"Don't look at me. I'm a Hellenist."

Justus hesitated, then offered, "Miriam, my parents came up with their personalized compromise. As a result, they practiced very few Jewish rules, especially after my grandfather died. Consequently, I haven't really bought into many of them."

Miriam appeared flustered. "Oh. OK." She looked down for a beat and moved to the door. "I'll tell Julius to not be concerned about our meal."

When she left, Justus settled next to Michal on the pallet. "I am very sorry," he murmured. He used the back knuckle of his right index finger to lightly touch her cheek.

She leaned her head into his finger to increase the pressure, her voice soft. "You didn't do anything wrong."

"I know . . . well, intellectually I know. But when I saw the ransom note, I nearly went crazy. I thought I would never see you alive again."

Michal placed her hand on his arm. "You didn't think you could get rid of me that easily."

Her light comment eased his self-reproach. "Never."

The sound of soldiers coursing through the hall outside Michal's door caused Justus to sit upright. He pressed his right hand on his left shoulder swathe. "Surprising, isn't it? I have lived over thirty years never knowing anyone who had been kidnapped and here I'm involved with two in about as many months."

The sound of the soldiers died away. Michal leaned her head against the wall behind her. "Why do you think Bukki abducted me?"

Justus felt a rising uncertainty. He shook his head, stared at the pallet, and tapped his forehead several times with his knuckles. "It certainly wasn't to find out the location of the Tomb."

"Why do you say that?"

"Because I tried to use its location as a bargaining chip while standing on the edge of the cliff. He showed no interest at all in knowing the location."

Michal took on a look of understanding. "Then that can only mean . . ."

Justus glanced at her as he completed her sentence. "Someone wanted us here and not in Jerusalem."

Michal thought about that. "But why?"

This point had puzzled Justus during the entire trip from the catacombs to the garrison's housing. "I can only think of one reason," he said.

"And that is?"

"He wanted to kill me."

Fear swept across her. "I don't understand."

"I don't completely either, but follow my logic. Suppose we are getting too close to finding out the truth . . ."

"About the Tomb?"

"Yes, or about Miriam's capture."

Michal looked thoughtful, her voice deliberate as she tried not to move her injured lip. "If we are too close to the truth, we would have to be silenced."

"And killing me, the Chief Advocate of Rome, would almost assure Caesar himself would demand revenge of the city in which I was killed."

"So, he would need to get you out of Jerusalem."

"And what better way to do that than seizing you and telling me to come alone with information about the Tomb?"

Michal processed the idea for a while, anger slowly showing. "He would have killed me."

"After he raped you . . . or at least that's what he told me."

She shuddered. "He would have had to kill me first."

Justus' reasoning began to race. "You know, we must be very close to finding the Tomb. Whoever wants us out of the way knows we are. I wonder how he knows."

The two sat silently, both in deep thought. Hoofbeats outside broke their contemplations.

Michal glanced at Justus, still humorless. "The clue you found about the tithe being under the hill of Golgotha is good, but don't you think there are many tombs under the hill? It is rather large, you know." She reached up and with two fingers gently rubbed her damaged eye. "And what about the two *i*'s?"

Justus gasped and barked a laugh. "Of course . . . that's it . . . You're a genius."

Michal looked at Justus as if he had two heads. "Huh?"

He leaned to kiss her softly, avoiding the cut on her lip. He grinned. "You just showed me how to find the Tomb."

"I did?"

"Remember, most of the really old tombs have symbols rather than words or letters."

"So?"

Justus reached out and softly touched the thin eyebrow of Michal's bruised eye, then her other one as he recited, "Two *i*'s . . . two *eyes*."

CHAPTER SIXTY-FOUR

Sethur hesitated in the subterranean foyer of the Jerusalem catacombs, salivating at the thought of being so close to immense wealth. As a scribe, he had never been poor, but he was constantly in close association with the very wealthy, which caused a thirst for the pleasures wealth could bring. Quelling his imagination from running too wild, he raised the lighted lamp and charged off.

The coolness of the empty caverns closed around him. It would be easy to walk off the distance from the north wall to Golgotha. He just hoped his guess at the above-ground location of the opening the Roman created was close to correct. Otherwise, he may be down here a long time.

Sethur jogged as fast down the main corridor as his light would allow. He had been in these catacombs multiple times, but this was his first time to hunt for a treasure. His vision caught a > scratched into the wall at the intersection of three corridors. The Roman was well versed in navigating catacombs. How did a Roman advocate know so much about such a lowly profession?

He continued following the signs Justus had marked on walls, weaving through different corridors until the pit was in front of him with stairs descending into it. He inched down the stairs, his hands beginning to shake. What if Melchizedek had booby traps around the Tomb?

At the bottom of the steps he stared at the opened passageway strewn with large stones, feeling a surge of adrenaline. *This is almost too easy.* He passed through the rugged opening into the Salem catacombs, tracing existing footprints made in the thick, fine dust.

The tunnel sloped deeper than the floor of the pit from which he started. He intently followed the tracks until he came to the intersection of another corridor. *Hmm . . . Whoever had made these tracks turned right, then came back the same way.* But Golgotha must be to the left.

Swallowing his uncertainty, he took deliberate steps into the corridor where the heavy dust laid unspoiled until he had paced off the correct number. These catacombs were even quieter than the ones under Jerusalem.

He felt an empty air of bewilderment. According to his calculations, he must go away from the city wall right here, but there was no tunnel to the right. He pushed firmly on the stone covering a nearby tomb, but it did not budge.

Sethur rubbed his beard, then clamped his thin lips together and pressed forward. After only a couple of steps, his light revealed the tunnel curved to the right. The discovery made his heart pound and his speed increase. Within ten paces, he detected the corridor was getting bigger. Moments later, Sethur froze. The meager light from his lamp bounced from the corridor walls, but disappeared into a large gaping blackness ahead. He fought the reflex to shiver, but lost. *What is this?*

He took half steps toward the black hole and stopped at the opening. Leaning in, he held his lamp high. The light showed a wall to the right with a tombstone close to the opening. He could see nothing to the left or straight ahead and remained stiff in breathless silence.

The room was so large his lamp would be of little help. Why such a large room under Golgotha?

He stepped into the room as if he were stepping on eggs. Holding his lamp as high as his short frame would allow, he took a minute to process the sight. Above the first tomb on his right was another one. There were two levels of tombs in this room. He edged along the wall, frowning. If this was where Melchizedek's Tomb was located, how would he ever be able to find it?

Sethur studied each stone for markings, a knot tightening in his gut. A frog, one with no marking, a bird, a cat, a sun, an arm . . . He turned to the wall opposite the opening and continued his inventory. A hand, a lion, a tree, a bee . . . He continued until he had completely traversed the far wall and encountered a third wall. He again could only move to his left.

As he started along the third wall, a feeling of defeat filled him. It was no use. There could be fifty tombs on these two levels alone. If he had torches, he would probably be able to see more levels above these two. There could be hundreds.

Sethur followed the third wall to its end, turned left and nearly ignored the remaining stones covering tombs as he scrambled toward the exit. Before stepping through, he turned back and lifted his lamp for one last look. Instantly, his muscles turned rigid. What was that?

A deep chill shivered along his back. He retraced his footsteps along the last wall, stopping after the third tomb. Above it was a faint, bluish glow.

Sethur gazed up at the image, but could not make out what it was. He took a few steps backward toward the center of the room for a better view and his jaw fell open.

Of course . . . how simple.

A pair of gemstone eyes glittered from a tombstone on the second level.

▹ ▹ ▹

Malchus was alone in his servant quarters, seated on the old water-barrel chair. There were no lights, but his thoughts were so far off, he didn't care about the darkness. He played over and over the command to stay away from the catacombs. Now that he knew they were located somewhere below the hill of Golgotha, with each replay, his anger mounted. The Passover Festival started at dark. He had lost another day and yet he was stuck here . . .

His internal dialogue was interrupted by a loud banging on the door. The noise startled Malchus and irritated him. His voice thundered. "Who is it?"

A firm male voice replied, "Please open the door."

Malchus stumbled to the door and his voice exploded outward. "I said, who is coming to my house this late at night?" Malchus waited only moments for a response, but when none came, he nearly ripped the door from its hinges. "What do you want?"

A man with black curly hair and a full black beard was poised in front of him, his countenance ice cold. "Are you Malchus?"

"Yes, so what?"

"I was told to come to you when Jesus was alone. My name is Judas."

CHAPTER SIXTY-FIVE

Justus felt rejuvenated after his long, uninterrupted sleep. He had little trouble moving his wounded shoulder and felt pleased with a single night's progress. Since he had slept through breakfast, his stomach reminded him it was empty as he passed into the dining hall where the Roman garrison was fed. It was typical for the central eating area to have no windows and although late morning, lamps were needed to see to eat.

The room was filled with soldiers reclining on the floor beside large mats holding their food. The laughing and talking was raucous. Justus passed through the room unnoticed, but his mouth watered at the smell of roasted quail and freshly baked bread.

He entered the smaller room where high ranking officers took their meals. Julius had propped himself up on a cylindrical cushion so he could eat with one hand. When he spotted Justus, he stood up and grinned. "I see you are healing. You've got to be sore though."

"I would rather be sore than be at the bottom of a ravine," Justus said, surveying the table mat. It held bowls of hardboiled eggs, dates, and cheese. Two plates held roast quail and bread.

"Good point," Julius replied.

At that moment, Michal moved into the dining hall, followed by Miriam. After morning greetings, they all reclined.

Justus broke off a piece of bread as he studied Michal. "Your wounds are healing faster than mine."

Michal gave him a charming smile. "I think the company physician has a magical ointment."

Justus chuckled and Miriam laughed out loud.

Julius looked thoughtfully at Miriam as he chewed. He swallowed, and turned to Justus. "Why do you think Bukki kidnapped Michal?"

Michal held a fig in front of her mouth, and said, "Probably to get Justus out of Jerusalem."

Julius glanced at her. "Why would he want that?"

Justus poured wine into a cup, and stared at it for several seconds. Finally, he said, "I think we are getting close to finding the Tomb Asher was hunting for."

Julius weighed Justus' words. "But why not deal with you in Jerusalem?"

Justus sipped from the cup. His voice had finality. "I think the idea was to kill me here."

"Ah . . . and if the Chief Advocate of Rome were slain in Jerusalem, Caesar would surely exact greater payment on Jerusalem than a single death."

"Exactly."

Julius leaned toward Justus, his voice soft. "How close are you to finding the Tomb?"

Justus set the cup on the table mat and shifted his weight from the couch pillow to his other hand. "Actually, I'm sure it's under the hill of Golgotha in the ancient Salem catacombs."

Julius appeared confused, so Justus went through the details of the entire mystery.

Julius took his cup and downed the wine. He had a foreboding look, and his voice took on a formal sound. "Honorable Justus, I can no longer keep your identity from Pilate. I must tell him who you are when we get back to Jerusalem today."

Justus had known for a while it was only a matter of time until his identity would have to be disclosed. He grimaced. The telling would limit him in searching for the Tomb. He also knew Pilate's past actions had shown him to be dangerous. Worse, Pilate could bring repercussions on Julius because of hiding his knowledge of Justus' identity.

"I understand," he told Julius. "I will tell him Caesar sent me incognito to find out the necessity of the Jewish custom of catacomb burial. It's not a total fabrication, for I know Caesar is having difficulty in dealing with sprawling catacombs under Rome, primarily due to Jews."

"Thank you," Julius said. "That will save my life and likely my rank. I truly appreciate it."

Miriam had been silent during the men's discussion, her look pensive. "I appreciate it too," she said.

Julius focused on Miriam, but spoke to Justus with a tight voice. "Do you think it was Bukki who kidnapped Miriam?"

"I'm pretty sure of it."

Julius turned and glanced at Justus. "Do you think he acted alone?"

Justus shrugged. "I don't know. He might have, but before he died, he said he would get his reward regardless of knowing the Tomb's location. So, he either already knew where the Tomb was located or was following the orders of another."

"A chief priest?" Julius asked.

Michal chimed in, "Seems most likely."

Everyone sat in silence.

Finally, Julius shook his head and sighed. "I will have Gaius post extra guards around Miriam's house when we return. I don't want anything to happen to any of you." He got to his feet. "We need to be leaving soon."

Justus stood and offered, "I'll tell Gaius we are ready to leave and to prepare our wagon."

"Thank you," Julius said.

Justus hurried out the dining room door to the building's exit, glad to be returning to Jerusalem. He wanted to search under the hill of Golgotha for the treasure as soon as he could. Opening the outer door of the barracks, he froze. His skin crawled as he stood in stunned silence, hearing only the soft cooing of a nearby bird, preparing for sleep.

My God. It's midday . . . but it's totally dark.

CHAPTER SIXTY-SIX

Malchus had been unable to sleep after last night's events, so he began his morning chores as the dawn broke. As soon as he finished them, he ran to the catacomb opening. He descended the stairs, his lamp already lit. He had a flask of oil over his shoulder.

His freedom dangled within reach. However, the deeper he descended the harder it was for him to squelch his nausea caused by the late-night arrest.

He reached the threshold, stumbled to a nearby wall, and leaned against it as his body shook uncontrollably. One hand shot to his right ear, and he gently massaged it. Over and over, he softly rubbed it, touching the front, back, lobe, curved top and inner skin as his incredulity intensified. *It's perfect. In fact, it's better now than it has ever been. But the pain . . . the pain.*

Malchus had internally relived the arrest multiple times, but he was driven to not allow it to interfere with his quest. He entered the caverns. However, the all-too-familiar corridors provided no stimulus to keep his thoughts from rebounding to the night before.

Judas had led them right to where the carpenter was in the garden. Everyone was afraid. They had all heard miraculous rumors about Him. They feared He would do something magical to harm them, so everyone just stood there.

I finally had to do something . . . I went up to take hold of Him, but one of His disciples cut my ear entirely off with a sword.

Malchus processed the memories again, cringed, and stifled tears as he strode ahead looking neither right nor left, but still touching his right ear. *Jesus picked my ear up and placed it back on my head.*

Malchus stopped, looked at the cavern's ceiling, and waved his hand out. *The pain immediately stopped. It was perfectly restored . . . not only as it was, but the wart on my earlobe is gone, the freckles on the top are gone and –*his chest felt constricted—*I can hear better with that ear than ever before.*

He dropped to one knee, his chest jerking with sobs. He wept for some time before he was able to regain control. As the emotion subsided, he stood and charged through the tunnel, his teeth clenched.

They were all wrong. The Nazarene was no liar or trickster. He must have been . . . He *was* the Son of God. And those idiots crucified Him.

Stepping through the connecting hole, he felt a deep chill. More footprints. The Roman must have returned.

Malchus felt it hard to swallow. His driving force for months had been the sure goal of freedom, but he felt it slipping away as surely as foot traffic had pushed away the ancient dust.

Defeat bowed Malchus' head. There were so many tracks, the Roman had probably taken whatever was in Melchizedek's Tomb. Now Malchus had nothing to give Caiaphas. He followed the footprints to a gaping black hole and sized it up for several moments before he stepped into it.

Instantly, he detected an unlit torch attached to the wall. Turning, he saw one on the other side. He held the lamp to one torch, lit it, and reeled back. *My God . . . a great room of tombs.* He lit the other torch, and his heart pounded.

A ladder stood propped against the same wall as the doorway. He approached it with baby steps. His heartbeats pounded in his ears. To the left of the ladder lay a large stone flat on the floor. Malchus held his lamp over it and shivered with amazement as his light was reflected back from gems outlining a pair of eyes. He swallowed hard and stared up the ladder at an open tomb on the second level. He was too late.

Holding his lamp with one hand, he used his other to spider up the ladder. A couple of rungs from the top, his legs went weak. This wasn't a tomb. He gazed at a deep indentation in the wall. Its smooth back held deeply carved letters:

```
R   N   A   M   M   F   I   B
```

```
Melchizedek
```

CHAPTER SIXTY-SEVEN

Other than traveling for a few hours in the eerie darkness before light returned, the trip from Ephraim had been uneventful. As the companions approached the city, the huge stones forming the wall were clearly visible, though heavy clouds hung low overhead.

The arch of the Herod Gate passed over Justus as he inspected the streets. "Hmm . . . how strange," he said. "Not only did darkness cover the land until about the ninth hour, but now we come into the city as Sabbath starts, and there's no one around."

Michal's black hair tousled as the wagon bumped over a stone in the pavement. She angled a questioning look at Miriam. "This is my first time in Jerusalem during the Passover feast. Is it common for the city to be so quiet and the streets to be so empty after the first day?"

Miriam regarded the nearly empty streets in confusion. "No, this is very uncommon. Usually pilgrims are either coming from or going to the Temple."

Justus guided the horses pulling the wagon to Miriam's street. Julius and his troop trailed closely behind them, the hoofbeat sounds bouncing off the houses as they past.

Justus had developed a plan and revealed it to Julius, but he'd waited until now to set it into motion, fearing Miriam would interfere. As Miriam's covered courtyard came into view, he said, "Miriam, I think you need to let Abigail and Perez go."

Miriam balked. "But why? Perez was faithful to my father for years, and Abigail has been invaluable during his coma."

Justus pulled on the horses' reins to slow the wagon further. "Bukki had to learn we were close to finding the Tomb from someone."

Miriam scrunched her brows. "But I trust them both."

Michal patted Miriam's arm. "We trust them, too. However we need to control everything about our search until we find out who wants to hurt all of us."

Miriam looked overwhelmed. "I really don't see how either could be involved in such a thing, but I'll rely on your judgment."

Michal wrapped her arm around Miriam's shoulders, pulling her scarf half down. Michal smiled. "Thanks. Don't worry. After all this is over, you can bring them back if you want to." Michal gazed at Julius as he dismounted, her smile growing to a grin. "Besides, you may be relocating to Shechem soon."

Miriam's cheeks reddened, but said nothing.

Justus drew up the horses pulling the wagon at the edge of the courtyard. Although the sun had set, the fire blazing in the courtyard provided a clear view of the area.

Perez and Abigail stood by the fire, inactive because of the Sabbath. As Michal and Miriam dismounted from the wagon, the two servants came to them.

Perez's boney features seemed distressed. "Lady Michal, a centurion came by yesterday and said you had been abducted."

Abigail looked at Miriam in confusion. "And he said you went after her with Roman soldiers." She turned to Michal, her voice dripping with misery. "We were very worried about your safety."

Michal's expression turned stern. "Everything worked out all right."

Miriam appeared distraught. "Julius and Justus rescued her. It was scary."

Julius came to Miriam's side with Gaius one step behind him. He turned to Gaius. "You are to post two guards at the door at all times. Keep others in the street on either side of the house. No one is to come into the house without the express consent of Miriam, Michal, or Justus." Turning to Perez, he thrust one finger. "That includes you."

Perez's normally sunken orbs appeared deeper as he nodded.

Julius bowed to Miriam, and his voice softened. "My Lady, I must debrief Pontius Pilate on everything. I will come back as soon as I can, but probably not before tomorrow."

"I understand. Be safe."

Glancing at Justus, he gave a slight nod. "I'll stop by Chief Priest Annas' house on the way and inform him of the death of his servant."

Perez gasped. "Which servant?"

Abigail's head bowed.

Julius and Perez bore into each other for several beats. "Bukki." He grabbed the reins of his horse and led it away from the courtyard with broad steps.

With her head still down, Abigail gave an upward look to Miriam. "Must I also get your permission to enter the house?"

Justus stepped between Abigail and Miriam. "Yes, it does apply to you. In addition, you may stay through the Sabbath, but then you must leave permanently."

Miriam placed her hand on Abigail's shoulder, her voice hushed. "I'm sorry. Too much has happened here. I think it best for you to leave."

Perez murmured, "My lady?"

Miriam looked sad. "I know you have been faithful, but you must go, too."

Perez took a deep breath and grumbled, "I shouldn't be surprised, after everything that has happened today."

Justus spun to Perez. "What did you say?" he demanded.

Perez looked up, dangerously defiant. "I was talking to myself."

Justus took a menacing step toward him. "What did you say about this day?"

"First the uproar at the pavement area, then the crucifixion, darkness in the middle of the day, and now I am told I must leave a job I've had for fifteen years."

Justus' blood went cold. "Who was crucified?"

Perez's chin lifted a fraction. He gazed directly at Justus and spoke a single word: "Jesus."

Justus clutched Perez's arm and stooped within inches of his nose. "Why?"

Michal gently pushed Justus away from Perez, her tone firm. "Justus, let's all go inside. It's been a long couple of days."

Justus glowered at Michal, then craned his neck, glaring at Perez. "Is he dead?"

"Yes, and buried."

Justus went white. He struggled to keep from collapsing.

Michal rushed to support him on one side as Miriam held his other.

"I . . . I . . . tried to warn him," he murmured.

CHAPTER SIXTY-EIGHT

Malchus was surprisingly calm as he had traveled from the Tomb, through the dark, quiet city streets to the palace of the high priest. His searching was finished and now the only riddle left was the fate of his freedom.

As he waited in the familiar foyer for Beulah to announce him to Caiaphas, he touched his right ear and a feeling of relief again washed over him. He had spent half a year trying to get his freedom by finding the Tomb of Melchizedek. Now he had found it . . .

No evidence of Caiaphas' usual air of superiority showed as he descended the stairs to Malchus. His voice was soft. "What is it?"

"I have found the Tomb."

Caiaphas froze and blinked several times. "Melchizedek's. How do you know?"

"His name was inside it."

Caiaphas took a step toward Malchus and looked angry. "You opened it?"

"No. It was already opened."

Caiaphas straightened and his head jutted forward. "What? Who?"

Malchus felt a lump in his throat. His pulse raced as he said, "I went to the Salem catacombs and saw several sets of footprints. I followed them to a large room in the bowels of the hill of Golgotha. It was filled with many tombs, but a single tombstone had been removed from the wall and lay on the floor."

Caiaphas glared. "What was inside?"

Malchus swallowed hard. "Well . . ."

A loud knock broke the tension of his response, and Annas stepped into the foyer. He gave a glance of surprise from Malchus to Caiaphas. "What are you two . . .?" He shook his head. "Caiaphas, we need to talk."

Caiaphas swiveled away from Annas, and glowered at Malchus. "Go on," he told Malchus.

Annas said nothing.

Sweat pooled on Malchus' forehead as he chose his words carefully. "Master, there was nothing inside. In fact, it was not a tomb at all, but a deep indentation in the wall, not big enough to hold anything of any size."

"But you said Melchizedek's name was in it."

A look of understanding crept across Annas, and he stared at Malchus.

Malchus cleared his throat and stammered, "Yes . . . the back wall was made very smooth . . . and there were eight letters . . . carved onto the wall. The name *Melchizedek* was below the letters."

Caiaphas gave Annas a questioning glance, then focused again on Malchus. "What did the letters spell?"

Malchus' words hung in space. "Nothing . . . I don't know. Maybe it is some ancient word."

Annas shouted, "What were the letters?"

"R N A M M F I B"

An eerie silence permeated the foyer, much like the silence of a tomb. Annas and Caiaphas exchanged puzzled looks.

Malchus stood trembling, his head bowed. He coughed into his closed fist. Summoning all the courage he had left, he forced the words out. "Master, you promised my freedom when I found Melchizedek's Tomb. Although not the first, I did find it. Am I free?"

Caiaphas gave Malchus a steely stare.

Annas clutched Caiaphas' arm and pulled him a step away from Malchus. He leaned to Caiaphas' ear, put up his hand to shield his lips, and whispered so Malchus could not hear.

Caiaphas' stood pondering the words, while continuing to look straight at Malchus. A faint hint of a lopsided grin formed. "Yes, Malchus, I give you your freedom—on one condition."

Malchus felt an unexpected surge of hope. "Anything, Master. What is the condition?"

"That you leave Jerusalem after the Sabbath and never return."

"Done." Malchus dashed out of the palace foyer and sprinted to his quarters. The condition was of no consequence. Malchus wanted to put as much distance between him and the high priest as possible before Caiaphas could change his mind. Mosaic Law prevented him from traveling more than a mile on the Sabbath, but he would go the limit right now.

▶ ▶ ▶

As the door thudded shut, Annas offered an easy smile. "Good decision. Our plan is unraveling in the worst way."

"What happened to Bukki?" Caiaphas asked.

There were no benches in the foyer, so Annas moved to the stairs and sat on the second step from the floor. "To get the Roman out of town, Bukki kidnapped the Grecian woman, left a ransom note for him, and took her to the Ephraim catacombs as bait. When the Roman came to rescue her, Bukki tried to kill him, but he was killed instead."

Caiaphas looked grim. "How did you find this out?" He paced the small distance from side to side.

Annas straightened his long robe and pointed toward the door. "The commandant of the Shechem garrison just told me, and I immediately came here."

Caiaphas ground out, "Does he suspect you?"

"I think so, but I told him I thought Bukki had run away. I acted as surprised as I could."

Caiaphas thumped his fist against his thigh. "What a cursed day."

"You have that right." Annas crossed his arms across his chest. "What do you make of someone else finding the Tomb?"

Caiaphas took two steps away and shook his head. "I'm flabbergasted. Obviously, it wasn't the Roman."

Annas' voice was tinted with wonder. "It must be someone who has been after the treasure for about as long as we have."

"Do you think it was Perez?"

"No. He's too . . . servile." Annas looked truly perplexed. "It must be a priest or a scribe, though. How else would anyone know about the historical potential of the treasure with the skills to look in the Torah for clues?"

"Hmm . . . doesn't look like much of a treasure. Just a word so old, no one knows what it means, probably some kind of religious advice."

Caiaphas was exhausted. He touched the wall to support himself for a moment. He suddenly longed for his simple childhood room in the casement wall atop Masada. A moment later he said, "We need to get as far away from this as we can. There is no treasure . . . only two women abducted . . . and we can't be a part of that."

"But what about the people who found the Tomb?"

"Let them be. There is no treasure. Whoever opened the Tomb has wasted their time also. Actually, the discovery may serve us well as we do damage control."

Annas inhaled deeply and stood. "Speaking of damage control, we need to convince Pilate to put a guard on the tomb of the Nazarene. All we need now is for his disciples to steal the body and claim he came back to life."

Caiaphas caught the pitch of the new topic, and his expression glazed. "Absolutely . . . first thing in the morning."

CHAPTER SIXTY-NINE

Justus was in a trance-like state as he perched on a bench in Miriam's front room. Crucifixion was an insidious form of capital punishment. The victims were laid on a wooden cross on the ground, their arms stretched out onto the crossing beams and each hand was nailed to the beam through the wrist. Their feet were crossed and a single nail was driven through the ankle bones, twisting the legs.

The cross was then hoisted up and dropped upright into a hole in the ground. The impact caused the full weight of the body to tear at the nails. The cross usually pitched one way or another, which added greater pain to the side of the victim where the force of gravity was pulling hardest.

With the sufferer's arms stretched so wide, exhaling became very difficult. Only by pushing up with his feet could he keep from suffocating, although this prolonged his agony.

Justus bucked the reflex to vomit. Visions of several Roman crucifixions passed through his consciousness with the image of Jesus superimposed on them. He shuddered. A desire to know more about the crucifixion burned in him.

He stumbled back into the courtyard to the fire where Perez still stood, alone. Although now died down, it cracked, sending a spark toward the street and causing a puff of white smoke to curl up to the roof. Justus was in a hot sweat. "When was Jesus crucified?"

Perez was barely able to conceal his disgust. "Mid-morning."

"Were you there?"

Perez bent his boney body closer to the low flames, breaking eye contact with Justus. "Yes, I was."

"Why were you there?"

Perez gave him a grimacing glance, but talked to the fire. "I was on my way to Chief Priest Annas' house to help prepare the Passover meal with his servants. When I arrived, it was nearly midday. The sunlight was just starting to diminish. The door maid told me everyone had gone to the hill of Golgotha . . ."

Justus felt rising wonder. "The hill of Golgotha?"

Perez raised straight in front of Justus. "Yes. So, I went to the hill. Jesus was on a cross with two others, one on either side of him. Many people were milling around. A few yelled taunts at him."

Rage began to simmer in Justus. His voice became deep and demanding. "Go on."

Perez moved to the nearby woodpile, picked up a small log, and dropped it onto the hot embers, causing a rain of sparks to climb the hot air. "There isn't much else. It became very dark. I could see several people standing close to the three crosses, but I wasn't close enough to hear what they said." He glanced at Justus. "I did get close enough to see a sign with the words 'King of the Jews' above Jesus' head."

The memory of a particularly horrific crucifixion Justus had witnessed passed before him. He tilted his head slightly, his voice much lower. "How is it Jesus is now dead? Usually, it takes a long time to suffocate on a cross."

Perez stepped back from the fire. "I was told he had been flogged so badly, that somewhere between the praetorium and Golgotha the soldiers had to get someone else to drag the cross the rest of the way. He must have been almost dead when he was nailed onto it."

Justus turned away, again feeling his gut retch. "Did you hear him say anything at all?"

"Only when he shouted."

Justus braced for the words. "Shouted what?"

"It is finished."

Justus gulped as he remembered those were the exact words Jesus had said to him only weeks before.

Perez spoke hurriedly. "I know nothing more. Please excuse me. I must prepare to leave tomorrow."

An unexpected surge of longing overtook Justus, as Perez traipsed across the courtyard to his private room. *I wish I could have talked to Jesus just one more time.*

From the corner of his eye, he saw the soldier in the street come to attention.

Julius appeared and gave the soldier a slight nod before he burst into the courtyard. "Have you heard about . . .?"

Justus nodded as he extended both hands, his voice distraught. "Yes, Perez told me, but I would like to hear more."

Julius looked and sounded unusually anxious. "Not now. I must get back to Pilate's palace. He is having an emergency meeting of the officers. I will tell you everything I know tomorrow, but I suspect you will be the one telling me things."

Justus had a delayed reaction. Finally, he said, "Why do you say that?"

"Because Pilate directed you see him early tomorrow morning."

Justus felt a sinking feeling. "He knows who I am?"

Julius stepped close to the flames regenerated by Perez's log and held his hands out. "Yes, as we talked, I had to tell him."

"Is he upset?"

"Actually, I don't think so. He sentenced Jesus to death today, and I think he is very bothered by it. I know he wants to talk to you about it."

Justus' imagination could not contrive Pilate's possible line of questioning.

Julius turned, glanced at Miriam's front door, and lumbered back into the street, his voice strong. "Tell Miriam I will see her tomorrow."

"Of course." Justus stayed where he was, lost in far-off visions.

After an hour, the fire became embers. Justus shivered in the coldness of night. He looked around the courtyard and realized it had become quite late. Passing the two door guards, he went into the house.

A lamp was burning in the empty front room, so Justus settled on a bench near the side of the table Michal had been using for her searches. Miriam and Michal had most likely retired for the night, but his imagination was racing too fast for sleep to be an option. *I knew this could happen. I tried to stop him . . . but, what if this is what he wanted?*

Justus shuddered. *Am I crazy? No one wants to be crucified. That's the worst way to die . . . ever.*

Powerful remorse crushed him. Bethany . . . It seemed like a lifetime ago, but it was only a few days. Jesus had raised Lazarus from the dead. Martha called him the Messiah. Oh, if he only could have been. It would be hard to picture a man who could be better.

Justus absentmindedly picked up a wooden strip and twirled it in his hand. His backside began to get numb, so he stood to get the blood flowing.

Wish I were sleepy. I would love to become unconscious for a while.

He peered absently at the scroll—left untouched since Michal had been kidnapped—and laid the 7-letter wide strip to cover a second set of 7 columns, after skipping the column next to the ones Michal had already covered on the 49 x 49 scroll.

The puzzle caught his attention. He picked up another wooden piece the same size and laid it on the next 7 columns after skipping a letter. He felt his pulse throb as he fixed on the 17th row. The letters *J, E* and *S . . .*

Surely not.

He grabbed two other 7-letter strips and dropped them onto the scroll. *Good God.* The name stood out prominently

J E S U S

Justus' imagination ran wild as he laid a 7-letter strip on the scroll covering rows 2-8. His body became rigid. He didn't need to cover any more letters, but completed the mechanics of the searching process anyway. An eerie feeling blanketed him as the strips highlighted the seventeenth column. Asher believed a new scriptural truth was found when imbedded words were found in close proximity.

A strange warmness ebbed throughout him. He smiled as he looked at the words standing out.

```
            M
            E
J   E   S   U   S
            S
            I
            A
            H
```

Suddenly, reality hit. *But . . . he's dead.*

CHAPTER SEVENTY

A faint knocking reverberated from the deepest recesses of Justus' subconscious. It became louder and louder until it sounded as if someone was pounding on his head. He bolted upright on the bench and tried to shake sleep away. Through his grogginess he realized someone was knocking on the door.

Gaius opened the door slightly, urgency framing him. "Honorable Justus, please excuse me, but Commandant Julius told me to bring you to the procurator's palace right now."

Justus glanced at his wrinkled clothing and heaved a dismal sigh. "All right . . . let's go."

Thick clouds blocked much of the morning sun and Justus shivered as a light mist funneled around him in a soft breeze. He had comfortably dealt with many military leaders in the past, but those times were always straightforward, with no hidden agendas. This day would be different. He clicked off the possible alternatives Pilate might choose, trying to develop a strategy.

Gaius came between Justus and a side door of the Antonia Fortress and told the guard, "This is the Honorable Joseph Justus."

The guard didn't look surprised. "He may enter. The procurator is waiting inside."

Justus took a deep breath and passed through the open door. The room was not an armory, but multiple weapons and body armor lined the wall opposite the door. Four benches were pushed too close together to be used for seating.

Pilate remained motionless, looking out of the only window,

Justus felt a little chill. He had heard many stories about how ruthless Pilate could be at times. He maintained his advocate demeanor, his voice strong as he said, "Governor, you wanted to see me?"

Pilate slowly turned. He had deep lines in his face. He wore no battle gear, but a small crown of golden leaves circled his head, contrasting with his short, dark-brown hair. He placed his fisted hands on each side of his hips. "I could have used your talents yesterday, Chief Advocate."

Justus heard the edge in Pilate's voice. "I apologize, sir. I was on special assignment . . ."

Pilate held up a hand and looked distressed. "I have been informed. I'm not angry because you didn't identify yourself. I'm angry about what happened yesterday."

Justus relaxed a little. His sandals scuffed softly on the stone floor as he approached the weapon wall. "I see. What happened?"

"I was forced to kill a man."

Justus swayed with the weight of Pilate's words. He turned full to Pilate. "Forced? How could they force you?"

Pilate waved, plopped down on the front bench, and gave a grim sigh. "They set me up so I could make no other decision."

Justus took two steps toward the rows of benches, but remained standing. He felt a pang of sadness. He thought he would be able to maintain a separation between hating Pilate for sentencing Jesus to be crucified and identifying with him for being a Roman procurator, but instead he felt he was merely interacting with a peer.

Pilate went on, "The chief priests brought this man to me early yesterday morning, claiming he had violated some law of theirs. They said he claimed to be a messiah or king or something." He stood and turned to the window again. "I asked the man myself if he was a king and he said he was. But someone can say they are king, a prince . . . a frog . . . a fig tree . . . anything. Claiming to be something means nothing." He took a long breath. "It certainly isn't a crime demanding crucifixion."

Pilate stared out the window. He looked as if he had forgotten Justus was in the room. His voice became softer. "My wife sent me a note saying the man was just and righteous and that she'd had a disturbing dream about him. So I offered to just scourge him and let him go. But no, they wanted more than blood. They wanted him dead."

Justus could feel Pilate's torment, but still didn't grasp how the highest authority in the region could be controlled by his people. He waited a minute for Pilate to continue, but the silence was unbroken. He rubbed his mouth twice. "You could have simply freed him."

Pilate spun around and glared at Justus as if he had just slapped him. "Passover is a big deal to these people. For years I have offered to release one prisoner to show my kindness and attempt to establish some type of rapport with the nation. I offered to release this 'king' of theirs, but they would have none of it. No, I'm convinced they were completely jealous of the man and used me to do away with him."

Justus tried to understand how that could happen, but he remained in silence. He took a small step sideways.

Pilate shot him a menacing glance. "They forced me by saying I was no friend of Caesar if I freed a man who was making himself a king in place of Caesar."

Understanding exploded within Justus. "Hmm . . . of course. They did compel you. All they had to do was report you to Caesar . . ."

"And I would likely be put to death for treason."

They exchanged uneasy looks.

Pilate stepped to the nearby wall, grabbed a short sword, and examined the blade. His demeanor went soft. "Justus, I'm sure you understand I was not appointed by the Senate, as your father was. I was appointed governor by Caesar himself. My loyalty must always remain with him." His words had chilling precision as he examined Justus. "However, had I known you were here, I could have appointed you to be his advocate. You could possibly have saved him without me being dragged into the middle of it."

Justus' gut rolled. *But I wasn't even in the city. I was baited to leave the city. I was the one controlled. Maybe someone did want to kill me outside Jerusalem's walls, but their real desire was . . .*

A soldier stuck his head through the door. "Please excuse me, Governor. Two men say it's urgent they talk to you."

"Show them in."

The soldier's frown deepened, and he spat out. "Sir, they are Jews. It's their Sabbath, and they think they will be defiled if they come in. They want to meet you out front."

Pilate grimaced and hacked the blade into the side of the bench, embedding it into the wood. "What is it with these people?"

Justus gave a calm look. "Sir, shall I stay and wait for your return?"

"No, come with me. These men may need your services."

Justus brushed off a sneer. "As you wish."

Justus trailed Pilate and stopped close behind him on the top of the stairs leading to the fortress' main entrance. He didn't recognize the two men, but could tell by his robe that one of them was the high priest.

Pilate raised himself to a kingly poise and his voice did not hide his disgust. "What is it you want this time?"

The high priest stepped closer to the stairs, with a dangerously impudent air. "Sir, we have just remembered that vagabond predicted after three days, he would rise again."

Justus hung on the high priest's words.

He continued, his tone gruff. "Therefore, give an order to have the tomb made secure and safeguarded through the third day, for fear his disciples will steal the body and tell the people he has risen from the dead."

The other priest chimed in, "That last deception would be worse than the first."

Pilate turned, clenched his fists, and spoke with a voice of contempt. "You have Temple guards. Have them make the tomb as secure as you can."

Both priests glared at Pilate for a few moments, turned around, and sulked out like they had been banished.

Pilate relaxed. "Those two were yesterday's ringleaders." He studied Justus. "So, Chief Advocate, why do you think they forced me to kill the man?"

Justus nodded. "I think you hit it right on the head. They love power and praise so much, they couldn't stand to be in Jesus' shadow."

CHAPTER SEVENTY-ONE

Jehu was in a foul mood. He, Attai, and Sethur had opened the Tomb the preceding morning, and found only a single, meaningless ancient word. He had holed up in his cramped room at the guard station the rest of the day and the entire night to avoid anyone seeing his deep depression. He had shirked all his Passover duties and was not even considering helping in any way with the Sabbath ones.

He picked a spear from the four leaning in the corner. It needed a new point, so he sat on the single chair in the room and braced the spear handle on the leather-covered bench. His activity, however, did not keep him from wallowing in his melancholy. As he unwrapped the thin leather bands holding the broken tip, he replayed the high of finding a treasure to the grim reality none was there.

It had to be there. The Roman found it in the Torah and Sethur confirmed it. The Torah said the tithe was under the hill of Golgotha . . . and it is never wrong.

A knock on the door interrupted Jehu's thoughts. He felt frustrated as Attai entered his office leading a young man. The youngster had rusty brown beard growth less than an inch long. His tunic was short, a small turban was tied around short hair, and his robe a coarse woven, dirty white. He was clearly a servant.

Jehu felt a tinge of impatience, and he remained seated. "What is it you want?"

Attai nodded sideways at the youth. "This is Simeon. He has been sent with a message."

Simeon's hands shook as he used them to help talk. "Chief Priest Annas has directed me to bring you a command of the high priest. You are to post a guard at the Nazarene's tomb."

Jehu bounded up from the chair. "You must be kidding."

Simeon gave him a surprised look and stepped back. "The high priest has directed it."

Jehu grimaced and waved the broken spear head perilously close to Simeon's chest. "For what purpose? He's dead. Do they think he's going get up, push away the stone, and walk away?"

Simeon stammered, "I . . . he . . . I was told to . . . to tell you."

Jehu snorted and turned his back to Simeon. "Just go. You've done your job."

The youth bolted from the room.

As Jehu heard the door slam, he grabbed the spear shaft with both hands and shoved it sideways onto the floor near the bench. The loosened tip shot off on impact and clanged twice on the stone surface. "I think the whole bunch of them have lost any ability to think."

Attai squeezed past Jehu and retrieved the broken spear point and separate handle. He looked thoughtful. "Maybe they are afraid his disciples will take the body somewhere and claim he has risen from the dead."

Jehu snatched the spear shaft from Attai's hand. "You have got to be kidding me. I think you've been around those guys too long."

"What do you mean?"

Jehu scowled. "If someone takes the body away and claims he has risen from the dead, the only response is 'OK, let me see him.' If he's never seen by anyone, he didn't come back from the dead. I mean, good grief, what kind of logic is that? Who in their right mind is going to say he's alive if nobody ever sees him alive? Who would believe it?"

Attai lobbed the dulled head into an empty corner. It bounced on the stone floor once, ricocheted into the wall, and fell to rest on the broken end, leaning against the rough surface. "I get your gist. You are right, of course. Also, if they say he's alive and they just put the dead body somewhere else, we will hear of it. There's always someone who can't keep a secret."

"Absolutely!"

Attai looked troubled. "What are we to do?"

Jehu hesitated for only a few moments. He examined the spear handle, reached below the bench, and picked up a new spear point. He sounded unusually calm. "Select three men. The four of you stay at the tomb until dark. Have four others relieve you then and stay at the tomb until first light. After that, you four relieve them and stay the remainder of the day." He gave a long exhale as he fitted the point to the handle. "We are only required to guard through the third day, so at dark tomorrow, our assignment is finished. Then we'll let the carpenter rest in peace."

Attai nodded. "As you wish." He paused to look at Jehu. "There is a situation."

Jehu shot a glance back. "A situation?"

"Bukki is dead. The Roman advocate killed him."

Jehu demanded, "Why would he do that?"

"Supposedly, Bukki abducted the Grecian woman and took her to the Ephraim catacombs. The Roman followed him, killed Bukki, and rescued the woman."

All Jehu knew about Bukki's recent activities flashed through his gray matter. He felt a tinge of impatience. "Why kidnap her?"

Attai shrugged. "I have no idea."

"Well, investigate as much as you can before you stand guard. This means I must interrogate the Roman . . . without him knowing it."

CHAPTER SEVENTY-TWO

Shortly after Caiaphas and Annas made their request, Pilate had allowed Justus to leave. He immediately found Julius at breakfast and debriefed him on the meeting. After breakfast it took him little time to make his way back to Miriam's house. As he crossed the covered courtyard, he exchanged greetings with the two door guards and rushed in. Though he had rolled the facts around mentally several times, he could not fathom a connection between Bukki luring him out of Jerusalem by kidnapping Michal and someone kidnapping Miriam.

Michal launched herself from her bench before Justus had taken one step inside and darted to him, looking distressed. "Are you OK?"

Justus hugged her and noted the room was as he'd left it earlier. "Yes, I'm fine. I spent the morning with Pontius Pilate. He revealed the strategy used by the chief priests."

Michal clutched Justus' arm. "Strategy? For what?"

Justus gave her a detailed account of the crucifixion and his meeting with Pilate.

Michal's expression was forlorn. "I'm sorry I let myself get kidnapped. Maybe you could have saved Jesus."

Justus offered a caring smile and lifted her chin with one hand. "Hey, it's not your fault. I was set up by your abduction, but you are not to blame." He took her hand and guided her to the bench she had been sitting on. He sat and gently pulled her beside him. However, rather than looking at her, he stared at the opposite wall and spoke slowly. "I'm having difficulty coming up with a reason for Bukki to kill me. He could have simply killed you and returned to Jerusalem. By the time

I would have found you and returned, Jesus would already have been crucified."

Michal shuddered. "A good question, but not one I want to think about."

Justus touched her arm. "I'm sorry. That was a cold way to put it."

Miriam entered from her room. She seemed hesitant. "Is everything all right?"

Michal smiled, stood, and went to her side as she replied, "Yes, but the story continues." She summarized the situation. "It's not clear whether our abductions are interrelated."

Miriam frowned and remained silent.

Justus stood, but added nothing to Michal's condensed version of the facts. He took note of Miriam's increasing depression and tried to find a better topic. "I had breakfast with Julius this morning, and he is coming soon."

Miriam instantly perked up and stepped toward Justus, placing her beside the high stand with the papyrus sheet. "I'm glad. For some reason, all these happenings seem to bother me less when he is around."

Michal and Justus exchanged knowing glances.

Miriam looked at the sheet, eclipsed with wonder. "Isn't it incredible what happened to Jesus and you finding *Jesus* and *Messiah* in the shape of a cross?"

Miriam's comment made Justus feel a deep chill, but he simply gazed at her.

"Dad said the proximity of two words was important to determining a new truth . . . and you can't get more 'in proximity' than this."

Justus joined Miriam at the table, a sudden tiredness coming over him. "How can a dead man deliver the Jews from Rome or anyone else's power?" Justus turned, moved to the bench, and stared at it without sitting. His voice was soft. "No, you can't be dead and be a messiah."

A loud knock was followed by Julius breezing into the room.

Justus wheeled at his entrance.

Watching his expression, Miriam asked, "Are you all right?"

"It has been an incredible night and morning," he replied. He marched to Miriam and looked long at her. "I'm fine." He glanced at Justus and added, "And, I am free for the rest of the day."

Justus nodded as he felt his mood lift. "So you can go with us?"

"Yes."

Michal shifted a step from Miriam to Justus, her face questioning. "Go where?"

"To the catacombs. I still believe Miriam's abduction had something to do with the Tomb, even if yours didn't."

Michal continued to him, smiling. "Let's go now."

> > >

The foursome quickly gathered what they needed to be able to see in the caverns. In less than an hour, they threaded their way to the pit Justus had used to find the connection between the Jerusalem and Salem catacombs.

Justus held his lamp high, showering the jagged walls of the pit with light, his jaw set firmly. "Follow me."

Michal, Miriam, and Julius filed down the stairs behind him.

Justus ducked through the hole he had created days earlier and froze, riveting the pathway. "Oh no! If there really was a treasure, it looks like someone has already found it. Look at all these footprints."

Michal twisted to see around Justus in the narrow tunnel. "Wonder how they figured out about the 'pair of eyes'?"

Justus shook his head as he moved deeper into the corridor. "I don't know."

The cave had an even more acid smell than the Jerusalem side. As they snaked through the Salem shafts, both Miriam and Michal held their hands to their noses to block the strong odor.

The four retraced the footprints in the dusty passages until they were in front of the black, yawning opening.

Justus' heart pounded as he took a half step in. He glimpsed a torch next to the opening and lit it. "This is a pretty large area." He moved far enough into the room so the others could join him. A strong chill snagged him and caused a deep shudder as recognition slapped him. They were directly below the hilltop where yesterday Jesus was crucified.

Julius lit the torch on the other side of the opening.

They all gaped in silence at the magnitude of the room of tombs.

Michal was the first to break the silence, her voice a whisper. "Wow, there are two levels of tombs on every wall."

Justus' remorse gave way to a surprising flood of excitement. "I'll bet Melchizedek's Tomb is at the top of that ladder against the wall." He bound for it, the others on his tail. Stopping near the bottom, he pointed at the tombstone on the floor. "There are the two eyes."

Michal glanced at them, then hopped up two rungs. Suddenly, she froze. "This isn't a tomb," she said.

Justus demanded, "What did you say?"

"No. It's only an indentation in the wall with letters carved into the back."

Justus' pulse thundered. "What are the letters?"

"R N A M M F I B. With the name Melchizedek below them."

Justus grabbed the steps with one hand as he strained to see over Michal. His booming voiced bounced off the walls. "Are you sure?"

Michal looked down at him with a frown, her voice sounding miffed. "Yes." She peered the opening again. "What kind of word is that?"

Justus hesitated only an instant, before snorting. "A cipher."

CHAPTER SEVENTY-THREE

The pure white robe with black embroidered pomegranates lining the edge accentuated the white streaks in Kore's uncut beard. He saved this outfit for the yearly Passover Festival.

An old man with a dark purple robe and a flowing white shawl maneuvered from the front of the crammed assembly to Kore, who stood at the side. He rolled up the Torah scroll, handed it to Kore, and shuffled to his former place on a front bench.

The last reading was complete. Kore glanced over the congregation, drew a deep breath, and crossed to center stage. The Passover celebration always generated large crowds on the Sabbath. Enjoying the focal point of attention, he raised his frame and held his right hand high.

His voice was loud and sounded like a preacher's. "As we have heard, the Lord charged our forefathers through the mouth of Moses. Every year from the fourteenth day of this month, Abib, until the twenty-first day, we are to eat nothing that is leavened and have nothing leavened within our dwellings."

He lowered his hand, shifted his weight, and pointed at the front row. "It is the sacrifice of the Lord's Passover, for He passed over every house that had the blood of a lamb placed on the lintel and the two side posts of their doors in Egypt. But He slew the firstborn of all those in the land of Egypt who had no blood on the door; from the firstborn of Pharaoh, to the firstborn of those in dungeons, even the firstborn of all the Egyptian livestock."

The synagogue comfortably seated a hundred men, but this day, all benches were filled and the walls were lined with standing pilgrims.

Silence pervaded the room and every man's attention was riveted on Kore. A few sandals scraped across the rough stone floor as some changed positions. Two coughs punctuated the air.

Kore beamed as his pride swelled. "Seven days we eat unleavened bread, and on the seventh, we feast. But, remember the Law . . ." He dropped his right hand in cadence with his directives, his voice curt. "You must set apart to the Lord all firstborn. The clean animals are the Lord's. Others must be redeemed by the blood of a lamb. And all your firstborn sons shall be redeemed."

The congregation rose, chanting in unison. "All the Lord says, we will do. All His ordinances, we will follow. All His ways shall be our ways. Mighty is the Lord." After reciting the benediction, they began migrating toward two doors at the back.

The room held so many worshippers, it took several minutes for all to file out. The purple-robed old man went to Kore and placed his hand on Kore's shoulder. "May your coming year be prosperous." He followed the others.

Finally, all had departed except Sethur, who had chosen to stand near the front, so his short height would not prevent him from watching the ceremony.

Kore still held the air of superiority he showed when speaking to the congregation. His voice sounded as if the multitude were still present. "May I help you in some way?"

Sethur looked truly perplexed. He combed his long brown beard with the fingers of his right hand. "Yes, there is."

"Is it something about Passover?"

Sethur looked hard at Kore for a few beats and stepped closer. His shrewish face narrowed on Kore. "No. I saw a strange word written in the dust near the Temple yesterday. I have researched all the documents I have access to, but cannot find it. I was wondering if you know of it."

Kore was surprised at the request. His pompous air evaporated. "What is the word?"

"RNAMMFIB."

Kore turned from Sethur to hide contempt for the mini-mystery. What a waste of time. "No, I'm sorry. I have never heard such a word."

Kore turned a slow gaze to Sethur, his voice dripping with scorn. "Many pilgrims come from distant lands. It's probably a foreign language."

Sethur looked doubtful. "It might be. However, if you know any of the sages who might have come to Jerusalem for the Passover, I thought I would ask them."

Kore pivoted to Sethur. Moments passed as he tried to conjure up the real reason a scribe would want to question a sage. Unsuccessful, he finally shrugged. "There may be many, but I only know of one."

"Who is it?"

"Mazis, from Masada."

CHAPTER SEVENTY-FOUR

Michal gawked at the two men from her perch near the middle of the ladder. She gave them a skeptical look. "What's a cipher?"

Justus grinned. "You know, like Caesar's Cipher."

Michal shook her head. "Caesar's Cipher? I have no idea what are you talking about?"

Julius glanced at Justus, then expressed tenderness. "Julius Caesar devised a method to write tactical orders to his troops in such a way that if someone intercepted them, they could not be understood."

Justus spoke hurriedly. "And every Caesar since has had his own version. My father has received ciphers from Caesar Tiberius."

Julius added, "Actually, I have received some from Caesar Tiberius myself."

The light flickered from the burning torches. The light's random motions crossed Michal's manner and amplified her look of confusion. She stepped one rung lower and focused on Justus. "If someone intercepting the message can't understand it, how does the true receiver understand it?"

Julius moved to the ladder and held the side opposite Justus. He spoke before Justus could answer. "There are two components to a tactical cipher: the messenger who brings it to you and then a second messenger who brings you the key."

Michal's eyebrows shot up. "A key?"

Justus had spent long hours in developing and cracking ciphers. The first one his father had given him hooked him for life. He had become a master at making and breaking them. His father still regularly contacted him when he wanted particularly secret ones.

Justus offered his hand to help Michal the rest of the way down. "Let me give you an example. One Caesar's Cipher variation was to do this." He guided her off the ladder and to an area with no footprints.

Justus bent and used one finger in the deep dust on the floor:

A B C D E F G H I J K L M N O P Q R S T U V W X Y Z

He glanced up at Michal, his voice instructive. "He would then write out another listing of the alphabet, but start four places over."

A B C D E F G H I J K L M N O P Q R S T U V W X Y Z

W X Y Z A B C D E F G H I J K L M N O P Q R S T U V

"So . . . to make a message—for example 'Hi Michal'—I would go to the top letters, but write the bottom letters. See?" Justus wrote in the dust:

DE IEYDWH

Julius chimed in, "Then a second messenger would go to the cipher receiver and instruct him to move four letters over."

Michal stared at the cipher in the dust, looking thoughtful.

Miriam nearly jumped to Michal, grabbed her arm, and blurted out, "Like Atbash."

Michal flinched and pursed her lips. "I think I've been in Greece way too long." She stared at Miriam for a second, then spoke slowly. "What is Atbash?"

Miriam dropped to her knees. "It's the same thing Justus did on the ground, but the alphabet is totally backwards." She spread the dust out, erasing Justus' cipher, and used her finger to write two strings of alphabet in the dust—one the correct sequence, one in reverse:

A B C D E F G H I J K L M N O P Q R S T U V W X Y Z

Z Y X W V U T S R Q P O N M L K J I H G F E D C B A

Miriam's countenance was bright, as she glanced at Michal. "This would be your greeting if I said the same thing using Atbash." She wrote on the ground:

SR NRXSZO

Michal gasped and stooped down next to Miriam for a better look. "I see. In your case, though, the messenger with the key would have to say something like 'backwards'."

The other three bellowed in unison, "Yes."

Justus' creativity raced as the new twist in their searching took hold. He touched Miriam's shoulder, his excitement growing. "Did Asher study ciphers?"

"No, but he had a good friend who did."

"What was his friend's name?"

"Mazis."

CHAPTER SEVENTY-FIVE

Jehu forgot his frustration at not finding the treasure when he heard the news that Bukki had kidnapped Michal and then died at the hands of Justus, her rescuer. He knew Bukki had kidnapped Miriam and was using her safety to force Asher to search the Torah for the treasure. He suspected Annas was the mastermind behind the plan, but had no proof. Now he needed to gauge Annas' involvement in Michal's abduction before he could address Justus on the primary issue—the meaning of the strange word in the fake tomb.

Jehu marched stiffly across the open courtyard of Annas' home. As he waited for the maid to allow him entrance, he glimpsed the nearby door of Bukki's apartment and an evil smile twisted his lips.

When the maid let him in, he waited as she scurried off to tell Annas of his visit. He absently looked at the benches in the foyer on opposite walls as he mentally rehearsed his line of questioning.

In minutes, Annas glided into the foyer. His long robe was gathered at the waist by a gold chain. A purple shawl completely covered his head and ran down the length of his long beard. His look was stern. "Simeon told me you didn't like the order to guard the tomb of the Nazarene. Is that why you're here?"

Jehu was so engrossed in the matter at hand, he was unprepared for Annas' question. He took his helmet from his head—to buy time more than give comfort. He looked directly at Annas and said, "No. I have placed guards at the tomb. I'm here on other business."

Annas hesitated, as a look of anticipation came over him. "What is it you want?"

"I have learned Bukki kidnapped the Grecian woman. The Roman advocate subsequently killed him." Jehu extended his hand. "Why would he do that?"

Annas half turned. "I have no idea."

"He was your lead servant."

Annas stood straight and gave Jehu a cold look. "I do not like your tone. Bukki was going through some emotional problems and evidently cracked under self-induced pressure."

"Problems?" Jehu set his helmet on the bench farthest from Annas. "What problems?"

Annas gave a wave of disgust. "He became obsessed with a mythical treasure."

"Treasure?"

"Abram's Tithe. Treasure hunters have searched for it for years. Surely you've heard about it."

Jehu felt elated but maintained a cool exterior. He nodded as he spoke slowly. "Of course . . . children's games. There is no treasure." He pivoted and stepped the short distance to the outside door. "But why would Bukki become obsessed with it?"

Annas paused and put a hand to his lips, as a moment passed. "He found out Caiaphas was having Malchus search for Melchizedek's Tomb in exchange for his freedom."

Jehu had long since known Malchus' motivation but had kept the knowledge secret. He returned to the bench, holding his helmet. "So?"

"I'm sure he thought Caiaphas had some special knowledge about the Tomb's location."

Jehu was secretly pleased. "Why would Caiaphas want to find Melchizedek's Tomb?"

Annas swallowed hard, a single drop of sweat falling down one sideburn. "He obtained information from a source I do not know suggesting there was information in the Tomb that would shed light on the claims and actions of the late Nazarene."

Jehu stepped uncomfortably close. "Do you think Bukki kidnapped Miriam?"

Annas looked like a bear backed into a corner. "Absolutely."

"Why didn't you turn him in?"

"I had no witnesses."

Jehu wheeled about to assure he didn't give away a hint of a smile. His voice was metered. "And—without two witnesses, there is no case."

"Precisely."

Jehu nodded. "Thank you, Chief Priest Annas. I appreciate your time." He snatched his helmet and strode out into the courtyard.

Now the Roman.

CHAPTER SEVENTY-SIX

The shadow from Jerusalem's west wall began to blend into the dusk as the sun set. Although there was enough light to still see, Justus kept his lamp burning as he led Michal, Miriam, and Julius from the catacombs.

He had been able to unravel every cipher he had ever encountered, usually in very little time. But RNAMMFIB had him stumped. Usually the letter *e* was easiest to find as it is the most-used vowel, then a sensible repositioning of the other letters could quickly be arranged. But . . . not with this cipher. Whoever came up with this one was a master.

Irritated, he paused to look down the street to the Herod Gate. Michal stopped at his side, but Miriam and Julius passed him and strolled ahead. A few people entered the city through it, but the streets were fairly empty. An owl's screech came from beyond the gate.

Michal wove her arm into his. "Do you want to visit Jesus' tomb?" she asked.

Justus was almost glad for her interruption, but he shook his head. "Not tonight. I'm going to Bethany in the morning. I'll stop by on my way."

Michal gently tugged his arm, and they ambled after Julius and Miriam. "Why Bethany?" she asked.

Justus looked at the roughly stoned street right in front of him. "I suspect some of Jesus' family are at Lazarus' house. If they are, I want to give my condolences."

Miriam turned, and Julius stopped with her. She called out, "Aren't you going to the tomb?"

Justus replied, "In the morning. It's nearly dark . . . and . . . the guards may think I'm up to some mischief."

Miriam looked stunned. "The guards? Why are they guarding a tomb?"

Although moving quite slowly, Justus and Michal came near the other two, and Justus replied, "The high priest is afraid Jesus' followers will steal the body and claim he has risen from the dead." Justus flipped his hand in the air. "I think it's a harebrained idea."

Miriam looked incredulous, but said nothing. She and Julius resumed their trek in line with Michal and Justus.

Julius shook his head, and his voice sounded disgusted. "If his followers are still in the city, which I seriously doubt, they won't be stealing anything." He leaned to look past Miriam at Justus. "In fact, I doubt if they will show themselves for days. Some Temple guards observed all of them fleeing in fear when Jesus was arrested."

Miriam took Julius' hand and shivered. "Let's get to my house." They set off at a brisk pace.

Arm and arm, Michal and Justus quickly fell far behind them. At the next intersection, three women carrying sacks cut right in front of them. Michal inhaled deeply as they proceeded down their street. "Mmm . . . smell those spices."

Justus watched the three disappear into the darkness. "Very nice. The Sabbath ended only a short time ago. I wonder if they are selling or buying."

"I don't know, but they were in a hurry."

Justus and Michal picked up their speed. They gained enough distance to watch Miriam and Julius enter the covered courtyard. As they approached the area, Miriam and Julius appeared to be talking to a man and woman whose backs were toward Justus.

Joining the group standing around the fire, Justus recognized Jehu and Abigail. He didn't attempt to hide his suspicious expression, his voice hinting contempt. "It's late to be visiting."

Jehu gazed at him blankly. "I'm not visiting. I am here on official business."

"What kind of business?"

Jehu spoke with a flat, matter-of-fact tone. "I have figured out Bukki kidnapped Miriam."

Miriam glanced at Justus, her voice low. "Why?"

"To force your father to find Melchizedek's Tomb."

Miriam edged closer to Julius.

The night was not very cold, but Justus stepped behind them to the woodpile and selected a long branch. He was surprised at Jehu's forthrightness and remained cautious. "Was he ordered to do it?"

Jehu scowled. "He acted alone. And you need to be very careful with accusations such as those."

Michal spoke up as she moved close to Miriam. "He was Annas' lead servant. How do you know Annas didn't order him to do it?"

"I interviewed Annas and learned Bukki's motive." He summarized his meeting with Annas.

Justus stirred the fire with the branch as he listened to the mono-logue. At the end, he was not at all convinced and said, "Before Bukki fell from the cliff, I offered to tell him the location of the Tomb, but he appeared totally disinterested. If he was obsessed with finding Abram's Tithe, why wouldn't he want the location?"

Jehu crossed his arms over his leather breastplate and slowly turned his head to Michal. His black helmet seemed to add a sinister quality as he stared at her for several seconds. "Perhaps he thought you knew something more important than the Tomb's location." He shot a glance at Justus. "Do you?"

Apprehension seized Justus powerful and sudden. *What does Jehu know?* He threw the branch in the fire. "I only know the location."

Jehu's brows furrowed, and he glared at Justus. "When will you go there?"

Justus exchanged fugitive looks with Michal.

Julius interrupted, his voice commanding. "That is no business of yours."

Jehu's demeanor instantly changed. He dropped his arms and took a step back as he looked at Julius. "Not only none of my business, but also none of my concern." He half turned to the street. "Why would I be interested in a child's fairy tale?"

Justus was taken aback. He had become totally convinced the Tithe was real and felt sure that breaking the cipher would lead them directly to it. But he showed no emotion and remained silent.

Jehu stepped onto the street, then suddenly turned back to Miriam with an oily smile, "Abigail tells me you are no longer in need of her services, so I asked her to prepare a house for some of my relatives who are soon moving to Jerusalem. Is that acceptable with you?"

Miriam glanced at Abigail. "That will be fine."

Jehu nodded and disappeared into the darkness.

Abigail bowed her head before Miriam. "I thank you all for your kindness." She picked up a sack.

Miriam touched her arm and restrained her. "Do you want someone to go with you?"

Abigail slightly shook her head. "I'll be fine." She pointed north. "The house Jehu wants me to prepare is right across the street. I'm going there now."

Justus and Michal traded suspicious looks.

Miriam glanced at the house. It was a small, two-room building with a single window. An alley was on one side and an extremely small, open courtyard was on the other. She sighed, "Well, if you need anything, just ask."

Before Abigail reached the street, Justus called after her, "Has Perez left?"

She turned back, her voice shaky. "He left with his things in the afternoon. He didn't tell me where he was going. I'm sorry."

Glad to hear he was finished with Perez, Justus simply shrugged.

Julius took Miriam's hand. "Do you care if I stay in Perez's room tonight?"

Miriam beamed at him. "That's a great idea."

"Thanks." Julius walked Miriam to her front door. After Miriam and Julius exchanged farewells, he slipped along the outer wall to the private entrance of Perez's adjoining room.

Michal shivered and stepped closer to the fire. "Looks like our attempt to get rid of Abigail and Perez was only half effective."

Justus grimaced. He stared into the blackness that had swallowed Abigail. "You're right. We need to be careful what we do out here in the courtyard . . . especially if we solve the cipher."

Chapter Seventy-six

Michal squinted. "Have you thought more about it?"

"Yes . . . and it's very difficult. "Justus grabbed a long stick from the woodpile and wrote the Atbash cipher scheme in the dirt close enough to the fire so it could be seen. Beside it, he traced the cipher from the tomb, RNAMMFIB. "See, Atbash yields nothing." He wrote below the cipher IMZNNURY.

Michal sighed. "Yeah. Nothing."

Justus squatted down and wiped away the reversed alphabet, then used the stick to reposition an alphabet below the original, but off-set by four letters. "And . . . starting four letters to the right yields, NJWIIBEX." He continued writing below the Melchizedek cipher. "Starting five letters to the right gives, MIVHHADW."

Michal looked up at him. "But aren't there thousands of combinations that you might try?"

"An infinite number."

"So, how can you solve it?"

Justus gave a grim sigh. He stared at the fire and dropped the stick into it. "I probably can't without the key."

Michal moved to the bench by the fire and plopped down on it. Her voice sounded defeated. "Melchizedek or whoever has been dead for thousands of years. There's no one who can bring us the key."

"I know . . . I'm afraid we have hit a stone wall."

Julius stuck his head out of the door of Perez's quarters, and called, "Justus, I've found something you need to see."

In four broad strides, Justus entered Perez's apartment, Michal close behind him.

Inside, Julius pointed to a hole in the dirt-brick wall. "He heard everything."

CHAPTER SEVENTY-SEVEN

Justus woke instantly, but he saw nothing in the room now black as a cave. His body was rigid, and sweat covered his forehead. Something was very wrong. He held his breath, trying to detect if someone or something was in the darkness with him.

His bed moved ever so slightly. A low-toned groan sounded and the bed moved again, this time noticeably.

He jumped up as a deep rumpling noise increased. An earthquake.

Justus stumbled into the wall. He slid both hands over the rough dry mud façade, tracing his way to the door, and flung it open.

Michal stood in her doorway, her short black hair sticking out on one side. The flickering light from the lamp she held at her waist made her look like an evil monster. Her voice was shrill. "Earthquake! Everyone out of the house . . . now!"

Justus raced after Michal as the wooden strips clattered onto the floor.

The fire outside was still smoldering. It gave an eerie glow through the dust falling from the mud-jointed reeds of the courtyard's canopy.

Julius was already out of Perez's apartment and barking orders to the four soldiers outside. He spun around, his manner radiating fear. "Where's Miriam?" Not waiting for an answer, he leaped into the house. Seconds later, he reappeared, carrying Miriam in his arms.

She wore only a long tunica. She rubbed her eyes with the back knuckles of each forefinger. As Julius descended the steps, Miriam looked up at him, her voice anxious. "What's wrong?"

Julius set her down in the street and sighed loudly. "There is an earthquake," he told her. "Didn't it wake you?"

The tremors began to subside, as a few stones from a nearby building fell harmlessly to the street.

Miriam glanced down the street in the direction of the sounds. She straightened her long, light-brown hair with both hands. She gazed at Julius for a few seconds through half-closed lids, turned, and stepped back into the courtyard toward the house. "Jerusalem gets many earthquakes. After a while, one gets used to them."

Justus searched the street. He could only see two torches moving. "Guess you are right. There are only a couple people milling around. It looks like hardly anyone has left their homes."

Julius remained in the street. He wore the short tunic of a Roman warrior. He studied the top of the city wall. "Familiar or not, I don't like them. I've experienced devastation from earthquakes in other countries."

Miriam gave him an amused look and then went back into the house.

Justus felt uneasy, but went back under the courtyard covering. "I have, also. Think I'll stay near the fire in the courtyard until the aftershocks are over. It'll be dawn soon anyway."

Michal sidled up to Justus, a coy smile. "I'll join you."

➤ ➤ ➤

Justus squinted in the bright morning sunlight until he passed through the Herod Gate and turned northwest in the shade of the wall. He and Michal had spent the dawning hours talking about ciphers and various ways of breaking them. They had also talked a little about Jesus' family. He was surprised when she declined to accompany him to Bethany.

He moved with a relaxed gait. Three vultures caught his eye as they slowly spiraled high in the sky to the west. *Wow. What a beautiful morning.* Even knowing it would be difficult talking to Jesus' family, he felt surprisingly refreshed.

Reaching the corner of the city wall, he stopped as a rooster crowed in the distance. He smiled softly and angled northeast toward Golgotha hill. His wide strides ate up chunks of distance. The hill was soon in sight. He raised his hand to block the low morning sun. Per standard operating procedures, the soldiers had long since disposed of the crosses.

He continued up the Golgotha slope, his anticipation increasing with each step. At the top, he froze and gaped at an opened tomb on a hill slope opposite Golgotha. *That must be the tomb. But why is it open?* He surveyed the slope, but saw no other tombs. *Where are the guards?*

Justus bolted to the tomb, bent down, and took a step inside. It took him only a second to see it was completely empty. He stepped out, and leaned against the outside wall for support. Unseen sheep bleated from the other side of hill. He stared at the large, flat stone lying on its side a few yards away.

Did the earthquake cause the stone to fall like that? He glanced back at the opening, scrambling for a reasonable explanation. Had Jesus' disciples moved his body because an earthquake had opened the tomb? But, what about the guards? They wouldn't have allowed it. Did the guards move the body? But where?

Justus stooped and peered into the tomb again. It was still empty. He shivered and took small steps to the city wall's northern-most point. When he reached the wall, he slanted a final look at the tomb for a heartbeat then charged southeast, trying to crowd out his confusion by focusing on his mission at Bethany.

The path to Bethany from the Mercy Gate was well worn. The dirt had been pressed solid, and no stones lay in the way. Justus made the walk in twenty minutes. He paused at the outskirts, near the house of Lazarus.

The city sloped upward from where Justus was standing. He browsed over what he could see of the small town, his thoughts finally leaving the empty tomb. A few people were talking in a street some distance away, but no one else was visible. He gave Lazarus' house a doubtful glance. It certainly doesn't look like anyone was at home.

Justus crossed the courtyard and knocked loudly, his booming voice tinged with desperation. "Lazarus? Mary? Martha? Is anyone home?"

Justus remained in place a few minutes and knocked again, but this time said nothing. His chin went to his chest as he waited longer than needed to conclude no one was there. Finally, he retreated several steps. He gave a long look at the door, turned toward Jerusalem, and kicked a rock lying at the edge of the only path in the garden.

From behind him a desperate voice called, "Justus! Wait."

Justus spun about. "James! Am I glad to see you!"

The two men embraced.

After a minute, Justus pushed James back, his voice quivering. "Are you all right?"

Tears streamed down James' cheeks. "It was horrible . . . simply horrible."

"Was your mother there?"

"Yes. And most of his disciples watched from one point or another."

Justus took a step from James, but remained focused on him. He swallowed hard, not really ready for what he knew was the answer. "Did he suffer much?"

James' shoulders slumped. "Yes."

Justus went back and wrapped his arm around James, his voice a whisper. "It's over now."

The two were silent for several minutes. Justus moved to a large stone under a fig tree in the courtyard. James sat on a nearby stone bench. Justus gave a short summary about Michal, explaining why he was not at the crucifixion.

Finished, he pointed at the door. "Where is everyone?"

"Mom was here the last two nights. She's really in bad shape. Lazarus and his two sisters, along with my brothers and sisters, left at dawn to take her back to Nazareth." James stood, took four steps to the edge of the courtyard, and looked up over Bethany. "The earthquake woke them early, though I don't think Mom has slept since Jesus died."

"I knew she would take it hard." Justus regained a little composure and asked, "Why did you not go with them?"

James extended his hand west. "Jesus' disciples are still in Jerusalem. I want to talk to them before I leave."

Justus rose from his stone chair and tilted his head. "In Jerusalem? Where?"

"Actually near Miriam's house. They all ate the Passover Supper in the upper room of a house one block away in the direction of the Herod Gate."

Justus put a single finger on his lips. "Why are they still there?"

"They are afraid the Jewish authorities will do something to them next."

Justus nodded slowly. "I guess I can understand their concern. The priests and Pharisees have tasted blood. Who knows how long before that thirst will be quenched?"

James turned and looked northwest. "Also, on the way, I want to go past the tomb again."

Both of Justus' hands shot up, spread wide. "But it's empty."

James' jaw dropped. "What?"

"It's empty. I just came from there. Evidently, the earthquake caused the stone covering to fall. I guess someone decided to move the body after that."

James wobbled several steps back.

Justus jumped forward and clutched his arm. "Let's go inside for a while. I'm sure Lazarus won't mind."

Justus held James up as they moved inside Lazarus' front room. The floor dining mat was scrunched to one side. Two benches were in the center of the room. The absence of any windows made the house gloomy, even though the sun shone brightly outside.

Justus helped him settle onto one of the benches. James' back was to the door. He joined James, as his own dammed-up grief seeped through. "Please forgive me."

James glanced at him sideways. "For what?"

"Had I been in Jerusalem, I could have defended Jesus." Justus looked at the ceiling and held his right palm half up. "James . . . it's what I do."

James shook his head, his voice definite. "The high priest was judge and jury. There is no way you would have been able to help him."

Tears topped Justus' eyelids and fell. "Pilate would have insisted I be his advocate. James . . . God has made me a very good one. I could have helped him."

James laid his hand on Justus' arm, and gave a reassuring look. "Don't do this to yourself. It's over. Even Justus couldn't have brought justice, this time."

His jingle caused Justus to flash a one-sided smile which instantly turned to anguish. "But I could have saved him."

Suddenly the room reverberated with a deep voice directly behind the men. "Instead . . . I saved you."

They froze for a split second, then exploded from the bench, knocking it over. In unison, they turned to Jesus.

He was dressed in a fine linen robe with a long shawl over his head. Both were a brilliant white and almost gave light to the room. His unblemished face was framed with a carpenter's precisely trimmed beard and moustache. His look appeared to be testing them.

James gasped, "But you were dead! I saw you myself."

Justus was a human statue with a gaping mouth.

Jesus gave Justus a twinkling gaze as He held up his nail-scarred hands. "It's time for you to decide. You have seen all the facts about me. What does your impeccable logic tell you now?"

Justus fell to his knees, his hands up in worship. His voice was trembling. "My Lord and my God. I believe you are the Messiah."

Jesus showed a broad grin as he pivoted to James, his voice loving. "And you, my brother?"

James appeared mesmerized. "You are my Lord. I, too, believe."

Still grinning, Jesus turned to go.

Justus jumped up toward Him. "Wait. This is not all, is it? You are the Messiah. When will You begin to reign?"

Jesus' look was gentle, and His words were almost like a song. "Soon I will send a Comforter. He will make all things clear to you. Afterwards, go and tell the world what you know about Me."

Justus and James were frozen.

Jesus placed his hand on Justus' shoulder and bent toward him. With an affectionate look, his voice became soft. "Justus, you have found Me. Yet . . . still you seek Me?"

In a blink of an eye, Jesus disappeared.

The two men exchanged incredulous looks.

CHAPTER SEVENTY-SEVEN

Justus shook his head hard and peered at James. "He was here, right?"

James slowly nodded, but said nothing.

Both men sat heavily on the side of the overturned bench.

James offered, "I see why the tomb is empty."

All sadness had been erased from Justus as he stared into space. "In fact, this clears up a bunch of things about Him I haven't understood."

The two sat for a long time lost in their individual thoughts.

Finally, Justus jumped up, his demeanor joyful. "James . . . He is alive, and I'm going to go tell Michal."

James joined him and gave a long exhale. "I'm going to Nazareth and tell Mom. That is, if Jesus doesn't beat me to it."

Justus shot him a knowing look. "You know . . . your mother really was a virgin, wasn't she?"

CHAPTER SEVENTY-EIGHT

Jehu leaned against the wall of the guard's quarters. He felt oddly unsettled as he stared out the window. The mild earthquake had wakened him earlier. Although he was still tired from lack of sleep and emotionally drained by the last few days' events, his thoughts about the ancient word and uncertainty about Justus' continued involvement prevented him from going back to sleep.

A strong breeze blew through the Temple courtyard. The bright morning sun was high above the city wall and forced him to squint. Even so, he focused on a man running at full speed from the west enclosure wall toward the guard's station. As he neared, Jehu noted the way he held his spear forward and concluded he was Attai. He stood up as a sensation of impending danger gripped him.

Attai reached Jehu in seconds, breathing too hard to speak immediately.

Jehu looked vexed. "Why are you not watching the tomb?"

"When I . . . arrived . . . to relieve . . . the four guards . . ." Attai's breathing became less labored. ". . . the tomb was open."

Jehu fell back a step. "What? How?"

Attai placed one hand on the guard quarter's wall. "My men said one came like lightening and moved the stone away."

Jehu shook his head in disbelief. "Were they drinking?"

"I don't think so. They appeared very frightened."

"What did they say happened then?"

"They told me they all fainted. None have any idea what happened after that."

Jehu felt disgruntled. He knew this was the very thing the priests were afraid would happen. The slothfulness of a few guards had put Jehu's position as captain in severe jeopardy. He leaned toward Attai with one hand out. "And the body?"

"When they awoke, they went into the open tomb. Nothing was inside, except the burial clothes in a pile near the fine linen cloth covering the body. And . . ." Attai focused on the ground in front of him.

Jehu could tell he was struggling, but he pressed him anyway. "Go on. What else did they see?"

Attai looked up, his voice just more than a whisper. "The linen strips which were wrapped around the head were in a different place, still wrapped as if around a head . . . yet, there was no head in them."

Jehu pushed Attai's shoulder forcing him up. "Did you go in and see this?"

Attai stared at Jehu for several seconds and appeared to swallow hard. "Yes, I saw it exactly as they said."

Jehu exhaled loudly. "Follow me. You must tell this to the chief priests."

The guard quarters were attached to the outer Temple wall, so it took few steps before both men entered the Temple through a side door.

A young servant was just inside the door sweeping. He was small, dressed in coarse cloth, and one arm was deformed. Jehu grabbed his good arm, his voice ringing with anger. "We must talk to a chief priest or the high priest immediately. It is of the utmost importance."

The servant looked frightened and dropped the broom. "I will inform them at once."

Jehu stared at the servant until he disappeared through an inner door, then said sarcastically, "The earthquake probably opened the tomb, and those idiots you selected were so filled with strong drink, they saw lightening and passed out. They woke up after someone had moved the body."

Expressionless, Attai glanced at Jehu but said nothing.

Only a few minutes passed until Caiaphas and Annas entered the small side room.

Annas appeared agitated. "What is so important?"

Jehu told them all Attai had reported.

Caiaphas didn't hide his disgust. "They fainted? Good God. Remain here. Annas and I will speak to the elders and come back to inform you what you must do."

An hour passed before Annas re-entered the small room carrying a large pouch. He handed it to Jehu, his expression authoritarian. "Take this money. Split it between yourselves and the other guards. Tell everyone the Nazarene's disciples came during the night while they were sleeping. They stole the body."

Jehu held the pouch out as if it contained snakes. "What if Pilate hears about it and demands some type of penalty?"

"We will make you all safe and free from trouble or care."

Jehu glowered at the pouch for several seconds, then gave Annas a cold gaze. "As you command."

The guards strode out of the Temple, both men's capes flapping behind them in the wind. They marched in time to the guardhouse and halted.

Jehu glanced back at the Temple and threw Attai the pouch with loathing. "Instruct the others what they are to say. It irks me they will be paid to tell what can only be the truth."

Attai returned a smug glance. "They will think they are lying."

➤ ➤ ➤

Malchus stopped on the dusty road and reversed directions to contemplate the Jerusalem skyline. The sun was directly overhead in a cloudless sky. A breeze wafted his long hair as his finger pushed aside a few locks to touch his right ear.

As he affirmed it was still perfect, the events of the three-nights-ago arrest fixed firmly in the forefront of his intellect. He had his freedom. But why Caiaphas' condition that he leave Jerusalem?

Malchus took several backward steps away from Jerusalem, still gazing at the Temple turrets with a look of growing determination. A wild goat munched on grass a few yards away and watched him intently.

No. I have done a great wrong and I must apologize to Jesus' disciples before I leave for good. He had searched for the Tomb that was supposed to have evidence about Jesus for Caiaphas to probably use against Him. He had led the arresting party. He had gained much and hurt Him even more. *I must tell His disciples how sorry I am. If they kill me, so be it. I must prove to them I have repented of my wrongdoings.*

Malchus hesitated for only a few beats, straightened, and marched toward Jerusalem, determination in every step.

CHAPTER SEVENTY-NINE

Justus had jogged nearly all the way from Bethany to the Temple area inside the walls of Jerusalem before resuming his normal strides, partly to catch his breath and partly to prevent unwanted attention.

In a short time, he saw the covering over the courtyard in front of Miriam's house and he slowed further. A stranger stood by the fire near Michal, who was bent over writing in the dust with a short stick. He forgot about telling her Jesus was alive as he studied the newcomer.

He was middle-aged and muscular. His bald head was framed by surprisingly thick white hair above his ears. He had a well trimmed, white beard, but his robe was coarsely made, and slightly tattered. He seemed delighted as he watched Michal make letters.

Justus said, "Michal, who's . . .?"

Intent on her writing, Justus' voice startled her and made her hand jerk. She bounced up and grabbed his arm, her teeth shining through a broad grin. "This is Mazis." Waving her hand, she added, "Mazis, this is Justus."

Suddenly awed, Justus peered at the man. "Really . . . I am pleased to meet you . . . and I'm glad you are here. But why . . .?"

Mazis interrupted Justus with the customary Jewish embrace and grinned broadly. "Fortune is good."

Michal grabbed one of Justus' arms and turned him as she burst out, "Mazis came to Jerusalem for the Passover Festival. He came here intending to stay with Asher, but we were in Ephraim."

Mazis picked up the explanation. "Since nobody was here, I stayed with nearby relatives outside the city walls. They informed me Asher had passed over, but they knew no reason why Miriam should not be here. So, I decided to stop by this morning before I return to Masada."

Michal drew a deep breath and continued in rapid bursts. "He came shortly after you had gone to Bethany. We told him all about what was happening with the search for Melchizedek's Tomb." She used the writing stick to point to Miriam's house. "I showed him how you had found the clue to the Tomb and the word *Jesus* crossing *Messiah* . . ."

Mazis was excited, and blurted out, "Both are quite clever. You should be proud of your findings."

Michal leaned between the two men and rushed on, "Then we came by the fire and I showed him some of the ways you have tried to interpret the cipher." She stopped only long enough to inhale. "After a short time, Miriam got bored and went inside."

Justus smiled slightly at Michal. Detecting she was finished, he angled his head to look at Mazis. "Do you know what the cipher says?"

Mazis' grin faded. "No. And I don't think it can be understood without knowing the key." He stepped close to the place Michal had been writing and looked at the letters in the dust. "Michal has shown me your several attempts at guessing a possible key, but with no success. I think your chances of accidentally stumbling onto the true one are less than one in a million."

Justus nodded thoughtfully and stepped around Michal to join Mazis. He examined Mazis for a second, and said, "Miriam told us you and Asher talked about Atbash. Do you know of any other ancient methods for making ciphers?"

Mazis glanced up from the writing on the ground, his voice thoughtful. "There are none I know as old as Atbash." He thoughtfully rubbed his beard up and down.

Michal had followed Justus to Mazis. Her gloomy appearance turned stern, her voice sharp. "So, are you saying you don't think we can solve the riddle and you can't give us other suggestions to try?"

Mazis focused on Michal and his lips curled up. "Actually, I think you are very close to the solution."

Justus shot him a confused look. "Why do you say that?"

Mazis paused for a second and walked to the opposite side of the fire as he spoke. "Consider what is known. Melchizedek receives Abram's

Tithe and, knowing he will never need it, places it into a tomb he also knows he will never need. Since he is God's high priest, he was told something by God which led him to put the two eyes on the tombstone."

Mazis stopped and looked directly at Michal over the fire, his expression expectant. "Whatever it was caused Melchizedek to realize someone would find his Tomb, probably a long time after it was closed. Obviously, Melchizedek didn't want just anyone to find his treasure"—he looked at Justus—"but God's choice."

Mazis broke eye contact and completed his circle around the fire. "A cipher was placed in the Tomb, so complex only one person would be able to find the key."

Justus shook his head and held both hands out from his waist. "But we don't have the key."

Mazis looked like the cat that just ate the canary, his voice quiet. "I think you do."

Michal's head thrust back as she asked, "You do? What is it?"

Mazis bent forward and looked up at Justus. He appeared to be ready to disclose an important secret and moved his finger at Justus as if he were tapping it on an invisible wall between them. "I don't know what the key is, but . . . I'm sure Justus soon will."

Justus straightened and looked at Mazis for a couple of beats, as he folded his arms across his chest. "Why do you say that?"

Mazis relaxed and waved his hand at the letters on the ground. "Michal tells me you have always been extremely good at breaking ciphers."

"Yes, that's true, but not this one."

"Perhaps . . . even gifted."

Justus dropped his arms to his side and slanted his head. "You think God gave me that gift . . . to solve this mystery."

"I do."

Justus was stunned.

Michal had an excited expression. "Of course. Look how you were able to find *tithe* and *Golgotha* in the Torah."

Suddenly, he clutched her. "Jesus is alive!"

Michal stepped back and gave an incredulous expression. "You mean he didn't die?"

"No. He died . . . but he has risen."

Mazis beamed. "See . . . you found a truth in the Torah Asher had hunted for all his life. Jesus is the Messiah . . . the Christ."

Michal held a look of wonder. "That explains a lot."

Mazis picked up a staff with a hook like the ones shepherds use to herd their sheep.

Michal blocked his exit. "Wait. You are not leaving, are you?"

"Yes. I must allow Justus to work."

Justus looked doubtful. "You have more confidence in me than I do."

Mazis' eyes appeared to twinkle. "Simply rely on God."

Justus grimaced. "Any other hints?"

Mazis leaned on his staff and said, "List everything you know about the mystery . . . every little detail. If you leave nothing out, you will find the key."

CHAPTER EIGHTY

Perez had been sure he would be able to get the job, but still felt weird since it had been so easy.

Two women were near the fire. One pushed a hand millstone to crush wheat kernels. The other was plucking feathers from a dead chicken. Both stopped and stared at Perez as he sauntered from Chief Priest Annas' house, across the courtyard to the door of Bukki's former room. For a moment, he looked at it blankly.

Again, he had a private room, but being lead servant for Annas would be much more demanding than serving Asher. He wasn't sure he was up to it. He held the door wide, allowing the afternoon sun to stream in.

It was more spartan than his room at Asher's house. It contained a single bench, pallet bed, and shelf, holding one lamp. He went in, leaving the door open, grabbed the lamp and headed back into the courtyard to light the lamp in the smoldering fire.

The two women hurriedly looked down and began to work as he approached.

Perez was worried. Somehow he must contact Abigail to tell her what had happened.

❯ ❯ ❯

The Herod Gate guard had just announced the ninth hour of the day. Since the afternoon was well advanced, pedestrian traffic through the gate had become quite heavy.

Sethur leaned against the doorpost, his forehead deeply grooved as he tried to see every person who entered and exited the city. Due to his many contacts, he quickly learned Mazis had visited Miriam.

Sethur didn't want Justus or Michal to know he was the one who had found Melchizedek's Tomb. So, he decided to stake out the gate most likely to be used by someone returning to Masada. If Mazis didn't come out this gate, an entire day would be wasted.

Jehu stood on the opposite side from Sethur, ignoring the traffic, but watching the gate guard closely.

Suddenly, the guard pointed at a bald-headed man strolling through the opening. Jehu motioned to Sethur, then took only a few giant steps, and firmly grabbed Mazis' arm. "Sir, I'm sorry to bother you, but I must ask you a few questions."

Mazis gave Jehu a knowing smile. "What questions?"

As Sethur joined them, Jehu nodded toward the giant door, which in its opened state, was touching the wall. "Let's go to where it is quieter." Jehu led the other two to the wall a couple of steps beyond the thick, wooden portal. "I am told you are Mazis of Masada," he said when they paused.

Mazis' demeanor remained unchanged. "I am."

Sethur drew his short frame up and grabbed Mazis' robe just below his chin in a tight fist. "But Mazis is a sage . . . a kabbalist. You don't look like a priest. In fact, you don't even look Jewish."

Mazis didn't attempt to get loose and gave a pleasant laugh. "I'm impressed. You're correct on all counts."

Sethur was surprised at the response. He let go of the robe and stepped back, still looking unconvinced. "Meaning . . ."

"I am a sage . . . a kabbalist . . . not a priest . . . and only half Jew."

Sethur held out both hands, palms up. "You mean a kabbalist doesn't have to be a priest?" he demanded.

Mazis shrugged. "And not even a full-blooded Jew."

"But . . . but . . ."

Mazis chuckled. "At times the Great Assembly chooses to accept certain individuals to further the Kabbala tradition, depending on their skills and abilities . . . but who told you I was a sage?"

Jehu stepped close, with an air of authority. "Kore, the Pharisee."

Mazis looked hard at Jehu. "Ah . . . Kore . . . Yes, I know him. So, are these Kore's questions?"

Sethur's tone softened. "There is only one question . . . and . . . it's mine."

"I see . . ." He waited for Sethur to go on.

Sethur nervously pulled at his brown beard. A man towing a two-wheeled cart with an old lady in it passed close by before turning into the city. When they were out of hearing, Sethur continued. "I saw a word traced in the dust near the Temple recently. It appeared odd, so I began to research it." Sethur gave a light wave of his right hand. "I looked in all the ancient records, but have no clue to its meaning. I was wondering—since you are a sage—if you might know what it means."

Mazis became businesslike. He stared at Sethur for several seconds, then said, "Is it spelled . . . RNAMMFIB?"

Sethur jumped back in shock.

Jehu inhaled sharply. "How did you know?"

Mazis had a roguish expression. "Lucky guess."

Sethur came close to Mazis. "Well, is it an ancient word with some particular religious meaning? Or a foreign language? Or maybe an abbreviation?"

Mazis looked from Sethur to Jehu as though weighing whether to tell them the truth. Finally, he shrugged. "The word has no lexicographic definition. It is a cipher."

CHAPTER EIGHTY-ONE

The night air had a deep chill, but the blazing fire in the center of the covered courtyard crackled. Michal sat on a bench placed the right distance away for comfort.

Justus crossed the courtyard with several more sticks.

She grinned at him. "So . . . you are going to find the key to the cipher."

Justus gave her a dubious look and threw the sticks in a pile near the fire. "Yeah . . . right. I don't have a clue what the key is."

Michal kicked a stick from the fire and grabbed the non-burning end. She leaned toward the other side of the bench. "Mazis said to list everything we know about the mystery. Let's see . . . there is the Torah, Genesis, Abram, the tithe . . ." Michal paused as she used the charred end of the stick to write the items on the flat wooden seat.

Her enthusiasm became infectious and Justus moved to the bench to watch more closely. "Pair of eyes, Jerusalem catacombs, Salem catacombs . . ."

Michal added, "Golgotha and the room of tombs below it."

"And two levels of tombs."

Michal's voice was thoughtful. "Caesar's Cipher and Atbash."

Justus was reflective. "Those aren't associated with this situation."

"How do you know?"

"I don't, but they are not visible in the situation."

Michal's jaw set firmly. "How would they be visible, other than their results?"

Michal stooped to pick up a new charcoal-tipped stick and continued to write. "Of course we must include the cipher." Her list was:

```
Genesis

Torah

Abram

Tithe

Pair of Eyes

Jerusalem catacombs

Salem catacombs

Golgotha

Room of Tombs under Golgotha

Two Levels of Tombs

Caesar's Cipher

Atbash

RNAMMFIB
```

She stared at it. "Are there any other things associated with the cipher?"

Justus was silent for several seconds. "No. I think that covers everything."

They pored over the list for a considerable time.

Michal softly repeated Mazis' words, "List everything you know."

Justus continued, his voice little more than a whisper. "Little details. We need a key . . . but we have already found a couple."

Michal glared at him. "What do you mean? What keys have we found?"

Justus stared impassively at the list. "Well, the word *Golgotha* was curved on the scroll. The curve was a key for the hill of Golgotha. The word *tithe* was located under the curved word *Golgotha*, which was a key to its location in the Salem catacombs. *Tithe* was spelled with two *i*'s, which was the key to the location of the tomb by locating a pair of eyes on the tombstone."

"OK . . . they are all keys. But how does that help?"

"Hmm . . . every little detail." Justus ignored her question as he pointed to each entry, saying the words to himself. After touching each line of words, he went to the top of the list and started again. He abruptly stopped with his finger on *pair of eyes*. "Pair of eyes . . . pair of eyes . . . pair . . . pair!"

Michal appeared perplexed. "What about pair?"

Justus sat for a few seconds, his face betraying the blossoming of a new idea. "What if the 'pair of eyes' was a key for not only finding the cipher, but also for understanding it."

Michal looked intrigued. "In what way?"

Justus hopped up and extended his hand toward her, his voice hinting of excitement. "What if one had to use 'pairs' to create a tool to decipher the word?"

"I'm not following you."

"I'm not sure where I'm going, so this may be hard to follow, but look." Justus grabbed a stick from his pile. In the dust in front of the fire he wrote the first half of the alphabet with large spaces between the letters:

A B C D E F G H I J K L M

Returning to the beginning, he filled in:

AN BO CP DQ ER FS GT HU IV JW KX LY MZ

"See, the first half of the alphabet is paired with the second half."

Michal moved to Justus' side, looked at the letters in the dust, and shrugged. "That's not a key."

Justus grinned, "Of course . . . you're right. However, what if Atbash is the tool, but on a paired alphabet." Justus quickly wrote under the paired alphabet he had just generated:

```
AN BO CP DQ ER FS GT HU IV JW KX LY MZ

ZM YL XK WJ VI UH TG SF RE QD PC OB NA
```

Michal wrote the word RNAMMFIB in the dust and placed under it the corresponding letters from the paired Atbash: IMZNNURY

She grimaced. "Nothing. It doesn't help at all."

Justus held his two hands together and tapped the fingers of one hand onto the other. "This Melchizedek character was one tricky guy. Why have pairs, unless you use them?"

"I'm not following."

"Well . . . you have a pair of letters below each letter of the alphabet, so you could use either the letter immediately below or the letter next to it in the pair. If you knew the crossing convention, you could use either letter in the pair."

Michal cocked her head at him. "Huh?"

Justus explained, "Say you decided to always cross to the other paired letter below the one you are trying to hide. Doing that, your name, Michal, would be spelled: AEKFMB.

A look of understanding came on Michal and she quickly wrote under RNAMMFIB: VZMAAHEL. She threw her stick down, her voice frustrated. "That doesn't work, either. Do you really know what you're doing?"

Justus touched her shoulder, his voice gentle. "I was simply showing you how one convention, crossing to the other letter in the pair, would work. I didn't say that was the one used."

"You know what he used?"

"Cross in every other set of pairs. The first two times, you don't cross; the second two times you do; the third two times, you don't; and the last, you do."

"Let me show you." He pointed to RNAMMFIB. The first pair of letters, R and N, you don't cross."

```
AN BO CP DQ ER FS GT HU IV JW KX LY MZ
↓           ↓
ZM YL XK WJ VI UH TG SF RE QD PC OB NA
```

CHAPTER EIGHTY-ONE

He wrote: IM in the dust. "The second pair, A and M, you do cross."

```
AN  BO  CP  DQ  ER  FS  GT  HU  IV  JW  KX  LY  MZ
  \                                            \
   ↓                                            ↓
ZM  YL  XK  WJ  VI  UH  TG  SF  RE  QD  PC  OB  NA
```

Justus continued writing: IMMA. "The third pair, M and F, is not crossed."

```
AN  BO  CP  DQ  ER  FS  GT  HU  IV  JW  KX  LY  MZ
                    |                            |
                    ↓                            ↓
ZM  YL  XK  WJ  VI  UH  TG  SF  RE  QD  PC  OB  NA
```

He added the third pair: IMMANU. "And we finish with crossing the last pair, I and B."

```
AN  BO  CP  DQ  ER  FS  GT  HU  IV  JW  KX  LY  MZ
      \                       \
       ↓                       ↓
ZM  YL  XK  WJ  VI  UH  TG  SF  RE  QD  PC  OB  NA
```

Justus finished writing the word: IMMANUEL

CHAPTER EIGHTY-TWO

Jehu and Sethur walked side by side across the edge of the Temple courtyard and stopped at the guard's quarters. It was completely dark, but the torches lacing the Temple wall provided flickering light in the night breeze.

Disappointed, Jehu gazed at Sethur. His voice had a tinge of sarcasm. "Do you think you can determine what the cipher says?"

Sethur glanced at a nearby torch. "Of course I'll try, but quite frankly . . . I don't have a chance."

"Anyone you know who is good at that type of thing?" Jehu asked.

"None at all."

Jehu untied the leather straps holding his breastplate and plucked off his helmet. He looked south. "I wonder if the Roman or Grecian woman can solve those types of riddles."

"I seriously doubt it. I have been told Roman commanders use them because they are nearly impossible to solve . . . and this one is probably thousands of years old. I think we have just lost the treasure."

Jehu combed his hand through his long, black hair. "Well, just in case. You know what to do."

▸ ▸ ▸

Michal stared at the letters in the dust for several seconds, amazed at the ease of the solution once they knew the key. She sent Justus a wondering look. "How did you know that?"

Justus shook his head, stood, and took a step to the fire. "I don't know. It just seemed obvious if pairs were the key, one should simply alternate crossing when crossing every time didn't work." He glanced back at her. "You know, crossing in pairs."

Michal had long since formed a high opinion of Justus' intellect, but as she reflected on what he had just accomplished a new respect grew for him. "Mazis was right. You have a gift."

Justus looked at the fire and shrugged. "I don't know."

Still looking at the word, she said, "Immanuel . . . what's it mean?"

"God with us."

Michal grimaced. "I know it means God with us. I meant, what does Immanuel have to do with the location of Abram's Tithe?"

"Maybe nothing." Justus sighed, and his voice became soft. "Abram's Tithe may just be a myth. Maybe Melchizedek simply provided the cipher . . ."

Michal jumped up, turned Justus toward her, and stood on her tiptoes to get her face as close as she could to his. "But the scroll indicated the Tithe was under the hill of Golgotha."

"You are right. Still, maybe it was never located in Melchizedek's Tomb."

Michal stepped away and looked at the word in the dirt for a moment. "Or . . . maybe he had a fake one and a real one . . . and we have not yet found the real one."

Justus' voice was mixed with mirth. "You mean the 'pair of eyes' was a key to the fake tomb?"

"Yes. And the fake tomb held the key to the real Tomb."

Justus stared at her for several seconds, then began to pace in the courtyard. "You may be on to something." He stopped at her side. "All the tombs had pictures on their stones, except two, and they had no markings. None had words, let alone the word *Immanuel* . . . and how can one draw a picture meaning God with us?"

Michal stood still for several seconds, trying to come up with an explanation but failing. She finally blurted out. "Maybe deciphering RNAMMFIB was a lesson, rather than a clue."

He gasped. "I wonder . . ."

Miriam bounded from the street into the courtyard, her complexion glowing. She rushed to Michal and grabbed her arm with both hands. "I've decided to move to Shechem. Julius' tour of duty there won't be up for two more years. And I have no reason to stay in Jerusalem." She whispered in Michal's ear, "I really enjoy being around him."

Justus smiled at the two girls as he smoothed the letters from the dust with his sandal.

Julius stepped into the covered courtyard. He had a broad grin, but he said nothing.

Michal hugged Miriam as she exclaimed, "I think it's a wonderful idea. It will be good for you to get away from here."

Justus smudged the charcoal words with his palm and moved to Julius. "Will you be helping Miriam build or buy a home?"

Julius shook his head. "I only know of three empty houses in the entire city." He glanced at Miriam and beamed. "If she doesn't like any of those, then . . ." He didn't finish his thought, as Miriam bounced to him and took his arm.

Michal moved to them more slowly. "When are you going to leave?"

Julius cleared his throat, but his voice was not quite formal. "Since the Passover festival has ended, Pilate has released my troops from extra duty, so we will all be leaving in the morning."

Michal felt a warm feeling come over her. She took Miriam's hand and gave a tug. "Come on. I'll help you pack."

CHAPTER EIGHTY-THREE

The preceding night Malchus had returned to the city under cover of darkness and waited until he thought the disciples would be awake before calling on them.

The sun was peeking over the eastern wall of Jerusalem as Malchus walked up the steps to the second-level room of the large house built into the side of the city wall. The warm sunlight calmed some of his anxiety at how they would receive him.

I hope I can make them understand how sorry I am. He knocked loudly on the door. Several voices behind the door instantly stopped. Nothing happened for several seconds.

Malchus took a step to the right on the top stair, then to the left. He looked down the alley he had come and back at the door. He clutched his hands together when suddenly the door opened just enough for a single eye of a man to be seen.

A young man's voice sounded as a loud whisper. "What do you want?"

"Are the disciples of Jesus inside?" Malchus asked, his voice normal.

"Why do you want to know?"

Malchus felt a surprising surge of fear as his practiced speech drained from his mind. "I want to ask their forgiveness."

The door closed, but immediately opened wider. A hand shot out, grabbed Malchus' arm and pulled him through the opening. The slamming door hit Malchus in the rear.

The room was large and only a couple of lamps were burning. It took Malchus several seconds to adjust from the bright sun outside to the dim light inside. In front of him was John. John and Caiaphas knew each other well, before Caiaphas had became high priest. During those years, Malchus had multiple dealings with John.

Malchus pointed at him. "Are you a disciple of Jesus?"

John smiled broadly. "Yes. But why do you come?"

Before he could reply, he felt someone tapping his shoulder. Malchus turned and cowered at the sight of the man who severed his ear during Jesus' arrest.

The man had an anguished expression and held Malchus by both arms. "You are the high priest's servant, aren't you?"

Malchus' voice was a whine. "You cut my ear off."

The man looked sheepish and scratched his hairless top. "I know . . . It was wrong of me. I'm sorry. Please forgive me."

John stepped between them. "Malchus, this is Peter. We were all under a lot of stress that night. Peter just reacted." He touched Malchus' ear and smiled. "It looks fine now."

Malchus felt the repeated feeling of wonder. "It's better now than it ever was."

Peter nodded and pointed in the direction of the Temple. "Why did Caiaphas send you here?"

Malchus looked at the floor. "He didn't. In fact, I am no longer his bond servant . . . I am now free."

"Why?" Peter asked.

Malchus' fear was replaced with impatience. "I found something he wanted, and he gave me . . ." He glanced from John to Peter in remorse. "That has nothing to do with why I'm here." Malchus gave a quick survey of the room. Probably fifty people were in it. "I wanted to ask you all for forgiveness. I was ordered to lead the group of men who captured Jesus that night. I did it, but I am very sorry. I had no idea it would lead to His crucifixion."

His tears topped the dam of his eyelids, streaking his face as he began rubbing his right ear, his speech disjointed. "Jesus picked up my ear and touched it to my head. I was completely restored. He must be the Son of God. I came to learn more about Him."

Peter flushed as he said, "You were the last person Jesus healed as a mortal."

"The last? You mean there really were others?"

"Many others."

Awe overtook Malchus. He stared blankly at the wall behind Peter for several seconds, then suddenly took on a questioning frown. "Why did you say 'as a mortal'?"

Peter's voice rang out. "Jesus is alive."

Malchus jumped back. "What? He never died?"

John wrapped his arm around Malchus' shoulders, grinning. "He really died . . . but He came back and has appeared to all of us in this room. He recently appeared to five hundred other disciples and to James, His brother. He appeared to the women who ministered to Him. We have his empty burials cloths here if you want to see them." John raised both hands into the air, his voice strong. "He lives again."

CHAPTER EIGHTY-FOUR

Justus held his hands out to capture the heat of the fire. He had awakened early and could not get the word *Immanuel* out of his mind. Rather than lie awake, he decided to merely start the day early. Michal had a good idea about the cipher being a lesson, but he simply didn't see what the lesson was.

Michal came into the courtyard from the house, interrupting Justus' thoughts. Her movement frightened two sparrows sitting under the roof. They exited with a loud flapping of wings.

The sun had not yet washed away the shadows of the surrounding houses, which had spilled onto Miriam's house.

Michal joined Justus at the fire, with an impish grin. "Solve any riddles last night?"

"No. I think your idea is a good one, but I certainly haven't learned the lesson."

Michal gave the fire her attention, her voice heavy with conviction. "If Mazis is right, you will."

"Hmm . . . maybe I'm a slow learner." Justus took Michal's hand. "James told me the disciples were in the upper room of a house nearby. I am going to see if they are still there. Do you want to come?"

Michal pondered his question, and then shrugged. "Why not? Miriam is nearly finished packing. Besides, if I try to help more, she'll get even more upset with me. She's trying to take everything she has, and I have insisted she doesn't need to."

Justus tugged on her hand and grinned. "Good."

In only a few minutes the couple made the two-block trek to a large house. Designed to save space, it was built into the side of the city wall, at the end of an alley. The main floor was the primary dwelling area. A large room built above it was meant to provide future space for sons who would marry and segment the upper room into smaller rooms for their brides.

The roof of the second level was made structurally solid, so it could serve as a courtyard with enough space for fires, ovens, grinding grain and other food preparation.

Justus led Michal up the stairs to the second level and knocked on the closed door. The door opened slightly, then wider.

Peter stood beaming and held his large hand out. "Justus, please come in . . . a pleasant surprise. I planned to see if you were at Asher's house tomorrow."

Michal and Justus filed into the large room in front of Peter, who closed and latched the door.

The room was crowded. Justus had seen several of the people when he visited Jesus in the Garden, but didn't really know any of them. The random voices of the crowd made it hard to hear normal conversation.

Justus asked loudly, "Why did you want to see me?"

"I have much to tell you and a few things to ask."

Justus exclaimed, "Actually, that's why I came. Jesus is alive."

"I know. Isn't it wonderful?"

Justus flinched. "Did He appear to you?"

Peter gave a broad sweep of his hand at the crowd and fairly shouted, "Yes . . . and not only me, but everyone here and many of His other disciples as well."

Taken aback, Justus wondered. *Am I a disciple?*

A man from the back of the room broke Justus' thoughts by yelling, "Not everyone in this room. I have not seen Him."

Recognition flowed over Peter. "Oh yes, I'm sorry. You just came. No, you were not here when Jesus came."

Michal looked intrigued. "Was Jesus really here?"

Peter's voice was lower. "Twice."

"Do you think He will come here again?"

A man elbowed his way between four men at the front of the assembly to say, "I certainly hope so. I would very much like to see Him."

Michal nodded. "Me, too."

Crows-feet formed at the edge of Justus' eyes, as he tried to pinpoint the man's identity. "I'm sorry. You look very familiar, but I cannot place you."

Michal chimed in, "This is Malchus, lead servant of the high priest. Remember? He was at Asher's funeral in the Temple."

Justus nodded. "But not in the catacombs."

Malchus' smile instantly faded. "Ah . . . the catacombs . . . I have spent far too much of my life in them."

The comment piqued Justus' interest. "Were you involved in many burials?"

"Not burials. Searching the tombs."

Michal perked up. "For Caiaphas?"

Peter folded his arms across his chest. He and John quietly stood by, but their expressions showed they had no idea what was being discussed.

Malchus gave a curt nod. "Yes, for Caiaphas. In fact, I followed you both when you found the connection between the Jerusalem and Salem catacombs."

Michal gasped. "Were you the one who was digging under the wall?"

Malchus gave an embarrassed look. "I was."

The affirmation caused suspicion to well up inside Justus. "What were you hunting for?"

"For the Tomb of Melchizedek."

Justus stared at him. "Why?"

Malchus sounded deeply remorseful and held up one hand. "The high priest was convinced there was some information in Melchizedek's Tomb that would help him understand if there was a relation between Jesus and the long-awaited Messiah."

Peter stepped forward, an obstinate set to his jaw, his voice definite. "Jesus *is* the long-awaited Messiah."

Malchus winced looking confused. "Did you learn that from Melchizedek's Tomb?"

"No, we learned it from Jesus. Look at what he has done—healed the sick, made the blind see, made the deaf hear, raised people from the dead, and now has come back from the dead." Peter shook his head and held out questioning hands. "Man, it's obvious."

Justus gave Malchus no time to respond, his tone accusing. "Wasn't Caiaphas really searching for the treasure?"

Malchus blinked several times. "Treasure? What treasure?"

"Abram's Tithe."

"What's that?"

Justus glanced at Michal.

She shook her head. "He has no idea."

Malchus turned to her. "Idea about what?"

Justus sucked in a deep inhale. "Bukki was holding Miriam ransom so he could get Asher to search for clues in the Torah leading to Abram's Tithe."

Malchus brows pinched together, and he held Justus' gaze for several heartbeats. "So that's why she was kidnapped . . . but what exactly is Abram's Tithe?"

Justus leaned in at him. "Some believe when Abram gave Melchizedek a tenth of the recovered wealth of Sodom and Gomorrah, he stored it in his Tomb. People have been looking for it ever since."

Malchus' shoulders slumped.

Justus continued, "It just seems Caiaphas or Annas were somehow behind the whole plot."

Malchus wasn't buying it. "Surely not the high priest."

CHAPTER EIGHTY-FIVE

The meeting with Peter and the other disciples had been enjoyable, and the exchanging of stories about Jesus' appearances awesome. Justus and Michal traded words of wonderment about the resurrection all the way from the upper room to Miriam's house. As soon as they entered the covered courtyard, Michal went in to tell Miriam the news, leaving Justus alone with the duty guards.

Justus stared into the fire, but his thoughts churned, far off. *Surely I'm not a disciple . . . but I have learned from Jesus. He told me I had a gift . . . but my gift is defending people . . . or is there another? It was easy to solve the cipher . . .*

Justus jumped when Julius touched him. "You startled me."

"I am sorry. I could tell you were lost in thought, but I didn't realize how deeply."

"It's OK. I'm simply having difficulty putting together everything that has happened recently."

Miriam bounded out of the house into the courtyard, leaving the front door wide open. She had a cape flowing behind her robe. Her head was covered with a finely woven shawl. A large, woven basket was in each hand, stuffed full. She held them by the braided rope laced through the top to get them closed. "Julius . . . I'm ready."

One of the door guards moved to close the door, but stopped when he saw Michal.

She stood in the open door, eyebrows raised. "I think she's been ready for a long time." She hopped down the steps.

The two girls embraced.

Holding Julius' arm, Miriam glanced at Michal. "I'll send word when I find a house."

Michal gave her a lopsided grin. "And we will notify you when we sell yours here."

Julius stepped away from Miriam to loosen the belt holding his sheathed short sword. He held it towards Justus. "Honorable Justus, I want you to have this as a token of my appreciation. You have helped me much."

Justus stepped back and shook his head. "This isn't necessary. Besides . . . I'm the one who should be giving you a gift for helping me rescue Michal."

"I know, but giving it to you means a great deal to me."

Justus took the sword and gave Julius a polite smile. "All right. Thank you very much."

As he fished in a pouch tied to the belt around his uniform, Julius turned to Michal. He bowed his head slightly, his expression still earnest, and held out a thin, silver dagger, handle first. Leather strands used for tying it to an arm or leg dangled down. "Lady Michal. I want you to keep this. My troops will no longer be here protecting you, so I want you to have this."

Michal looked skeptical, but took the dagger. In a formal voice, she replied, "I too thank you, though I'm not sure how well I could use it."

Justus gave her a frolicsome smile. "Actually, she's much better at running away."

Michal lunged at Justus, feigned anger on her face. "You'll regret that."

Miriam and Julius laughed, and the four exchanged farewells and hugs. Soon Miriam and Julius left the courtyard, followed by the two door guards who carried Miriam's belongings.

Justus put his arm around Michal's waist as they both waved until the party was out of sight.

Michal moved closer to the fire. "They make a good couple."

"I agree."

They stood for a couple of minutes in silence.

Michal sat on the bench. The smudged list from the day before caught her attention. Although not readable, she cycled through it mentally in seconds. She snorted. "Huh . . . we didn't write down the most obvious detail."

Picking up a branch to place on the fire, Justus stiffened. "What do you mean? They're all there." He rehearsed them, "Genesis, Torah, Abram, tithe, pair of eyes, Jerusalem catacombs, Salem catacombs, Golgotha, room of tombs under Golgotha, two levels of tombs, Caesar's Cipher, Atbash, and the cipher."

"Nope."

"OK, smarty, what's missing?"

"Melchizedek."

Justus dropped the stick. His pulse quickened and a creepy sensation seized him. "Of course . . . that's the answer."

Michal looked incredulous. "The answer? You're kidding . . . aren't you?"

Justus radiated understanding. "Why would he sign his name to a cipher in a fake tomb?"

"I don't know. You're the cipher breaker. You tell me."

Justus took a step toward the fire, placed both hands on his hips, and spoke to the flames. "Isn't it odd the room of tombs had so many tombs in it?"

"I guess, but that was thousands of years ago. Maybe they did things differently then."

Justus rubbed his chin, his voice metered. "Maybe . . . but . . . maybe not. And two levels . . ."

Michal felt lost. "What are you getting at?"

He pivoted to her. "How many tombs were in that room?"

"I don't know . . . 30 . . . 40?"

Justus gazed at her for a couple of beats, his lips blossoming. "How about . . . 52?"

CHAPTER EIGHTY-SIX

Both Justus and Michal held torches as they inched down the narrow stairs to the connecting tunnel between the Jerusalem and the Salem catacombs. It had taken them little time to gather the needed equipment to again come to the catacombs to search for the treasure.

Michal also held an unlit lamp, and Justus carried a long prying bar.

Reaching the bottom of the pit, they threaded through the narrow opening into the Salem catacombs and down the now-familiar corridors to the great room of tombs. As they entered, each lit the torches fixed to the inside walls near the doorway.

Michal revolved as she checked the tombs, her appearance uncertain until she completed counting. "You are right . . . twenty-six on the bottom and twenty-six on the top."

Justus glanced from Michal to the tombstones near him and grinned. "Look . . . a slightly greater space is between every other tombstone."

Michal exhaled in wonder. "Yup . . . they're in pairs. Barely noticeable, but pairs, nonetheless. What does it all mean?"

Justus wrote the paired alphabet and the paired Atbash on the dusty floor, his excitement building.

AN BO CP DQ ER FS GT HU IV JW KX LY MZ

ZM YL XK WJ VI UH TG SF RE QD PC OB NA

"This is the Atbash deciphering tool to find the word *Immanuel.* And, as you suggested, the effort was merely a lesson." Justus glanced up at the open tomb. "Suppose the tombs are arranged exactly as our deciphering tool. The fake tomb is the twenty-third, so let's assume it corresponds to the twenty-third letter." He underlined the letter in the dust.

AN BO CP DQ ER FS GT HU IV JW KX <u>L</u>Y MZ

ZM YL XK WJ VI UH TG SF RE QD PC OB NA

"See, the letter *L*. We know the name Melchizedek has 11 letters, so let's move back 11 pairs, but, following the cipher's pattern, not cross." Justus underlined the letter *A*.

<u>A</u>N BO CP DQ ER FS GT HU IV JW KX <u>L</u>Y MZ

ZM YL XK WJ VI UH TG SF RE QD PC OB NA

He went on, "Continuing as we did in our solution of the cipher, the first two were not crossed, but we go to the Atbash pair and the next two are crossed. Look . . . crossing to the bottom . . ." Justus underlined the letter *M*.

AN BO CP DQ ER FS GT HU IV JW KX <u>L</u>Y MZ

<u>ZM</u> YL XK WJ VI UH TG SF RE QD PC OB NA

"And go back 11 pairs . . ."

<u>A</u>N BO CP DQ ER FS GT HU IV JW KX <u>L</u>Y MZ

<u>ZM</u> YL XK WJ VI UH TG SF RE QD PC O<u>B</u> NA

He underlined the letter *B* and froze.
Michal blurted out, "*Lamb*."

Justus stared at the letters as a feeling of reverence clutched him. "When Jesus appeared to James and me after He rose from the dead, the last thing He said to me was that I found Him, but was still searching for Him. Good God. He was killed on the Passover . . ." He grabbed Michal's arms and looked deeply at her. "He was God's Lamb. He was sacrificed, just like the lambs were when the Israelites used lambs' blood so the Angel of Death would pass over them in Egypt."

She pulled away and gave him an uneasy look. "That's a beautiful picture of reality, but what does that have to do with the Tomb?"

"It tells us where the Tithe is."

Michal looked totally unconvinced. "It does? Where?"

Justus searched for understanding in Michal, but seeing none his voice became soft. "In the tomb marked with a picture of a lamb."

Michal gasped. "Of course."

As Justus grabbed the ladder and started for the door. Michal called to him, "I didn't pay attention to all the pictures. Is there one with a lamb?"

Justus smiled as he passed Michal, carrying the ladder. "I don't remember either, but the lesson suggests the first one on top."

Michal glanced at the letters Justus had marked in the dust and noted the one with the second letter underlined and her loud voice betrayed her inspiration. "The one corresponding to the *A*."

"Yes."

Justus placed the ladder against the wall, grabbed a lamp, and scaled several steps.

Michal sounded impatient. "Well?"

Justus studied the stone for several seconds before catching the faint image of the small drawing of a lamb at the very top. "It's here." He scooted down, traded Michal the lamp for the prying bar, scurried back up the ladder to remove the stone from the tomb.

After several long minutes, he warned, "Look out below. I think I have it." Justus put the bar into a crack at the top, pushed with all his strength and the stone became dislodged. It crashed onto the floor of the great room causing a cloud of fine dust to mushroom.

Justus leaned into the tomb opening. Though he held no lamp, the torches were near enough for him to make out several irregular, shadowy shapes inside. He brushed away some of the dust on the closest pointy object causing the light to glitter from it and sucked in a loud gasp. "Michal . . . it's here! The treasure is here."

Justus' skin prickled as a husky, male voice answered, "Thank you for finding it."

CHAPTER EIGHTY-SEVEN

As the sound of the voice died, the room became as silent as the tombs it held.

Justus felt a knot in his stomach. He looked down to see Jehu, Attai, and Sethur.

Sword in hand, Jehu gave him a devilish grin and blocked the bottom of the ladder.

Attai had covered Michal's mouth and held a knife against her throat. He stood in the opening as he glared at Justus.

Sethur moved between them, almost comical in his shortness.

Jehu used his weapon to motion Justus down the ladder, his voice precise. "Come down slowly and keep your hand away from your sword."

Justus' palms became wet with sweat as he nodded and stepped one rung lower. "So, it was you who found the first tomb?" he asked.

Jehu answered, "No, it was Sethur who saw the 'pair of eyes'."

Justus finally reached the floor. "You helped Bukki?"

"Not at all. In fact, Bukki had no idea we were watching him. Neither did Perez or Malchus. They were much less patient than we were."

"What about Annas and Caiaphas?"

"What about them?"

Justus scowled. "Were they involved?"

Holding a lamp, Sethur shook his head and with a look of impatience, scaled the ladder like a monkey.

Jehu chose his words carefully. "I'm not convinced they were, but only they know for sure. They are very corrupt and quite resourceful."

Attai moved his hand from Michal's mouth, but kept the knife firmly against her flesh.

Justus pretended to relax. "What do you intend to do to us?"

Jehu sneered. "These are catacombs. They hold the dead." He looked at Sethur above them and gave a wicked grin. "And would you look at that . . . one will soon be empty . . . ready to accept a couple of dead bodies."

He suddenly barked at Justus. "Unbuckle your sword and drop it to the ground."

Justus remained frozen.

Jehu pressed the blade on Justus' throat, his bearing dark with rage. "Now."

Justus slowly unbuckled his belt, as he focused on Jehu, but did not drop it.

As soon as Sethur had reached the Tomb, he began inspecting its contents. Finished with the hasty inventory, he could not contain his excitement. "God of our Fathers. This Tomb is filled with gold and silver. We will be richer . . ."

All attention focused on Sethur just as a dull thud sounded, and Attai crashed to the ground.

As he fell, Michal fell with him to prevent the knife at her throat from cutting her.

Jehu spun around to Malchus, his saber moving away from Justus.

Malchus was barely one step in the room and raising the large stone he had just used on Attai.

In an instant Justus realized Malchus had sneaked up behind Attai from the corridor to the tomb room and struck him. Justus drew his sword as Malchus launched the rock.

Jehu swerved, avoiding the missile. He lunged and sank his point into Malchus' side.

At the same time, Justus hacked Jehu's other arm and blood splattered on the floor.

Jehu gave a loud scream, but still swathed the air in retaliation.

Justus parried the thrust and a deafening metal-on-metal clang echoed in the room.

Sethur spidered down the ladder, cutlass brandished.

In the time it took Sethur to reach the ground, Michal retrieved Attai's knife and stuck it deeply into his arm.

He yelled, dropped the weapon, and hit Michal's chin with his fist.

Blood sprayed from her mouth. The force of the blow caused her to trip on Attai's unconscious body, but she somehow maintained her balance.

Jehu and Justus continued with a violent barrage of thrusts and parries, exchanging offensive and defensive positions.

Malchus lay in the corridor moaning.

Sethur grabbed his fallen sword with his left hand and stabbed at Michal, but completely missed her.

As Michal avoided his thrust, she hammered her right elbow as hard as she could into Sethur's face.

A sickening breaking sound came from his nose as blood splashed over him and Michal. He fell back and landed next to Attai's body.

Michal stuck the blade into Sethur's back.

Justus' strength and skill as a warrior quickly turned the tide of the battle.

Jehu tried desperately to keep Justus from striking a fatal wound, so he constantly retreated, circling the room backwards over and over.

Michal plucked up the stone used by Malchus. Weaving back and forth, she searched for a chance to hurl it at Jehu. When his back was totally turned to her, she catapulted it with all her strength.

The stone struck his left shoulder and knocked him off balance.

Justus tried to deliver the killing blow, but his foot hit the tombstone with the pair of eyes. He pitched forward and tumbled to the ground.

Jehu charged past Michal, hitting her in the side of the head with his sword handle, and went for Justus.

Justus spun onto his back, anchored his weapon on the floor, and used his foot to hit Jehu's leg.

Jehu was charging so fast, he could not avoid the obstacle and his momentum caused him to spill out of control. He wailed as the blade slid out of his back, then lay still on top of Justus.

Justus pushed him off and slid in the direction of Michal's prone body, his voice raspy and his breathing heavy. "Are you all right?"

Michal lay still. Finally, she turned to look at him, blood trickling from her mouth and beads of sweat dotting her forehead. Before Justus could reach her, she looked over him and gasped.

He heard the scraping sound of metal leaving its sheath and rolled over. The tip was inches from his head.

Attai swayed as blood from his head wound looked like a miniature waterfall down his shoulder. "Not yet, you Roman half-breed. You have yet to taste my steel."

Justus heard a sound like a bee buzzing by his ear and saw a thin steel handle pop out of Attai's chest exactly over where his heart would be inside.

A shocked look froze on Attai. A second later he crumpled onto the floor.

Justus fell onto his back next to Michal and gave a long exhale. "Lucky . . . or are you that proficient?"

She gave a sideways glance, her voice snooty. "We girls had to do something to pass the time."

Justus savored the quietness and felt all his muscles relax as he continued to lie on his back, gazing at the dark ceiling. Finally, he turned to Michal.

Her forehead was smeared with dust which had turned to sweaty mud. Blood trailed down her chin and a large, purple bump rose behind her ear.

He lightly touched her cheek and said, "Will you marry me?"

She slanted a glance at him without moving. "Hmm . . . I don't know. You can't even protect me."

Amusement filled Justus forcing a chuckle. "I haven't seen you need it yet." He softly kissed her forehead.

She snuggled closer. "Of course, I will."

CHAPTER EIGHTY-EIGHT

Michal and Justus had gone directly from the Tomb to the garrison. A Roman physician treated Michal's wounds while Justus told Gaius about the treasure and the fight. Gaius ordered guards to the catacombs and two soldiers to stay with Justus and Michal.

Five hours had passed since the encounter in the room of tombs when Justus and Michal arrived back at Miriam's house. The second night-watch announcement had just sounded. It was midnight.

Michal went directly to her room, but Justus stayed in the courtyard and coaxed the barely hot embers back into a roaring fire. Feeling exhausted, not only from the late hour, but from the adrenalin high he had during the altercation, he stumbled into Asher's old room and fell asleep fully clothed.

Loud knocks on his room door caused some consciousness to return. The room was gloomy, but light filtered in around the door. For a minute he had no idea where he was.

The knocking continued, followed by Julius' strong voice. "Justus . . . are you all right?"

Justus rolled his head from side to side as the haze of sleep dissipated. "Yes, I'm fine. I'll be out in a second." He moved slowly to allow his stiff muscles to overcome the soreness. A minute later, he pushed open the door.

Michal and Miriam were sitting close together on a bench. Julius was speaking to Gaius. All stopped talking and focused on Justus.

Justus glanced at Julius. "I'm glad you gave me the sword. It came to good use."

Julius stepped toward him with a look of relief. "I too am glad." He moved his hand toward Gaius. "Soldiers came to Ephraim. They told Miriam and me what had happened, so we immediately came."

Justus looked at Michal. "Are you feeling OK?"

She stood and went to his side. Her lip was red, but not swollen. She appeared to move easier than he could. "Yes, I'm fine. But you need to listen to Gaius."

Justus felt a shiver. He looked at Gaius. "What's wrong?"

Gaius had a formal tone in his voice. "Honorable Justus . . . as we discussed last night, I directed some soldiers to remove the four bodies and post soldiers at the room of tombs to guard the treasure."

Justus took a step away from Michal. "Yes . . . and?"

"They reported back to me the opened Tomb had nothing in it."

Justus forgot to breathe for a moment. "Empty? Impossible!"

Michal slid her arm around Justus, but said nothing.

Miriam stood from the bench. "Would the guards have stolen it?"

Julius moved to her and took her hand, but his tone sounded official. "No, they would not have done that." He glanced at Justus. "Justus, you know how we prevent that type of dishonesty."

Roman soldiers could have one hand amputated if they were caught stealing and then were placed in the front battle lines for a sure death.

Justus nodded, trying desperately to figure this out. "How long was it before the guards went to the catacombs after I reported what happened?"

Gaius looked flustered. "Actually . . . quite a long time. The second night watch was about to end, so it took a while to wake additional troops, brief them, equip them, and have them perform the cleanup."

Justus rubbed his forehead, lost in thought.

Julius countenance softened. "Do you think someone stole the treasure during that period of time?"

Michal looked skeptical. "Who? No one even knew we found it."

Justus suddenly stared at the hole in the wall.

Michal caught the move and grimaced. "But Perez has been gone for some time. No one was in that room since Julius left."

"Perhaps we are to learn another lesson," Justus said.

Julius appeared thoughtful. "Lesson?"

"How did Jehu know to follow us?"

The room became so quiet they could hear each other breathe.

Only a beat passed for Michal to clamp her lower lip, her tone seething. "Abigail."

Justus gave Michal a strained look. "Come with me. We need to pay our regards to our neighbor."

The group, including the two duty guards, marched to the house Abigail was supposed to be preparing for Jehu and formed a semi-circle in front of the door.

Justus knocked loudly, his voice piercing. "Abigail! We know you are in there. Open the door."

After a few moments, Abigail flung open the door.

Justus barged in. The others flowed around him and searched the house. It was unfurnished, with the exception of a pallet to sleep on in one corner. Dust was thick and the whitewashed walls were grey, with one beginning to crumble.

Justus stood on one side of Abigail, Julius on the opposite. She wore no scarf, so her red hair was striking. She looked like a cornered fox.

Justus' voice was rough. "How much did Jehu pay you to spy on us?"

Abigail averted his gaze. "How did you know?"

"Pretty obvious. He retains you to prepare a house for relatives across the street from Miriam's house and then shows up in the catacombs just as we find the treasure."

She gave him a furtive look. "Treasure?"

"Don't be so innocent. You know about the treasure."

Abigail's teeth chattered uncontrollably, and her breathing became ragged. "I don't know what you're talking about. Jehu told me he thought you were up to some mischief and wanted me to tell him when you left the house."

Justus grabbed her arm. "Did Jehu put Perez up to eavesdropping through the hole between his room and Miriam's front room?"

Abigail bleached. She stammered. "No . . . not Jehu. Annas."

Michal had just joined Justus from the side room and cried, "I knew he was guilty."

Justus grabbed Abigail's arm and squeezed. "Where is Perez?"

"At the house of Chief Priest Annas. He is now lead servant."

Gaius completed his tour of the dwelling, joined the group, and touched Justus' arm. His voice was controlled. "There is no treasure here."

Justus pivoted and yanked Abigail through the door. "You're coming with us."

The band snaked their way through the crowded Jerusalem streets to the courtyard of Annas' house.

Perez circled from directing several other servants, looking from Abigail to Justus. "What do you want?"

Justus pushed Abigail hard into Perez. "The treasure."

Perez looked frightened. "What treasure?"

Justus leaped to clutch Perez's tunic and pulled him close enough to smell what he had eaten for breakfast. "I think you know exactly what treasure."

Perez swallowed hard and nodded, "Let me get my robe, and I will take you there."

After Justus released him, he took two steps toward his room, then suddenly changed directions and bolted across the open courtyard to the nearby street.

The others raced after him.

Perez wove haphazardly around people in the busy street as he dashed away from his pursuers.

Michal easily outdistanced the others and was about to nab Perez at the Herod Gate.

He lurched sideways, grabbed the spear from the surprised gate guard, and twisted to stab at her.

She performed several revolutions, avoiding the thrusts.

It took only seconds for the stupefied gate guard to recover, draw his sword, and plunge it into Perez's back.

Perez slumped to the ground and moaned loudly.

Justus was too far back to help in the engagement, but arrived as Perez hit the ground. He fell to his knees by Perez.

Gaius and Julius pulled up simultaneously and stopped the guard from further action.

CHAPTER EIGHTY-EIGHT

Justus held Perez's head up and demanded, "Where did you hide the treasure?"

Perez gasped for air as blood filled his lungs. His appearance showed victory. Justus pressed him, his voice desperate. "Where is the treasure?"

Perez's expression became glazed over as he coughed and exhaled blood to inhale no more.

Justus dropped Perez's head into the dirt, and stood to join the others as they stared at the dead body.

Michal broke the silence when she asked dully, "Do you think Abigail knows?"

Justus spotted a ring belted around Perez's waist with several keys threaded onto it. Suddenly, he smiled. "Doesn't matter . . . I know where he put it."

CHAPTER EIGHTY-NINE

Julius, Gaius and twenty Roman foot soldiers appeared as stark pillars at the southern opening of the Temple enclosure. All were dressed in battle uniform, but only ten had weapons. The other ten each held a large wooden box. Air whipped through the opening and a shadow would occasionally race over them as a cloud blew past the midday sun.

Justus was so sure what he would find in Asher's Temple room, he had hired four Jewish men to accompany them. And, even though he had been in the area once, he went to the Jerusalem synagogue with orders from Pilate to have Kore escort them into the Temple.

The soldiers lined the entrance and stood at attention.

Dressed in his usual long robe, Kore walked slowly into the Temple courtyard, his untrimmed beard bent by the breeze.

Justus marched behind him. Michal, Miriam, and the four employees filed after him, each carrying a large basket.

As they neared the Temple's side entrance, Caiaphas and Annas stood stiffly. Five Temple guards were stationed behind them. Kore did not look at the priests as he passed them to ascend the stairway.

Justus paused for a beat in front of Caiaphas and returned his cold stare before following Kore.

Kore reached the landing in front of the door of Asher's searching room. He turned to Justus with a disgusted look. "Give me the keys."

Justus struggled to maintain a civil voice as he held out the key ring. "Here."

Kore examined the ring and tried four keys before finding the correct one. He opened the door wide and led the others into the room.

No one needed to search the room, for a large pile of objects pushed a black tent cloth up from the bed on which Asher had slept.

Michal darted to it and pulled back a corner of the tent. "It's here."

Miriam joined Michal on the opposite side with a look of wonder.

Justus leaned back at the four men still standing on the stairway. "Take everything in the corner between the women to the Roman soldiers outside the Temple enclosure."

The men squeezed past Justus and began filling their baskets.

Kore looked mesmerized.

It took the men five trips to empty the room, but in an hour they had finished. On their last trip, Justus and the women followed the four basket carriers to Julius.

Julius chuckled as Justus approached him, his voice low. "Quite a treasure."

Justus glanced at the box of a nearby soldier, now filled with gold and silver. He nodded and took Michal's hand, but looked at Julius. "Would you come with me to the great room of tombs and bring four soldiers?"

Julius swept his hand in the direction of the filled boxes. "Of course, but do you mean to move the treasure there?"

"No, have them take it to the fortress." Justus turned to Michal and smiled. "There's something I want to show you."

Michal looked puzzled. "What?"

Justus touched her nose, his voice mirthful. "It's a surprise."

❯ ❯ ❯

In less than an hour, Justus, Julius, Michal, and Miriam stood in the great room of tombs with four Roman soldiers lining the corridor outside it. The two torches were lit. Both Miriam and Michal held lighted lamps. The ladder remained on the wall to the now-empty Tomb and the prying bar lay in the dust near the wall.

Michal examined the area, then gave Justus a questioning look. "So . . . where's the surprise? We have already found Abram's Tithe."

Justus came close to her. "Have we?"

"Yes, and you know it. Now . . . what's this all about?"

Justus snatched the prying bar, squatted as he smoothed out an area of dust, and wrote the familiar deciphering letters.

```
AN BO CP DQ ER FS GT HU IV JW KX LY MZ

ZM YL XK WJ VI UH TG SF RE QD PC OB NA
```

His voice sounded excited. "Bring the lamp closer."

Michal stood at his right shoulder.

Julius and Miriam were poised opposite them.

Justus looked up. "Michal was correct in suggesting the whole deciphering thing was a lesson. But I think we have still underestimated Melchizedek. What if he foresaw someone might get as far as we did."

Michal looked mystified. "But we found the treasure."

Justus pointed up with the bar. "What if our reward is only equal to the lesson we've learned?"

Michal gave him an exasperated look. "What are you talking about?"

"The first lesson was the word *lamb* and it led us to the correct Tomb." Justus underlined the letters:

```
AN BO CP DQ ER FS GT HU IV JW KX LY MZ

ZM YL XK WJ VI UH TG SF RE QD PC OB NA
```

Michal angled to look at him. "The first lesson?"

Justus glanced around at the four walls. "There are twenty-six tombs on the top." He stood and looked directly at Michal. "And on the bottom."

Julius and Miriam exchanged bewildered looks.

Michal's expression changed to one of understanding. "Oh . . . we stopped too soon."

Miriam looked around the room. "What?"

Justus grinned as he recorded Michal's look of recognition.

Michal's face lit up. She stepped to the lower row of tombs directly under the ladder. "We stopped too soon." She pointed at the second tomb on the bottom from the entrance, her voice sounded like she was talking to herself. "Cross over in the pair . . . no markings."

Justus held a pleased expression. "And if you count eleven more pairs on the bottom row, I'll bet another tomb has no markings either."

Miriam pointed to each of the pairs, but said nothing aloud until she counted eleven. "No markings." Miriam looked at Justus, her voice sounding confused. "So . . . what does all this mean?"

Michal laughed. "It means . . . they are filled with treasure also."

Miriam gasped. "No way."

Justus inserted the prying bar at the top of the tombstone where Michal stood and soon had it on the floor. "Ha, Ha! Gold and silver."

Julius snatched the prying bar, strode to the tomb in front of Miriam, and removed the other stone. "Same here." He wiped the sweat from his brow and grinned at Justus. "You are rich beyond compare. What are you going to do with all this?"

"That's why I need your five soldiers. Have them transfer all the wealth to the fortress and meet me there."

CHAPTER NINETY

Annas matched Caiaphas' pace, stride for stride. Pontius Pilate had demanded they come to the Antonia Fortress by the ninth hour. It had been two hours since he and Caiaphas watched Justus, Michal, Miriam and four men empty Asher's searching room of gold and silver. During those hours, they frantically worked to devise a plan to take Abram's Tithe from the Romans.

As they turned north from an opening in the Temple enclosure, a strong wind caused both men's headdresses to flap on their backs. In ten minutes they turned into the polished stone court in front of Pilate's palace judgment hall and stopped dead.

Pilate stood three steps up from the court. He was dressed in full battle gear, except in place of the conventional helmet he wore the governor's crown. One step lower, Justus and Michal stood on his left while Miriam and Julius stood on his right. Twenty Roman foot soldiers lined the court, their stance wide with spears pointing toward the priests in one hand, tall shields resting on the stone floor in the other.

No one moved in the court. Annas glanced at Caiaphas and swallowed hard. This was not going to be easy. A single thrush whistled as it darted from a palace turret.

After a long minute, Pilate pointed and said, "It's time you two answered some questions."

Annas and Caiaphas exchanged surprised glances.

Annas held out both hands. His voice sounded kind. "Procurator. We have reason to believe . . ."

Pilate stepped down with one foot, frowning as he yelled, "Silence!" He retook his position and folded his arms across the shiny metal breastplate, his voice authoritarian. "You will answer the chief advocate's questions."

Caiaphas' black beard accented his now-ashen face. He looked at the soldiers, then at Pilate, but remained silent.

Justus stepped onto the court in front of the two priests. He pointed at Annas, his voice sharp. "I want to know why you had Bukki kidnap Miriam and then Michal."

Before Annas could respond, Caiaphas stepped beside him and spread both hands out, his voice booming. "Why would he do such a thing?"

Justus scowled, his voice condescending. "To find the treasure."

Annas saw an opening, and he focused on Pilate. "Any treasure from a tomb of a priest belongs to the Temple."

Pilate arched his back and shouted, "Answer his questions or my men will take you to a place where you will."

Twenty shields raised in unison, filling the court with a momentary roar.

Cold sweat broke across Annas' forehead. His arms fell to his side. "As you wish, sir." He stepped toward Justus, his voice conciliatory. "Bukki acted alone. He had severe emotional problems. It was only days ago I learned from Jehu what he had done. He was obsessed with the treasure, and I guess he lost his sanity."

Michal looked disgusted, as she spoke in a loud voice, "But Abigail told us you ordered Perez to eavesdrop."

Annas felt his gut tighten, but his tone was flowery. "Lady Michal, I'm sorry. A minor indiscretion." He glanced at Caiaphas, extended his hand, and looked at Michal. "Asher was working with us to locate the Tomb. When he died, we thought there was a chance Miriam would be successful in the search. But after I interviewed you and her, I was sure you would not help us. So, I asked Perez to . . ."

Justus interrupted. "So, you were searching for Melchizedek's Tomb?"

Caiaphas chimed in, "We did want to learn the location of Melchizedek's Tomb so we could discover if there was a link between the Nazarene and the coming Messiah. Like so many before him, Bukki went mad thinking Abram's Tithe was in Melchizedek's Tomb. He's the one who was behind the kidnapping, not us."

Annas looked from Caiaphas to Justus and spoke in a softer voice. "That's why we had the scribes make the large papyrus sheets you desired."

Only the wind whipping through the palace colonnades could be heard. Justus glared at Caiaphas for several seconds, turned on his heel, and went back up the steps beside Michal. He glanced at Pilate, then focused on Annas as a smile hinted at his lips. "The Tithe was in the Tomb."

Annas felt a ponderous weight bear on him. "Is that what you were removing from Asher's searching room a few hours ago?"

Michal took Justus' hand and looked up at him as she answered flippantly, "In a way."

Caiaphas held out his arms, his attention on Pilate. "Procurator, Abram's Tithe belongs to Israel. It's our National Treasure."

Pilate looked at Justus, but said nothing.

Justus returned his gaze. "I'm sure that's what they would have said if they had found it."

Hatred surged into Annas, and he defiantly shouted, "It belongs to Israel, not Rome."

Pilate showed an obscene grin. "It now belongs to the chief advocate." He leaned down to place his hand on Justus' shoulder. "Justus, tell him what you will do with it."

Justus had a broad grin. He pointed to Caiaphas, his voice commanding. "Assemble the Sanhedrin in front of the Temple in one hour, and I will tell you all what I will do with your National Treasure."

⟩ ⟩ ⟩

The glimmer of contentment Justus had felt at the Antonia Fortress had grown into a full air of triumph. He was sure Caiaphas and Annas had conspired to order Bukki's actions, but he didn't have one witness to call, let alone the two required by Jewish Law, to convict them. However, what he did have would deliver a worse blow than a felony conviction.

He strolled across the Temple courtyard, Michal at his side. The Sanhedrin was lined up in front of the main Temple entrance watching him lead the procession.

Behind them were the four Jewish men Justus had hired to help empty Asher's searching room. Each carried a chest with treasure nearly spilling out.

Justus stopped short of the porch and watched as the men lined their boxes in front of the council.

Justus moved his gaze from the riches to the assembly, his voice firm. "I come to you today following the Law of Moses that originated with our forefather Abraham. He gave a tenth of the recovered wealth of Sodom and Gomorrah to Melchizedek. I have found that treasure and now give a tenth of it . . . to God."

Caiaphas stepped forward and looked incredulous. "A tenth?" He waved at the boxes. "That is nearly all the wealth you removed from Asher's room today."

Justus bent and picked up a gold goblet. He held it in front of Caiaphas and chuckled, "But only a part of Abram's Tithe was in Asher's room." He pushed the goblet inches from Caiaphas. "I . . . found it . . . all."

Caiaphas glared at Justus, his face purple with seething rage.

Annas stepped from the line of priests and turned Justus toward him. He looked distressed. "You mean nine-tenths is not here?" He turned to the gold and silver, his voice a hiss. "There was that much?"

Justus soaked in the priest's loss for only a beat, then turned to the council, his voice loud. "I trust this esteemed assembly will use my tithe to glorify God."

A middle-aged man stepped forward and showed a look of genuine gratitude. Although not as tall as Justus, his head was higher than any priest in the lineup. He had a ruler's bearing. "Honorable Justus, my name is Nicodemus. I assure you the Sanhedrin will use the tithe according to the Law."

Justus threaded his arm around Michal. "Good." He turned Michal and let his hand slip down her arm, as he gave her a soft nudge.

They crossed the courtyard at an average pace, the four hired hands a little distance behind them.

Michal looked up at Justus, her voice happy. "Wow . . . you really got those two."

Justus glanced sideways and spoke with a chuckle. "Yeah. It's funny how the loss of something you never had can hurt so much."

As they approached the exit from the Temple enclosure, Michal clasped Justus' hand. She nodded toward Julius and Miriam standing close together about a hundred feet beyond the wall. Still out of earshot, Miriam was smiling as she gazed at Julius.

"I wish they could have seen the priest's expression," Michal said.

"Me too." Justus gave her a slanting look. "But they'll get some benefit."

Michal looked questioningly at Justus, but said nothing.

He pulled her to a stop just outside the enclosure. "I think part of the treasure will soon be their wedding gift."

Michal grinned broadly. The hired hands passed them and continued down the street. They paid no attention to Justus and Michal. Suddenly, Justus swung Michal into a deep alcove in the wall where they were partially hidden by a thick growth of vines. She looked up at him, white teeth showing from her smiling lips. Leaning against him she gave him a warm look and said, "You're richer than most kings. No need to be an advocate anymore."

Justus gazed deeply into her dark pools, a new feeling washing through him. He kissed her lightly. As he pulled back, her lids remained closed and he held her close to murmur in her ear, "You're right, but I love being an advocate." He bent to kiss her again but paused to say, "Besides, you'll love Rome."

Her eyes shot open, and she pulled back with an arch look. "Rome? . . . You mean Athens, darling."